STAYING FOR LA LLUVIA
RITMO Y PASIÓN

SHELLY CRUZ

SHELLY CRUZ WRITES, LLC

Copyright © 2026 by Shelly Cruz
eBook ISBN: 978-1-7358437-8-0
Print ISBN: 978-1-7358437-9-7
All rights reserved.

Visit my website at www.shellycruz.com
Cover Designer: Murphy Rae
Editors: Developmental: Attacus Atlas House, LLC; Copy/Line Edits: Split Leaf Saturdays
Interior Designer/Formatting: Author J.L. Lora
Proofreaders: Sapphic Library Author Services

Except as permitted under the U.S. Copyright Act of 1976, no part of this book may be reproduced or transmitted in any form or by any means, electronic or mechanical, including photocopying, recording, or by any information storage and retrieval system without the written permission of the author and publisher, except for the use of brief quotations in a book review.

In addition to the rights protected by copyright law, the author expressly prohibits the use of this work, in whole or in part, for the purposes of text and data mining, scraping, or for training, developing, or populating any artificial intelligence (AI) systems, machine learning models, large language models (LLMs), or any other generative AI technologies, now known or hereafter devised, without the express written consent of the copyright holder. Any use of this work for such purposes without a specific, separately negotiated license constitutes a violation of the author's copyright and is subject to legal action.

Please protect this art by not pirating.

This book is a work of fiction. Names, characters, places, plots, and incidents are products of the author's imagination and/or are used fictitiously. Any resemblance to actual persons, living or dead, events, or locales is entirely coincidental.

Staying for La Lluvia

CONTENT WARNINGS

Infidelity (off-page, not between main characters).
Drug use (off-page and on-page).
Sexually explicit content.

*A la memoria de mi papá. For the stories you told,
the Boricua heart you gave me, and the passion that defines us.
Bendición, Papi.*

PROLOGUE

Xavier

My apartment is hot and stuffy. Sweat slides down the sides of my face, but I'm not sure why. The AC is blaring at sixty-two degrees. As I reach for the rolled dollar bill on the table to snort another line, the heavy wooden door flies open, slamming into the doorstop and causing me to jerk my head up. My sister appears, her silhouette a contrast to the blinding light.

"Hey, sis. You're late to the party," I slur, a slow, crooked grin spreading across my face.

Her designer heels click on the tiled floor as she rapidly approaches me. "You're sweating, and you smell like you haven't showered in days."

I raise my arm to take a whiff of myself. Damn, she's right. When was the last time I showered?

"Ugh, I can't believe you're still snorting those fucking pills." She snatches the rolled bill from my fingers.

When popping Percocet wasn't getting me high like I wanted, I started cutting and snorting them. "Always so judgmental. At least it's not cocaine."

"Right, because that makes it so much better!" She swipes her hand across the table, dispersing the line I had just readied.

"Hey" —my head bobs— "I was about to take that." She's my older sister, but since our mother died when we were kids, she's always filled the role.

"I know! And now you're not! What is this shit you're listening to?" The sharp rap of her heels echoes like fireworks, and she pushes the stereo's power button, instantly filling the room with piercing silence. My fingers immediately start rubbing the area around my ears to relieve the pain.

I push myself up to turn the power back on, but my legs are weak and I fall back into the couch, causing the room to spin and the nausea to surface. "I was working on something. The label is gonna love it. It's gonna be my next platinum record."

"The label doesn't love anything you're doing. They're about to drop your ass." My manager mentioned something similar last week, but once they hear this album I'm working on, everyone will realize I'm back.

She's standing before me, hands on her hips as she scrutinizes me. "Come on, let's go."

Her words are like a serrated knife blade killing my buzz. "I'm working. You wouldn't understand the pressure I have doing this job."

She cackles. "Sure, keep telling yourself that."

"What did you come here for, to ruin my high and judge me? Why don't you leave?"

"*Abuela* is dead. That's what I came here for."

Her words sucker punch me, and I fall back into the cushions. *Abuela* is my home. The woman who raised me when my mother died. I can still smell the sweetness of the scalded milk as she poured freshly brewed coffee into *la taza del café con leche* she made for us every morning. "Don't play like that. I just talked to her and told her I was going to pick her up to take her to the beach house."

She shakes her head while exhaling. "You haven't talked to her in months. If you weren't high all the time, you'd remember I told you she was sick. Now she's dead. I held her hand as she prayed for your recovery on her deathbed."

I want to understand the words Xiomary is saying, feel the sadness she's trying to convey, but Mr. Percocet has me in a chokehold, preventing me from crossing into the emotions death stirs.

"Our flight leaves for Puerto Rico tonight. The funeral is on Friday. You need to get up."

The thought of getting on a flight right now, the altitude and change in pressure, and the tight spaces, sours my stomach.

"I can't make it Friday. We're working on the new album." My eyes roll up as my head falls back.

"You're so high, you don't even understand what I'm telling you! Keep it up, and you'll be next."

"I'm not dying. Not yet. *El Flaco Casanova*'s next album is going to be his best!"

She stares at me while blinking. "Get your shit together, Xavier, and take a shower. I'll be back to pick you up in a couple hours." Her voice fades as she closes the door behind her.

Now that she's gone, the silence turns up the volume. My heart aches, and the loud thumping rings in my ears. I draw a vial from my pocket in search of the only thing that will make it all stop.

CHAPTER ONE

Rocío

THE CARS HEADING northbound whiz by, and I look up at the crisp blue sky, promising another beautiful South Florida day and clashing with my splintered heart. Drumming my fingers on the steering wheel, I huff and glance at the time on the dashboard—8:17 a.m. My stomach churns as I inch my way toward the courthouse. The traffic is practically at a standstill on I-95, and I won't get there by nine if it doesn't let up soon. Stretching my neck, I look back and to the right, searching for any possibility of changing lanes. If there's any way I can get over and get off at the next exit, I can take the surface roads and be inside the courthouse with time to spare.

Desperate for a distraction to help pass the time, I use the car's voice command system. "Call Nikki." We've been friends for thirteen years, but it feels like yesterday when our law school professor paired us as partners during our first-year writing class. I quickly went from not knowing anyone to having her by my side day and night as we navigated endless case briefs and research. We've been tight ever since.

I really need her to pick up. "Hi, Rocky," she says after the fourth ring. "You ready for your hearing?"

My hearing. The day I've been anticipating yet dreading for nearly two years.

"Not really," I admit. "I mean, I know it'll be quick, but having to face the judges and lawyers I work with every day is mortifying!"

I never would've imagined I'd be the one needing a divorce lawyer. Nerves eat away as I inch closer to the courthouse. For as long as I can remember, I always wanted to be a lawyer. Before moving to Miami, I cut my teeth as a paralegal, working for a badass divorce attorney in Boston. She was one of the most sought-after lawyers in the city and working alongside her solidified my decision to attend law school. Watching her help people navigate the emotional wreckage of failed marriages helped me choose my desired area of law. I wanted to have a practice just like her but needed to learn to be a trial lawyer before opening my own firm. As soon as I became licensed, I went to work at the Miami-Dade County State Attorney's Office for a few years before hanging my shingle.

"Rocky, you literally help people like yourself every day," Nikki reminds me. "You should not feel mortified at all! Besides, it was all Victor's doing. He's the one who couldn't keep his dick in his pants. *He* should be mortified, not you."

Victor. The Miami boy with the charming smile who weaseled his way into our study group and stole my heart, only to shatter it years later. I'd planned to return to Boston after graduating law school, but falling in love with Victor changed everything. Those plans evaporated quickly at the thought of us not being together. Although he was born in Argentina, he was raised in Miami. His parents and siblings still live here. Moving to Boston wasn't an option for him because of his young daughter, and I wasn't willing to leave him behind. Much good that did me. In hindsight, it was probably an early sign of things to come.

"It's been over two years since that day. Why does it still hurt like a motherfucker?"

The day after we took the bar exam, we moved in together. We were thick as thieves the first few years of our relationship, first as boyfriend and girlfriend and then as husband and wife. With Victor, I was invincible. I loved him with everything I had. I admired his drive to succeed and enjoyed sparring about different legal issues. Our careers started taking shape—him, an esteemed criminal defense lawyer and me, a family law attorney. Our relationship was solid, stronger than we'd ever been. Except I was oblivious to what was happening right under my nose.

"You loved him since the first time he joined our study group. It was written all over your face. Of course it's gonna hurt. He's an asshole—I could kill him for hurting you the way he has."

Two years, five months, and twenty-three days ago, I was preparing for the biggest case of my career, representing the soon-to-be ex-wife of a prominent Miami business executive in a high-stakes divorce. Millions of dollars and custody of their three children hung in the balance as we prepared for a five-day trial. But just as the judge was about to take the bench, the husband's lawyer asked for a few minutes to speak with me. They made the settlement offer my client had been waiting for since the divorce process began. My client was ecstatic she wouldn't have to relive years of emotional and financial abuse through the stress of a trial, testifying, and listening to her husband's antics on the stand. Rather than a grueling days-long trial, we drafted a marital settlement agreement, and had it printed and signed by late afternoon. The judge was so pleased with how diligent we were, she agreed to hold the final hearing right then to finalize the divorce.

"I haven't seen his face in months. I'm not sure how I'll react when he's a few feet away from me in the courtroom."

The client's case settled, and I had suddenly found *days* of free time. The early mornings and late nights of intense trial prep had taken a toll, so the unexpected break was a gift, a chance to breathe that I wanted to take advantage of. But when I pulled into the driveway of our office, I saw Victor's car, and my stomach sank. Something was off. He should've left to pick up his daughter, and the office should've been empty.

Instead, he was inside. Naked and balls-deep fucking another woman. Her dark, silky hair splayed across our Italian leather couch.

"When you see him, tell him to go fuck himself!"

Every time memories of that day resurface, I wish I had been witty or had some great line to tell both of them off. But no such thing happened. Instead, I stood there like a statue, speechless and stunned.

Shaken.

Shattered.

Sobbing.

"If I could use such words inside the courtroom, my job would be kinda fun and way less stressful." I huff. "I'm just glad we were finally able to settle, and I don't have to endure a nasty public trial."

The day I walked in on Victor was also the day I moved out with a whirlwind of tears as I hastily packed my things. It took me several months to get my shit together before I was able to file for divorce. The weight of Victor's betrayal tore me up from the inside out, knocking me so far off balance, I was unable to keep my bearings. So much so, I had to hire my friend to represent me. And the irony wasn't lost on me—I was a divorce lawyer, unable to face her own divorce.

My situation finally helped me fully grasp what most of my clients experience. Although divorcing people is my job, I never envisioned it for myself. I was an utter failure and free-falling down the mountain. The death of everything I'd known since moving to Miami.

"Listen, you'll be fine. Today feels heavy because it's officially the end, but it's *been* over. You've already worked through it with your therapist and came to terms with it. You have a new life now—he's old news."

In my new apartment, I became a recluse. Left only for work—for court appearances, really, because the rest of the time I worked from home. Victor's betrayal uprooted both my personal and professional life, since we were also law partners. The heaviness of it all prevented me from going out, and I had to learn to work from home after dissolving our law firm and moving out of my office—another painful reminder of what I'd lost.

"You sound like me when I'm counseling my clients," I reply. "Honestly, I'm not sure why it's hitting me so hard again. But you're probably right, it's officially official. I'm closing that chapter of my life. It's so final."

For months I refused to go out, attend any events, network, or socialize. Even showering was a chore. My parents and friends checked on me regularly, brought me food, cooked for me, and would try to motivate me. Nothing worked. One of my sisters even flew down from Boston to stay with me for several weeks, but I was a wreck. It was Nikki who finally broke through by suggesting I speak with a therapist. She'd met a psychologist while working on a case and thought she'd be a good fit for me. I'm grateful Nikki convinced me to schedule an appointment with Dr. Pérez, because she became my lifeline, slowly guiding me back to myself. I'm not sure how I survived without her.

The traffic moves and the green exit 3B sign appears ahead. I crane my neck and when there's an opening, I veer right to switch lanes.

"Well, we already know I'm right." Her gravelly chuckle

streams through the speakers. "Now that you're single again, you gonna go on that date with the lawyer from César's firm?"

As a federal public defender, Nikki met her husband César when he was working in the same office. He's since left and works at one of the biggest entertainment law firms in Miami.

The car rolls down the exit ramp, finally getting me moving again. I just might be on time. "Definitely not! Girl, the ink isn't even dry, and you already want me hooking up? I'm not ready for that yet."

"You're definitely ready! You've been on your own for more than two years. It's time! Besides, I'm not saying you need to get serious—just dress up, have someone whisper sweet things to you, look at you like they want to eat you up, and maybe actually eat you up!" she jokes. "Did I mention he's a hottie? If I weren't married, I might date him, but since I can't, I can live vicariously through you."

"We'll see. Let me get through this morning and I'll let you know." The courthouse appears up ahead, and I scan the street for parking. It's lined with vehicles all the way down the block, so I pull into the garage. "Need to park. Call you when it's over."

"I'll be waiting." I know her bubbly voice is meant to cheer me up, but it's falling short today.

As I approach the entry to the courthouse, I hesitate, peeking up at the imposing structure. I've walked through these doors thousands of times, but today, it seems to loom extra-large, a tower of glass and steel engulfing me in its shadows. Before entering, I pause to glance at my reflection in the glass to my left. I chose to wear my red power suit with the A-line skirt falling at my knees. The one Victor said I should never wear for court appearances because red is too bold a color. The one that exudes confidence, like wearing invisible armor. *You can do this,* I remind myself, striding through the front entrance.

People meander in the foyer outside the courtrooms, fidgeting with their hands, whispering to their neighbor, or scrolling on their phone to seek distraction. Usually when I'm here, I'm discussing the upcoming appearance with my client or attempting to relax them by informing them of what to expect. But today feels like my first time. My nerves are frazzled, despite knowing this uncontested final hearing should take less than five minutes once we're in front of the judge. My eyes scan the area, looking for Victor or my lawyer. Finding neither, I tug my jacket sleeve up to glance at my watch.

The seats at the far end, near Courtroom C, remain empty and I toss my bag on one seat and sit, grabbing my phone to check emails.

"Hey, Rocky."

Even after everything, Victor's voice still caresses me and my skin tingles. He's sporting a cocky grin as he lowers himself next to me, too close for comfort. He's let his hair grow out, the light brown strands curling behind his ears, just like I loved. My back straightens, and I pull my legs closer together.

"What do you want?" The weight of his stare digs at my skin. He's wearing a navy suit with a white shirt and that damn lavender tie—the one I bought him after passing the bar exam. What a jerk! Wearing that tie, today of all days.

"Good morning to you, too," he retorts, his thin lips smirking. His hand lands on my bare knee and gives a light squeeze.

My belly flutters at his musky scent, and part of me wants to reciprocate what he's offering. Why does his touch still ignite desire? But I know better than to let him lure me in. Turning to meet his pale blue-gray eyes, I hold his gaze and shove his hand from my knee. "Good morning. Now, what do you want?"

"I'm trying here, Rocky. I even wore your favorite tie." He grasps the bottom of the lavender fabric, giving it a tug. "I want to know how you're doing." His voice softens, and he shimmies closer to me, the woodsy scent of his cologne tickling my nose. He hasn't shaved in a couple days, and a memory of his scruffy beard scraping the sensitive skin of my inner thighs invades my thoughts. Heat pulses through me. Why does he still affect me this way? I'm so mad at my traitorous body.

"You're such an asshole!" I lift my chin defiantly.

"Rocky, good morning." Silvia, my lawyer, interrupts us, and I could not be happier about the intrusion. She always looks so sharp with her sleek, chin-length bob and large, black-rimmed glasses.

"Good morning." I rise, lean in and kiss her, cheek to cheek. With my tote bag in hand, I follow Silvia to one of the rooms along the wall so we have some privacy, the weight of Victor's eyes on me as I put distance between us.

Thank god Silvia and I met several years ago at a work conference we both attended. As divorce lawyers new to family law practice, we became fast friends who often discussed the legal issues of our cases. Our love for the law grew into a friendship where we bonded over spicy romance novels. When it was time to file for divorce, she was the one I wanted holding my hand.

She takes a seat and pulls her iPad out. "You okay?"

"I will be. I wasn't sure how I'd handle seeing him again after so long. Apparently, my body is a traitor because having him so close got me all flustered." I shake my head and sit across from her. Her hand stretches and grasps mine.

"This too shall pass. You know how these final hearings go. Finality makes people feel out of sorts and brings all the emotions back up. Makes old wounds feel fresh." She squeezes my hand, and I nod in agreement. Logically, I understand—I've given this speech countless times. But somehow, being on this side of the pep talk makes all my professional wisdom fall flat. "Anyway, I know you're familiar with the process, but anything you want to review before we go in?"

I shake my head. "I'm good, I just want it done. I'm horrified that I have to face the judge and her staff as a soon-to-be divorcée instead of the lawyer."

Silvia shakes her head. "Don't be. Half the judges in this courthouse have been divorced and they know all too well how it goes. It has no bearing on you as a lawyer and won't affect you. You're overthinking it."

"You're probably right, even if it doesn't settle my nerves right now."

"Aguirre v. Aguirre," the bailiff calls out. I follow Silvia out and into the courtroom. Inside, the judge is already on the bench, her clerk sitting to her right. Victor and his lawyer are settling in at the respondent's table.

"Good morning, Your Honor," I greet the judge as I pull the chair out at petitioner's table, then hang my tote on the back of the chair. As I glance around, the courtroom appears larger than it usually does, the judge's bench intimidating me in a way it never has.

"Good morning, Your Honor," Silvia says. She turns to Victor's lawyer and extends her hand out. "Silvia Maria Gonzalez, pleasure to finally meet you in person." Although this divorce proceeding has been dragging out for almost two years, it wasn't until Victor hired his current lawyer that we were able to settle. Silvia was able to pull it off through extensive back-and-forth emails and lengthy phone calls.

It's not that we had significant assets, but we did have our home and two other properties we owned together, as well as our retirement accounts, bank accounts, and a few other investment accounts. I wanted everything evenly split and to make a clean break. But Victor was being obstinate and unreasonable. Knowing Victor, he was probably fired by his first lawyer because of his inability to listen to reason.

"It's good to see everyone this morning," the judge responds.

The clerk calls the case, and the lawyers inform the judge of our settlement. The judge begins the colloquy to inquire about the agreement, if we're satisfied with it, and whether it was signed voluntarily. She then turns her head toward me. "Are you requesting the court restore your name to Rocío Fontana?"

"Yes, Your Honor," I respond, looking toward the judge but staring at the letters carved on the wall behind her, *We who labor here seek only truth.*

With a few final formalities, it's done. Yet everything is the same. Disappointment bubbles where excitement should be brewing. Disappointment at the finality of crushed hopes and dreams making way for a new path I never wanted to travel. "Thank you, Ms. Fontana and Mr. Aguirre. You've both been restored to the status of single."

CHAPTER TWO

Xavier

The elevator up to the fortieth floor is making all the stops today. I adjust my baseball cap to sit lower over my sunglasses, grateful they're hiding my eyes. Usually, I don't mind being recognized, but today, anonymity is where it's at. Didn't get much sleep last night after a late night out. I had totally forgotten I had to meet my sister today until I saw her text message this morning.

My older sister is a partner at the law firm that occupies an entire floor of the Miami Tower and is the most prominent entertainment law firm in the city. Three years ago, she transferred from their LA office to Miami because there was a higher probability of making partner here than in Southern California. She all but told me to come into the office to sign some contracts and meet with one of the attorneys she works with.

Xiomary is six years older than me. Although we have the same mother, we have different fathers. Her dad was never in the picture and mine raised her as his own. After they both died when I was twelve, we went to live with our grandmother in Puerto Rico. We never wanted to go, but there was no alternative, because my *abuela* moving to the suburbs of Boston was out of the question. Instead, we moved in with her to the house where my father grew up.

When the elevator finally reaches the lobby, I stride across it to greet the receptionist while flipping my cap around. "Hello, Daniela. Is my sister in her office?" I lean against the desk, removing my sunglasses.

"Hi, Xavier." Her green eyes light up. She stands and quickly circles around, leaning in to kiss me, cheek to cheek. "Mary is still in a meeting and running late. She told me to have you wait in her office. How are you?" Her hand brushes my upper arm.

Mary. How I hate when she uses that name. I remember the first time I heard someone call her Mary, I was so confused. We still lived in Boston and were at the mall when a boy called her over. Although I'm younger, I was acting territorial because a boy was messing with my sister. I rushed up to him shouting, *her name isn't Mary, it's Xiomary!* In the moment, she yelled at me and dragged me away. But later, she screamed at me again and forbade me from calling her Xiomary unless we were at home because no one could pronounce it, and she was embarrassed about people's constant questions surrounding the spelling, pronunciation, and meaning of her name.

"*Ahí*, you know how it goes. Keeping busy. How are you?" A smile spreads across Daniela's face, deepening the dimples on each side of her mouth. I don't visit Xiomary's office often, but the times I have, Daniela has always been subtly flirtatious, with her soft words and lingering glances. She's a beautiful girl with blonde curls cascading down her back, but not my type.

"I'm well, thank you for asking." She tucks her hair behind her ears. "It's good to see you again. It's been a while since you've been here." She turns on her heel. "Mary has a new office, follow me."

Daniela struts down the hall to our left, as I fall in step alongside her. Once we arrive at the door, she steps aside to let me enter. Xiomary's new office, which is now in the back corner, is twice the size of the last one she occupied. Makes sense that after becoming a named law firm partner she'd get a bigger office. "Thank you, Daniela."

"My pleasure. If you're thirsty, she has a small fridge"—she points to the wall behind me—"over there."

Daniela leaves and I stroll over to the floor-to-ceiling windows with the views looking south, the jagged peaks of the downtown Miami skyscrapers dominating my view, and the Rickenbacker Causeway Bridge off in the distance. "Check out my sister in this office," I mutter under my breath.

I kick back on her leather couch along the left wall and slide my phone from the left breast pocket of my jean jacket. I'll catch up on emails and text messages while I wait for Xiomary. There are a few emails from my manager in my inbox with subject lines related to the tour we're planning—I'll read those later when I'm back home and have time to consider. There's another email from the design team at *Pulso Urbano*, who I'm working with for tour merch. *Pulso Urbano* is the streetwear brand of designer Renzo Nova, a Nuyorican who's made headlines with his edgy menswear in the past few New York Fashion Weeks. We recently signed a contract for exclusive designs for each city on the tour and are waiting for mockups. I skim the email, but when I see Maritza, my assistant, has already responded, I close it out.

"Hey, *chiqui*," Xiomary says as she strolls into her office, her long silky hair pulled back in a ponytail. For as long as I can remember, she's called me *chiqui*, short for *chiquitito,* because I'm her younger brother. She stopped growing at five foot seven, while I grew to six foot three. It got weird when I outgrew her at fifteen, but it's grown on me. Now, she only uses my given name when introducing me to people, or when she's furious at me.

"What up, sis?" I place the phone on the end table and rise, wrapping her in a hug and kissing her on the cheek. She's identical to our mother with her high cheek bones, dark brown eyes, and thin lips. "I'm digging your new office. Look at you, making boss moves!"

She sits on the couch to my left. "You know me, always hustling." Xiomary has always been driven. She graduated at the top of her class in high school and in college. When she finished in the top ten in her class at law school, she was angry with herself because she let the top spot slip away. Xiomary is always working on something, searching for the next talent to sign, or project to create.

"You made partner and you ain't even forty yet!"

"You played a role in that, too. Since your comeback, you've sent me tons of new clients. That client portfolio is worth a pretty penny."

Several years ago, while driving home with a buddy of mine, he lost control of the car after someone rear-ended us, causing us to slam into the guardrail along the highway. The accident left me severely injured with several broken ribs, a broken shoulder, arm, and hand. But the physical trauma was only the beginning. The trickle effect of the accident was devastating and took a toll on me and my music career. Painkillers started as a way to ease my pain but quickly consumed me. I was on the brink of ruin while chasing my next high—putting off my family, friends, and music for pretty little Percocet pills that were, and are, my arch-nemesis —all while under the Latin media's watchful eye. Those vultures circled overhead, eager to document every stumble, every fall. I've been working my ass off for the past two years to get my shit back together.

"I trust no one more than you, sis." The vibrating on the table behind me interrupts our conversation, and I reach for my phone. *"Dímelo."*

"Hey, *Flaco*."

"What's up, Roly? I'm here with Xiomary to sign the designer contracts."

"Yeah, I saw her email. That's gonna be an incredible gig. He's the IT designer right now."

Rolando has been my manager since the beginning of my career. I was a young kid up and coming to the reggaeton scene, wide-eyed and raw with potential, and he was well known in Puerto Rico for backing several notable artists who helped make the Latin and Caribbean hip-hop rhythm and beats part of the mainstream music scene. He continued to support me even when I was spiraling, lost in a haze of pills and self-destruction. Roly's not just my manager, he's family.

"Anyway, I won't keep you," Roly adds. "*Tengo que cancelar* dinner tonight. Nina's car broke down and she needs me to help her. Sorry, man."

"You're straight. Don't worry about it. Take care of your kid and we'll catch up mañana."

"Roly is bailing on dinner," I tell Xiomary. "It'll just be us, lucky you." I wink.

"Between our schedules, it's been a minute since we've had time to just sit and catch up, so it works out perfectly. Anyway, let's talk about what I needed you to come in for. First, I need you to sign the contract for the luxury watch designer from Brazil. We finalized the details and all that's left is your signature."

Since getting clean, I've had to decide in what direction to take my career. I love writing music and singing, but performing and traveling is exhausting. I intend to tour a few more times, but at some point, I'll want to scale back. Together with Roly and Xiomary, we discussed ways to diversify my income, and brand partnerships were the next step.

"What, no electronic signature this time? Dragging me into

the stone age, sis?" I sit back, stretching my arms out along the back of the couch. She rolls her eyes, but I catch the hint of amusement.

"No, they want wet ink signatures for whatever reason. I'll have them ready for you to sign before you leave. The other thing is, one of the partners here at the firm signed Roxana Gatani and—"

"What?!"

Xiomary's eyes widen.

"Sorry to interrupt you, but you signed *La Gata*? When?"

Roxana Gatani, who goes by the stage name *La Gata*, is one of the biggest Latin pop stars right now. She's been singing for several years but really jetted to the top of the Latin charts two years ago, when one of her songs hit number one. After that, she started collaborating with various artists. Early last year, when I was doing smaller shows in Latin America, I met one of her producers, who recommended we meet. He had this glint in his eye, like he'd just struck gold. "I've got a song," he'd said. "Perfect for you and *La Gata*."

Boy was he right. It was like catching lightning in a bottle. "*Sombra Fiel*" catapulted to number one in the Latin charts and held that spot for numerous weeks before finding itself in the top ten, where it's been sitting ever since. I was ecstatic because I was in the process of rebuilding my music persona, and it was just what I needed to get back in the game. For me, it was more than just a hit, it was redemption.

"Well, I didn't sign her. Another attorney signed her about three weeks ago."

"I didn't know she needed a new lawyer, or I would've connected you."

"I forgive you." Her right hand smacks my thigh. "Roxana is releasing a new album, and the label is kicking off the promo tour here in Miami." Roxana was signed as a *Ficha Mundial* Latin Entertainment artist when I was getting clean and putting my life back together. "Since you released a song together, she wants you to make a surprise appearance during the event. I told her lawyer you'd do it, but then I realized maybe you're not available." She lifts her shoulders in uncertainty.

"I don't have much going on in the coming weeks. What day is it?"

"March 16."

I confirm the date on my calendar. "I'm in."

Xiomary stands and starts exiting her office. "Come on, let's go meet her lawyer."

"Why?"

She stops and glares at me. "Really, *chiqui*? He asked to meet you while you're here." She shakes her head and turns back to walk out the door. "Let's go." I rise and follow my sister into the hall and make the short walk two offices over. The door is open, but she raps on it before walking inside. "Hi, César." She halts and turns. "This is my brother, Xavier."

A dark-haired man sits behind the sleek mahogany desk, his suit jacket hanging on the back of the chair. He stands, moving with the same easy confidence my sister does when negotiating on my behalf, and juts his hand out. "César Molina. Pleasure to meet you."

I extend my arm to meet his hand with mine. "Xavier Delgado. Nice to meet you as well."

"Your sister is always talking about you and how proud she is. Happy to finally put a name to the face."

My sister wraps her arm around me and rests her head on my shoulder. The gesture is familiar, so comforting, it takes me back to our childhood days. "I'm extremely proud of everything he's accomplished, and what he still has yet to achieve."

My arms encircle her as a warmth spreads across my chest, because she's still proud of me despite my past with drug addiction. "Thanks, sis." We separate and each take a seat in the chairs across from César.

"As Mary probably already told you," César says, "Roxana's performing here in Miami in about three weeks. When she was in the office a few weeks ago and met your sister, one thing led to another, and the connection was made that you're Mary's brother. Roxana immediately asked if you'd make a surprise guest appearance at her concert. Your sister tentatively said yes, so we're hoping you'll make it official."

When I was rebuilding myself and Roxana wanted to collaborate, it was unexpected because many big-named artists ignored me or tried to distance themselves. I'm eternally grateful and forever in her debt.

"Absolutely. Xiomary already cleared the date with me. I'd be happy to. Looking forward to seeing Roxana again." The chemistry we had performing *"Sombra Fiel"* in the studio was electric. I can only imagine when we're live at the stadium, it's going to be explosive.

"That collab of yours was something else." César leans back in his chair. "It's been dominating the Latin charts for months, so it makes sense for you to make the appearance."

"We haven't performed it live yet. This will be the first time," I chime in. "I hadn't realized, even better. The crowd is gonna go wild!" His grin stretches from ear to ear.

"The crowd always goes wild when he's on the stage," my sister adds while glancing over at me. "They love him."

Having Xiomary's support means everything. She's the only family I have left since *abuela* passed away. When I was at rock bottom strung out on pills, I was ashamed at how much I'd let her down. Despite all of her studies, she always made it a point to be present, even if it meant via video call.

There was never a day we didn't see each other or speak. We'd do homework or just chat, catch up on life's happenings. She's my older sister, but she mothered me in our mother's absence.

"When does Roxana arrive in Miami?" I inquire, looking between César and my sister.

"She'll be here four or five days before the show," César responds. "No exact date yet."

"I'll reach out to her to coordinate and discuss what she has in mind for the performance."

"Great. I'll work on the documents we need and send them to Mary to review. You'll be able to e-sign them. That way, you won't have to come back into the office."

Xiomary is standing, and I join her. "Good meeting you, César. Thank you."

"Likewise, Xavier." My sister is already in the hall when I exit César's office.

Once back in Xiomary's office, I settle into the chair across from hers. "He seems like a nice guy. Have you known him long?"

"Just since transferring to the Miami office. He's friendly." My sister is sitting behind her desk, clicking away at something on the computer. "I'm printing the contracts." She glances at her watch. "I have a meeting in forty-five minutes."

Her stomach growls.

"Always working so much and taking care of others but never yourself? You haven't even eaten yet! Let me go get you some lunch."

She pulls the sheets of paper from her printer and spreads them across her desk. "I forget a lot of things; eating isn't one of them. I had Katia order sushi. It got here a few minutes ago."

When Xiomary joined this firm, she insisted on Katia being part of the package. Katia is my sister's legal and personal assistant and their loyalty to one another runs deep. Katia even moved to Miami when my sister transferred.

I sign the last page of the contracts and slide them across the desk. "Do you want me to pick you up for dinner later?"

"No," she says, shaking her head. "I have a late meeting, so I'll drive over. There's valet parking. I'm not worried about it."

"*Dale*. Eight thirty at Bistro Danzón."

CHAPTER THREE

Rocío

VICTOR LEFT the courtroom together with his lawyer. I wanted to avoid him, so I stayed behind chatting with Silvia for approximately half an hour before she had to attend another hearing. I'm hoping it was enough time, but as soon as I exit the building, he's leaning against the wall, waiting for me.

"What do you want, Victor?" I ask as I scurry past him.

He's alongside me as we stride toward the garage. "I just want to…I don't know…see you, talk for a minute."

I halt and turn to face him. His eyes are soft, a smirk gracing his beautiful face. Smug bastard! "Talk? Really? We're way past talking!" I turn on my heel and continue my stride.

He grasps my wrist, pulling me toward him. "Rocky, I'm sorry. Truly, for everything. I—"

My lips purse as I glare down at him. When we first started dating, the one thing about Victor that made me hesitate was his height. Although he's tall at five foot nine, next to my six-foot stature, he's short. But his charm and wit won me over, and I convinced myself that height didn't matter. Instead, I chose to focus on his other qualities.

"Your sense of entitlement is something else." I yank my hand back, shake my head, and turn. I continue toward the garage, the entrance just across the street, but he's still keeping pace to my right. "We're done, it's done. Just"—I stop and face him again, my heart racing a mile a minute—"we're done!" There are so many things I want to say but choose to swallow my words because we've already been through all of them, and the outcome won't change. My energy needs to be focused on my future, and Victor is my past. "Goodbye, Victor."

When I see there are no cars, I cross the street and push the elevator button repeatedly, because, you know, pushing it over and over makes the elevator arrive faster. The signal dings the lift's arrival, and I scurry inside, press the 3 button followed by the closing arrows button, willing the doors to close.

Once inside my car, I exhale while tightening my grip on the steering wheel. My heart thumps in my chest and crawls up my throat. That was everything I expected and so overwhelming at the same time. Being so close to Victor affected me in ways I thought I'd moved past. Beneath the anger bubbling at the surface, my belly stirred when his scent tickled my nose, reminding me of how much love I felt for this man and how much I missed the days when my heart burst with excitement each time he was near me. I suppose loving him for so many years makes it harder for me to shake him off, regardless of his indiscretions. Thankfully, I have a session with Dr. Pérez early next week. I'll need help to untangle this Victor-sized emotional knot in my stomach.

At the time we scheduled the hearing, Silvia recommended taking the entire day off, anticipating my emotions would be all over the place. Since it's a Friday, it will give me a three-day weekend, allowing me time to process and recoup. At the time, I thought she was being extra. Now, I'm glad I heeded her advice—advice I'm adding to my toolbox for my clients.

"You've both been restored to the status of single."

The judge's words weren't as satisfying as I expected they'd be. Reclaiming my maiden name should've filled me with optimism for the fresh start that lies ahead, but it barely registered as the judge voiced the words I'd hoped would spark joy. Instead, disappointment flooded me, and with remnants of memories and shared dreams in my mind, pain squeezes my heart.

"*Buenos días*, Pedro." I wave to the concierge manning the desk in the lobby of my building, his familiar face a small comfort today. When I moved out, I needed a change and to be as far from South Miami as I could, while still being close enough to my office and the Miami courthouses. I rented a two-bedroom apartment in a high rise building on Collins Avenue in the middle-beach area of Miami Beach, mostly because I wanted security to prevent Victor from coming around, but also because I wanted to be near the ocean.

I used to love the beach, and the first few months after moving to Miami, I'd go regularly. Once Victor and I were an item, those beach trips dwindled because he wasn't into it. He'd easily convinced me that we needed to study and didn't have time to waste lying in the sand. At the time I didn't care. Looking back, I realize I lost so much of myself in him and in our relationship.

"*Buenos días, Señorita* Rocío," Pedro responds. Since the day I moved in, his kindness and the softness of his words are always welcome, like an embrace *de mi abuelo* Juan, whose arms I'd run into as a child growing up each time I visited my grandparents' home.

Inside my apartment, I toss my pockabook on the kitchen counter, kick my shoes off, and plop myself on the white modular couch, which sits along the wall of the open living space. When I saw this apartment, it was the stark opposite of the large four-bedroom house I shared with Victor. The cozy space with white walls and ceilings was sterile and screaming for personality. But I let the living room sit empty for nearly a year, the blinding white a reminder of the clean slate that was thrown at me. One I hadn't been ready to face, until I came across a print at a local art shop on Las Olas Boulevard.

The woman in the print, titled "She Became Herself with Tears," called to me as she shed a lone tear, except her dress is entirely made of tear drops. Her head is tilted back, facing the sun, ready to receive warmth and light. When I saw her, I knew that I was also ready to radiate as I once did. She reminds me that despite the rainstorm of tears I've lived in for the past few years, I'm here persevering. That I survived the storm. As I contemplate the portrait, I'm gazing at it with a new perspective. There is nothing left officially tying me to Victor, and life from here on out will no longer include navigating divorce proceedings.

I grab my phone to call my father. "*Hola*, Roo." He answers on the first ring as if he's been waiting for my call. My entire life, my father has always called me Roo. It's his special name for me, so I don't like anyone else using it.

"*Hola*, Papi. It's done." I rest my head back.

When I was nearing my law school graduation, my parents moved from Boston to South Florida, since my father had retired. For years, they talked about moving to Florida when my father hit retirement age, and when they learned I would be staying in Miami, they took advantage and made the move. Although they don't live in Miami proper, they're not far from here. Their quiet neighborhood in Pembroke Pines, about forty minutes from me, is home to several of their friends from Argentina.

"*¿Como te sentís?*" he inquires.

How *do* I feel? Emotional after finalizing the divorce. It still stings, and I hate that Victor still drums up these emotions. "Okay, I guess. I thought making it official would somehow change things, but no such luck. Today I'm numb just like every other day."

"*Dale tiempo, que el tiempo cura todas las heridas.*" His voice is gentle.

Ah, time cures all wounds. How cliché. "I mean, it ended over two years ago. How much more time needs to pass?"

"Soon, *hija*. You can't put a deadline on your feelings. You and Victor *estuvieron juntos muchos años*, and all those years filled with memories and emotions don't just disappear. One day, you'll wake up and feel better. You'll see." He pauses. "Did you call your mother?"

My mother is the last person I want to talk to right now. She's so good at passing judgment, criticizing me, and doing all the right things to push my buttons. "No, you can tell her. I'm not really in the mood *para escuchar* her judgment today." I can already hear the outrage in her voice because her daughter is divorced, asking about reconciliation, questioning how I'll survive. God forbid I'm forty-one and single, what an outrage. It doesn't matter that I'm a lawyer and law firm owner, my mother still measures me and my success by the man whose bed I share.

"She means well, you know how she is." I can picture my father rubbing the back of his neck, tugging on the hairs at the nape. My parents have been married for nearly fifty years, and for all of them, he's been a patient man. Some days, I'm not sure how he does it.

"Yeah, I do, but I'm still not calling her." I'm closer to my father than my mother, as are my two sisters. He's much easier to talk to. When I told my parents I was filing for divorce, my mother was devastated—told me Victor "*es un chico bueno*" who just made a mistake, and I should be able to forgive his indiscretions and stay married because nobody is perfect. She spent a good part of the conversation that day trying to convince me to not file for divorce and stay with my husband. As with many of our conversations, it ended with me leaving frustrated and annoyed at her canny ability to question my decisions and her staunch inability to accept my choices.

"*Ay*, Roo, she loves you. Besides, she's not going to change now that she's almost seventy-five years old."

I chuckle because, even if she were years younger, she wouldn't change. She's stubborn and set in her ways. "Please just tell her I called *y que nos vemos mañana*." I try to spend time with my parents every Saturday, if I'm in town. Although my mother and I have a convoluted relationship, they're still my parents and my father serves as a buffer for us to have easier conversations. Besides, they'd never forgive me if I stopped seeing them regularly, and I'd never forgive myself if something were to happen to them.

"*Listo*, I'll tell her when she gets home from the market."

"Okay, Papi, I'll see you tomorrow. I'm going to the gym and maybe catch up on some emails."

"*Bueno,* Roo. *Te quiero.*"

"Love you, too." The call ends, and I drop my phone on the couch.

Frazzled thoughts swirl, and I push myself up and cross the living room toward my bedroom. I need to shake off these erratic feelings. Maybe hitting the gym will do the trick.

After a grueling forty-five minutes on the stair machine and a shower, I'm prepping some lunch when my phone rings, alerting me to a call from the lobby.

"Hello."

"*Hola, señorita*. This is Pedro. There is a delivery for you, someone from Beach Flowers. Should I send them up?" Flowers? Who the heck would send me flowers? And on the day I got divorced? It has to be Nikki. She's the type to send me a congratulatory bouquet.

"Yes, please. Thank you, Pedro."

The young woman at the door hands me a vase full of red roses and blue irises arranged with purple statice—the same flowers that adorned the guest tables as centerpieces at mine and Victor's wedding—and I instantly know Nikki didn't send them.

"Thank you, miss." I hand her some folded bills and close the door behind her. The small envelope on the plastic holder reads my name in Victor's handwriting and my nostrils flare.

Rocky, I'm sorry. I really fucked up. Hope one day you can forgive me for all the damage I caused. You'll always be my girl.
— Love, Vic

Tears stream down my cheeks, and anger bubbles in the pit of my stomach. "Fuck you, Victor!" I shout. I toss the card on the counter, grab my phone, and go out to my balcony to get some fresh air, hoping the salty ocean air will help calm the storm that's churning inside. My apartment is on the tenth floor of the building and has expansive views of Miami Beach. The sparkling turquoise water is usually calm and inviting, but today, it does nothing to tame my turbulent emotions.

Sending flowers is such a Victor move—selfish and without regard for how receiving them will affect me. There's a small part tucked away at the back of my heart that wants to call him, hear what he has to say, believe maybe this time it could be different. But my head knows better than to allow Hurricane Victor to pull me into the intensity of his emotions.

In the last few years of our relationship, Victor became a master of chaos. He'd claim to be "at work" late or on weekends, leaving me to fend for myself at our social engagements. Plans would be canceled at the last minute, always with work as the convenient scapegoat. There were times his daughter was with me, let down by another one of her father's broken promises. It started happening so often that we would argue about it, and eventually everything else. It wasn't until I moved out that I learned it was all a farce. He'd create cover stories or start arguments unnecessarily to cover his tracks. Cunning and deceit at its finest.

My ringing phone breaks through my thoughts, Nikki's name scrolling across the screen.

"Hey." I answer the call on speaker.

"Your phone shows you're already at home, but you didn't call me after court. How'd it go? We still going out to celebrate later?"

In our early law school days, Nikki and I started sharing locations with each other as a safety precaution. We became accustomed to it and with the perils that sometimes accompany practicing law, we continued using it.

"Yes, we're still on for dinner. As for the hearing, the actual court part with the judge was easy. Being in the same space as Victor is another story." I shake my head.

"What did he do now?"

I recap the day's encounters with Victor, including his most recent intrusion that's sitting on my kitchen counter. "I just don't understand how he keeps going. We're finally divorced. It's done, there's no going back. Why can't he just accept it?"

"You're not really surprised by any of his actions, are you? You're the best thing that's ever happened to him. It wasn't until he got caught with his dick in his hands that it hit him. Now that you're gone, he's realizing how he fucked himself."

"I am pretty incredible." It's taken me almost two years of therapy to be able to voice that out loud.

"Damn straight and don't you ever forget it! So, now that you're Ms. Fontana again, can I set you up with Rodrigo from César's office?"

"You're really pushing this, aren't you?" I shift in my seat, pulling my legs up onto the chair.

"I mean, I just want you to go out with someone, have fun. Let him wine and dine you. But I also don't want you to go out with a psychopath. Since I've met him, I know he's a nice guy who's laid back, which is why I'm pushing for it. This way, your first time back out in the dating pool will be a chill experience. Like I said, it doesn't have to be serious. Set your boundaries from the beginning and have fun."

My left index finger starts drawing circles on my thigh as I contemplate Nikki's words. Of course, I know what she's saying is true, but my heart isn't ready for any of it. "I haven't been on a date since I met Victor. I don't even know what to do anymore."

"Dating is dating, and right now, it's nothing serious. Just go out for drinks, or dinner, and be yourself. Maybe have sex after a few drinks."

She's not wrong, and the thought of actual sex is pretty enticing.

"I could stand to get laid. Don't get me wrong, I love my toys, but I really miss some old-fashioned dick!"

"So that's a yes? I can tell him to call you?"

"Fine. Give him my number."

Nikki squeals with delight. "YES! It's about time you say yes to me."

"Don't get too excited. Just because I agreed for him to have my number doesn't mean it'll go anywhere. Seriously, no promises!"

"Doesn't matter. Saying yes means your mind is open to whatever the future holds, and that's what matters to me."

I glance at my watch. "What time are we meeting for dinner tonight?"

"Our rezzie is at eight thirty."

"Is Alondra still coming? I haven't spoken to her yet."

I met Alondra through Nikki because they've been friends since their high school days. During one of our law school study sessions at Nikki's house, Alondra joined us because she was working on her master's degree in accounting. Our friendship built from there, with me slowly integrating into their already established relationship.

"Yes, she's picking me up, and we'll meet you at Bistro Danzón."

CHAPTER FOUR

Rocío

BISTRO DANZÓN IS LOCATED in the Brickell neighborhood of Miami, and I decide to take an Uber, knowing Nikki and Alondra will insist on sipping champagne to celebrate my reclaimed single status. After a couple of hours with those two, I'll be in no shape to drive home.

Once inside the car, I shoot them a quick text in our group chat.

> ME
> I'm OMW.

Alondra responds almost immediately.

> ALONDRA
> OK, see you soon. We have a table past the bar.
>
> NIKKI
> Hope you wore dancing shoes.

We've been wanting to have dinner at Bistro Danzón since it

opened late last year. It's a bougie Latin fusion restaurant with a dance floor and live music several nights a week. Reservations have to be made weeks in advance. Once I had my final hearing date, I gave it to Nikki so she could secure us a table.

"Thank you," I say to the Uber driver when he pulls up to the restaurant. Valet attendants assist drivers leaving their vehicles, and a doorman holds open the heavy mahogany door. Inside the lobby, people mill around. The hostess stand is in the center of the foyer area, the expansive dining room filled with round wooden tables throughout and numerous blown glass chandeliers hanging from the vaulted ceilings. The stage is to the back left of the restaurant with a small dance floor, which is visible from every table in the house. I spot the bar along the right wall and slip through the crowd in search of my friends.

I find Alondra, who's wearing a terracotta red halter with a twist top, her pixie cut with dark blonde bangs styled to the side. She has piercing blue eyes and the tiniest nose ring that shimmers when the light hits it.

"You're here!" Alondra shrieks, pushing her chair back and embracing me. Her arms are tight around me, and I return her affection, allowing myself to feel comforted and supported. "Hello, Ms. Fontana! How's it feel to be single again?" she asks as we separate.

I turn toward Nikki while leaning in to kiss her hello. "Hi, Nikki," I say.

Nikki has dark curls that belong in one of those curl product ads—healthy, bouncy ringlets of perfection. I've spent years trying to get my curls to look like hers, but I never get close.

"You're just in time. I already ordered the bottle of champagne to toast your newfound freedom," Nikki responds.

"Freedom I was forced into," I retort, shaking my head as I look back at Alondra. "I'm okay. It hasn't quite hit me that I'm single again."

"You've been single since the day you moved out. Today was just a formality. You'll come around. I've never been married but did go through that nasty breakup with David a few years ago. I know, not the same, but ugly nonetheless."

A few years after meeting Alondra, she got engaged to a guy named David, who she'd met at the accounting firm they worked at. She was a staff accountant, and he was the CFO of the company. She was pregnant and making plans to get married, but she called it off when she found out he wasn't the man she thought he was. Turns out he was a fraudster, because the FBI knocked on her door early one morning and turned their house upside down. His double life was exposed—he'd been skimming the books of their employer to the tune of millions of dollars. He's currently serving a ten-year sentence while she raises their daughter as a single mom.

"Enough talk about exes," Nikki interrupts. "Let's get ready to toast because here comes our waitress." I take a seat with my back to the bar, across from Alondra. When I look to the left, a young woman with dark hair pulled back in a ponytail is carrying three champagne flutes with a yellow labeled bottle of champagne. We all watch as she pulls the foil off the top and tilts the bottle, anticipating the festive popping sound of the cork. Instead, it's a soft popping sound followed by a hiss of escaping bubbles.

"Well, that was anticlimactic," says Alondra.

"Right?" adds Nikki. "We were hoping for the loud popping sound."

"Yeah, we're encouraged to not do that because the tops of these bottles are unpredictable." She stretches her arm and begins pouring the liquid into our respective glasses. "This way, we can control it more, but definitely not as fun to open," the waitress says. She places the bottle in the ice bucket between Alondra and Nikki. "I'll be right back."

We each lift our glass, meeting in the center of the table. "To you, and all the amazing things that are coming your way," Nikki says.

"And all the incredible sex that's on the horizon," Alondra adds.

"Now *that* I can toast to. I haven't had sex with anyone since Victor, and I may start shriveling up if I don't do something about it soon!" We all drink from our glasses.

"You'll need to find a friend with benefits to help clear out those cobwebs," Alondra says, smirking.

"I might have already found one for her," says Nikki.

"Who? Spill, I need all the *chisme*!"

"Hi again, ladies. Ready to order?" the waitress interrupts us.

"Girls, I was thinking we can order the chef's tasting menu because it includes appetizers and desserts," Nikki says.

Both Alondra and I agree, and after the waitress leaves, Alondra says, "Now, back to Rocky's friend with benefits. Who is it?"

"I haven't met him yet, so it remains to be seen if I'll get any benefits," I say, sipping my champagne.

"His name is Rodrigo, he's a lawyer at César's firm, and he is fine as fuck!" Nikki sips from her glass then turns to look at me. "Girl, you'll finally earn the right to call yourself a cougar."

"Wait, what? How old is he?" My eyes widen.

"Thirty-four."

"Nikki, what were you thinking? He's practically a kid! Why would you want to set me up with someone so young?"

"Settle down. First of all, he's not a kid. He's a grown ass man who's thirty-four years old. He's not that much younger than you. I was thinking you could have some fun with him."

"I'm forty-one. I can't go out with someone seven years younger than me!" Never in a million years could I have imagined to be single after just turning forty-one.

"Why not?" Nikki asks, as she gives me side-eye.

Why can't I date someone younger than me? I haven't really thought about anything past the number.

"I'm waiting." She rests the champagne glass at her lips.

"To start with, we have nothing in common. Also, he's thirty-four, which means he's actually thirty emotionally. Men are always emotionally younger than their actual age. I don't have time for all that."

"Are you gonna marry him?" Nikki quips.

"What? No, of course not!"

"I'm still not seeing the problem. If he were seven years older than you, then it wouldn't even be a thought." She sips her champagne again. "Oh, and you're both lawyers, so you do have something in common." She raises her eyebrows and gives me a "so there" smirk.

"You should've told me! Had I known, I wouldn't have agreed to give him my number."

"*¡Ay, por favor!* You're so frustrating! This is why I didn't say anything. Because you're already making excuses and saying no, and you haven't even met him!"

Nikki shifts her attention to Alondra. "What do you think?"

"I mean, I've never dated a younger guy so I'm not sure. I don't see anything wrong with it." She shrugs. "You're both consenting adults."

My head shakes. "I don't know. Does he know how old I am?"

"No, I didn't tell him."

I huff. "I can't with you, Nikki."

"Woman, chill! You look incredible, and I didn't tell him for the same reason I didn't tell you. Why predetermine something if you have no idea?" Nikki reaches for the champagne bottle to top off our glasses.

"I think you should at least give it a try. You have nothing to lose except cobwebs," Alondra adds.

"He already has your number. I gave it to him today after you gave me the okay. When he reaches out, just talk to him. Although, knowing him, he might text."

"Wonderful." My head shakes, and I pull from the flute.

There was a band playing, so after dinner and polishing off two bottles of champagne, we head to the dance floor for a few songs. We sway and spin, lost in the music, until Alondra notices the time and we call it a night. Her daughter is sleeping at her parents' house, but they have to leave early so Alondra has to pick her up.

As we're walking past the bar toward the exit I hear, "Rocky. Rocky!" I turn and see Celeste, an attorney who I worked with at the state attorney's office.

"Celeste, hi! My gosh, we haven't seen each other in years. How are you?" We exchange cheek to cheek kisses.

After quickly introducing everyone and chatting for a few minutes, Alondra says, "Rocky, we have to go."

"Okay. I'm gonna stay behind, catch up with Celeste." We say our goodbyes and as Alondra and Nikki are walking away, I say, "I'll let you know when I'm home."

Celeste and I were trial partners during the three years I was at the state attorney's office. We spent a lot of time together—both at the office and outside of it. When I left for private practice, she stayed, and our friendship gradually faded. In retrospect, I see how much I allowed Victor to influence my friendships, too.

"I have a seat in the corner here." She points to the bar area behind her. "Join me. I'm waiting for my boyfriend to have a late dinner. We need to catch up." Celeste and I settle into the seats in the corner. My stool is against the wall, so I turn it slightly to face her to make conversation easier. The bar is full, and when I'm finally able to flag the bartender over, I order another glass of champagne so that I can accompany Celeste with her drink. After the bartender places my champagne flute on the bar, we chat for a bit and catch up with each other's happenings until Celeste's boyfriend makes an appearance. "You're welcome to join us," she says to me.

"Thank you, but I'm calling it a night. Enjoy your dinner." We say our goodbyes and they make their way into the dining room.

Drinking alone at the bar—a fitting end to my first night as a newly single woman. I smirk at the cliché of it all and pull from my champagne flute, which is nearly empty. Probably a good thing because I'm starting to feel buzzed.

"What are you celebrating?" a deep, rich voice asks. I shift in my seat and see a tall man standing to my right, leaning into the bar. He's wearing a black baseball cap flipped backward to the side, and a jean jacket.

"What makes you think I'm celebrating?" I respond, lifting my eyes to scan his features. The dark stubble of his neatly trimmed beard has clean lines around the edges, outlining his strong jawline and thin lips. He's pretty, yet edgy.

"You've been drinking champagne with your friends all night." The steady tone of his voice caresses me and my skin tingles.

My eyes hold his dark brown gaze. "So, you've been here a while?" I ask.

Without breaking eye contact, he signals the bartender. "Bring her another of whatever she's drinking, and the usual for me." His usual. That means he's a regular at this bar. "I was having dinner across the dining room when you caught my eye. That dress"—his gaze drops to my cleavage before he rakes it down and back up connecting with mine again—"was made for you. I've been wanting to say hi so here I am." He adjusts the stool Celeste was sitting on just a few minutes ago and lowers himself, sitting sideways so he's facing me.

In anticipation of our celebratory dinner, I had purchased a black sleeveless tank dress with a slit up the left thigh. Although it's a bit shorter than I usually like, I love everything else about it. The models pictured online in this dress show the hem falling below the knees, but because of my long legs, it falls two inches above my knees. It hugs my curves and has a deep V-neck that accentuates my breasts.

"Mind if I join you?" he says, as he invites himself to sit next to me. The huskiness of his words sends a shiver down my spine.

"Maybe I don't want any company right now," I quip.

He licks his lips, then says, "Keep telling yourself that, but your eyes are having a completely different conversation with me."

I guess I'm not so good at this anymore. Aren't I supposed to play hard to get or something like that? The rules of this game feel foreign after so long.

"What's your name?" I ask him, keeping my eyes locked with his.

He hesitates and lifts his chin, his eyes assessing me while deciding if he's ready to share his name with me. "Xavier. You?" The way his name rolls off his tongue tells me he's a Spanish speaker.

"Rocky." The bartender places our two glasses on the bar top. I grab the stem, sip, and place it back on the bar—never letting my eyes stray from his.

"It's nice to meet you, Rocky." He reaches for my hand and

takes it in his, raising it until it's hovering just below his mouth. I swallow, the anticipation of his lips touching me making my heart race. As if in slow motion, I watch him drop a single kiss on the inside of my wrist—his lips hot as they graze my skin. "You haven't answered my question. What are you celebrating?" He rests my hand back on the bar top.

"Myself."

"Every woman should celebrate herself." He rolls his lower lip between his teeth, and I fixate on his lips. What would his kisses taste like? Would they be rough like his voice, or soft like his gaze?

"Why's that?"

His response is immediate. "It shows you know you're worthy and deserving of joy and all the good that life offers."

I swallow. This guy's voice is like warm chocolate, its velvety smoothness coating me like a silky blanket.

I bite the inside of my left cheek and reach for my flute to drink because I have no comeback for that. My skin prickles, and I'm unsure whether it's the champagne coursing through my veins or this man with the sultry voice who's inches away from me.

"You're suddenly so quiet. You don't agree?"

"No, that's—" I shift in my seat, suddenly keenly aware of our proximity to each other. "Yes, I do."

"I'm gonna be honest with you." He grabs his glass, and I watch as he brings it to his lips, the soft fizz of the carbonation shimmering. He places his tumbler back onto the bar and scoots in my direction. His hands find my barstool and he tugs, bringing us closer, just enough for his clean scent to tickle my nose. His eyes find mine again. "I really want to kiss you right now."

"That's not what I was expecting to hear."

"What were you expecting?"

"I don't know, but it wasn't that." I swallow and the thumping in my chest intensifies.

"Okay, but I still want to kiss you."

"There's a lot of people here. Besides, we don't even know each other."

"Kissing can be considered getting to know each other, no?" His teeth scrape his bottom lip. "We can go somewhere more private. Would that be better?" He has a comeback for everything.

"Maybe." Did I really just say that? Okay, that's definitely the alcohol talking.

"What needs to happen for that maybe to be a yes?"

My mouth opens and closes. I'm never at a loss for words, and now he's left me without them twice in the span of minutes. I sip more champagne because, apparently, it's giving me wings right now. "Keep talking."

He chuckles and slides his hand across the bar top, resting it flush with mine. The sliver of skin rubbing against mine is warm. "Looks like you and your friends were having fun dancing." He scoots a smidge closer. "Shaking that ass in this dress." His finger caresses the side of mine, causing my skin to prickle.

My heartbeat quickens, and I swallow the lump in my throat.

"Were they here celebrating you as well?"

I nod and drink some more.

He leans in, his lips hovering at my ear. "When you say yes, I want to celebrate every part of you, too." His hot breath shoots straight down my core.

Although the bar is full and music streams through the speakers, it's as if everything around us has faded away. "Let me go to the restroom." I push the chair away from him, grabbing my pockabook as I turn away. "I'll be right back." As I scurry to the bathroom, my heartbeat races and the thumping in my chest intensifies. Once inside, I pull my phone out and dial Nikki's number.

"Are you home?" she asks.

"No. I'm still at the restaurant and there's this insanely hot guy flirting with me and I'm flirting with him, and I'm buzzed and horny. Is it crazy that I want to go home with him?"

"Wait, what?"

For the next few minutes, I explain how the night progressed. "And here I am, hiding in the bathroom calling you. So, tell me I'm crazy and that I should take my ass home to one of my trusted toys."

"I'm the wrong friend to call if that's what you want me to tell you today of all days. Didn't you just say if you don't have sex, you're gonna shrivel up? You're newly single and need to have some fun, so go get un-shriveled!"

Hearing Nikki give her stamp of approval on my impulsive plans gives me the push I need to make this happen. "All righty then, it's decided. Looks like I'm getting laid." I bite my lip and smile at my reflection.

"I have your location, so I'll keep an eye on it."

"Okay. I'll check in tomorrow."

I drop my phone in my pockabook and turn to the mirror. My curls are frizzy and wild, emulating what I'm feeling. After washing my hands, I dry them by running them through my hair, allowing the dampness to tame the frizz. "It's only one night. You got this, Rocky," I whisper to myself.

As I'm walking back to the bar, I pause to watch Xavier twirling his glass, his head slightly dropped. From this angle, I can't see much other than the dark hair along his jawline and just the tip of his nose. I inhale, filling myself with strength. "Here goes nothing," I murmur under my breath before sliding back into my chair. "I'm back."

"Is everything okay?" he asks. My eyes meet his, and I nod. "Do you want another drink?"

I shake my head because I don't need any more alcohol. "Maybe just became yes."

CHAPTER FIVE

Xavier

Her response catches me off guard. "Yes?"

She nods as she's licking her generous lips that still have a faint red color.

"Yes, what?"

She shifts in her seat and leans into me. "Yes, I'd like you to kiss me," she says, her voice breathy.

I lower my head to meet her gaze, her floral scent invading me. "I can do that."

"Okay, but not here," she blurts.

I lean back, contemplating her for a moment, looking for any signs of hesitancy. Her emerald-green eyes are fixed on mine, and they turn up at their corners, causing a smile to stretch across my face. "Where should we go?" My fingers drag along the skin of her forearm.

She licks her lips. "Um, a hotel?"

I can't just show up at a hotel, risk being recognized, and have the paparazzi waiting for me when I'm leaving. I'd rather take her back to my building with its high security and surveillance cameras. "You good with going back to my place? It's nicer than a hotel."

Her eyes search mine and she nods. "Yeah, we can do that."

"My car's out front. Let's go." I pull my wallet from my back pocket and drop a hundred-dollar bill onto the bar, signaling to the bartender so he can see it. I've been coming to Bistro Danzón since it opened its doors last year, and the same bartender has been working the bar on the nights I've visited. Since the first night he met me, he's been chill, even if eventually he did tell me he recognized me. It's refreshing, especially when so many people become starstruck, shoving phones in my face for selfies before even saying hello. I'm just another guy who happens to also be a *reggaetonero*.

It's only now that we're walking side by side that I notice how tall she is, nearly shoulder-to-shoulder next to my six-foot-three height. I glance down and she's wearing Doc Martens. Not the shoes I'd expect to see a woman like her wearing. Images of those long, thick legs wrapped around me flip through my mind, and the pressure in my jeans intensifies. When we reach the door, I rest my hand on her waist, allowing her to exit first. The valet attendant outside sees me and, moments later, hands me the key to my arctic gray Porsche Cayenne parked immediately to the left of the restaurant entrance. As she's waiting by the passenger door, I sidle up next to her and stretch my arm to grasp the handle, allowing me to get closer to her. "It's gonna be a long drive home with you sitting so close, yet so far," I say.

I open the door, but she pauses and meets my eyes, smirking, then rises to get close to my ear. "Let's see how we can make the time pass quickly," she says in a husky breath. As she puts space between us, she's licking her lips. What will her plump lips feel like wrapped around my cock?

Inside the car, I buckle my seatbelt then pull the car into traffic. We drive a few blocks before we find ourselves at a standstill. "You good?" I ask, glancing at her.

She purses her lips and nods. "I need some music," she says, then stretches her hand out to turn the volume up, the *Caliente* station is still tuned in from earlier tonight. "Otherwise, I'll get in my own head and that's not good for either of us." She's nervous. It's written all over her, legs crossed and fidgety fingers tapping along her thighs.

"This okay?" I inquire, stretching my hand to rest on the skin just above her left knee.

"Yes." She nods then rests her left hand over mine.

After driving for several miles in silence with just the music filling the space, Rocky says, "I like this song, I've never heard it."

I'm a bit surprised at her statement considering "*Volví*" by Aventura and Bad Bunny was one of the biggest Latin hits a few years ago. "This is a huge hit, you've never heard it?" I quickly peek at her, then look at the road again, my fingers still drawing circles on her warm skin.

She shrugs. "I'm more of an AC/DC kinda girl." Well, that explains why she doesn't recognize me and asked for my name.

My hand nudges her leg toward me. "I'd be happy to help you widen your musical preferences." I chuckle, and she uncrosses her legs.

She juts her tongue out, dragging it along her top lip. "Is that right?"

"What makes you like this song?"

"I like the rhythmic style of rapping." She grabs my hand and places it on the inside of her thigh, letting her legs fall to the side. "But it's also sensual."

"Sensual. Yeah, definitely that," I say, my fingers drawing

circles on her soft skin. "You understand the lyrics?" I ask, unsure whether she understands Spanish.

"I do." The song ends, but there must be a Romeo Santos marathon because his song *"Propuesta Indecente"* begins playing, the pulsating rhythmic beats enveloping us. "His voice is so sexy," she says. I need to not let her distract me and keep my eyes on the road, but she's squirming in her seat. Stretching my arm, I inch my hand up her thigh, my fingers still making circular motions. "Why'd you stop there?" she inquires.

I glimpse at her. "Show me what you want." Her right hand disappears, and the seat begins sliding back. She lifts her right leg and places it on the dashboard, letting her knee rest on the window as she tugs on the hem of her dress. She grasps my hand in hers and drags it toward her panties, her thighs hot as I approach her core. With her right hand, she slides the black fabric and then guides me toward her pussy. I lean into her slightly, and my fingers begin exploring her hot wet core, causing her to mewl.

"More." Her raspy plea is making my dick harder than it already is, and I shift in my seat to alleviate the pressure. My index and middle fingers find her entrance and push, causing her to gasp. "Yes, just like that, Xavier."

Fuck me, she's so wet. "Damn, *beba, estás mojaíta.*" I'm stroking and circling at a slow pace, and she's rewarding me with her whimpers and moans. Our exit is up ahead and I'm eager to get to my place so I can feel all of her. As the car slows, her hips roll in tune with the strumming sounds of the bachata music streaming through the speakers. A loud wail escapes her, and tremors vibrate across her body. When I look over at her, her head is resting back, eyes closed, and her bottom lip between her teeth.

"You like that?" I ask.

She nods. "Just a little bit," she says, with a lopsided grin.

"There's plenty more where that came from."

"Good. I'm feeling greedy tonight."

We're waiting for the last traffic light before my building to turn green. "When we pull up to my building, the valet will greet us. You should put that tasty pussy away." I smirk, bringing my fingers to my mouth, savoring her. "Mmm, *qué rico*."

"I bet you are, too," she says, as she's adjusting herself.

We leave the car with the valet attendant and walk into the lobby. "Good evening, *Flaco*," the doorman says.

"Hello," I say, grasping Rocky's hand in mine.

"Good evening," she says.

The concierge is sitting behind the desk in the center of the lobby. He gives a curt nod and says, "Xavier."

I acknowledge the concierge as we pass his desk and call the elevator. Inside the lift, she's leaning against the wall. I swipe my card and then push the 34 key, allowing the doors to close behind me. When they're shut, I place my hands on each side of her, boxing her in, searching her eyes. "Can I get that kiss now?" She nods and my lips crash with hers. Her breath is hot, and I suck on her bottom lip.

The elevator announces our arrival at the thirty-fourth floor, and we exit into the lobby. "Is this the only apartment on this floor?" she asks, eyes searching.

"Yes, just you and me, *beba*." I pull my key and push the door open, landing us inside my kitchen and living area.

Once I'm at the far end of the white quartz countertop, I stop. "Come over here," I command, and she obeys. I grasp her hips and hike her dress up. "Let's get you up here," I say, helping her sit on the counter. "Lay back."

She props herself on her elbows, watching me bring my mouth to her center, her panties soaking wet from earlier. "*Quiero saborear* that pussy," I say, tugging her undies to the side. My mouth meets her hot lips, and I suck and swirl as she writhes underneath me, whimpering. "You like that, *mami*?" I peek up at her, her head hanging back and her hips circling as I flick her with my tongue. I push two fingers in and hook them up, causing her to gasp. My thumb strokes her while my two fingers rub her from the inside. She yanks the cap off my head and throws it to the side, then drags her nails along my scalp as she starts wailing. I drink her in, tasting her sweet honey.

When her body relaxes, I pull my hand from her and guide her up to sit face to face with me. I push my index and middle fingers inside her mouth so she can taste herself. "*Chupa*," I instruct. "Taste *lo deliciosa que tú eres*." Watching her savor herself as her tongue swirls around my fingers with her mouth moving up and down their length makes my dick twitch, because that's what her lips will look like wrapped around me.

She releases my fingers. "That was—I don't have words for what that was, but you, sir, have a magic wand where your tongue should be."

"I haven't brought my magic wand out yet," I tease, then suck her lips with mine before helping her down from the counter.

She adjusts her dress then brushes her finger on the black bandana wrapped on my left wrist. "What's this for?"

When I was a teenager, I started wearing a bandana wrapped around my left wrist to cover up a cut I had gotten. It became part of my image once I was singing, so I kept it. "*Una bandana* I wear."

She loosens the knot. "Lemme see."

"*Ahora te enseño todo.*" I tug the bandana and walk toward my bedroom, Rocky's fingers grasping the other end of the black fabric as she follows me.

Inside my bedroom, as I'm removing my shirt, Rocky's leans on the bed, gazing at me. "*¿Todo bien?*" I ask.

She nods and kicks her boots off, stretching her hand so her fingers can trace the eagle tattooed across my chest, its wing spilling over to my right shoulder onto my bicep, where the wing's tip lands at the top of the Woman of Caguana tattoo. Her eyebrows draw in to one another as her eyes peruse the ink adorning my skin, while her fingers trace the lines with a feather-like touch.

My hands grip the sides of her dress. "You ready to take this off?" She covers my hands with hers and pulls up, the black fabric shimmying up her thighs then hips, until the skin of her soft belly is exposed. After I toss her dress to the side, my hands land on her heavy breasts, the nipples hardened underneath her lacy black bra. She reaches back, unsnapping the constraints, and once free, they fall into my hands. The dark skin around her nipples is pebbled, and I guide my mouth to the tip of her right breast, pulling it between my lips. Her hands fumble with my belt buckle while she's working at unfastening it.

"Do you have a condom?" she asks, her eyes searching mine as she's shoving my jeans down.

"*Por supuesto*," I respond. I reach into the nightstand and pull a few gold packets from the drawer, tossing one on the bed and the others on the nightstand. After I position myself in the center, Rocky turns and slides my briefs down my legs, then crawls toward me, wrapping her hands around my hardened length.

Curls cascade over her shoulders as she's licking her lips and then swirling her tongue along my tip, causing an electric tingle to shoot up my shaft. "Mmm, you taste so good." Her eyes are hungry, lust burning at their rims as she takes what she wants.

I gasp as she savors me this time, but before I get lost in her sucking me off, my hands guide her away from me then reach for the condom, while locking my eyes with hers. "*Mami*, we'll get around to you sucking my dick. But right now, I want to fuck you, feel your weight on top of me. Come over here and let me fill you." I toss the foil wrapper to the side and roll the rubber down my cock. "*Mira lo que tengo pa ti*," I say, gesturing to my hand as it glides up and down.

"Mmm, look at you, ready to feed my greed," she says, grabbing me in her hands as she positions herself over my erection. When she impales me, I hiss and squeeze her rounded hips. "Fuck, you feel so good," she says, letting her head drop back as she takes me in. Her tightness grips me as I'm stretching and filling her. She rolls her hips and adjusts herself, sending a tingle up my spine. There is nothing I love more than feeling the weight of a beautiful woman riding me.

She leans in, pushing her breasts in my mouth and I palm one in each hand. My tongue swirls on one hardened nipple and my fingers squeeze the other. She groans, and I thrust up and watch as her eyes roll back and her mouth goes slack, her body consumed in pleasure.

Her dark curls are strewn across the pillows and she's lying on her back. Her curves are soft, relaxation emanating from every inch of her. I shimmy closer, our bodies sheen with sweat, the sex haze setting in. My nose lands at her earlobe and she looks up, pressing her skin to mine and tickling me with her floral scent. I prop myself up on my shoulder to look down at her. She's lying on her side with slumber in her eyes. "*Mami*, that was incredible."

She nods, a lopsided grin gracing her flushed skin as she settles into the bed, making herself comfortable. "It really was."

My fingers linger at her hip bone, drawing small circles on her olive skin. "So, earlier when we were driving and "*Volví*" came on the radio, you were playing when you said you hadn't heard it before, right?"

Her head shakes. "I wasn't. My playlists consist of AC/DC, Metallica, *Soda Stereo*, Fito Páez. Stuff like that."

"It's kinda crazy such a popular song isn't known by everyone, but if you're not into that type of music, makes sense, I guess."

Weary green hues consider my words. "My sister was a huge rock music fan, especially *Soda Stereo*. With her being seven years older, I idolized everything about her," she shares, offering me a cautious smile.

"My sister was super into *Soda Stereo*, too. Still is." Xiomary would blare their music from the stereo in her bedroom, forcing me to listen to it. Initially, the music irritated me because I thought it lacked depth and sounded like thrashing instruments. But it grew on me, and when I began paying attention, I started enjoying the melodic bass and rhythms infused with sensual and poetic lyrics.

"You like *Soda* then?" she asks, her eyes lighting up.

Nodding, I say, "Yeah. They're one of the few rock bands I have on my playlist."

"Have a favorite song?"

"'*En la Ciudad de la Furia.*'"

Her hand gently smacks mine as excitement spreads across her face. "Get out! That's my favorite song!"

The lyrics speak about the anonymity the darkness in the city brings and finding refuge in that. "Yeah, the way it depicts the chaos of city life."

"Gustavo Cerati was an incredible singer. Left this world way too young."

"My sister cried when she heard the news. I remember watching so many of their older performances and interviews. It's then that I learned I love hearing people speak with an Argentine accent."

Her eyes flash to mine. "*Yo soy de Argentina.* Guess that means you like my accent, too." Rocky bites her lip and shifts.

Her green eyes are soft, and they crinkle in line with her upturned lips.

My hand spreads over her hip and I pull her flush to me, letting her feel how hard I am for her again. "I like more than your accent."

"I bet you do," she teases, lifting her leg to cross it with mine.

"You were kinda timid in the restaurant, guarded almost." Sitting at the bar, she tried playing it off as if her body wasn't welcoming me, but her eyes betrayed the words coming out of her mouth. There was deliberate hesitation in her movements, keeping herself at a distance but warring with the self-imposed restriction. "Once we got in the car, you invited me right in." My hand palms her ass cheek. "Then, it was like you took off your armor and were ready to play ball."

"What can I say. It's been a minute…" She pauses and closes her eyes, taking several deep breaths.

When she doesn't finish her thought, I ask, "A minute what?"

Her eyes flutter open, and she pulls her bottom lip between her teeth, indecision racing across her face. "I haven't orgasmed like that in years. You must think I'm some pent-up crazy woman," she whispers, an airless laugh escaping her.

"Years?" My eyebrow lifts in curiosity, my fingers dragging along her thigh.

She purses her lips and nods. "Earlier today, when you asked what I was celebrating? I was celebrating me, but I was doing it because today, I am officially divorced."

Divorce wasn't a word I expected to hear tonight. My jaw clenches thinking about her with another man, one who she divorced. What kind of man would let a woman like her escape? If she were mine, there's no way I'd let her go. His loss is my gain, so maybe I should be happy. "Lucky me to be the beneficiary of such a celebration."

"I don't know, that tongue of yours might make me the lucky

one." She smirks, and rests her head on the pillow again, closing her eyes.

"You can try your luck with my tongue anytime," I tease.

"Thank you for being the cherry on my sundae today."

My fingers continue exploring the lines of her skin. She has the tiniest beauty mark just above her belly button, and I kiss it. "How long were you married?"

"Almost ten years."

Damn, that's a long time to be married. Now I'm intrigued and need to know everything. "Why'd you get a divorce?" Silence balloons as I continue caressing her skin, so I peek up at her.

I'm about to ask if she's okay when her body stiffens and her eyes quickly open, briefly crossing with mine before she stares up at the ceiling. Suddenly, she sits up, swinging her legs over the side of the bed, stands, and reaches for her underwear. Her slumber instantly evaporated.

"Hey, I'm sorry," I say, stretching my hand in search of her. "We don't have to talk about it. Please, come back to bed." When she continues as if I hadn't spoken, I rise from the bed. I'm not ready for her to leave. I was just getting started on digging into who she is. It's not often I meet someone who doesn't know me as *El Flaco*, and it was nice having her enjoy me as Xavier without expectations. "Where are you going?" I ask, approaching her as she's standing at the foot of the bed, pushing her arms through the dress. I wrap my arms around her, pull her to me, and drop kisses along her jawline.

"I need to get home." Her head falls back, giving me access to the silky skin along her neckline and my lips savor her, her scent invading me. There's a magnetic pull to her. She clearly wants to be here; her words may shut me out, but her actions contradict them.

"Need to, or want to?"

Her eyes meet mine before flitting away. "Need to." The more her words contradict her behavior, the more layers I want to peel back. Why would she deny herself?

"Anyone ever tell you you're a terrible liar?"

She shakes her head, but still won't look at me.

With my middle and index fingers I nudge her chin up, green meeting brown. "When can I see you again?"

"You can't. Tonight was a one-time thing." She lifts her chin, but her eyes skirt away.

The knot in my stomach tightens as she voices her rejection, which is foreign and unwelcome, twisting like a thorn in my side. "Why's that?"

Her left hand is resting on her thigh and she's rubbing her thumb and index fingers in a back-and-forth motion, as if struggling with her own decision. "I had a really great time, but that's all it was."

With both of my hands I grab hers, interlock our fingers, and raise our arms between us. I'm intrigued with this woman, want to get to know her more, but she's closing the door and shutting me out, which only makes me want her more. I've never been one to beg—except this feels different. She's different. I inhale, forcing myself to accept the decision she's made for us. "Okay, let me take you home."

She shakes her head. "No. I'll call an Uber."

As we're riding down the elevator, her arms are crossed, and she's quiet, staring at the door. What happened that caused her to flip a switch from being naked and supremely relaxed to stoic and fully dressed in under a minute? The elevator dings and she scurries toward the exit. There are no cars out front, and she tightens her purse over her shoulder and begins pacing as we wait for her ride. Silence hovers and looms, and I stuff my hands in my pockets while my eyes follow her as she walks the length of the glass up and back. Rocky's unwillingness to share intrigues me.

When she sees the headlights, she dashes out and I follow. She's opening the car door but before getting in, I grab her hand and pull her back to me, cover her mouth with mine and suck her plump lips, causing her to sigh. I get close to her ear and say, "I can still taste you on my tongue. You know where to find me when you change your mind."

CHAPTER SIX

Rocío

EVEN THOUGH I got home late from Xavier's last night, I forced myself to go to the gym this morning. It's been a new routine since splitting with Victor, and it helps me sort the shit in my head. I'm supposed to be driving to my parents' house for our usual Saturday lunch. Instead, I'm driving up Collins Avenue returning to my building because I forgot my phone at my apartment. Sitting at the red light, a pale blue SUV pulls up next to me and memories from last night flash through my mind.

The pressure of his fingers.
The whip of his tongue.
The way he gripped my hips.

I can still hear his gruff voice whispering as he thrusted into me, and my legs clench. The car behind me beeps, snapping me back to the road in front of me. I'm approaching the front entrance of my building and am happy to see that there is only one other car right now. I leave my key with a valet attendant and take the three steps up to the entrance.

As I cross the lobby, Catalina, Victor's teenage daughter, is rising from one of the couches and walking toward me, her short sundress swaying as she strides across the marble floors. She's the only thing left tying me to Victor, but despite the anger I feel toward him, I love her too much to cut her out, too. Cata has her mother's high cheekbones and full lips, but Victor's gray blue eyes and dark hair. "Hi, Kiki," she says.

When Victor and I started dating, Cata was two, but I didn't meet her until the summer after our first year of law school, when she had already turned three. She struggled pronouncing Rocky. Every time she tried saying it, she'd say Kiki instead, and it stuck, but she's the only one who calls me that. I've been in her life since. Although when she was younger, my relationship with her mother, Lorena, wasn't easy, as time passed, our relationship improved. That had more to do with Victor's behavior toward Lorena than me, but the dynamics of it ultimately affected me as well. Luckily, Lorena understood that Cata only benefits when we all get along and she let me in, allowing us to build a friendly rapport. In turn, it became easier for Cata on the days she stayed with her father.

"Hi, Cata. What a surprise!" I open my arms, and she steps into them, returning my embrace.

Near the end of my marriage to Victor, Cata sensed the growing tension between us. As a result, her grades suffered, and she began to lash out at both of us. Our marriage ending affected her deeply—so much so that Lorena called me because Cata's behavior was starting to spill over into her home as well.

Two and a half years ago

"Hi, Rocky," Lorena says, her voice slightly strained and softer than usual.

"Hey, Lorena. Everything okay?" I ask.

"You have a few minutes?" she responds.

"Yes, of course."

"Cata finally shared what's been going on with her."

I adjust the volume on the phone to hear Lorena better. "I suppose that's good, right?"

"It is. Thankfully, it's nothing to be concerned about, at least I don't think so."

A breath escapes me, causing my body to relax. "What's going on with her?"

"She told me she's afraid of never seeing you again now that you and her dad are splitting up."

My heart pangs as I listen to her share about Cata's feelings. "Oh, Lorena, I hate that our divorce is affecting her so much!"

"I told Cata I didn't think she'd stop seeing you, which is why I'm calling. I'm hoping you'll come take Cata out for dinner, tell her you'll stick around?"

Tears slide down my cheeks. "Of course. I was never going to leave her."

"I'm going to the beach with friends, and we parked at the lot next door," Cata says. "I tried calling but you didn't answer, so I figured I'd stop by and say hi." She forces a lopsided smile, but her eyes don't meet mine.

During my final few years with Victor, Cata spent nearly all of her time at our house with me because he was rarely home.

Looking back, the one positive thing that came from that time in my life is the bond between her and me.

"Come on, let's go upstairs. I forgot my phone when I went to the gym this morning, which is why I didn't answer. Unfortunately, though, I have to leave because my parents are waiting for me." We enter the elevator, and she pushes the 10 button.

"Yesterday was court to finalize the divorce. Does it feel weird?"

"No, not weird." I shake my head. Although I've seen Cata numerous times since moving out of the house, I didn't expect to see her so soon after finalizing the divorce. "I'll be honest, it wasn't an easy start to my day, but your father and I have been over for a long time. I think most of the feelings I had were nostalgic." She's pulling her hair and twirling it around her thumb and index fingers, a telltale sign she's feeling anxious.

"We'll get to hang out soon, right?" Her eyes are wide and bright, her lips softly curving up.

After that day Lorena called to encourage my continued relationship with Cata, I took Cata out for dinner so she could share what she was feeling. It was then that I promised her I'd always be a part of her life, so long as she wanted me around. The elevator door opens, and we turn right toward my unit. With the key in my hand, I stop at the door and face her. "Of course. What's really going on, Cata? Is everything okay?"

She nods. "I guess with the divorce being official, I just wanted to know that you and me will still be friends." Her shoulders rise and she drops her eyes to the floor.

"Hey." I extend my hand, lift her chin so her eyes meet mine. "You and I aren't friends, we're more than that! You're still my family, even if your dad and I are divorced. I may not be your mother, but I certainly love you like you're my kid. I promised you I'd always be here so there's no getting rid of me now." I pull her into my arms and squeeze her tightly, reassuring her.

"Thanks, Kiki." She puts space between us and as I'm turning to stick the key in the door, she says, "I love you."

Meeting her eyes, I respond, "Love you, too. Your father and I divorcing will never change that." My eyes linger, searching hers for understanding.

When we're back in the elevator, I say, "Sorry I can't hang out today, but let's plan dinner soon."

Her eyes light up and a smile stretches across her face. "Okay, we can go have sushi. *Mamá* doesn't like it, so you're my sushi buddy."

"What about your father? He loves sushi, too."

"You know him, I can never count on him for anything! We were supposed to have dinner last night, but after I waited an hour for him to pick me up, he canceled."

My heart hurts for Cata because despite his behavior, her eyes yearn for him, even if she won't admit it. "I'm sorry he did that to you again."

The pattern is familiar—so many nights Victor would schedule father-daughter dinners, only to cancel. He would cancel on her almost as much as he canceled on me. The two of us were led to believe work was what kept him away from his "two favorite girls." Lies, all of them.

"You guys aren't married anymore. You don't have to apologize for him." She steps into the lobby, and I follow behind.

"I know. Old habits die hard. But remember what I always told you"—my hands seek hers, intertwining our fingers, her warmth filling me—"when your father behaves the way he does, it doesn't have anything to do with you. His behavior is a reflection on him. Those words don't always make you feel better when he acts the way he does, but it's important you remember them. Okay?"

She sighs. "Yeah. I remember." Her arms stretch and they

envelop me, she rests her head on my shoulder. "I love you, Kiki. Tell your parents I said hi."

My lips land on her temple, and I tighten my arms. "Love you, too, kiddo. They miss you too, so we'll plan another day for you to see them. Listen, you're taking the public beach access next to the building?"

"Yes." She's nodding in unison.

"Okay. Text me when you meet up with your friends, please."

"I will." She walks out the door and to the left.

Once inside my car, I peruse my phone and see two missed calls, from Cata and my mother, and a few text messages.

> **NIKKI**
>
> Chisme is best served con cafecito. Come on, woman, I'm dying to know everything!

I respond and tell her that I'll swing by her house after having lunch with my parents.

Before opening my parents' front door, I take a deep breath, channeling patience and preparing myself for whatever mood my mother might be in. "Hello," I call, closing the door behind me and strolling into the kitchen. When my parents moved to South Florida, they left behind a lot of their furniture, but the kitchen looks nearly identical to the one of my childhood home—decorative ceramic dishes adorning the wall, flowered dishrags hanging from the stove and towel racks, and the same tea kettle my parents have used since I was a kid. My stomach growls, the scent of my mother's cooking wafting through the air.

"*Hola*, Roo," my father says, kissing me on the cheek.

I get my height from my father, who's about three inches taller than me. Although he's seventy-six, his curly hair is still thick and mostly black, barely peppered with grays.

"Hi, Papi."

I drop my pockabook on one of the chairs and approach my mother, leaning in to drop a kiss on her cheek. "Hi, Ma." My mother is a shortie next to me, standing at five foot two.

"Hi, nena. Your hair is loose, go over there while I'm cooking, *por favor*." She shoos me away while calling after me. "*Sino*, grab a *pañuelo* and cover it. We don't need any hair falling into the food."

My entire life, my mother has never wanted us in the kitchen if our hair wasn't tied back and covered. She'd scold us for having loose curls around her while working with food. Although my mother's hair has been short nearly my entire life, her head is always donning a handkerchief when working with food. I cross to the other side of the kitchen and pull a bandana from the stack she keeps in the middle drawer to the left of the refrigerator. After pulling my curls into a bun, I tie the colorful fabric around my scalp, covering up my mane.

"What's for lunch?" I ask. If it's one thing my mother is good at, it's cooking. It's the one thing she's always prided herself on, making family dinner and cooking for all of our family gatherings. Growing up, my friends would love when they could eat over because everything she makes is delicious.

"*Milanesa con papas fritas* and a salad." I peek at what's on the stove as she's turning a cutlet in the frying pan. "Now that you're here, *pongo las papas a freír*. Jorge, *pasame las papas, por favor*." My father hands her the bowl of sliced potatoes. She removes them from the water they've been soaking in and turns on the oil where she'll drop them.

Of all the food my mother makes, breaded steak cutlets with homemade fries and salad are what I love the most. I would ask for it all the time growing up. "My favorite," I say with a half-smile.

"That's why she made it," my father adds. I glance at him and he's pouring lemonade into a glass, his lips turned upward at their corners. "*¿Querés?*" he asks, extending the lowball glass to me.

He's smirking at himself, because he knows how much I'm torn about not wanting to spend time with my mother yet feeling guilty when I don't visit, especially because neither of my sisters live close. I recognize my mother made my favorite meal because she loves me. I've never thought she didn't, but our personalities clash and our discussions often end in an argument. It's exhausting. He says we argue because we're so alike—headstrong and tenacious. I couldn't disagree more.

"No, thank you. Just water for me today." I'm still feeling a bit dehydrated from all that champagne we drank last night, but my parents don't need to know that.

While my mother finishes making lunch, I set the table. One of the pieces of furniture that made the trip to South Florida with my parents is the round kitchen table we had. The oak table took up much of the space in our small kitchen, but it's where we gathered every night to have dinner *en familia*. Rare were the times that we were allowed to miss *la cena*. It was our parents' most cherished time of day. Every ding or scratch across the faded wood evokes a memory. It now sits in the center of their Florida room, overlooking their backyard.

My mother is adding olive oil and white vinegar to the salad, tossing the spinach and lettuce leaves with a fork and spoon. "How do you feel today, *hija*?" she asks. She plucks a sliver of red onion and a cherry tomato and pops them in her mouth.

"Fine. Went to the gym today before coming here."

"*Vos ya sabés* that's not what I'm asking you." Her attention remains on seasoning the salad.

I was hoping to not get into anything with her but I'm incapable of ignoring her jabs. "Actually, I don't know what you're asking. Why don't you just ask me what you want to know?" My mother has an impeccable manner of delving into topics you don't want to discuss, without actually ever asking you directly. She's done it my entire life, but it still drives me crazy. Staying neutral as he's always done, my father has taken his seat at the table and is looking at his phone.

"You saw Victor? ¿How is he *ahora que están divorciados*?" I wish her asking me how my cheating ex-husband feels now that the divorce is official surprised me, but it doesn't.

"The hearing went well. It was quick," I quip, my words sharp as they roll off my tongue. "I felt a little weird when the day started but am happy it's over. I'm finally single again! Thanks for asking!" I shake my head while grabbing a glass from the table and push it into the water dispenser on the fridge with more force than I intended.

She places the salad bowl onto the table and then covers it with a clean rag. "I know you're okay. Your father told me." Her even tone twists the thorn in my side.

"It doesn't matter, Ma!" I take a sip of water and look at her. "I'm your daughter and you should ask about my feelings, not his. He's not part of our lives anymore!"

"*Ay, hija, no sé por qué te enojás tanto.*"

How she can keep an even tone and straight face while asking me why I'm so upset is infuriating. "Because he's my cheating ex-husband who had zero respect for me!" I know I shouldn't raise my voice, but sometimes I can't help it with her. My father is still looking down at his phone, tuning us out because for him, it's just another day with Mirta and Rocky. Most of my life I've wondered why my father put up with her, the way she talked down to him and always had a "glass half empty" outlook on life.

"Nena, he's a man. Men do that sometimes. *No fue tan grave para que lo divorciaras.*"

My mother believing infidelity isn't that bad is fundamentally contrary to everything I believe. I have no idea how this is the woman who raised me. "Maybe in your book that's fine. But for me, it's an unforgivable break of trust, so yeah, it warranted me divorcing him. I really don't understand why it's so hard for you to comprehend!"

After my separation, I asked my father about his devotion to my mother in spite of the way she often talks down to him. His response was, "We've loved each other since we were young, and she's all I know. She's not perfect and neither am I. *No puedo imaginar mi vida sin ella.*" They're from a different generation when couples stayed together regardless of the circumstances.

"*Eso es problema tuyo, no tiene nada que ver con él,*" my mother shoots back, then turns to tend to the food still cooking on the stovetop.

A loud groan escapes me at her accusation that my inability to forgive is my problem, not Victor's. "Okay, this conversation is over. I'm not discussing it anymore. Victor is no longer part of my life, he's finally my ex-husband! You need to accept it and move on, Ma! Papi, I'm going outside. Call me when lunch is ready, please."

"Stay, nena. *No hablo más,*" she says in a soft, even tone as she pokes a cutlet and turns it over in the frying pan. Although she knows her words infuriate me, she is incapable of holding her tongue or apologizing after. Her way of moving past it is just not talking about it anymore. Then she'll just start discussing something else, as if she didn't just piss you off.

I take several deep breaths to calm myself and sit next to my father when he peeks up at me, his hand stretching to gently pat mine while shaking his head. "Don't fight," he whispers. "Just enjoy lunch."

The drive south from my parents' townhouse in Pembroke Pines to Nikki's palm tree-lined street in Miami Lakes was quicker than usual because there wasn't much traffic. As I approach the gate along the side of the house, the voices from the backyard get louder. César and Nikki are sitting at the table inside the screened-in patio, their two kids and some of their friends splashing and jumping into the pool.

"Hi Rocky," César says. I kiss him hello. "You're just in time. I was telling Nikki about the album launch party *La Gata* is having in a couple weeks after her concert. You should come."

"I'm sorry, who?" I kiss Nikki hello, then I drop my pockabook on the table and slide a chair out.

"You're kidding, right?" César exclaims, grabbing a handful of pretzels from the bowl on the table.

"You know she's a rocker girl. Rock music is all she and Victor used to listen to," Nikki adds. "But she'll come to the launch party anyway because it'll be fun, and Rodrigo will be there."

Last night, Xavier asked me about my music taste too, surprised that I had never heard the song that played in his car while we drove to his apartment. Once I shared the names of some bands I listen to, I was not expecting him to say his favorite *Soda Stereo* song was the same as mine.

"Rodrigo? From my firm?" César inquires, lifting an eyebrow.

"Oh." She shrugs and scoops up some pretzels from the bowl. "I must've forgotten to mention that I'm trying to set Rodrigo and Rocky up."

"Isn't he younger than her?"

"See"—I smack Nikki's arm—"even César thinks he's too young for me."

"That's not what he said," she quips, shooting me a sharp look. "And yes, he is younger than her but that's not an issue." She stares at César, her eyes widening.

"Cougars are trendy now, aren't they?" He's laughing at his own words under his breath.

"Okay, enough about my non-existent love life," I huff. "Who's the artist?"

"You probably heard her songs on the radio at some point. She's the super popular Latina artist, the one that collaborates with all the big reggaeton stars."

"I think I know who you're talking about. If it's who I'm thinking, it's the artist that Cata loves, the Colombian one, right?"

"Yes, that's her," César adds.

"César just signed her as a client a few weeks ago. It's a work event for him, so he's getting Alondra, you, and me concert tickets and invites to the album release party."

"Why not! I have nothing on my social agenda for the rest of the year. Sign me up!" I rise and turn to slide the door open. "Need some water, I'll be right back." As I'm pulling the door closed behind me, Nikki stops it and follows me into the kitchen.

"*¿Cafecito?*" Nikki asks, grabbing the Moka Express from the stovetop.

"Yes, please."

"So, spill! Who's the mystery man?" I push the refrigerator door shut after grabbing a bottle of water.

"All I know is his name is Xavier." He rocked my world last night. I didn't expect to enjoy my time with him as much as I did.

"What else?"

My shoulders lift. "*Nada.* I mean, we went back to his place, which was in this bougie building. His apartment takes up the whole floor."

"Oh, so we know he has ridiculous money."

"With a place like that, he must." I pop the top off the water bottle and sip.

"And his fancy apartment didn't make you curious to ask what he does for work?"

I shake my head. "Nope. The less I know, the better." At least, that's what I keep telling myself, since he's been on my mind all morning. Our sexual chemistry was intense, but it was his genuine interest in talking and asking questions that softened me, got me sharing some personal details.

"*Ay*, Rocky. *Por lo menos* you could've asked some questions. If you've learned nothing from me over the years, you've at least learned *como ser chismosa*."

Nikki loves to know all the gossip that's happening with people she knows, and even with those she doesn't. "Aside from what I shared, the only thing I know for certain is he's fine as fuck." I lean in and whisper, "And his tongue is magic."

"You *do* look quite relaxed; he must've fucked you good."

"I don't know if it was my shriveled-up lady bits talking, but I've never had anyone go down on me like that." An image of me propped up on his counter, legs spread for him, flits through my mind and gives me goosebumps.

"I mean, your husband was a selfish prick who only ever thought about himself. I'm not surprised." She scoops coffee grounds into the filter.

"First, he's my ex-husband! We need to get the terminology right! Second, I'm pretty sure I let the champagne do the talking. He drove us to his house, and we got frisky on the drive up." Remembering how his fingers explored me as we drove to his place sends a tingle up my spine. "Well, I let him get frisky with me. I came so hard with just his hand, I was seeing stars."

"She's back! Yes!" Nikki has a smile plastered across her face; you'd think she was the one who hooked up last night.

"After orgasm number five, I lost count. He must've thought I was some pent-up crazed woman." I chuckle.

"Hopefully he fucked Victor right out of your thoughts. When are you seeing him again?"

"I'm not. He started asking personal questions, and I split. I talked myself into one night and that's what we had." When I realized he was digging with the goal of getting to know me better, I knew it was time to leave. I hadn't even been divorced twenty-four hours, and I wasn't ready to start sharing myself again. I won't share that with Nikki because in her mind, I've been single since the day I left Victor.

"What? After all that great sex? You can't be serious!"

The sex was incredible; would it be so bad if I went back for another incredible night?

"I am. Although, I've been questioning my decision all morning."

CHAPTER SEVEN

Xavier

MARITZA and I are at my studio working through some details for the upcoming tour. Early last year, I purchased a small run-down house in the Design District of Miami, then renovated and converted it into my office and recording studio. This way I have a dedicated space to work on my music, and we have a place to gather and brainstorm. Before I got involved with drugs, I mostly worked out of the house I lived in at the time. Now that I'm back on my feet, I prefer to keep my work and personal space separate. I still have an office at my penthouse, but now I conduct most of my business from here. It also allowed me to have a full recording studio where I'm able to lay down tracks, including collaborating with other artists, without having to go elsewhere to record.

"What's going on with the venues?"

"Mexico City is confirmed, and *Ficha* has already started promoting and selling tickets," Maritza responds. When Roly was coordinating the tour stops with *Ficha Mundial*'s tour manager, we were told to start in Mexico City because of the label's other tours happening in other cities. They wanted to ensure at least one of their artists was in Mexico on those dates. "But the venues in Tegucigalpa, Honduras and Asunción, Paraguay, aren't available on the dates we want."

"What's the plan?" I inquire.

After my collab with *La Gata* blew up last year, shit got hectic, and I couldn't keep up. Xiomary urged me to hire a personal assistant, probably more for her than me, because I was calling her and Katia for everything. Katia recommended Maritza for the position, and it couldn't have been a more perfect fit. We've been working together for a year and a half and we just vibe, affording me the time to focus more on my music and branding.

"Roly and I spoke with the tour manager, and we agreed that we'll need to find different venues in those two cities because they've already started promoting and selling tickets for the confirmed venues," Maritza says. "We won't be able to move any of the other cities and dates."

"Let's go with the smaller venues we had originally planned on," I add.

Talks of going on tour started before I recorded with *La Gata*. But since the success of our collab, we've had to change nearly everything. The song spending months at the top of the Latin charts drove more sales and downloads of my individual music, which resulted in Roly recommending larger venues, causing us to scrap the entire plan and start from scratch.

"By the way, VIP tickets already sold out for the shows where tickets are live." This is the first tour we're doing a VIP experience for fans, since Roly says a majority of the artists are doing them nowadays, it's almost expected.

"In all the cities where tickets are live?" I agreed to do them because Roly thinks it's what we should do, but I didn't think they'd sell out. After the shitstorm that was my life, I really wasn't sure if I'd be well received upon my return.

"Yup," she responds, grinning. "And tickets are live in every city except for the two we need to book. Well, except North America, those will probably go live next week, after Xiomary approves the contracts."

"Damn, wasn't expecting that." I lean back in the chair, allowing myself to absorb the news that the fans are as excited to see me performing as I am to be getting back out there.

"Xavi, you shouldn't be surprised. Your fans love you. And they especially love a good comeback story. Anyway, I'll let Xiomary know we'll be getting new contracts for those two cities."

"Roly won't like it, but there's no way around it." When we scrapped the original tour plan, Roly was adamant about playing at arenas and not amphitheaters, insistent that the music sales would support the bigger venues—and so far, he's been right.

"Oh, I almost forgot," Maritza adds. "Misu, the producer from Argentina, wants to schedule you for recording sessions." She looks up at me from behind the desk. "Is that something you want to do before the tour kicks off?"

I peek at my watch. "We'll be in Buenos Aires for two shows. It makes sense for us to try and work the sessions into the time we're down there. Let him know I'm happy to do it, but it'll have to wait till then."

"Okay, I'll make a note and run it by Roly." After she finishes jotting down a few things, she crosses the room to the kitchen area to grab a soda.

When Maritza started working for me, she had recently graduated with her bachelor's degree in event management and marketing. She's taken the lead on planning the upcoming tour, and Roly has given her more responsibility because she's incredible at it. I'm lucky that the first assistant I hired was a perfect fit and Xiomary often reminds me to make sure Maritza is not only well compensated but always appreciated for the work she does.

"Mari, while you're in there, bring me a water, please."

"Here you go," Maritza says, extending me the bottle.

"Thanks."

"Katia called me and said the deal with the Brazilian designer is done. I'll reach out to them and coordinate. We need to schedule a photo shoot and create the social media and marketing plan."

"Yeah, I signed the documents last week and—" My phone rings, interrupting us.

"*Dímelo*," I say, answering when I see my friend Orlando's name.

Landy and I met when I first came to Miami during the early days of my career. At that time, he was producing music with a small label. Since then, he's gone independent and opened his own recording studio in Wynwood, allowing him to work with more artists. When I signed with *Capicú*, one of the labels at *Ficha Mundial* Latin Entertainment, I told Xiomary she had to negotiate Landy producing my music into the contract or there was no deal, and they agreed.

"Yo, real quick," Landy says. "The album files were just sent to mastering. Macho's gonna start working on them when he finishes his current project. Said if he likes the mixes, we should be able to listen to the album in two weeks."

I shift in my seat and rest my elbows on my knees. "What do you mean if he likes the mixes?"

Macho Diamante is the mastering engineer Landy works with on all the music he produces. Macho's known for making the roughest of tracks shine like a diamond—hence the name.

"His usual mixing engineer wasn't available, so he's working with someone else."

"Damn. Macho's masters are always tight, so I have faith he'll get it done." Roly strolls in, greeting Mari with a cheek to cheek kiss and then crossing to where I'm sitting on the couch, extending his hand, and giving me a grip and slide handshake.

"One more thing, I was approached about creating a collab with you and Santo Toro."

Mateo Santoro, who goes by the stage name of Santo Toro, is a young artist who's making noise on the scene. He's had a few number one hits in his native Argentina and his first just made the Latin Billboards. I don't know much about him yet and will need to do a bit more research, make a few calls before I agree to collaborating with him.

"Let's talk about it more *y te aviso*. Mari will schedule something for us."

I slide my phone onto the table and quickly update Roly and Maritza. "Mari, please schedule a lunch or dinner for me and Landy."

Roly takes up residence on the couch to my right. "While you're at it, Mari, please schedule a meeting for *Flaco* with the CPA. She called me on my way here and needs to discuss a few things with him."

"We just had our monthly finance meeting last week. Is everything okay?"

"As far as I know. She didn't sound concerned or say it was urgent," Roly adds.

"Mari, please set it up," I instruct. "Whatever she needs."

Mari nods.

For the next two hours, the three of us review the first print concepts from *Pulso Urbano*, the company we've partnered with to create exclusive tour merch. Each tour stop will have a city exclusive poster and t-shirt design, and what we've seen so far hits at the intersection of streetwear and concert tees. We'll also be selling obsidian black and ultraviolet oversized hoodies, distressed mesh jerseys that mimic basketball jerseys, except stylized as streetwear, vintage acid-wash tees with listed tour stops, chrome-colored bandanas splashed with ultraviolet, and water bottle carriers with an integrated LED strip that can be synced via an app to pulse with the concert's bass. Now that we've approved the artwork, they'll create some samples and send them out. Although I get final approval on the tour merch, *Ficha* has to be on board with whatever we select.

"Okay, guys. I'm out," Mari says. "I'll be running those errands we talked about earlier. I'll check in later."

"*Dale*," I say, and rise to kiss her goodbye.

Once she's gone, Roly says, "I'm sorry about dinner the other night. I know you wanted to talk details with Xiomary about the tour."

"We good. It worked out in my favor." I shift and rest my arm on the back of the couch.

"Yeah, how's that?"

"If you'd have been there, we would've talked shop all night until my sister left, and I wouldn't have had a wandering eye. *Y nunca hubiera conocido a la mujerona que conocí.*" I probably wouldn't have met Rocky and that would've been a crime. Watching the way her curves swayed in that dress and her ass bounced to the music, I knew I had to meet her. And once I did, I wasn't mistaken. She was reserved yet confident. A woman who's comfortable in her own skin and isn't afraid to take control while in my bed. "Haven't been able to get her out of my mind." I pull my lower lip between my teeth, picturing Rocky with her legs spread for me as I made her writhe and moan to the tune of my licks.

"Oh, shit, it's like that?" He smacks his hands together.

My head gestures up and down. "She was something else, Roly. She had this quiet confidence. I haven't met a woman like that…I don't think, ever." She was eager yet reticent. When she fully relaxed, she was in the moment, but once her thoughts started churning, she'd put the brakes on. You could see the internal battle as she put her walls up.

"I haven't heard you talk about a woman since Lisandra."

Hearing that name takes me back, stirring memories of a different life of two young people living the party life and in love. Lisandra and I were together for a few years before I got into my accident. She wore my ring on her finger, and I thought she'd be Mrs. Delgado. "I was twenty-three when I started dating her. I ain't that guy no more."

After I got hooked on Percocet and chose them over her, she cut me off without a second thought. Back then, I was too high to care, too high to realize how much I hurt her. Lisandra leaving me was just another excuse I made to rationalize popping pills. Putting blame where it had no business being. When I finally got clean, I thought about reaching out but learned she had moved on and was in a committed relationship. I had already destroyed so much in my life, I didn't want to add yet another thing to my list. Maybe someday I'll get the opportunity to apologize for how my selfish ways wrecked the plans we had set out for ourselves.

"You're the same kid I met, except now you have your shit together."

When I was younger, I wanted to be famous. Making money was a bonus. Now that I'm older and back in the game, my priorities have shifted and setting myself up for the future is where it's at. "I've been focused on getting my career back on track. And it's not like I was looking for anything the other night, but she caught my eye from across the restaurant."

A few nights ago

I glance around Bistro Danzón as I wait for Xiomary to finish a call she's on. Our table is along the left side of the dining room, across from the bar. As I peruse the large space, searching for familiar faces, my eyes land on a table of three women to the left of the bar. A woman in black with dark curls cascading down her back throws her head back in laughter. When she's done laughing, she adjusts herself in the chair, her posture erect and steady, occupying the space in front of her by extending her arms on the table. The live music picks up again and one of the women stands, encouraging the others to stand as well. They turn and shimmy their way through the tables toward the dance floor. Despite the tight spaces, this woman's steps are deliberate and measured as she navigates the dining room. The three women sway and spin with one another, but it's the woman in the black dress who's intrigued me. She moves with easy confidence, as if nothing or nobody can affect her. As her body sways to the rhythm of the conga drums, she's smiling—a smile that stretches from ear to ear and radiates around her.

"Sorry about that," Xiomary says, interrupting me. "It was one of my LA clients."

My eyes shift to my sister. "It's okay," I respond, glancing back toward the woman in the black dress. Before my night is over, I need to meet her.

"Life's best surprises often strike when least expected." He shifts, settling into his corner of the couch.

Nodding in agreement, I say, "She made me feel some sort of way. I don't know." Her words were measured yet her eyes held a certainty in them. She wanted more but forced herself to close the door. The way Rocky took what she wanted to make herself feel good was such a turn on. It's a rare quality I love discovering about women.

"When are you seeing her again?"

"That's the problem. Other than her first name, I don't know anything about her. She had no intentions of doing anything other than spending a few hours with me."

"Well, you're *El Flaco Casanova*, women everywhere want to spend a few hours with you." He chuckles.

El Flaco Casanova is the stage name that was given to me in my early days of reggaeton. On the streets of Carolina, Puerto Rico, where we went to live with my grandmother after our parents were killed, I was known as *el flaco* because of my tall, slender stature. My mother, Patrizia Casanova, was a Venezuelan born to Italian parents, and her last name completed my stage persona. Add that my songs are often laden with rhymes about sex and women, and the name embodies my music.

"That's the thing, I'm pretty sure she has no idea who I am."

Roly quickly shifts in his seat to face me. "What, how's that possible?" He raises an eyebrow. "*¿No era latina?*"

I shrug. "She's from Argentina. When I approached her at the bar there were no signs of recognition on her face. Then, when we were in the car, '*Volví*' came on the radio, and she didn't recognize it. She said it's because she's more of an AC/DC girl."

"And all you have is her name?"

"Yeah—Rocky. And I'm not sure that's actually her name. As soon as I started asking personal questions, she freaked out and called it a night."

It was like she flipped a switch. One moment, she was relaxed from her most recent orgasm, allowing herself to just be present. Her skin was glowing and slick with sweat. The next moment, she was getting dressed. She revoked permission to continue in her relaxed state. Rather than tell me she wouldn't answer my question, she ended it. Her mind and heart were at odds. While she turned me down, she was incapable of meeting my eyes, yet allowed me to continue indulging in her softness.

Roly suppresses his laugh. "Damn, *Flaco*. That must be a first for you."

I shoot him a sideways glance. "I went back to Bistro Danzón the next night to ask the bartender if he'd ever seen her, but he hadn't. He thought it may have been her first time in."

"Oh, you went looking for her. So you're serious, then?"

Rocky's forced reluctance piques my interest, makes me want to do everything I can to find her and peel back her layers.

Nodding, I respond, "Serious as a hawk on a hunt. But I think I'm at the end of the road. She took an Uber, it was her first time at that restaurant, and she had just gotten divorced that day, which means she was just out for a good time. I've googled her first name y *nada*, nothing but a bunch of dudes or movie information in my search results." My head shakes in disappointment.

"Maybe she'll go back to the restaurant soon and the bartender will recognize her," Roly suggests.

Rocky's rejection struck a chord, making me pine for her more. What we can't have often becomes what we want the most. That, and she has no idea who I am, or that I loved talking with her as we were lying in bed. It was the first time a woman was interested in me and not *El Flaco Casanova*.

"If he sees her, he already knows to reach out to me," I tell him. When I returned to Bistro Danzón, I slipped the bartender a couple hundred bucks as an incentive to keep an eye out.

My phone starts vibrating on the table and when I reach for it, Roxana's name flashes on my screen, indicating an incoming video call. "*Dímelo*," I answer.

"*Hola*, Xavier. How are you?" Roxana has long, dark blonde hair and vibrant blue eyes.

"Good, good. I'm here with Roly."

"He's your manager, right?"

I nod. "Yeah, glad you remember him from the studio."

Roly slides across the couch and shows his face to the camera. "Hi Roxana, it's nice to see you again. And congratulations on the collab. It's beyond what any of us expected."

Roxana beams at Roly's words, her eyes lighting up as she nods in agreement. "It's incredible. I credit the producer. He saw Xavier at that show in Medellín and knew." She goes off screen and quickly returns. "*Flaco*, the crowd is going to go crazy when you come out on the stage." Her smile illuminates the screen.

"I can hear the screams already." I beam, my body buzzing with excitement in anticipation of being on stage performing. "Especially since this will be our first time singing it live," I add.

Since the song's release several months ago, we haven't had the opportunity to be in the same place at the same time. Although we've both done interviews, sometimes on the same show but via video, we've never performed it outside the studio. We've had conversations about when it would happen and thought maybe the Latin Grammys later this year would be the first time. We don't know that the song will be nominated, but Roly said there's some talk about having us perform at the award ceremony and he told me, "Your performance all but secures your nomination."

"What I have in mind is for us to sing it as the last song of the night—close the show out with the two of us on stage. The crowd won't be expecting the song on the setlist, so it'll be a complete surprise."

"*¡Va a estar duro!*" I say and Roxana nods in agreement. "Listen, last week I met your lawyer, and he told me you'll be in Miami a few days before the show. You're welcome to use my studio while you're here, just let me know. We can also meet and rehearse a day or two before the concert, if you want."

"Thank you. I'll probably take you up on that. I had thought about having you come to soundcheck, but I don't want any leaks of your appearance, so that's a better idea."

"It's all good. Once we rehearse at the studio, we'll be straight."

"You guys are attending the album release party, right?" Roxana asks.

I glance at Roly, and he shrugs. "When is it?" I ask.

"The night after the concert, the seventeenth." Roly is taking notes as Roxana shares the information.

"The label is having it at a private estate on Star Island. I'll have my assistant, Gabriela, connect with Maritza to give you all the information, and to ensure your team and their plus ones are on the list. They're arranging transportation or something because apparently getting onto the island is tricky."

"Yeah, *Ficha* likes to have their events there because it's a private island that's gated with security," Roly says.

"Great, see you soon," Roxana adds.

CHAPTER EIGHT

Rocío

THE CONCERT TONIGHT is at the stadium in Miami Gardens. We decided to meet at Nikki's house since she lives in Miami Lakes. This way we can take an Uber to the stadium and then drive home with César, since he'll be there before us.

"Hi, girls," I say, walking into Nikki's kitchen where Alondra and Nikki are sitting at the large center island with quartz countertops, sipping wine. I hate that looking at it reminds me of the one I shared with Victor, since Nikki and César renovated about a year before I split with Victor by the same guy who had done our kitchen. The white cabinets make it look clean and bright and rather than a table, they use their island for seating, since it seats up to eight people.

"Damn, those jeans are *super* cute! Like, *te levantan las nalgas y todo*," Alondra says, slapping my ass as she likes to do ever since I started going to the gym.

"Thanks. I'd like to think that the torture I put myself through on the stair machine at the gym is paying off. That thing is brutal."

"I'm allergic to that machine. Well, the gym in general," Nikki chimes in, laughing before drinking the last of her wine.

"Are we having dinner before the show?" Alondra asks, adjusting her red halter top.

"I hope so, I'm already getting hungry. I'll definitely be starving before the show starts if we don't," I add.

"César mentioned there's a private pre-show event with food. Once we check in and get our badges, we'll meet him."

"*¡Por fin!* All his years as an entertainment lawyer have paid off. We finally get to go to a show that's worth it," Alondra says.

"I downloaded a few of her songs to listen to before the concert so I don't feel totally out of my element," I say.

"Honestly, Rocky. Sometimes I wonder what rock you live under!" Alondra quips.

"The rock's name was Victor—heavy and useless—but thankfully, that weight has been lifted, and I'm slowly coming alive again."

"At least your cobwebs have been dusted off," says Alondra, chuckling.

"Dusted off? Nah, he blew that shit away! I haven't stopped thinking about that man for the past two weeks." The way he thought about my pleasure before his own the entire night. Then while lying in bed, he was thoughtful and gentle. He made it really difficult to stick to my self-imposed "one night only" rule.

"You could always go to his place—he did say you know where to find him," Nikki chimes in.

"I thought about it, but I wouldn't know what to say. He lives in that fancy building with security that has one apartment per floor. A bit out of my league."

"Ah, why out of your league?" Alondra scrunches her nose. "You're beautiful and smart and successful! That man would be lucky to have a woman like you."

Why out of my league? I had a successful man with money

and look where that got me! "I suppose," I respond, lifting my shoulders, "but I'm not looking for anything serious right now."

"Why does it have to be serious though? He could be your friend with benefits," Alondra suggests.

"Especially since you know how good the benefits are," Nikki adds.

"Those benefits would be wicked good!" I contemplate. It felt incredible to feel wanted and desired like I did that night. Xavier looked at me like he wanted me to be his next meal, and I can't remember the last time I felt so beautiful. I could get used to something like that again. But that would also mean effort on my part, even if I don't plan on having anything serious. After being burned so badly, I need to protect myself. "I don't know. I have a trial in a few weeks so maybe when that's over. In the meantime, I'll have to rely on my trusted toys. They'll be loyal till the end."

"Except your toys don't talk dirty to you," says Alondra.

"He's the first guy I've experienced dirty talk with. Victor was never like that with me."

"Victor was a selfish asshole," Nikki exclaims.

"He wasn't always selfish," I recall. "In the early days, we had fun. There was a time we had a lot of sex. Really good sex."

"That's one thing I'll say about David, his dirty talk alone would wind me up something good. I loved it," Alondra adds.

Nikki glances at her watch. "Enough about your raggedy exes. Let me call an Uber."

"It got me going. Something I never knew I needed in my life, but probably won't be able to live without," I say.

"Okay, the Uber will be here in a few minutes. Let's go have some fun," says Nikki, adjusting the turquoise blouse tucked into her black pants.

"Yeah, yeah, we know you have a great husband who does all the things," Alondra teases, chuckling.

We gather our stuff and wait for the car in front of Nikki's house. Once inside the vehicle, Alondra asks, "What are you girls wearing to the album release tomorrow night? I know César said we should dress up as if we were going out for a night on the town, look chic."

"I'm wearing a cute blue dress that's blingy," says Nikki. "I have these super cute heels that I recently bought. César will have on one of his nicer suits with a matching colored tie."

"Aww, matchy, matchy, *qué cute*! What about you, Rocky? Have you decided?"

"I'm torn between a black one-piece jumpsuit or a fuchsia cocktail dress I bought a few years ago and never wore. We'll see which one I'm feeling tomorrow when it's time to get dressed." After I told César and Nikki I'd attend the album release party, I rummaged through my closet in search of the perfect outfit.

"Fuchsia, for sure. Rodrigo will be there," Nikki says. "And you need to show off those Stairmaster legs."

"He hasn't even reached out." I shake my head. And since Nikki gave him my number instead of the other way around, it would be weird reaching out first, wouldn't it? "He probably did some digging and found out I'm older than him and lost any interest he may have had."

"Nah, he's been in trial for the past couple of weeks. I've seen him at the courthouse several times. They had some huge case, but they wrapped it up earlier this week."

"Ah, yeah. I know how that goes. When I'm in trial, I like to be in the zone." Trial work is exhausting because, although the actual time in court is like a regular workday, as the trial lawyer, I'm always putting in extra work in the early mornings and after the court day finishes. So much time goes into the trial that I have little left in me to do anything other than eat and sleep, and even those are scarce.

"See, you have something else in common," Nikki chimes in, smirking.

The Uber drops us off near the South Gate, where we have to check in to get our badges so César can meet us. There are people milling around but you can tell that it's still early because the crowds haven't descended yet.

"Do you think we'll have to make the line?" Alondra asks.

"Nah, César said this is the VIP entrance. Besides, the gates for the regular show don't open until six-thirty." As we approach the glass doors, Nikki halts and turns. "I need your licenses for security." I dig for my wallet, pull out my license, and hand it to Nikki.

After clearing security, we approach the tables where a man is helping someone at one table. We walk up to a thin woman with pale skin and light brown hair behind the other table. "Hi," she says, looking up at Nikki. "Name, please."

"Hi. Niurka Molina. There are three of us."

"I'm sorry, can you pronounce that again?" the woman shoots back, a slight twang in her tone.

"Niurka, with an N, like Nancy. Here's my ID." She hands over her driver's license.

"I'm not seeing your name on the list. Give me a moment." The woman grabs her mobile phone and dials. When the person answers she gives them Nikki's name, hacking the pronunciation. "My manager said she'll call me right back."

"Thank you," Nikki murmurs.

The woman peeks at Nikki's license again, then extends it out to Nikki. "I've never heard your name before, where's it from?"

"I'm Cuban," she responds, her tone flat. Nikki turns to us, eyes wide, terse lips, and flaming red cheeks. She's upset and this woman behind the table isn't helping with her flippant tone.

Nikki was born in Cuba but like many here, moved to Miami with her parents and siblings at a young age to escape the thumb of communism. She's the oldest of four siblings—all of them with names having Russian origins because of Cuba's dependence on the Soviet Union during the Cold War.

"*Hola, mi amor*," César says, and the three of us turn on our heels to see César stepping off the escalator to our left.

"Hi," Nikki responds, her shoulders softening.

"Sally, this is my wife, Niurka, and her two friends. They need friends and family passes, not the regular VIP passes."

"Your lanyards," the woman says with an outstretched hand. "You have to wear this at all times. Your seat numbers are on the back." Nikki takes them and hands one to each of us.

"Thank you," César says, as we collectively walk toward the escalator.

Alondra flips the badge around. "Holy shit, this says row B. Does that mean we're in the second row?" She hangs the pink lanyard around her neck. The lanyard has the words *color de rosas* in black lettering with pink glitter stones outlining the letters.

"Yes," César responds. "We're on the right side of the stage, in the section reserved for friends and family, but it's second row."

"I've never had floor seats for a concert. I may not know the artist, but this is gonna be awesome!" I add, grabbing the pink badge in my hand. "And the passes say all access! What does that mean?"

"With those badges, you can walk anywhere in the venue without any issues," César explains.

"Wow, that's incredible!" It feels amazing to have this type of concert access. I've never experienced a concert with VIP perks, nor is it something I ever imagined.

After getting off the escalator, César halts and pulls Nikki into him, kissing her.

"Eww, get a room," Alondra says, chuckling.

"Don't hate 'cause you don't have a man right now," Nikki retorts with a smirk.

"I'm definitely hating right now." Alondra laughs under her breath.

"That woman was rude," Nikki tells César.

"Yeah, she's with this new VIP experience company Roxana hired, and it's been an issue all day."

"I thought Nikki was gonna go off," Alondra chimes in.

"I wanted to but also didn't want to ruin our night."

"*Bueno*, don't let that woman take up any more space. Let's go into the bar and enjoy the night," César chimes in, changing the subject. Once inside the bar area, there are people milling around, drinks in hand and chatting. The room has a good number of people, but it's by no means full. "It's open bar, and the food" —he points toward the back—"is along the wall." My eyes follow his finger and my stomach growls at the mention of food.

"You did good, César," Alondra tells him. Nikki nods in agreement and drops a kiss on his cheek.

"Roxana will come up to meet people soon, she's doing an interview with the local news, but she's almost done. She'll mingle in here for about an hour and then sound check, which is a few minutes before six. We can go down to watch that."

"This is wicked cool, César. Thank you!" I add.

"You're welcome. I hope you enjoy it, rocker girl." He winks. "I have to go back downstairs, but you ladies enjoy the food and drinks. I'll be back with Roxana soon."

After César leaves, we head to the bar to order drinks. "Order me a tropical mule, please," I tell the girls. "I'm gonna go check out the food because I'm starving."

"Grab some for us, too," Nikki requests.

The table is filled with various foods such as crispy coconut shrimp, chicken and cheese tequeños, beef skewers, empanadas, rice and black beans, and salad. I fill up two plates with a variety of items and bring some empty plates so that we can share between the three of us. We're gathered around a high-top table, finishing up our food and drinks, when we see César walk through a door in the back, followed by a woman with long blonde hair and a small group of people. As they approach us, Nikki leans in and says, "Here she comes."

The noise level in the room increases as everyone anticipates seeing and meeting Roxana. As she enters the room, people crowd her, phones in hand while asking for a picture, forcing her bodyguards to make space, but Roxana's smile remains the same, her demeanor calm. I've never seen something like this. How is she able to maintain her posture and keep her cool? I don't think I could stand a single phone being shoved into my face for a selfie. The buzz of excitement swirls as she approaches a group standing at the table next to us. César looks over at Nikki and nods.

"He told me he'd try to stop by our table with her right after getting here. I'm guessing they'll come here next."

"I've never met anyone famous," Alondra says. "I'm actually a little nervous. What do we say?"

"Just say hi. She's human like the rest of us," says Nikki.

"Not everyone can be as calm and collected as you, Captain Obvious." Alondra gently smacks Nikki's arm.

"She's used to meeting celebrities because she and César often go to work events for his clients," I add.

"I was nervous the first time I met some of César's clients," Nikki says. "But I always remember one guy saying being a celebrity has changed over time because, before cell phones, people would stop and have a conversation with him and now everyone has a phone in hand, wanting a selfie. He told us he preferred when people talked to him before asking for a picture."

"That makes sense," I add. "It must be exhausting being in the public eye all the time. I can't even imagine."

"Here they come," Alondra whispers.

"Roxana, this is Nikki, my wife, and her two friends, Alondra and Rocky."

Roxana is petite with dark blonde curls that fall to her waist. She's absolutely gorgeous with piercing blue eyes. She's fit and curvy, her golden skin on display in her black skirt and crop top, with pink sparkling rhinestones. She has ink covering both of her arms and up the side of one of her legs.

"It's really nice to meet you," Nikki says, extending her hand out. "I'm a big fan, so thank you for having us." Roxana leans in, giving her a kiss on the cheek. She then turns to Alondra, doing the same.

"I'm happy you're here and excited for you to experience today's show."

"It's so great meeting you. Thank you for having us," Alondra says.

After giving Roxana a cheek kiss, I say, "Nice meeting you, Roxana. Thank you for having us. We're wicked excited for your show tonight."

"You girls will be at my album release party tomorrow night, right?" Roxana says, looking between the three of us.

"Yes, we're super excited about it too," Alondra responds.

"Good, they're a lot of fun *y más íntimos* than any of the other events I do."

"It'll be the first time we've been to one," Nikki tells her.

"It definitely won't be the last, at least not as long as I'm working with César." Roxana glances at César then back to Nikki.

"I was at your show in Miami last year," Alondra chimes in.

"It was *super* good, probably the best concert I've been to." Alondra's smile is spread across her face, her eyes glowing in excitement.

"Did you ladies go to that show together, too?" Roxana asks.

My head shakes. "No, tonight will be the first time for me."

"Well, you're in for a treat. It's going to be incredible. And don't leave early because I have a surprise at the end." She winks and flashes a toothy smile. Her bodyguard signals that they need to move to the next table. "I'm being told we have to go, but before I do, let's take some pictures."

We all take pictures with her as a group before a few selfies with each of us, and then she continues making her rounds.

"Wait till I show Cata these pictures. She's gonna flip!" I say.

A few hours later we're at our seats, the stadium nearly full as I glance around. According to César, Roxana will be performing to a sold-out crowd. Because this is a special concert put on by *Ficha Mundial* Latin Entertainment, there is no opening act.

The stage is so close. The heat emanates from the lights, the speakers and stage equipment stretching dramatically different from this angle. When the stadium lights dim, the roar of the crowd reverberates. Fans begin chanting *Gata*, calling for their artist to make her presence known. The energy is electric and as the sound level increases, the screen at the back of the stage illuminates in various shades of pink with the words *color de rosas* in black scrolling across the display, followed by introductory music.

Two rows of dancers fill the stage from each side, lining the catwalk that leads out to the open area of the stage. Each dancer holds two poles with lighted pink fabric. Roxana's voice rings out, "ME-AH-ME," and the crowd goes wild—screaming, whistling, and words of adoration filling the air. Roxana emerges from beneath the tunnel created by the dancers while singing to the tune of afrobeats.

"Hace tiempo que no te veo
Últimamente I've been flying solo
Esta vida de soltera me tiene con ganas
Y hace rato que rodeas y me llamas
No sé lo que piensas ni lo que te tramas
Pero estoy lista para tenerte y disfrutarte en mi cama."

Her words caress the crowd, and I instantly recognize the song from the ones I downloaded because the lyrics spoke to me as a newly single woman who was able to indulge in all that Xavier gave me that night. The entire stadium is singing along with her, holding their phones up and swaying. Although she is a "new to me" artist, my skin prickles as I experience the emotional connection her fans share with her. I wasn't sure if I'd enjoy a concert by an artist whose music I don't listen to, but if this is an indicator, it's going to be a great night.

I glance at my watch, and Roxana has been on stage for nearly two hours. Alondra is to my right, and I link arms with her, letting the music carry us as we take it all in. Nikki is singing along, César's arms wrapped around her from behind and they sway together. As the song is coming to an end, *La Gata* is saying goodbye to the crowd, thanking them for their love and support. The music ends and she exits the stage, followed by her dancers, and then the musicians. But the lights remain off. Whistles and cheers from the crowd fill the air. Although the stadium is dark, dancers begin roaming the stage as smoke fills the air. There has to be more.

The crowd starts chanting *otra, otra* repeatedly, calling for her to come back out onto the stage for one more song. After a few minutes, she reappears and the crowd roars, the sudden swell of noise followed by echoing shouts, applause, and whistling.

César turns toward us and says, "Wait till you see what's coming. She has a special guest, and it's gonna be epic!"

"*¡Gracias, Miami! ¡Los quiero!* To thank you for all your love over the years, I want to bring out a special guest." The crowd erupts in cheers, the chaotic yet unified noise building the anticipation. The energy around us is rumbling, the continuous undercurrents of murmurs adding to the overall excitement of what's to come. Roxana welcomes *El Flaco Casanova*, and the piercing screams and whistles explode around us.

I lean into Nikki and ask, "Who did she announce?"

Nikki yells, "He's a reggaeton artist. Last year they collaborated on a song, and it was super popular."

A thick fog-like smoke fills the stage and through the dramatic effects emerges a tall figure, accompanied by electronic synths and tropical beats. *La Gata* halts at the end of the walkway and starts singing about him being here and he can't stop her. He follows, turns to face her, and responds by singing he's crazy to be with her and he didn't know if he'd see her again. His voice is deep and rhythmic, with an edge that complements her soaring vocal lines. Their voices are a perfect blend of pop and urban sounds.

The crowd is going wild with *El Flaco Casanova*'s sultry voice. Roxana turns to walk down the stage away from us and the man turns to walk toward us. My heartbeat increases to a rapid flutter when I recognize his thin nose and neatly trimmed beard. The same beard that tickled my thighs and the lips that made me soar. Xavier is rapping, blending Spanish and English in a flow of rhythmic lyrics that is firing up the crowd.

"Holy shit!" I say, grasping Alondra and Nikki's arms to steady myself.

"What's the matter?" Alondra asks, leaning into me.

Nikki turns, and I say, "That's Xavier, the mystery man from two weeks ago."

"Where?" asks Nikki, searching the area.

"On stage. That's him, singing with *La Gata*. The line of his nose and his beard are unmistakable!" My legs squeeze together remembering how his facial hair brushed my sensitive skin.

"Get out!" Alondra squeals.

"Girl, as if this night wasn't amazing already!" Nikki says. She's dancing and singing along with *La Gata* as she's belting out how much he confuses her. Xavier continues crossing the stage in our direction and Nikki begins screaming in an effort to get his attention.

I squeeze her arm. "What are you doing?"

"Now you can stop questioning your decision."

I'm frozen in place. I imagined a thousand different ways I may have run into him again, including me going back to his bougie building in Sunny Isles Beach. Him rapping on stage while thousands of women swoon over him was *not* one of them.

As he approaches the side of the stage, his glance briefly crosses mine. He continues walking but when it registers that it's me, he steps back, locking his gaze with mine. The microphone hovers at his mouth as he continues singing.

"Te hablo en serio mi deseo
There's no way you wouldn't know
Not sure why *apretaste el freno*
Tú sabes que nosotros tenemos tremendo flow."
All.
While.
Staring.
At.
Me.

CHAPTER NINE

Rocío

"My phone finally has service again," I say as César pulls out of the stadium lot. I've been furiously trying to get a signal since seeing Xavier on stage, but with the number of people in attendance at the concert, it was impossible.

After Xavier and *La Gata* finished performing and exited the stage, the stadium staff started shuffling people out, trying to clear the floor. I wanted to see him, confirm it was actually him and not my mind playing tricks on me, because it's still all so surreal.

"Phones almost never work when there's that many people in one place," Nikki adds, glancing back from the passenger seat.

My phone displays full bars and I open the browser, typing in *El Flaco Casanova*. His name appears at the top with the words *American Rapper and Singer* underneath, followed by a few pictures. "Oh shit, it says he's thirty-one years old!"

"Really working that cougar thing, aren't you?" César teases.

"Apparently, the universe wants me sleeping with younger men." I had no idea he was ten years younger than me, but how would I know? It's not like we asked those kind of personal details, although if it had been up to him, we would've.

"Madame Universe, please send some of whatever juju you're blessing Rocky with over my way," Alondra says, chuckling, as she's looking up and out the window.

When I click on the largest picture, it fills my screen, his soft brown eyes staring back at me. *Holy shit, it really is him.* I long press and save the image and continue gawking. Picture after picture displays his closely shaved beard, accentuating his strong jaw, evoking memories of him as he licked me up and down. I squeeze my legs together to tame the tingling sensation.

"Girl, this man is fine!" Alondra says while peering at my phone.

"Tell me something I don't know," I respond as I continue gaping at pictures of him and saving them as I go. In all of them, whether on stage or elsewhere, his eyes are soft or turned up, relaxed shoulders and lips upturned. His smile is disarming, full of charisma, and lights up his entire face. There's a boyish charm to him that peeks through the rough, tattooed exterior. Despite finding dozens of pictures, I've not yet seen any of him bare-chested. There were a few of just his tattoos or where he was pulling up the hem of his shirt, but never fully off.

"Did you find the article about his ex-girlfriend yet?" Nikki inquires.

Ugh, of course there's an ex-girlfriend. "Nope, not yet. I'm still drooling as I scroll." When I go back to the search bar and type his name again, the auto-populated search terms that appear: *El Flaco Casanova girlfriend, El Flaco Casanova songs, El Flaco Casanova net worth, El Flaco Casanova age*, and many more. Damn, he's pretty popular and I was oblivious to him the entire time we were together. When I select the girlfriend prompt, several news articles appear along with pictures of a gorgeous woman named Lisandra Torres, a well-known agent in the boxing world and the daughter of a storied Puerto Rican fighter. She's beautiful with dark tight curls and curves—think sexy and sculpted, like someone who lifts but also loves rice and beans. I know it's not rational, but seeing pictures of them together, her hand wrapped in his, or his arm grasping her hip causes jealousy to twist in the pit of my stomach. I've been trying to convince myself it was just one night, but the more I try, the harder I fail. Seeing him now with Lisandra makes me wish he were mine, that it's my hand his fingers are intertwined with, my hip he's possessively grasping.

My mouth goes slack as I read an article titled "The Drug Habit that Cost Him His Career: *El Flaco Casanova* Chose Drugs over His Career and His Girl." I don't know what's worse—the fact that he's a drug addict, or that reading about their breakup makes me feel warm and fuzzy. Is it wrong? Probably, but I'm learning to not apologize for my feelings. Besides, feelings never ask permission, they just shove their way in and make themselves at home.

"Um, apparently he got involved in drugs and that's why she broke up with him."

"Allegedly," César chimes in. "These stars, they deal with a lot of sensationalism. So take everything you read with a grain of salt."

"Is there any truth to all these stories?" I ask while clicking the news tab at the top of the search results and skim the headlines.

Downward Spiral, *El Flaco Casanova* Hits Rock Bottom and Loses Everything: His Career, His Home, and His Fiancée.

Rock-Bottom Split: After Xavier Delgado, who goes by the stage name *El Flaco Casanova*, hits rock bottom, his girlfriend leaves him to fend for himself.

Addiction Defeated: *El Flaco Casanova* proves redemption is the ultimate comeback.

"Not sure, I don't really know him," César responds, glancing back at me through the rearview mirror. "I only met him a few weeks ago. I do know his sister. She speaks very highly of him."

"That's gotta speak for something, right?" Nikki adds.

The headlines are dramatic, talk about him going off the grid and counted him out, predicting his career would end and never recover. But the tabloids are in the business of selling stories. As I'm reading, I'm torn between what I read and what I know about the man who made me orgasm more times than I can remember. How much truth is there about his drug addiction? How much should I allow it to influence the choices I make?

I've usually made it my practice to steer clear of drugs, in general. Sure, I smoked weed and popped an ecstasy pill here and there in my early twenties but always hated how they made me feel and have seen the destruction they cause. Because of that, I tried to distance myself from those who partied a bit too much. I don't want to judge him based on celebrity gossip, but I'd be lying if I said I wasn't worried. From the little I've seen, he didn't seem like a drug addict, but then again, it can be an easy thing to hide. I was slightly put off by those stories but I also know how the media loves to drag celebrities through it for the sake of selling. I want to ask him about it, but really, do I even have the right to ask?

"Wait," Nikki blurts, turning in her seat and handing me her phone. "This is one of his recent Instagram posts. It looks like the bar top at Bistro Danzón. Was this the night you met him?"

I grab the phone from her, gaping at the picture. It's his right hand stretched across the bar, his silver watch peeking out from the jean jacket he wore that night. A rocks glass stands next to his hand, the champagne flute I was drinking from not too far behind it. When zooming in, the remnants of my lipstick staining the glass rim appear. The caption reads, *Excited pa lo que viene.* "Holy shit, I think it is!"

"What does that caption mean? What's coming?" Alondra asks, pulling the phone from my hand.

He must've taken this picture when I left him to go call Nikki from the bathroom. It's the only time he would've had to snap it. "I have *no* idea!"

"Um, you. You were coming that night! That's what his caption means," Nikki quips, throwing her head back in laughter.

The car comes to a halt as we pull into the driveway at Nikki's house. As we gather in the driveway to say goodnight, Alondra asks, "You're still going to the album release party tomorrow night, right?"

"Of course she is, what kind of question is that?" Nikki retorts.

"Good night, ladies," César says, kissing each of us cheek to cheek.

"I'll be right in," Nikki tells him.

"I'm not sure I should."

"I'm not sure I should? What are you even talking about?" Nikki cries out.

"I mean, this dude is a huge megastar who I have no business being with?"

"Are you even listening to yourself right now?" Nikki huffs. "You absolutely should go. If that man could've jumped off the stage when he saw you, he would've!"

Alondra grabs my hand and spreads her fingers wide, locking them with mine. "Look, here's some advice from the girl who's been single since the David debacle. It's hard to let your guard down after you've been burned. I compare every single guy I date to David, which makes me my own worst enemy. Maybe it's because I have a daughter but whatever the reason, doesn't matter. I'm so in my head about every little thing that it makes finding the right guy like hunting for a drop in the ocean."

Alondra talking about her dating failures pulls at my heartstrings. "Girl, you trying to make me cry tonight, too?"

"A good cry is always a good thing," Nikki chimes in, wrapping her arms around us.

"No, I'm not trying to make you cry. I'm trying to prevent you from creating the same hurdles I have. You don't have a daughter so it's already easier. But please, don't let Victor be how you measure every guy from here on out. Because if you do that, you're setting yourself up for failure."

"Love you, Alondra." My heart is beaming as I wrap my arms around her and tighten. She and Nikki always keep me grounded, reminding me of who I am when I get in my own way.

"Back atcha, babe!" she whispers while tightening her arms.

Nikki wraps her arms around both of us. "I had an amazing time tonight, ladies. Thank you for making it incredible."

"Me too," Alondra and I say simultaneously.

Nikki is walking toward the front entrance, and as I'm about to get into the driver's seat, I halt. "Hey, Nikki," I shout.

"Yeah?" she responds, turning on her heel.

"Will you guys pick me up tomorrow night for the party?"

CHAPTER TEN

Xavier

I'M SITTING in the back of the SUV with Roly while Mari is sitting up front with Adrián, my security and driver. I had Mari put the Classic Rewind station on because I'm not in the mood for any conversations right now. Hearing this rock music has thoughts of Rocky spinning through my mind, hoping she's here tonight so I can finally reconnect. With the causeway traffic leading to Star Island, it took us longer than expected to get here. Adrián gets us through the gated security of Star Island and pulls the SUV up to the house, parking in the circled drive. There are very few vehicles because most guests are being shuttled here, which is a security measure required by the community.

"You good, *Flaco*?" Roly asks. "*Te veo medio nervioso.*"

Anxious is what I am, not nervous. When I first saw Rocky in the crowd last night, I doubted my own eyes. I thought maybe she was a figment of my imagination because I'd been craving to see her and searched everywhere for her. But when I took a second look, there was no mistaking the contours of her neck, her piercing green eyes, and the curls cascading down her back. They were the same curls framing her face as she sucked me off.

"Yeah, I just need to find César and ask him about Rocky."

"You think he knows her?" he asks.

"He was standing one person away from her. It would be a crazy coincidence if he didn't. And you know I don't believe in coincidences."

As we approach the arched front entrance of the home, my eyes dart around in search of César. He was practically next to Rocky at the concert, and I need to know if it was a fluke or if I've finally found her. After we exited the stage, I had asked Roly to go out and find César but by the time he made it out there, the stadium employees had cleared the area, and everyone was gone —shattering my hopes.

We enter through the front entrance of the massive home *Ficha* hosts their events at. After greeting several people on my way toward the back, I see César just outside the French doors. "Found him," I say to Roly, gesturing with my chin toward the back entrance.

"Okay, I'll meet you. I'm just gonna say hi to a few people," Roly says.

When I approach César, he's in the middle of a conversation with another man. Rather than interrupt, I stand between the both of them so they can see me. People mill around, sipping cocktails or snacking on the passed hors d'oeuvres. After a few moments, César catches sight of me. "Hello, Xavier. It's good to see you. This is Daniel, another attorney at my firm. Daniel, this is Xavier, he's Mary's brother and one of our clients."

Daniel extends his hand, gripping mine in his. "Pleasure meeting you. Mary speaks very highly of you."

"Nice to meet you, too," I say. The music streams in from the patio, "*Ley Feminina*," one of Roxana's new songs, filling the air around us.

"Too bad Mary had to miss this. She had a few things to handle in LA and flew out early this morning," César adds.

"Yeah, I would've liked for her to be here."

"Excuse me, gentlemen," says Daniel, and he slips off into the crowd behind him.

"César, I wanted to ask about the concert last night."

"Incredible show. It was loud when Roxana came out, but when you joined her, it was crazy. Good call on her part to plan it the way she did."

"Pardon me," a short woman says, extending a tray. "Crab cake?"

"No, thank you," both César and I respond.

Turning back my attention to César, I say, "Roxana always creates a frenzy, but the crowd's energy when Roxana announced me was fire. I knew the crowd would erupt, but it was more than I could've imagined." The energy in the stadium was electric. It was like the entire fandom was in synergy.

"The two of you on stage are something else!"

"Thank you. Listen, I saw you standing in the crowd and to your right there was a group of three women. I recognized one of them, her name is Rocky. Do you know her?"

His eyebrows raise. "Rocky is my wife's best friend, well, one of them. They went to law school together."

We didn't get to finish what we started because I'm nowhere near done fucking that woman. "We met a few weeks ago but we didn't get to finish our conversation," slips from my lips instead as relief floods through me.

He flashes a crooked grin and responds, "Well, she's here. She's with my wife and their friend, Alondra. They're probably out on the terrace."

The tightness I've felt since last night shifts to an electric excitement of anticipation, a surge of energy thumping in my chest.

"Has Roxana arrived yet?" I ask.

"Yes, she's here. She's upstairs giving an interview."

"Great. I'll look for her in a bit. In the meantime, thank you. I'm gonna go see if I can find Rocky."

"She's wearing a pink dress. My wife has a blue dress that sparkles"—he tugs the small kerchief in his left pocket—"this color."

"Thanks, man." I turn on my heel and push through the crowd, in search of a bright pink dress or a sparkling blue one. The expansive terrace overlooks the glittering lights of Miami Beach. Tables are strategically placed to encourage mingling, with a bar along each side and a small stage in the middle. In the distance, a fleck of bright pink appears, but a tall man is blocking the person wearing it. I step to my left and recognize her curls framing her face. The vibrant fuchsia color accentuates her heavy breasts. A smile spreads across her face and her eyes drop as she laughs gently. My heart swells at catching sight of her.

"*Flaco*." I halt and see two women.

"Hi," I respond.

"Can we get a picture with you?" the woman in a black dress asks.

"Sure."

"You and *La Gata* were amazing last night. Any plans to make more music with her?" the short blonde asks.

"Not sure, anything's possible," I say, keeping my eye on Rocky.

The women flank either side of me, and the blonde to my left lifts her phone up, positioning for a selfie. I consciously smile wide, ensuring it meets my eyes.

The woman snaps a few pics, and when she drops her phone, we separate. My eyes dart to where Rocky was standing and she's still in the same place. "Thank you," the other woman says.

"We're huge fans and that performance last night with *La Gata* was amazing!"

"I'm glad you liked it, thank you." Usually chatting with fans is something I enjoy, but right now, I want this to end so I can go get my girl.

"Will you be announcing your US tour dates soon?" the blonde asks.

"Yeah, we're wrapping up the details. Keep an eye on my socials, we'll post all the details when we announce."

"Thank you, *Flaco*."

"It was good meeting you ladies." I turn to shuffle through the throngs of people gathered, trying to keep my head down while pushing forward.

There's a sizable crowd, and I work my way toward Rocky with a laser focus. As I finagle my way through, a few more people stop me along the way to say hello or ask for a picture. Damn, don't people see I'm on a mission? When I approach Rocky, my eyes fall on the black bra strap peeking out from the left side of her dress. Once I reach her, my stomach twists because this dude she's talking to is making her smile.

Rocky is mid-sentence as I approach her, and when she recognizes me, her eyes widen and her words falter. "*Hola*, Rocky," I say, leaning in to drop a kiss on her cheek, letting my lips linger longer than they would if it were anyone else, and she gently pushes her cheek into my lips. After reluctantly separating, my fingers slide underneath her bra strap, adjusting it back into place. Her olive skin is warm and soft, like it was when she was naked in my bed. The man is scrutinizing me as I stake my claim on this gorgeous woman. *Mine*.

My presence doesn't surprise her, but my touch does, her hand reaching for mine. "Oh, thank you. Hi, Xavier." She rests her hand on mine, and I squeeze.

"*¿Como estás?*" I ask, locking gazes. Her dark green eyes are bright, shimmering in the evening sky.

"Good." Her look is sharp and assessing. Silence balloons between us despite the crowd that surrounds us. The man to my left steps closer to Rocky.

"Um, sorry…" Rocky shakes her head. "This is Rodrigo. Rodrigo, this is—"

"*El Flaco Casanova*. Yes, of course. I work with your sister, Mary. She talks about you often so it's nice to finally meet you."

"Likewise. Mind if I steal her away for a sec?" I ask, shifting my body away from him and toward Rocky.

"No, of course not. Rocky, I'll see you later."

"Okay, Rodrigo. Good to finally meet you." Her hand lifts, giving him a soft wave as he turns to walk away. "We'll talk later."

"Hi," I say, pulling my bottom lip between my teeth.

"What was that?" she asks, her eyes narrowing. "You were acting like a jealous boyfriend." Her lips turn up, smirking.

"You look beautiful. *Y ese vestido te queda…*" I bite my bottom lip. The dress is hugging her curves and lifting the globes of her ass, and I can't get the image of her naked and riding me out of my head. I adjust my stance to alleviate the pressure between my legs.

"Avoiding my question?"

"No. I heard it, but first I needed to let you know *qué hermosa te ves* in this dress."

"Thank you," she says, her eyes fluttering. "So, is jealous boyfriend the vibe you're going for?"

"Would me being your jealous boyfriend be a bad thing?" My hand lifts, tucking her curls behind her left ear while I lean into her, my lips grazing the skin near her ear. "I've been craving that pussy of yours." As I'm putting distance between us, her heavy breaths tickle my nose.

"You can't just say that," she softly gasps as I search her eyes.

"Why not?" Like the first night I met her, her eyes and body language contradict what she's saying. I watch as she swallows, searching for words to convince herself that the crackling energy surrounding us right now isn't happening.

"Because—"

I wait for her to continue but she remains silent. "Yeah, that's not gonna fly. Try again."

"You've answered all my questions with questions." Her lips purse, and she crosses her arms.

"Okay. Ask me again."

"Why didn't you tell me who you are?" She turns to face me, taking a tiny step closer to me.

"That wasn't your question."

"Well, it's my question now," she retorts.

"I did tell you. I'm Xavier."

She lifts her chin and squints. "You know what I mean."

"*El Flaco Casanova* is my job, not who I am."

"You still could've told me."

"Would it have made a difference?" I hope her finding out who I am doesn't change how she is with me because I'm not sure I could handle it.

Her body shifts and her arms remain tightly across her body. "Maybe."

"Why?"

"It just would have."

"It wouldn't have"—I place my lips at her ear again—"you still would've come in my mouth and screamed my name while you did." I smirk, and my dick twitches thinking about her legs spread for me.

She releases a soft gasp, and when I'm facing her again, she's breathing quickly. I'm waiting for her to say something, but she seems to be at a loss for words. Instead, I whisper, "I bet if I dip my finger inside of you, you'd be hot *y lista pa mí, mami*."

She drags her tongue along her dark pink stained lips and drops her eyes. "We can't do that anymore." She's forcing the words from her mouth.

"We can and we should."

Her head shakes as she swallows.

"Give me one good reason why we can't."

"You're too young for me."

"Oh, now all of a sudden my age matters?"

"*Flaco*, it's good to see you," a man I met recently says as he approaches us, but I'm not recalling his name right now. Not that I want to because what bad timing. His hand stretches out and I grasp it in mine, shaking it. When he sees recognition hasn't set in, he says, "It's Héctor. Héctor del Valle. We met at Landy's studio a few months ago. You were on your way out when I had just arrived."

"Yes. It's good to see you again, Héctor." The truth is the only thing I'm thinking about right now is getting Rocky in my bed and this dude is wasting my time.

"Anyway, Landy mentioned you may be here, so I wanted to say hello. We're not here to talk business, but that collaboration with *Santo Toro* Landy told you about, I brought that to him."

"Yeah, Landy briefly mentioned it, but we haven't had time to discuss it. We're scheduled to discuss it soon. Let me get with him and then I'd be happy to talk more."

"Great, thanks. And sorry to interrupt." He turns and walks off, and I shift, facing Rocky again.

"So, I was reminding you that age doesn't matter." I shuffle closer to her to search for her hand, needing her to feel our connection. When my fingers find hers, I wrap our pinkies together "*Tengo ganas de verte.*" I need to see her and haven't stopped thinking about her since she left me that night. Now that I've found her again, I'm not letting her get away.

"We can't." The words fall from her lips but they're empty and barely a whisper.

I search her emerald hues, looking for a sign that she wants nothing to do with me. Instead, her eyes assess mine, asking me to make her feel again. "You're such a bad liar," I say, "but, if you truly don't want to see me anymore, say it again, and look me in the eyes while you do. I'll walk away with no questions asked." I tug on her pinkie. "Otherwise, tell me what you really want para *dártelo*."

"Xavier—" My name rolls off her tongue and she pulls her bottom lip between her teeth. I love hearing her say it or scream it as she comes undone for me.

"*Dime, mami.*"

The pulsating beats of the Latin rhythms float around us, filling the space while she contemplates her answer. She lifts her chin as she licks her lips. "If I say yes, what happens next? How will this work?"

My smile stretches from ear to ear. "Just be in the moment, *mami*. We don't have to think about all that. *Lo que tú quieras*," I say, so she understands she's the one leading us. "I just want to spend more time with you." Her eyes drop to my lips before lifting and searching mine. There's something just beneath the surface that's holding her back, making her question herself. Until I'm able to learn what it is, she'll have to be the one holding the reigns if I have any chance of spending more time with her.

My words hover as she processes the idea. As she's thinking about what it means and the seriousness of my proposition, her eyes never stray. "So, friends with benefits?" She pulls the right side of her bottom lip between her teeth.

That's not where I wanted her mind to go but if it'll get her to say yes, I'll take what I can get and convince her otherwise when the time is right. "Call it what you want, if it comes with you saying yes."

"Rocky. We saw Rodrigo by the bar, so we came to find you thinking you'd be alone. But that's obviously not the case," says a woman in a sparkling blue dress. "Hi, I'm Nikki." Her right hand juts out toward me.

Reluctantly, I separate myself from Rocky and turn to Nikki, taking her hand in mine and dropping a kiss on her cheek. "Hi, Nikki. Xavier." After releasing her hand, I turn to the other woman and extend my hand to her. When she takes it, I say, "Nice to meet you…"

"Alondra."

"Nice to meet you, Alondra." I drop a kiss on her cheek.

"Sorry, these are my two friends, Nikki and Alondra." Rocky is shaking her head.

"Xavier, that performance last night was incredible!" Alondra chimes in.

"Thank you, glad you liked it."

Silence thickens and Rocky's arms drop to her side. Her fingers begin drawing circles along her thighs. "Have you all been friends a long time?" I ask, wanting Rocky to relax.

"Since Rocky moved to Miami," Nikki responds.

"Where did you move from?" I direct my question to Rocky.

"Boston. I came to Miami to go to law school and then never left."

"I'm from Boston, too, but moved to Puerto Rico when I was twelve."

"Look at that, you have something in common," Nikki says, looking at Rocky, her eyes widening.

"Seems so," Rocky responds, her eyes still resting on mine.

"Nikki, I have to go to the bathroom, why don't you come with me?" Alondra says, grasping Nikki's hand in hers.

"Right." Nikki looks at me, then Rocky. "We'll see you in a bit." Then she and Alondra scurry off.

"Sorry, that was awkward," Rocky says, shaking her head. "This whole thing is awkward."

"There is nothing awkward about us, *mami*." I step closer to her again, closing the space between us so we can pick up where we left off. "*Eres hermosa* and I want to get to know you better. It's a simple yes or no."

CHAPTER ELEVEN

Rocío

Yes or no. Two short, simple words, yet they're thick and laden with significance. Can I really just have a casual sexual relationship with this man who happens to be a superstar singer? Is that even possible? But also, the way he worshipped me that night was like nothing I've ever experienced, and I could really use a few more of those orgasms. If I were to ask Nikki and Alondra, they would encourage me to enjoy the ride—literally.

Possibility hovers and swirls in the air between us. When Xavier appeared, adjusting my bra strap that was peeking out, his touch ignited me from within. Our attraction is undeniable and although he's clothed in black from head to toe, I can still visualize his lean torso, his golden-brown skin slick with sweat as he filled me. Right now, our bodies are in close proximity and our pinkies are barely linked with one another, yet the same electricity crackles around us.

I take a deep breath. "Let me think about it." I want to say yes. But agreeing to this freaks me out for a lot of reasons. My head keeps telling me to stay away—between his fame and his money, he's surrounded by women all of the time, most of them fawning over him. Then there's the media who is always lurking and in search of their next big story. Our age difference would give them something to salivate over. Yet his voice stirs something inside of me, when he's conversing with me or talking dirty to me. Plus, the way he praised my body made me feel things I haven't felt in years. What happens when he's done with me? Or worse, I find him in bed with one of the thousands of women pining after him? I'm not sure I could handle that again.

Two and a half years ago

The suitcase is strewn across the floor as I empty the contents of my dresser into it.

"Rocky, please stop this madness and talk to me," Victor pleads, wrapping his hand around my forearm.

I shove his hand away. "Don't fucking touch me!"

"Rocky, it meant nothing. She meant nothing. Please, just talk to me."

Anger bubbles and I toss the pile of shirts into the suitcase. My back straightens and I close the space between us, looking down into the gray-blue eyes I've loved for years. "She meant nothing?! I don't think your dick would agree. When I walked into the office you were moaning like the whore that you are!"

"Rocky, I'm sorry. I wasn't thinking." His shoulders slump. My heart wants to believe his words, but my head knows better than to be tempted by his lip service.

"Yeah, well, you were obviously thinking with your dick." I slam the suitcase closed and storm into the closet to search for another, Victor trailing behind me like a lost dog.

"Rocky, please, don't leave. I can change, I promise I'll never do anything like this again."

Rage churns while Victor speaks. "What's that saying your mother always uses? Todo rollo, ¡nada de película! *Your promises mean nothing, Victor! They're empty. And you're right, you'll never do anything like this again because I'm done! Done with you, your lies, and being made a fool. It all ends today!"*

Alondra's words ring in my ears. *Don't let Victor be how you measure every guy.* The pain his infidelities caused dulls a little more each day but it's still there, reminding me of what I've been through. It would be easier to avoid getting involved with Xavier and everything that he is, but why should I deprive myself of someone who has taken interest in me and made me feel so incredible?

Xavier releases my pinkie and extends his hand. "Okay. I want to spend more time with you, but only when you're ready." He slides his phone from his pocket and hands it to me. "Punch your number in."

My eyes hold his dark gaze, contemplating his words, but then I tug it from his fingers and start typing. As I'm punching in the numbers, a text message from Lisandra pops up. If my memory serves me well, that's his ex-fiancée's name. I finish saving my number and hand back the device.

His lean digits push at the screen as the phone inside my pockabook vibrates. "I just texted you." I slide it from my purse and unlock it, showing him I received it.

"Oh good, you found her," César says as he's approaching us.

I put some space between Xavier and me, hoping it'll help my thoughts clear.

Rather than look at César, Xavier's eyes remain on mine. "Yes, thank you for that."

"Have you seen Nikki?" César asks me.

I force my eyes to César's. "Her and Alondra went to the bathroom," I say. "They should be back any minute."

"Thanks, Rocky." César shifts toward Xavier. "Roxana was asking for you. I told her I'd come find you. Whenever you're done here, she's off the stage to the right."

"Thanks, man. Would you mind letting her know I'll be over in a few minutes?"

"Sure thing, man." César nods and turns to cross the terrace toward the stage but stops and looks back at me. "Rocky, let Nikki know I'll be right back."

I nod. "Okay."

"*No te olvides de mí,*" he says, licking his lips, reminding me not to forget him, as if that were possible.

With a shake of my head, I peek up at him, his dark brown eyes nearly black under the night sky. His height is imposing and sexy. I had grown accustomed to being taller than Victor and convinced myself it wasn't a big deal. But here, standing next to Xavier as he looks down at me, is a subtle reminder of the concessions I've made in the past. "I don't think I can." What did I just say? Jeez, can I ever not fumble?

Nikki and Alondra appear in the distance and when my eyes meet Alondra's, she halts and lifts her chin to me. I nod. She continues her strides toward us, Nikki trailing behind her.

"Nikki, César was just looking for you. He said he'll be right back."

Xavier's fingers brush my hip then wrap around my wrist, his thumb caressing my radial vein. "I have to go see Roxana. *No te vayas.*" He dips his head and drops his lips to the corner of my mouth and my skin burns under his touch. When he separates, the air is cool against my heated skin. "Nikki. Alondra." He gives a curt nod and then disappears into the crowd before us.

"What in the panty-dropping universe is this?" Nikki exclaims as she sidles up to me. "That man has it bad for you, woman!"

"No, he doesn't," I retort, my heart hammering in my chest.

"Um, he would've fucked you right here if it were socially acceptable," Alondra says.

"What am I gonna do?" I ask, looking between my two friends. Do I follow my head, rational in its thinking to protect myself at all costs? Or do I follow my heart, or in this case my body, and allow myself to indulge in all things Xavier?

"You're going to sleep with the man and let him do all those things you raved about," Alondra says.

The thumping of the music matches the erratic beat of my heart. "But what if—"

"Stop. We're not going there," Nikki says, cutting me off. "Look at me, Rocky." Her hand reaches for mine and our fingers intertwine. "You deserve this, whatever this"—her free hand draws circles in the air—"is. Don't overthink it. Turn your lawyer brain off and just do it. Let the orgasms come as they may. Whether it lasts a week or a year, just enjoy it."

"He's ten years younger than me," I say.

"It doesn't matter. If he were ten years older than you, you wouldn't even mention it. Besides, it's nobody's fucking business," Nikki says. "Also, most importantly, I want to live vicariously through your sexcapades with that fine specimen of a man."

"What are you scared of?" Alondra asks, as she wraps her hand around my free one.

"I don't know." My eyes dart around the people crowding us from all sides, all engrossed in their own conversations. I meet Alondra's blue eyes. "I guess it's because I never imagined myself here. My mind still tends to go back to the life I thought I would have forever." And the man I trusted with my life, who betrayed me in a way I never thought possible.

"If anyone understands, it's me." Alondra's hand squeezes mine. "But I speak from experience when I say, your mind will always try to compare and rationalize in an effort to protect your heart from the destruction it's already been through. I'm not saying to go fall in love with the guy, but try to turn off those thoughts. Let yourself feel without the weight of expectations."

"After the past few years, you've earned it," Nikki adds.

I exhale and nod, accepting Nikki and Alondra's words. "Okay, I'll try. Not sure how the whole 'don't think about it' part will work but maybe he'll fuck me right into Forgetsville." I chuckle at the absurdity.

"That's my girl," Nikki screeches.

"*Hola, mi amor*," César says as he's approaching us, wrapping his arm around Nikki when he arrives. "What are you all excited about over here?"

"Rocky is finally getting out of her own way. Her and Xavier—"

My hand smacks Nikki's arm, interrupting her mid-sentence. "Do you ever keep anything to yourself?"

Nikki's shoulders rise. "What? It's just César."

"Well, he was anxiously asking for you," César says.

My head swivels toward César. "What do you mean, he asked for me?"

"When he got here earlier tonight, he was asking if I knew the group of women standing with me at the concert last night because he recognized you. After I told him you're Nikki's best friend, his whole body relaxed."

"Makes total sense. He's *super* into Rocky," Alondra says.

Nikki chimes in. "She's being modest. He can't get enough of her and—"

"I'm right here," I say, cutting her off. I get her and César share everything but I'd rather them not talk about my potential sex life in my presence.

"*Ay*, Rocky. *Siempre tan seria*," Nikki says, shaking her head. For as long as we've been friends, Nikki has always ragged on me for being too serious or too modest.

"Anyway, he seems like a nice guy, at least from what his sister has shared," César says.

"And don't believe all the crap you read online. You know how the media likes to twist shit for salacious headlines," Nikki adds.

The slew of headlines relating to his drug use flash through my mind, and I push the thoughts away.

"Come on, let's get closer to the stage," César says. "Roxana is going to come out to say a few words and then sing a few songs from the new album. Since she included the single with Xavier on the album, I think they will be singing that one first."

Collectively, we move toward the stage, creating a path through the crowd. We find a spot to the right of the stage and nestle our way near the front. A vibration in my bag tugs my attention. When I grab my phone there's a text from an unknown 787 number at the top of the screen.

> **XAVIER**
>
> Te ves hermosa tonight. It reminds me cuantas ganas te tengo.

Xavier's message sends a shiver up my spine. He really does have a way with words, which makes sense considering he raps for a living. Just thinking those words makes me realize how insane this whole scenario is. What do I even respond with?

"What are you smiling about over here?" Nikki asks. I turn the phone screen toward her so she can read his message. "Girl, if he is telling you he wants you in the first text message he's sending you, imagine all the things he's gonna whisper to you inside that bedroom."

My eyes repeatedly scan his words, and my chest tightens. It's both terrifying and wonderful. "I feel like a kid, all giddy inside."

"What are you writing back?"

"I have no idea. This man leaves me speechless, time and again. I'm not sure what to do with it."

Roxana's song "*Melancolía*" begins playing and the DJ turns up the volume. "What are you *chismeando* about over here?" Alondra asks, huddling around us.

"Her man texted her," Nikki responds in a raised tone.

I extend my arm so she can see the screen. "*Como un perrito*, making sure you know he's not giving up," Alondra says, comparing him to a cute puppy.

"What do I reply? Because my lawyer brain wants to say hi and then try and schedule plans since my flirtatious side has been under lock and key and is rusty."

"Short and sweet. Tell him *que tú también le tienes ganas*," Alondra responds, as if telling him I want to sleep with him is as easy as asking for the time.

"Just like that, so forward?"

"*Ay, por favor*. I'll type it for you," Nikki says, pulling the phone from my hand.

"Stop"—my hand yanks the phone back as my eyes bore into Nikki's—"I got this. Chill! I may be rusty but I'm capable of responding to his text." My fingers make quick work of responding before I let my thoughts run rampant.

ROCÍO

y yo a vos 🌀

"There, I responded," I say, turning the phone toward Nikki and Alondra.

The stage lights dim, and the tropical beats begin floating

around us, drawing whistles and cheers from the crowd. Roxana's voice fills the air, and I recognize the song when she sings, "*Hace tiempo que no te veo*," as the same one they performed last night. When Xavier begins rhyming about how crazy he is about her, screams of joy erupt. His voice is deep and soothing, the lyrics flowing like a warm Miami breeze.

I'm in so much trouble with this man.

"Mmm, listen to that voice," Nikki whispers to me. "Now I know why he gets you all worked up."

"You're so bad, Nikki," I say.

Roxana and Xavier finish their song to chants of fans asking for more music. Roxana takes the microphone. "¡*Gracias, Miami*! *Color de Rosas* has been a labor of love *y estoy súper emocionada* that you're all finally going to experience it! '*Sombra Fiel*' was so much fun to perform *con El Flaco*." Whistles and cheers fill the air as Roxana turns to look at Xavier.

He nods, his smile stretching across his gorgeous face. "*Gracias, Gata. Trabajar contigo* was incredible"—his head bobs up and down—"we should make more music together." The crowd erupts.

"Maybe we should," Roxana responds, encouraging the crowd. "This album helped me during a time of transition, and I hope you all love listening to it as much as I loved creating it." As Roxana continues, Xavier slips away into the darkness behind the stage. My phone vibrates, and when I peek at the screen, Xavier's name pops up.

> XAVIER
> Inside. 2nd floor, 3rd door to right of rotunda.

"I'll be back," I say, before I second-guess myself. I disappear into the crowd and search for the entrance to the house. With everyone outside listening to Roxana on stage, it's quiet inside. I locate the massive double marble staircase near the front entrance and look around before taking the steps up. After locating the door, I take a deep breath, grip the handle, and whisper to myself, "Okay, Rocky, let's do this."

Inside the room is large, with floor-to-ceiling glass along the far wall. He's standing at the window with his hands stuffed in his pockets, looking at the Miami skyline. His slender stature takes up much of the window's length. As I'm locking the door behind me, he pivots.

"Now that I know *que tú también me tienes ganas*, I couldn't wait another minute. Come here, *mami*." He strides across the room and pulls me to him, his large hands squeezing my rounded hips as our lips crash. His spicy amber scent clamors for my attention as his tongue juts out, pulling my bottom lip between his. My hands explore the skin at the nape of his neck. He separates from me, resting his forehead against mine and then pushes a stray curl behind my ear. Our eyes lock, and we take each other in—savoring the moment.

"Hi," I say, drawing in his breath with mine.

His thumb lands on my lips, and he drags it across. "*Esta bemba*," he says.

"What about my lips?"

"*Me vuelven loco*." His words are like sunshine on a cloudy day, warming me from the inside. He drives me crazy too, except I'm not ready to share that with him yet.

"So, how does this work?" I ask, peering up at him while putting space between us.

His thumbs drag across my cheeks. "*No sé*, but it doesn't matter. We're here."

"Here"—my eyes scan the room with white walls and a large bed in the center—"locked away and hiding in some random room at a party."

"Lie back. *Déjame saborearte*," he says.

Having him go down on me while hidden away in this private estate is both terrifying and exhilarating. "Now?"

He nods while guiding me toward the bed. "Yes. Less thinking, more doing." When the backs of my legs hit the mattress, we halt. His hands reach for the hem of the dress, and he tugs up. "I love this dress on you, but I'm ready to see what's underneath. *¿Estás lista?*"

I'm as ready as I'll ever be. I nod and place my hands over his. Together, we hike the fabric up around my waist. I allow myself to sit back on the bed. Xavier pushes my thighs apart, the tip of his tongue dragging up the skin toward my center. When his fingers reach the damp black fabric, he tugs it to the side and begins exploring.

"*Mojaíta*, just like I said." He smirks, then drives his index and middle fingers inside of me, causing me to gasp. His mouth meets his hand and the combination of his quick movement and the pressure of his mouth push me over the edge in seconds. I bite my lip, swallowing the moans I want to let free. He continues to gently kiss me and draws his fingers from inside of me right to his mouth. "*Deliciosa.*"

Xavier lies on the bed to my left, and I turn to meet his gaze. "Your magic tongue strikes again."

"*Tú no sabes na*," he says. "The magic hasn't even started yet."

"I'm here for the entire magic show." He grins at my words.

"Come home with me." His hand rests on my torso and his words are soft. "And before you answer, *no me digas que no.*"

It's as if he knows I'm about to say no, and guilt washes over me. "I can't tonight, I have an early commitment." His smile drops as he searches my eyes. Although I feel guilty, I need to see Dr. Pérez because she rescheduled our session from earlier this week to first thing tomorrow.

His right eyebrow lifts. "Commitment?" I nod because I'm

not ready to share too many personal details with him just yet. "*Entonces, ¿cuándo?*" he asks, inquiring when we'll see each other as he's drawing small circles on my belly.

"Not sure. Can I let you know?" My body wants to say yes, but for some reason I haven't convinced myself that I can take the leap. I thought by coming upstairs and being here with him it would be easier for me to say yes, but apparently my thoughts are bullying their way back and reminding me to protect my heart.

"Not the answer I was hoping for *pero está bien*," he says, forcing a crooked grin as he feigns acceptance. He rises and hovers over me. "*Te espero*," he says, letting me know that he'll wait for me, before his lips cover mine, pulling my bottom lip between his.

A knock at the door startles us, causing Xavier to separate from me and jump to his feet, and I follow. "Yeah," he says, resting both hands against the white door.

He's met with silence from the other side. "We should get back downstairs," I say.

Xavier turns cupping my face in his hands. "Don't make me wait too long."

CHAPTER TWELVE

Rocío

THE NOTIFICATION from my phone wakes me and I stir, stretching my legs and rolling my ankles. I must've forgotten to turn on the do not disturb option when I went to bed last night. I extend my arm to grab my glasses from the nightstand, followed by my phone, pressing the unlock button and punching in my code. Who's texting me this early on a Saturday? When I open my messages, I see Rodrigo's name at the top of my inbox.

> **RODRIGO**
> It was great to finally meet you last night. I'd love to see you again.

Despite the sweet message, disappointment weighs down my chest. *Not Xavier*. After the way I left things last night, I'm not surprised. He wanted me to go home with him, and although my body was screaming yes after he'd just made me orgasm with his magic tongue, I talked myself out of it. Sure, I have to see Dr. Pérez at ten, but I still could've spent a few hours with him back at his place. He's beautiful and makes me feel desired, but we're so different and those differences are all I can see right now. Like, hello—he's a superstar! Not to mention he's ten years younger than me. I feel like I'm setting myself up for failure. How long can he really be with a forty-one-year-old woman?

I push the sheets back and, after making a quick bathroom stop, shuffle toward the kitchen. I need coffee. When I moved to Miami, I wasn't a huge coffee drinker—had the typical cup or two of drip coffee in the morning to get started. But that changed once I started drinking *cafecito cubano*, which is an integral part of the Miami culture. *Cafecito cubano* is espresso, except Cubans prepare it by adding sugar to the first drip of coffee, creating a thick *espumita* at the top, which is the perfect blend of the foam of tiny bubbles from the freshly brewed coffee and the sugar. Once I became accustomed to drinking *cafecito*, drip coffee didn't hit the same.

Once the Bialetti Moka Express is on the stovetop, I grab the *criollitas* package from the pantry, my favorite Argentinian crackers I get from Buenos Aires Bakery and Market in Miami Beach. I reach for my phone, immediately opening the text message exchange with Xavier from last night. In hindsight, I'm an idiot for having said I'd let him know when I'll see him again. Maybe Dr. Pérez will give me some insight into what the fuck is wrong with my ability to execute on a decision about dating and moving on. Maybe after I've had a chance to unpack my swirling doubt with Dr. Pérez, I'll text him.

Instead, I respond to Rodrigo. Although we only spoke for a few minutes before Xavier staked his claim, I enjoyed our conversation. He was kind, had a good sense of humor, and is good looking. Plus, he's also taller than me. Seems tall men are something I crave after Victor. But at the same time, I'm hesitant because he's a lawyer, and Victor may have ruined that for me—at least for the time being. I know I shouldn't let Victor's indiscretions sour future prospects, but I can't help it. The constant uncertainty and wavering are mentally exhausting.

ME

Great meeting you too. Let's plan something.

When the coffee starts bubbling out, I lift the pot from the burner and pour the first liquid brewed into my stainless-steel frothing pitcher, where I already added sugar. As I beat the coffee and sugar, Nikki's voice pops up, telling me how proud she is that I'm keeping my options open. After the coffee finishes brewing, I pour it into the metal vessel and blend it with the creamy sugar mixture before adding it to my warmed milk and finishing it off with a dash of salt.

With my coffee, crackers, and tub of butter, I settle in at my counter. I should probably catch up on emails but instead decide to check socials. I don't want to get sucked into work knowing I have to leave in a little over an hour. Although it's Saturday, I still have to get to Midtown for my appointment, and traffic in Miami is never light. A picture of my sister, Julieta, together with her husband and their three daughters appears on my screen, telling me she updated her profile picture. When's the last time we spoke? I scroll through my phone log and find my answer. Oh, crap! It's been a week since we've spoken.

Julieta is seven years older than me. Although we have a good relationship, because of our age difference, I'm not as close with her as I am with my younger sister, Micaela, who's two years younger than me. Julieta left to study nursing at the University of Maine right after high school, where she met her now-husband. Because they moved in together during college, Julieta never moved back home. It's surreal to think their oldest daughter turns eighteen later this year, with two years between each of the girls. Last time I saw them was a few months ago for the girls' winter school break, when they flew down to spend the holidays and catch a break from the brutal New England winter.

A text notification from Rodrigo appears at the top of my screen, and I tap it to switch over to the message.

> **RODRIGO**
>
> Dinner next week? There's a new Brazilian steakhouse in Brickell that I've been wanting to try.

Dinner with Rodrigo could work. It'll give me time to get to know him a bit more. But, at the same time, it could go sideways and then I'm stuck being there when I'd rather be somewhere else. Shaking the negative thoughts away, I start typing my reply before I talk myself out of something for no other reason than my indecision always leads me to say no for fear of who knows what. Before I can finish typing, a bubble reading "Ma" pops up. I'm not sure I've had enough coffee to deal with my mother.

"*Hola*, Ma," I say.

"*Hola, nena*," she says. She goes on to tell me she still needs to go grocery shopping so lunch will be a bit later than usual today. She says she's invited their friends over for lunch and needs to pick up some extra things before she starts cooking. We chat for a few minutes about the menu, and before hanging up, she asks me to pick up some pastries at the Argentinian bakery on my way to the house.

After I make a second *café con leche* with the rest of the coffee, I grab my phone to read my texts and chuckle when I read Rodrigo's messages.

> **RODRIGO**
>
> Um, maybe I should've asked, do you eat meat?
>
> Oh shit, that sounded wrong, do you eat steak?

My fingers toggle over the screen's keyboard, contemplating my response. I hit send before I talk myself out of it.

> **ME**
> I see what you did there 😉 But yes, a steakhouse is a good choice.

> **RODRIGO**
> I promise I don't always trip over my own words.

> **ME**
> We all trip sometimes, you're good.
>
> Does Wednesday work? I have a late afternoon meeting at an office on Brickell so I could meet you after, maybe 6ish?

I don't normally have dinner that early so I'll have to plan accordingly. I'd hate to show up and not order much and have him think that I'm one of those girls who doesn't like to eat on a date.

> **RODRIGO**
> I'll make it work, I don't usually eat that early but for you, I'll make an exception 🙂

> **ME**
> I don't usually eat that early either but since I'll be in the neighborhood, it works.

> **RODRIGO**
> It's a date.

The three animated dots stare at me as I await Rodrigo's next words. I can't believe I'm finally going on a first date since I met Victor all those years ago. And with a man who's seven years younger than me. A few weeks ago, I never would've considered a younger man, and now I have two younger men and I'm not really sure how I feel about it.

> **RODRIGO**
> I'm gonna be honest, I can't stop thinking about you in that pink dress last night.

Flirting through text—I remember when Victor used to send me sweet messages in our early days. I'm not really sure when he stopped, or when I started noticing. Reading Rodrigo's words gives my confidence a nice boost.

> **ME**
> It was a great dress.

> **RODRIGO**
> Yes, but the woman makes the dress.

I bite my lip, remembering how Xavier admired my dress before hiking it up and devouring me. I'm terrible, thinking of him when it's Rodrigo I'm talking to. What does that say about me?

> **ROCÍO**
> Thank you, you're too kind.

I've been with Dr. Pérez for half an hour and her smooth, gentle tone has a way of soothing my swirling emotions. She sits across from me, legs crossed—one hand holding her notepad and the other, her purple pen. I spent the first part of my session telling her about meeting Rodrigo, then my unexpected run-in with Xavier at *La Gata*'s concert the other night, our encounter at the release party, all the emotions it evoked, and my hesitancy to move forward with him.

"You experienced a pretty profound betrayal and your trust was shattered. You questioning your decisions and judgment are a protective mechanism."

Her words simmer as my eyes roam the office, the muted blue walls adorned with several paintings of birds or flowers. "I guess, but I thought I wouldn't be so hung up by this point."

"What makes you think that?"

"It's been over two years. I've been solo the entire time, not one single date."

She makes a note, then looks up, meeting my gaze. "There is no timeline, Rocky."

"You sound like my father." I shift in my seat, crossing my legs. "I did text with Rodrigo this morning, and we're having dinner on Wednesday night. So, that's a start."

"That's great. And Xavier? Are you seeing him?"

My shoulders lift in uncertainty. "I'm not sure. We ended things last night with him asking me to go home with him and me saying no. He did tell me he'd wait for me. I may text him later."

"Why did you say no?"

"I have no idea. The more I think about it, the more I realize I wanted to say yes."

Dr. Pérez lays her hands on the notepad sitting on her legs. I catch the tiniest of smiles creeping in before she catches herself. "Whatever you decide, take things at your own pace and give yourself grace. Be transparent with yourself and with your intended partner."

"You think I should tell them how Victor fucked me up?"

"Do you want to tell either of them?"

Her words settle in. Telling either of these guys about why I'm divorced is something I'll have to do if I intend to have any kind of relationship with either of them, but talking about it will open up old wounds. There's still this tiny part of my heart that lives in the past, in the life I once had and thought would be forever. "I'm not sure, part of me does and part of me doesn't."

"Why's that?"

"I'm dreading sharing any of that part of my life."

She rolls the pen between her thumb and index finger. "You just met both of these men. Don't you think it's too soon to feel that way?"

"I suppose it is," I respond, nodding in agreement. "If I say something too soon, I'll almost certainly be met with pity. But it would also help Xavier understand this uncertainty that clouds my every decision, which is something Rodrigo hasn't experienced yet."

"You don't have to overshare from the onset, but as you get to know each other, acknowledging your past and your trust journey can be helpful in building your foundation with the new person."

"We'll see. I'm thinking neither of them will be around for too long."

Her left eyebrow arches up. "Why do you think that?"

"For starters, I'm not looking for anything serious. But also, they're both years younger than me—Xavier, ten years and Rodrigo, seven. I'm certain they'll get what they need and move on."

Dr. Pérez's head turns slightly to the left. "What makes you so certain?"

Honestly, I have no idea how to answer that question. But the age difference is the one thing I keep coming back to. Men love younger women, not older women. I'm a bit perplexed as to what a guy like Xavier sees in someone like me. Or Rodrigo for that matter. "The age difference is the only thing."

"But you already scheduled a date with Rodrigo."

"He's a lawyer. It makes sense for me to date someone like him."

"Is that why you're keeping Xavier at bay and approaching each of these guys differently?"

"Hmm." Her question isn't something I'd thought about. "Maybe it's because Xavier is famous. He could have any woman he wants. Why me?"

"Why not you?"

Why not me. Great question. This is the same thing Alondra pointed out to me. It's taken me two years of sessions with Dr. Pérez to be able to look myself in the mirror and tell my reflection I'm incredible. I'm more than enough to be with a man like Xavier, yet here I am, still on the fence. "I have to think about that and let you know."

Dr. Pérez's pen scratches something on the notepad in her lap. "You know the answer, you're just not ready to say the words out loud."

She's probably right. She usually is. But I've still not fully embraced the ability to see all my great qualities.

"Let me ask you this," she says, dropping her pen, "if your age was something that bothered Xavier, do you think he'd have pursued you the way he did? That he would have sought you out after spending that first night together?"

Would he have? I mean, this guy could choose any woman to be by his side, so I don't think he'd waste time with me, unless he really wanted to be here.

"I suppose not." I shrug. Nikki and Alondra don't see an issue that these guys are younger than me. It's not something I ever thought too much about until now, but society's expectations seem to be that women should date older men, not younger men. How will our age difference look to others from outside? Does it matter what others think if they're not in the relationship? "Maybe it's a societal thing."

"Well, over the years, you've told me your mother often judges you, and you make choices for yourself, despite her judgment. Whether the judgment is from your mother or someone else, it's no different."

My lips purse as I contemplate Dr. Pérez's last statement. She glances at her watch, signaling that our session is nearing its end. As usual, my time with her helps me vocalize what's churning inside, mentally decluttering the confusion my thoughts create. The clarity our discussions bring makes me feel lighter.

"That's time, Rocky. I think today's session was productive. You've given yourself a lot to work with until we see each other again. Since today is Saturday, I'll see you in ten days rather than two weeks."

Lunch at my parents' house started later than usual and lasted a lot longer than the typical Saturday when it's just the three of us. We lingered at the round table sharing stories of the past, when we were all younger. Their friends came to the United States from Argentina not long after we did. They were introduced to my parents through a mutual friend and became quick friends. They lived not too far from our family home, and our families would often spend holidays together. Their four kids grew up together with us and they're more like siblings than friends. Although they moved to South Florida last year, I hadn't seen them in several months so it was nice catching up. Not to mention, when they're around, my mother's judgment is tamed because she tries to keep it tucked away, hidden from the scrutiny of others.

I was itching to get home, and I'm finally comfy in my black lounge pants and my favorite fuzzy slippers. As the sun is setting, it's coloring the sky over the Atlantic soft shades of pink and red, with hints of purple hues. I love sitting on my balcony at this time of day—it's different than watching the sunrise from this same spot. Today, the scattered clouds hover over the calm waters and glimmer from the light of the sun setting behind me. The water that is often vibrant turquoise under direct sunlight leans toward steely gray as dusk settles in. It seems later than it is, but when I glance at my watch, it's almost five. What's Xavier doing tonight? Maybe he's up for hanging out. I grab my phone, search for his name in my inbox and begin typing.

ME

Hi.

I'm staring at my phone, hoping the elusive three dots pop up to show me he's typing but *nada*. I shake my head and place it on the table to my right. *Get a grip, Rocky*, I say to myself. He'll respond in due time, and when he does, I'll over analyze everything then. But what's he doing on a Saturday night? A guy like him probably goes out on the weekends instead of staying in, which is my preference lately. My phone vibrates against the glass underneath it, and when I glance at the screen, Xavier's name zaps a surge of electricity from my palm to my heart.

XAVIER

Hi mami.

He's called me *mami* since the night he had me sprawled across his quartz countertop. The first time he said it, I wasn't sure how I felt about it—especially since Victor tried calling me *mami* when we had started dating, and I shut it down real quick. But the way the pet name rolls off Xavier's tongue just hits different—his deep voice soothing my insecurities and calming my erratic thoughts while simultaneously getting me fired up. I like it. No, I love it! The flurry of butterflies swirl in anticipation of hearing him murmur it.

> ME
>
> This is me not making you wait too long. ¿Qué haces esta noche?

I hit send before I regret asking about his plans tonight. The knot in my stomach twists and pulls at the taut strings creating a bundle of nerves as the three animated ellipsis dots bounce up and down in a continuous loop. What's he typing that's taking so long?

> XAVIER
>
> In Brazil for work. Te llamo when this meeting ends.

It's like a splash of cold water hits me and my shoulders slump. Of course he's not in Miami when I finally got up the nerve to reach out to him.

CHAPTER THIRTEEN

Xavier

THIS MORNING, Maritza and I flew into Rio de Janeiro to meet with the marketing team at Joaquim Carvalho Luxury Watches. After I signed the contracts a few weeks ago, they were eager to get this scheduled as soon as possible. We're discussing the logistics of tomorrow's photo shoot for their new line. I've never been to Rio despite having performed in several other cities in Brazil, but probably won't get to see much since this will be a short stay.

Rocky's text message a few minutes ago was a welcome distraction. Last night, she talked herself out of coming home with me, trying to convince herself more than me that she'd think about seeing me again. But I knew she wouldn't be able to stay away, resist the way electricity crackles when we're together and the way her body responds to me. Her eyes betray her, telling me she wants what I'm offering despite her words saying otherwise. I've had the taste of her on my lips all day, her luscious curves in that pink dress etched in my memory.

"Tomorrow, our team will pick you up at the hotel at five a.m.," the marketing director says in a thick accent. "You'll be transported to the first of the locations we have scheduled. Because we like early morning light best for our outdoor shoots, we'll probably only get two locations on each day. The progress on day one will determine our schedule for the other days. We'll also work in some studio shots across the days you're here. There will be coffee and breakfast waiting for you."

Damn, five in the morning is early. "How long should we expect to shoot each day?" I'm already thinking about getting back to Miami to see Rocky now that she's finally coming around.

"You'll be with Efigênia Santos—she's Brazil's best photographer. She usually gets us what we need in very little time. Maybe five or six hours per day."

"How many days do you expect us to be here?" My leg bounces beneath the desk.

"We should be done by Tuesday."

Three days is a long time. "Great."

"Unless you have anything else you want to discuss or go over, that's it for us today," she says.

"We're straight," I say.

"We just need the hotel information," Maritza adds.

"Ah, yes. You're booked at the Fairmont Rio Copacabana. Edvaldo," she says, pointing to her right, "will take you there now. He'll be at your disposal during your time in Rio."

"Thank you. Look forward to working with you," I say as I stand, extending my hand to her.

"We're excited for your campaign, Xavier," she says, meeting my outstretched hand and pulling me into her, allowing our cheeks to meet for a kiss goodbye. "Joaquim and our entire team look forward to having you be the next face of our brand. Enjoy dinner with him tonight."

"You're not joining us?"

She shakes her head. "No, Joaquim's husband will be joining

you. They both travel a lot so when they're both in Rio, they accompany one another everywhere."

After settling into the backseat, Maritza sits to my left and Adrián sits in the front. Edvaldo pulls into traffic to navigate the busy Rio streets. The narrow streets are lined with kiosks and vendors and pedestrians. The traffic is stacked, making Miami traffic look like child's play. I grab my phone from the breast pocket of my denim jacket, find Rocky's name, and hit video.

"Hi." Her voice is soft and breathy as she appears on my screen. Ringlets are poking out of whatever she used to sweep up her hair.

"*Hola, mami.*" Tension releases from my body as her lips curl upward, illuminating her face.

"What are you doing in Rio?"

"We flew here early this morning. I recently signed a contract with a designer, and we'll be taking pictures for the marketing campaign."

"Oh, that's wicked cool! What kind of designer?"

"Watches."

"So, will I be seeing you on the billboards?"

"I don't know, *pero si me verás en tu cama*," I say, watching her cheeks turn crimson. Telling her she'll see me in her bed is nothing compared to all the other thoughts racing through my mind. But Maritza is next to me, so I need to check myself, even if she's gotten good at ignoring me.

"How long will you be in Brazil?"

"We should be back in the 305 Tuesday night."

She drags her bottom lip between her teeth before saying, "I'd like to see you when you're back."

My heart pounds in my chest at the words I've been waiting to hear.

"This is it," says Edvaldo, putting the car in park and hopping out.

"Yes, but hold that thought. We just got to the hotel. Let me get to the room, and I'll call you back." She nods before I hit end.

Edvaldo walks with us to an office on the left side of the reception area where we're greeted by a woman in a dark suit. "*Oi*, Edvaldo," she says.

"*Oi*. This is Xavier Delgado, Maritza, his personal assistant, and Adrián, their security. We checked them in earlier today."

"Welcome to the Fairmont Rio Copacabana. Let's head up to the fourth-floor reception. We'll pick up your keys and then continue up to your suites on the fifth floor. João here"—she points to the man walking behind us with our luggage—"will bring your luggage straight to your rooms." We follow the petite woman down the hall to an elevator and I slow my stride to create space between us. Once on the fourth floor, we exit into an open area that's bright, quiet, and adorned with fresh flowers throughout. The young woman behind the desk greets us, hands the petite woman three key cards, and we continue following her to another elevator. Way too many elevators and walking just to get to our rooms.

"Here we are," the petite woman says, pushing the door open. "This is the first suite." She taps the door to her left. "Then the others are next to it."

The woman hands me the keys, and I give one to Maritza and the other to Adrián.

"Mari, take the first one. I'll take the one in the middle, and Adrián can have the one on end," I say, hoping to speed things along.

Maritza nods and steps into the room but turns around to ask, "What time should we leave for dinner?"

My gaze turns toward Edvaldo. "Mr. Carvalho is meeting you at nine thirty. It's not too far from here, but we should leave by nine p.m."

"We'll meet you downstairs at that time. Thank you." He nods and turns back toward the elevator.

"See you in a bit," Maritza says, closing the door behind her.

Once inside my suite, I walk to the sliding door to see the expansive views of Copacabana Beach's golden sand and the iconic Pão de Açúcar with its distinctive rounded peak, dark green smatterings covering parts of the peak. *Damn, that view is incredible,* I say to an empty room. I wish Rocky were with me to experience it. *Slow down, Xavier. If you're too eager, you'll push her away.* But she texted me, like I knew she would. Now I have to make sure I'm at the forefront of her thoughts until I can get back to Miami. Pulling my phone from my pocket, I check the time and then press Rocky's name.

"Hi again." Her smile stretches across her face.

"*Hola, mami.*"

"All settled into your room?"

"Nah, just got here. But check this," I say, hitting the small camera icon with the circled arrow. I unlock the sliding door stepping out onto the balcony. The muggy evening air smacks me like a heavy blanket, typical of an August Miami day.

"Wow," she says. "That view is amazing! I've only ever seen it in pictures."

"Same, and it's so much better in real life." The smoky aroma of grilled meats from the restaurants below waft up, and my stomach growls.

"Everything always is."

"*Es verdad.* I'd rather be seeing you here with me and not on my phone." I can't see her face, but I can imagine her cheeks turning red. Sweat begins sliding down the sides of my face and I go back inside, flipping the camera back to me. "So, you were saying before we were interrupted, you finally stopped resisting and you're ready to see me?" I chuckle.

She nods, pushing a stray curl behind her ear. "Yes, but of course when I decide I'm ready, you're not even here."

"I'll be back before you know it *y después no podrás deshacerte de mí.*" She needs to know that once I get my hands on her, there's no getting rid of me. I want to unwrap everything she's keeping tucked away and hidden.

"Who says I'll want to?" She gives me a crooked grin.

"You won't. *Te prometo.*"

"Don't make any promises you can't keep." Her lips purse.

"*Nunca, mami.*"

Her eyes drop and she shakes her head before looking back up to the screen. "What are you doing tonight?"

"Dinner with the designer, his husband, and Maritza."

"Who's Maritza?" she asks, curiosity layered in her words.

"My assistant. My sister insisted I needed one, even if I swore I didn't. Now, I can't imagine how I survived without her."

"I get that." She nods in agreement. "My paralegal runs my life and my firm. If she leaves, I have no idea what I'd do."

"Have any plans tonight?" I lean back into the cushions.

"I did, but he's in Brazil so I'll probably read or watch some TV"

My belly flips knowing she wanted to spend time with me tonight. "What are you reading?"

"Nothing right now, I'm in between books."

"What kind of books?"

She purses her lips before pulling the bottom one between her teeth. "Mostly romance."

"With or without sex in them?"

She's shaking her head as she grins. "With. I like my books

smutty." Her words are disguised as coy, but the glint in her eyes gives her away.

"*Entonces quiero que me leas* the sexy parts while we're lying in bed," I say, licking my lips. My erection pushes at my jeans at the thought of her naked in bed while reading to me.

"While fully dressed or already naked?"

"*No importa* because if you're fully dressed *te quito to*." There's no way she could be fully dressed while reading about sex. I'd just peel it all off, trace the lines of her skin with my lips.

"You're so bad!"

"*Mira cómo me tienes, bien bellaco*." I'm horny as fuck and she hasn't even heard all the things I want to do with her. I want to get lost in her breath, find myself in her touch.

She squints. "What's that mean?"

I raise an eyebrow. "You for real?"

"Yeah. Just because I speak Spanish doesn't mean I understand all the different words." She shrugs as she settles into her seat.

"It means I can't wait to be inside of you again."

"It does?" she asks, crinkling her nose.

"Not literally, no. The word means horny but it's basically the same thing."

Recognition washes across her face. "If I'm being honest, *yo también quiero eso*." The way her Argentine accent rolls off her tongue with an "sh" sound when she says "yo" makes my dick hard and reminds me of our conversation about *Soda Stereo* the night we met.

"I like you being honest with yourself. Then you'll stop trying to talk yourself out of what you actually want."

Both of her eyebrows shoot up. "Um, I don't do that."

"Righhhht. I've told you—you're a bad liar. Even through the phone."

She's laughing. "Okay, maybe I do."

Maritza's name pops up on my screen, and I hit ignore. When I check the time, it's quarter past seven, which means I need to shower and get dressed. "*Mami*, I need to get ready for dinner, but I'll check in later."

She inhales, then lets out a long sigh. "Okay. Enjoy dinner. Talk later."

"*Dale*."

I'm eager for our flight to land in Miami. Although it's nearly nine p.m., I'm hoping to see Rocky. Four days in Rio dragged on, despite being busy most of the day with the photo shoots. "Mr. Delgado, is there anything else you'd like before we prepare to land?" our flight attendant asks. When I purchased my jet last year, Roxana recommended this flight attendant to work my flight, since she also works *La Gata*'s flights.

"I'm good. How much longer until we touch down?" I ask.

"We should be on the ground in about thirty minutes."

"Thanks." I grab my phone to send Rocky a text message.

ME

> Mami. My flight is landing in about 30 mins. Can I see you?

Before I can put my phone down, she responds.

ROCKY

> I'm home and already in my PJs. Maybe tomorrow?

> ME
> You won't be wearing them long if you invite me over.

The three circles roll continuously, my leg bouncing up and down in anticipation. The delay in her response tells me she's coming up with yet another excuse not to see me.

> ROCKY
> Good point.

> ME
> Is that a yes?

Electricity courses through me as I watch the three dots bounce. Ever since she told me she's ready to spend time with me I've been eager to get back to Miami and see her.

> ROCKY
> Te espero.

She finally said yes, and my heartbeat shifts to a powerful thumping, forcing my pent-up desires to explode and spread warmth throughout me. I'm typing a response to her message that she'll wait for me when a picture appears on my screen. She's lying down and wrapped in a red blanket. I can already taste those pretty lips on my tongue.

Adrián gets the keys to the SUV from one of his guys, and we jump in. As we're pulling out of the Opa Locka Airport, I say, "I need you to drop me at Rocky's place first, then you can take Mari home."

Last year after my collaboration with *La Gata* exploded, I hired Adrián as my driver for the times I didn't want to take one of my own vehicles. As "*Sombra Fiel*" continued at the top of the charts and my popularity grew, it helped to have Adrián around when going to certain places. Xiomary wanted him with me full time, especially because he's former military and has worked security in the entertainment business for a few years. I'm not a fan of being accompanied twenty-four seven but do my best to keep my sister happy.

"Whatever you need, boss. Just need the address," he responds, meeting my eyes through the rearview mirror.

"She lives in the 52 Ocean building on Collins and 52nd." I shift in my seat, a current of energy surges within me.

"Xavi," Maritza says, turning around in the passenger seat, "Roly just texted and asked if we can move up our meeting from Thursday to Wednesday because we need to finalize the last details of the tour."

"I'll let you guys know tomorrow." I open Rocky's messages. "What's our ETA so I can tell Rocky?"

"GPS says twenty-two minutes," he says, as he's driving down the Gratigny Parkway.

ME
Be there in 20, prepárate.

Nervous energy spreads as anticipation of seeing Rocky builds. I've been thinking about her since the first night we met. We finally reconnected, but she's been holding back, only allowing herself to share small pieces of herself. That ends tonight. Once I have her, she's mine. I don't want to scare her off, but she needs to be ready for me because I'm a one-girl-at-a-time type of guy.

"Once I drop Maritza at home, I'll come back to the area to be close."

"Not necessary, Adrián," I say. I'm planning on spending the night with her, even if she doesn't know it yet. "When I need you, I'll let you know."

Maritza and Adrián drive off, and I flip my hat around, pulling it low over my sunglasses as I walk into the lobby to her building. The circular atrium is bright, even at this time of night. The lobby is empty but for the security guard sitting behind the desk. As I approach the seating area located in the middle, Rocky appears from the hall on the left, her black shorts exposing her thick legs, a sweatshirt, and black fuzzy slippers.

"*Hola, mami*," I say, wrapping my arm around her waist and pulling her to me. A current passes between us as our bodies connect, and the butterflies that swirled are now flying in synchronicity.

"Hi," she says, her voice soft. After separating, she turns and gives the man behind the desk a soft wave. "Good night."

"Good night, Ms. Fontana," he responds, nodding his head.

Inside the elevator my body presses against hers, my erection rubbing against her belly. "*¿Estás lista?*" I mumble while trying to simultaneously devour her.

CHAPTER FOURTEEN

Rocío

AM I READY? Probably not, but I don't want to think about it too much because then I'll send him home. When Xavier texted me, I was curled up on the couch reading. On most nights I'd be reading on my Kindle, but I forgot to charge it and it's dead, so I was reading on my phone when his message popped up. Otherwise, I probably wouldn't have seen it. I haven't been able to stop thinking about him since the album release party. After my first text message on Saturday night, he video called me a few times a day while he was working in Brazil, keeping him at the forefront of my thoughts. It's only been three days, and I'm already hooked.

"*Sí*, I'm ready." The words are barely a whisper.

Last night, he asked if he could watch me pleasure myself, and I kinda freaked out. Not that doing it in front of him is an issue, but it was doing it on video that made me nervous. I mean, it's unlikely he'd record it without my consent, but I don't know him all that well yet. Besides, I've seen too many shady things in my years as a divorce lawyer that have left me jaded and wary. It seems I'm often saying no to him, which makes it seem like I have an excuse at the ready. It's just a matter of time before he gets tired of my reticence and moves on.

The elevator dings, and my hands instinctively go to my hair to tame the curls as I step out into the hall. Inside my apartment, I drop the keys on the counter and lock the door. "It's not much," I say, slightly self-conscious of my tiny apartment with minimal decorations.

"It's everything *por que estás tú*," he says, pushing his hands into my curls and crashing his lips onto mine. My hands furiously find the hem of his shirt and push them underneath, my palms feeling the soft skin of his back. As my hands explore, I guide him toward the couch. I find his bottom lip and suck while my fingers work at undoing his pants. When I finally unbutton his jeans, I push them down and put space between us, his erection standing tall as it peeks out from the top of his underwear.

He shoves his hand inside his briefs, wraps his hand around himself, and begins sliding it up and down. "*¿Esto es lo que tú quieres, mami?*" he asks, his eyes searing mine.

I nod and push the white fabric down, letting him free. He sits and I drop to my knees, taking his length in my hands. It's hot and wet from his arousal, and he gasps as my hand glides along its length. My tongue draws circles, lapping his arousal, and I take him in my mouth. His hisses and moans fuel me to make him feel more.

More tempo.

More suction.

More tongue.

"Fuck, *si sigues así, me voy a venir*," he mutters. Him coming in my mouth is exactly what I want, so I pick up my pace, letting him know where I'm taking him. While my right hand glides up and down in rhythm with my mouth, my left hand finds his balls, gently squeezing as I push him to the back of my throat. He threads his hands in my hair and gathers the curls, holding them back from my face. "That's it, *mami, quiero sentir esa boca.*" His plea to feel my mouth stokes the burning desire, and I gently drag my teeth along his length as I pull it out, causing him to writhe underneath me.

"*Esa bemba me tiene loco.*" He lifts his hips in search of getting deeper inside. When I push him to the back of my throat again, I shake my head and squeeze his balls at the same time. He grunts as he's coming undone. Unable to continue holding my hair back, his hands drop to his sides, his breathing labored as he empties himself. When his breath calms, his hands find my cheeks and guide me up. His eyes are dark, lust burning at their ridges. "Show me," he commands, his thumb finding its way between my lips. I adjust myself and then open my mouth, obeying his instruction. Cum covers my mouth and his thumb rubs it into my skin. "Fuck, *qué hermosa que eres* with my cum on your face." Desire swirls in his gaze as he watches me swallow. His hands slide up my face and then thread my curls as he pulls me to him, kissing me, tasting himself on me.

I want him inside of me, but the condoms are in my bedroom. Reluctantly, I stand and hook my finger in the bandana wrapped on his left wrist to walk in that direction as Xavier paces behind me. Inside the room, I toss my sweatshirt onto the wingback chair, then open the door on my night table. As I'm pulling the box of condoms from the bottom, his hands squeeze my hips and then he presses his hardened length into me. I drop the rubbers on the bed but before I close the door on the nightstand, Xavier asks, "Is that a vibrator?" His hand reaches around me and grabs my purple cock-shaped dildo.

Instantly, my cheeks flame, and I nod. "Yes, but that's not for today," I tell him while taking it back and tossing it in place.

Xavier's hands squeeze my hips as he grinds his hardened

length against my ass. "*Eso es lo que usas* when you think of me fucking you?"

Nodding, I push back into him, greedy for more. "*Sí.*"

"*Entonces otro día si lo usaremos.*" Promise laced in his words that we'll use it together another day. "Today, *tenemos este*," he says, palming himself with one hand while reaching for a gold packet with the other.

As he sheathes himself, I sidle up next to him, dragging my fingers up his firm legs. Black ink adorns each of his limbs, various art designs distributed up and down their length. I kick my panties off and to the side, giving him a nudge with my foot.

"Lie back *y ábreme esas piernas*." My legs fall open at his command, and his right arm hooks under my thigh, lifting and opening me up for him. His dark brown hues are raging with lust as he eases into me, stretching me inch by inch until he's seated completely inside of me. His hips pulse, slow and deliberate, in tune with his kisses, each stoking my burning desires.

"Xavier." His name is a cross between a moan and a grunt.

"*Dime, mami.*"

I lift my hips, searching for more. In response he drags his length out, painstakingly up and back and my hands squeeze his buttocks. Suddenly, his pace increases and he hooks his left arm under my leg, spreading me. "Ahhhh." His thickness causes me to whimper with each thrust, wail with each outstroke. A tingly warmth at my clit tickles and spreads across my body, and my eyes roll back as the pressure of his cock plunges into me over and over. My body quivers and shakes as an orgasm crashes over me.

"*¡Mami, ese toto está bien rico!*" His punishing strokes continue as he praises my pussy, his hands squeezing the back of my thighs. My eyes meet his and the intensity of his gaze is too much, forcing me to close them. I, again, raise my hips, my body craving more of him. He adjusts himself, the pressure of him filling me satiating my ravenous desires. As he methodically rolls his hips, his balls brush my sensitive skin, pushing him over the edge. "*¡Todito pa ti, mami!*" he grunts as he comes undone.

Our breaths are heavy and labored as he releases my legs and lies next to me. My arm drapes over his torso, my fingers caressing his golden-brown skin, slick with sweat. "Welcome back from Brazil."

His lips curl up as his eyes meet mine. "The welcome party hasn't even started yet."

The alarm on my phone is going off, and it stirs me awake but when I turn to reach for it, Xavier's hand tightens on my hip. "*No te vayas,*" he mumbles.

"I'm not leaving. I just want to turn the alarm off." His grip loosens, and I'm able to grasp my phone and silence it. Usually, a seven fifteen wakeup call doesn't bother me too much, but most nights I'm sleeping well before midnight. Last night, we were up until nearly three in the morning, eating late-night snacks, naked in the kitchen and drawing orgasms from each other—me riding him, him taking me from behind, and him going down on me.

His arm tightens around me. "What time is it?"

"Seven fifteen. I don't want to get up yet."

"So don't. *Quédate conmigo.*" His hand palms my ass and massages the generous skin. I'd like nothing more than to stay in bed with him. "Call your boss and tell them you're sick."

"I am the boss, and I am sick. Sick of working."

"*Tú eres la jefa*, you can do whatever you want then." His hand tightens at my hip again and he presses his erection to me.

"I suppose, but I have obligations and stuff to do."

"Right now, the only thing you need to do is me."

His words teeter between desire and dominance as visions of him fucking me flash through my mind, kindling my desires. Chuckling, I say, "I'll put you at the top of my to-do list, then."

"Your obligations will still be there later, no?"

What good is it being the boss if I can't do what I want, when I want? It's probably bad for business, but I went to bed too late last night. I'm definitely feeling my age this morning after sleeping only a few hours. My legs are often sore after a brutal workout at the gym. But this morning, my aching legs give me the chills, remembering how he spread me open, had me begging for his cock. "Let me look at my calendar and see what's on the schedule for today." I know I don't have court, otherwise last night would've never happened. After I put my glasses on, I open the calendar app on my phone. I have a late morning call that I can have rescheduled, and then the meeting this afternoon in Brickell. And my date with Rodrigo. Shit! I'm going to have to cancel that. There's no way I can sit through a date with Rodrigo after the night I just had with Xavier—and the morning we're still in the midst of.

"*Entonces, jefa*, what's the verdict?"

My body shifts and turns toward him again. His eyes are still closed yet he's wearing a smirk. "I'm gonna text my paralegal to reschedule my late morning meeting."

His grin stretches across his face and his eyes shoot open, widening when he sees the frames sitting on my face. "*¿Tú usas lentes?*" His eyes widen as they peruse the glasses sitting on my face. Last night, by the time I took out my contacts and laid down, he was asleep.

I find my paralegal's name on the phone and send her a quick text message, then drop the phone back on the nightstand. "Yes, when I'm not wearing contacts, I need them. *No veo nada* without them." I've been wearing glasses for as long as I can remember but have always hated wearing frames. In high school, I started wearing contacts because I didn't want to deal with being made fun of for suddenly having to wear glasses. My astigmatism gets slightly worse each year so I will always need something to correct my vision. I've now reached the point that, without them, a lot of what I see is blurry, making it impossible to go without.

"They look sexy." He bites his lip and stretches his hand out, adjusting the frames on me. "*Quiero que me lo mames* while you're wearing them." Heat rises to my cheeks, although after the hours-long sexcapades of last night, him telling me he wants me to suck him off while wearing my glasses shouldn't surprise me.

My hand reaches for his and I thread our fingers. "I'll see what I can do."

"I have to shower. Want to join me?" The office waits, but I can't bring myself to end my time with him just yet.

"*Solo si me dejas bañarte.*" His hands land on my hips, and he buries his nose in my neck.

"Mmm, I'd like that." He surprises me with each passing minute. When he showed up last night, I thought he'd leave whenever he was done with me. Then, I thought he'd skip out after I went down on him first thing this morning. Yet, here he is at eleven in the morning, asking to bathe me. Seems he doesn't want our time together to end either.

His nose drags down my neck and along my shoulder. "Maybe you shouldn't shower, you smell like us *y me tienes loco.*"

Seems he's got me all crazed too. "Let's go." I wrap my hand with his and lead us to the bathroom.

"Call Nikki," I say, prompting my car to dial her number. It's nearly one in the afternoon and I'm just now driving to work. I don't think I've ever gotten to the office this late "just because."

This morning, after gracefully going down on Xavier while wearing my glasses and with my curls pulled back, he made us breakfast consisting of scrambled eggs with ham, tomatoes, and onion, toast, and *café con leche*. When he asked if I had the ingredients for breakfast, it caught me off guard. I wasn't expecting him to be there as long as he was. When he also wanted to cook, I tried convincing him it wasn't necessary, even if deep down I wasn't ready for our time together to end. I savored every minute with him as he rattled off the names of the Latin American cities he'll be visiting on his upcoming tour while sipping *café con leche*.

"Hi," she says, exhaling loudly.

Nikki sounds frustrated. "Hey, you okay?"

"Yeah, I'm fine. I've just been up since six and it's been a fucking day dealing with one asshole after another."

"Want to talk about it?"

"And rehash the level of assholes I've dealt with? Nah, I'll just get annoyed all over again. I'm good. How's your day so far?"

"Can't say I had the same kind of day."

"Yeah, why's that?"

A smile spreads across my face, reminding me of the morning Xavier and I had. After I texted my paralegal, Xavier was hard as a rock seeing me with my glasses on. He was obsessed with the red frames and wanted me to wear them while I sucked him off and then straddled him. I felt giddy as I watched him sip his *café con leche* at my counter in nothing but his tighty-whities. Despite having orgasmed twice before breakfast, I wasn't satiated and I asked him to shower with me, where he enjoyed stroking me while he washed every inch of my body, then took me from behind. He's insatiable, and it's rubbing off on me! "Xavier spent the night last night, and we had a busy morning."

"Oh shit! I was not expecting you to drop that. *¡Necesito todo el chisme!*" Without getting into too many details about our activities, I told Nikki about him coming over straight from the airport. I learned that he has his own private jet that he uses to travel, which explains how he arrived at my apartment so quickly after landing.

"He wants to see me again. And after the morning we had, I'm canceling my date with Rodrigo."

"Looks like that cougar thing is working out for you!" She chuckles.

"I'm trying not to think too much about it because it'll just ruin everything."

"Rodrigo is gonna be heartbroken. César said he's been talking about his date all week!"

A brief flash of guilt crosses my mind. "I was actually looking forward to it. But I barely have the bandwidth for one guy, never mind two. Besides, it wouldn't be right to sit across from Rodrigo after the last twenty-four hours." My car slows, stopping at the red light on 41st Street and Pine Tree Drive.

"It's the right thing to do. He's a nice guy."

"So, what should I tell him? I don't want to lie but also don't think I should divulge all the things."

A few days ago my mind was made up—I had no intentions of having anything serious with anyone. Then Xavier appeared and my body betrayed my mind, gave in to the allure of his deep voice and promises of mind-blowing orgasms. After

Victor's infidelity, I swore off relationships and men. But that was just my anger protecting me, protecting my heart. That's not to say my guard is down, but my body is taking a stance, screaming that swearing off men is not an option—at least not right now.

"Maybe let him know you started seeing someone. He's probably not gonna ask for details."

He's definitely not asking for details. Besides, I don't owe him anything—we barely know each other. "If whatever this is with Xavier goes anywhere, I'm sure he'll find out eventually."

"By then, he will have moved on."

Traffic along 41st street at this time of day is way heavier than it ever is in the morning when I'm typically driving to the office. The sidewalks are full of parents walking their children home from school, since Wednesdays are early release days. As I wait for the traffic to inch forward, I glance at the palm trees lining the street. There are city workers perched up high, trimming the palm fronds. "Rodrigo's a texter, can I do it via text?"

"I mean, he probably would so I don't see why not. Besides, you guys haven't even talked much so I think it's fine. But what I do know, *soy una vieja* and I've been out of the dating game forever."

"That makes two of us. This morning was rough after only sleeping like four hours. Last night, the later it got, the more my age whispered warnings of the time lapse." I can't remember the last time I had so much sex in one stretch. "It's a different world out there! Nothing like it was when we were young."

"*Ay, mujer*, you're talking as if you've been out in these dating streets living it up. You haven't actually gone on a first date yet, unless you count sleeping with Mr. Skinny Casanova." She's laughing.

"You're terrible!" I respond. Nikki always has a comment about everything; her referring to him that way is so typical, and a shudder of annoyance rushes through me. Not sure why, but it rubs me the wrong way when she said it instead of his name.

"Why? It's true."

"Can you ever be serious? After more than two years of sleeping alone, I spent the night at my apartment with a guy and you're cracking jokes about him and his stage name." My tone is sharp.

Nikki's breathing is heavy. "Sorry, Rocky. You know my humor is usually inappropriate, especially when I'm off-kilter. Please don't be upset with me. Not sure I could handle that right now."

"You sure everything is okay?" I ask, remembering how she responded to my call.

"César and I had a huge blowout this morning. It's thrown off my entire day."

Her tone is flat, which is very out of character for her. "Oh, Nikki, I'm sorry. You want to talk about it?"

"I'm in the office and these walls have ears. Maybe later."

CHAPTER FIFTEEN

Xavier

ADRIÁN PARKS the car outside of Rocky's office at 169 East Flagler, a few blocks from Xiomary's building. Unlike the sleek, modern building Xiomary's office is in, Rocky's is inside the historic Alfred Dupont building adorned with art deco embellishments. This building is iconic in Miami's history, and it served as the headquarters for the Florida National Bank from the time it was erected until the mid-1980s.

I know she said she had court in the morning, but I have no idea what her afternoon schedule looks like, so I hope she's in her office. Yesterday, after we woke up together at her apartment, I didn't want to leave. It's been twenty-four hours, and I'm already fiending to see her again. After leaving her apartment, I met with Roly and Maritza. We were looking at the samples of the tour merch, together with the finalized designs for the limited-edition city tees and posters. As we flipped through pictures, the only images my mind focused on were of Rocky spread and eager for me. By the time our meeting ended, it was past nine o'clock and Rocky had said she was tired and that she had court in the morning. I'm not used to hearing the word "no," and I'm hoping she doesn't make a habit of it. We made plans to see each other today when she was done for the day but here I am, like a kid on Christmas morning waiting to open gifts.

Once on the seventh floor, I locate her office by the sign that reads, "Rocío Fontana Law, P.A. *Su familia. Su futuro.* Our priority." Inside, there's a young woman at the front desk. When her eyes connect with mine, recognition washes over her.

"Um, hi." The young woman is staring at me, her eyes wide and lips parted. "You're *El Flaco Casanova*, right?" she says, pushing her hair behind her ears.

Nodding, I say, "Yes, that's me."

"Wow." She shoots up from her seat and extends her hand out. "Can I get a picture with you?"

I give her a crooked smile. "Of course. Let me see your phone." I crouch down and position the phone in front of us, snapping a few selfies for her.

"Oh my god, my friends are gonna freak out when I tell them I met you!"

"What's your name?"

Her head shakes. "I'm sorry. You came to our office and here I am fangirling." She smooths her dress and straightens her back. "I'm Veronica. Welcome to the office."

A chuckle escape. "Thanks. It's nice to meet you, Veronica. And you're good." I wink.

"How can I help you?" She adjusts herself in the chair.

"I'm here to see Rocky."

Her eyes glance at the phone on her desk. "She's on a call right now. Do you have an appointment?"

I shake my head. "No, I don't."

"Yeah, I don't see you on our calendar for today. I definitely would've known if you were about to walk into our office."

"If you could let her know I'm here, I don't mind waiting."

"Yes, I can do that. Have a seat, if you'd like." She gestures to the couches in the lobby. Veronica rises from her chair and scurries down the hall. Whispers come from the office, although I can't make out the words.

Before sitting, I glance at the large painting hanging above the dark leather couch along the wall to my right. It's Lady Justice, and she's wearing a white tunic similar to a Greek goddess, a cloudy blue sky the backdrop. I'm about to take a seat when Rocky's warm and rich voice caresses me from behind. "Hi, Xavier. What are you doing here?"

I spin and take a few steps across the lobby to get close to her. "Hi, *mami*," I whisper, resting my lips on her warm cheek. It's not the kiss I want to give her but we're in her office and she wasn't expecting me—I don't want to freak her out, especially with her employees here. "I'm here to see you." I give her a big, toothy smile.

Her eyes search mine, and she purses her lips. She's about to say something but decides to keep it to herself. "Let's go into my office." My eyes drop to the round globes of her generous ass as it shakes with each stride she takes down the hall. The red suit she's wearing accentuates her hips, the hips I held onto as I rammed her from behind in the wee hours of the morning. My pants tighten just thinking about how she gripped me. Red is her color and she should wear it all the time.

Inside her office sits a large dark wooden desk in the center and floor to ceiling bookshelves that take up the entire wall behind it. To the left the windows stretch the length of the wall, making the office bright, with a view of the neighboring buildings. She closes the door, turning the lock on the handle, then crosses the office and sits on the edge of the desk. I follow, place my hands on the desk on each side of her, taking her mouth in mine—sucking her full lips. She rests her hands on the back of my neck and nudges my hat, causing it to tumble to the floor.

"*Mami, te quiero chingar bien rico encima de este escritorio,*" I declare, dragging my nose along the length of her neck. I want nothing more than to fuck her on this desk right now but doubt she'd let me.

Her chest rises and falls in steady breaths. "We can make that happen," she says, letting her head fall back to give me easier access to her, "just not today."

My hands find her breasts and squeeze. Her nipples harden through the fabric of her blouse. As I attempt to finagle my hand into her bra, her fingers wrap around my wrist, stopping me with a shake of her head.

"As much as I want you to touch me everywhere, my staff is just outside of this office so we can't." Her usual vibrant green eyes are a smoldering deep emerald—dark and hungry—devouring me while her hands keep me at bay.

I step back, respecting her request and put space between us. "I couldn't wait to see you. *No pasaba el tiempo.*" It felt like time was standing still as I waited for the hours to pass. Unable to resist her, my hand stretches to drag my fingers across her plump bottom lip.

"What are you gonna do now that you've seen me?" Her tongue juts out, sucking my thumb between her swollen lips.

"I would do everything, if you'd let me. *Pero dijiste que no se puede*, at least not right now." Her tongue swirls around my thumb before I drag it across her lips, smearing the mauve color more than it already is. My dick is rock hard, and I want to take her across this desk, staff and all, but she already told me she won't—at least not while they're here. I'm disappointed but get it. Not to mention, I respect that she sets boundaries and isn't swayed by my persistence. "You have a passport?" I ask, distancing myself from her to alleviate the pressure in my groin.

"Passport? What for?"

"*¿Lo tienes o no?*" Hesitancy is written all over her face as she contemplates my question, her lips slightly pursed.

She nods. "Yeah, I do."

"Then tomorrow we're leaving for South Andros Island. I want you all to myself, no distractions."

Her eyes widen. "What? I can't go to the Bahamas with you."

"*¿No puedes irte conmigo?* Or you can't go away?"

"That's not—" Her fingers fidget at her side, her eyes searching mine. "Of course I can go away with *you*, I just can't tomorrow."

"*¿Por qué no?*" Her eyes skirt away from mine.

"Tomorrow's Friday, and I have to work."

"*¿Tu eres la jefa, no?* You have court?" She shakes her head but doesn't say anything. "Then what? Why can't you go?" She's staring at me, her fingers rubbing her upper thighs. Silence hovers in the air as I watch the thoughts churning through her mind. "You want to know what I think?" I ask, crossing the room and halting in front of her, letting the tip of my nose brush hers.

"*¿Qué?*" she whispers, her breath hot.

"*Tienes miedo.*" My mouth covers hers and my tongue juts out, dragging along her teeth, wanting my touch to calm the fear she's creating for herself.

"I'm not." She huffs, meeting my pace.

"Scared *porque te hago sentir* and you don't know what to do with all those feelings." My lips land on hers again, sucking her bottom lip between mine, savoring it. "*Miedo* because you want me to fuck you *pero también* you want me to make love to you. *Miedo* because you don't know which you want more. *Miedo* of what will happen if you give in to me."

Her chest rapidly rises and falls. "Maybe."

"Maybe what?"

"Maybe everything." Her hands wrap around the back of my

neck, pulling me impossibly close as she deepens her kiss—an urgent conversation between our mouths, tongues intertwining and exploring. A sigh escapes her, and I growl as my dick presses at the seam.

"So then, you'll come."

"Yes, I want to come," she says, her words breathy as her hand palms my hard cock.

I'm unsure if she responded to my question of coming with me, or if she declared that she wants me to make her come. I'm going with the latter. "*Quiero que te vengas to'ita pa mi.*"

She's nodding while still devouring my mouth. Despite her hot breath and needy moans, she halts, and scoots to the right, freeing herself from my grip. Reluctantly, I don't follow, respecting the boundary she's creating while searching her eyes, lust burning at their brims. "Wasn't so hard, was it?"

"Actually, it was." She gives me a crooked grin.

"*Si tú quieres*, I'll let you feel how hard it can really get." All she has to do is say yes.

"You don't play fair."

"When I want something, I'll do whatever it takes. *Y yo te quiero a ti.*" In case she doesn't already know how much I want her.

"*Y yo a vos*," she admits.

"I've been meaning to ask," she says, shifting in her seat toward me.

We picked her up at her building, and Adrián is driving us to the Sunset Harbor Marina. "*Lo que tú quieras, mami.*"

Her lips are in a straight line, and her fingers rub the side of her leg. "What's the situation with the paparazzi? Will they be following us everywhere we go?"

My head shakes. "Nah, you don't have to worry about that. The marina is private property, and the resort is exclusive with a private villa and beaches. We good."

She nods and gives me a crooked smile that doesn't reach her eyes.

Adrián drives up to the entrance and we grab our things, heading to the boat slip. We're meeting Landy's brother who pilots my yacht when I want to take it long distances.

When *"Sombra Fiel"* catapulted me out of the hole I'd buried myself in, I bought this yacht and named her *La Tempestad*—a reminder that I'd weathered my drug-induced monsoon and was barely able to survive on some days as the tremors, muscle aches, nausea, and vomiting ravaged me while detoxing. When the drugs were finally out of my system, I was stuck in an emotional tundra of my brain telling my body it needed another pill, but my heart refused to give in, wanting to be clean. Wanting to be free from the binds Percocet had me in. There were nights when I wasn't sure I'd make it through, the profound sense of despair and anxiety all consuming. After the longest sixteen days of my life, I had once again felt a sense of calm despite the ever-swirling emotional turbulence and cravings. But each time the rain ends, the sun eventually shines, and I'm forever grateful that I too was given the opportunity to feel the warmth of its rays again.

After getting clean, there were days I doubted if I'd ever find my place in this world again. Don't get me wrong, there are still days where the craving of popping a pill is stronger than everything else around me, but my sponsor's voice always loudly whispers, "Play the tape through," reminding me that popping pills makes me feel euphoric in that moment, but the shame and guilt that washes over me through my hangover are far more devastating and impactful than the actual drug.

"You good, *mami*?"

Although South Andros Island is less than two hundred miles from Miami, to get there we have to cross the Atlantic Ocean, and I'm not experienced enough to do that, which is why I need someone to pilot my yacht. Besides, I'd rather spend the time with Rocky. We boarded the yacht a few minutes ago, and after getting the captain situated with our plans, I turn to Rocky, whose hand is outstretched and dragging along the back of the white seats.

"When you said, 'my yacht,' you actually meant your yacht. Holy shit, Xavier. This is a nice boat."

Last night, Rocky and I had dinner at a hole-in-the-wall Cuban place in Little Havana. I've been going there since I moved to Miami years ago, and it's my go-to spot for homemade Cuban food, often stopping in two or three times a week. She was asking questions about the trip across to the Bahamas and was surprised when I mentioned my yacht.

My eyebrows raise. "Of course that's what I meant. What else would I have meant?"

"I don't know. Guess I'm just not used to people actually having yachts." She shrugs.

"Have you ever been on a boat?"

She's nodding. "Yes. A few cruises and also a friend's boat, but smaller than this."

"And the Bahamas, have you been?"

"Only Nassau when one of the cruises stopped for the day."

"So no, you haven't really seen the Bahamas then."

"Will I get seasick?" A horizontal crease appears across her forehead.

"The waters are calm today and the swells are less than two feet," Landy's brother responds.

"I'm not sure I totally understand what that means, but hopefully the water being calm is enough to keep me from getting sick."

"Why didn't you tell me before we left, *mami*?"

Her fingers push her hair behind her ears. "It would've sounded like another excuse and I'm trying really hard not to make excuses."

"If you'd told me," I say, tracing her jawline, "I would've gotten you some of those pills."

"I bought some last night. I'm gonna take it now that we're getting ready to leave."

"Okay. He's the best at what he does so you should be good," I tell her, gesturing toward Landy's brother. "*Cualquier cosa*, you let us know."

The trip across the Atlantic was relatively smooth. Although we did get some strong currents in the Gulf Stream, Rocky handled it like a champ. When she told me she was prone to getting seasick, I was worried it may ruin her entire weekend. We docked the yacht at the private marina in Congo Town and are waiting for the immigration officials.

The man in a light collared shirt and army-green trousers boards the vessel and is eyeing our passports. He opens up the first one and then looks up, first at Rocky then at me, his gaze lingering several seconds before closing both books and handing them to me. "Enjoy your stay in the Bahamas," he says.

As the official is walking away, I open up Rocky's passport. "Is your last name Aguirre or Fontana?" I ask.

"Aguirre was my married name," she says, her gaze locking with mine. "I just haven't changed everything over yet."

"*Y Rocío es un nombre hermoso*. Why do you go by Rocky?" I ask, intrigued as to why she doesn't use her given name.

"Growing up in Boston, no one could pronounce my name, and I hated it. Everyone struggled and it made me wicked self-conscious about myself. Julieta, my older sister, hated it almost as much as me, so she started calling me Rocky, and it stuck. I didn't love it, but it was way easier for everyone to pronounce so I didn't protest. All these years later, nearly everyone calls me it—except Julieta, who chose the name and now says it's a terrible nickname. So she calls me Rocío." Her shoulders rise as she tugs her passport from my hands.

"I'll just call you *mami*," I say, wrapping my arms around her, burying my nose in her messy curls.

"I'll have the yacht ready for you to take it out tomorrow morning," Landy's brother tells us as we disembark.

With Rocky's hand in mine, we stroll to the main marina building where a driver from the Caerula Beach Resort is waiting to take us to our private villa. I've only been here one other time, and it was for a wedding I attended with Lisandra not long after we started dating. One of her childhood friends was getting married, and they had events spanning across four days. When I had Maritza book the villa for this weekend, I asked her to get any villa except the one I had with Lisandra.

Once inside the Pink Sands Villa, Rocky goes straight for the French doors that open up to the beach. "It's wicked pretty."

"Wicked pretty. If I didn't know you were from Boston, using wicked would give you away." I give her a lopsided grin.

"Yeah, can't help it." She shrugs as she pushes the doors, salty air filling the room.

"I absolutely love the beach." She kicks her sneakers off and peels off her socks. "Let's go down to the water." After removing my shoes, I sprint to catch up to her and once alongside her, I tangle my fingers with hers.

The sand between my toes is soft and feels more like powder than sand. "Me, too."

"There's no one here. It's like we have the beach to ourselves."

"*Casi.*" My chin gestures to our left where a couple is strolling away from us.

"Here I thought we might be able to swim naked." She bites her bottom lip as she's peeking up at me, desire dripping from her every pore.

Her mention of the word naked and my dick is already standing at attention. "The villa has a private pool in the back *si quieres bañarte desnuda.* As much as I love you naked"—my fingers squeeze her rounded hips—"*eres mía* and I don't share." We're in a secluded place but the last thing I want, or need, is prying eyes to catch a glimpse of my girl naked and landing us on *las malas lenguas* of the Latin media.

"A private dinner in our villa, huh?" Her fingertips drag along the table set for two on the veranda.

My eyes search her emerald hues. "*Te dije*, no distractions."

"What's on the menu?"

"Besides you?"

She gives me half a smile and nods.

"I haven't ordered yet, the menu's over there." I point to the counter behind her.

Earlier, hotel staff came to set up, leaving everything ready. The menus are next to the beverages—water, sparkling water, white wine, red wine, and various sodas. She reaches for the red wine and pulls the cork, pouring half a glass then extending it to me. "You drink red wine?"

I shake my head. "I don't drink."

Her eyes widen. "Oh." She slides the wine glass back toward her. "I'm sorry, I just…assumed since we met at a bar."

"It's okay." I lean into the counter and reach for her.

She grabs my hand in hers and our palms meet, hovering between us. "Why don't you drink?"

My heart thunders in my chest. I've not shared about my parents with anyone since Lisandra. I take a deep breath and squeeze Rocky's hand. "My father was an alcoholic, and he destroyed my family because of it." She searches for my other hand and closes the space between us.

"I'm sorry for assuming." Her eyes drop, and she shifts in place.

I release her hand then nudge her chin, forcing her eyes back to mine. "Hey. You don't have to apologize. I'm used to it, which is why I drink club soda with lime. People just assume I'm drinking vodka sodas." My lips graze hers.

Before drugs took over my life, I had my share of drinks. When I noticed I was drinking too much, I stopped for fear of ending up an alcoholic like my father. Lisandra thought it made me look weak if I didn't drink at all the events we attended, which is how I started drinking club sodas. At the time it bothered me, but then Percocet roped me in and everything else fell by the wayside.

"You shouldn't have to be used to it. It's a choice you made and people should respect it."

"*De verdad*, it's okay." My lips turn upward.

"Does it bother you if I drink?"

I shake my head. "*Nunca*. I would never ask you to do that."

She nods. "Okay." She glances at the menus then at the shimmering blue pool. "Not sure what I want more, to order food or take a dip in the pool."

"You did say you wanted to swim naked. I'll go with option two."

She grabs the hem of her shirt, lifts up, then tosses it on the counter, her luscious breasts spilling over the top of her bra. Her hardened nipples are visible through the white fabric as she's reaching back to unsnap the constraints. Her heavy breasts fall and my dick strains inside my briefs. As she's pushing the hem of her pants down, I do the same. She's immersing herself in the pool, her hand stretched back in search of mine. "Are you coming?"

I take the few strides toward her and step into the water. "Not yet, but I'm sure you'll help me with that."

CHAPTER SIXTEEN

Rocío

THIS MORNING, Xavier piloted the yacht and we anchored several miles offshore. Out here, we're surrounded by pristine turquoise water and sun. Just Xavier and me. We swam, ate, lounged, swam some more. "When you said no distractions, you weren't lying." We've been secluded and in our own private world, which is exactly what Xavier brought us to the Bahamas to do. It's nice being away from the daily grind and away from my phone. I can't remember the last time I took time off to relax and unwind. I'm stretched across the sun pads covering the foredeck, sunbathing without a bathing suit—something I've never done before.

Xavier pops up and leans over me, blocking me from the sun. "Never, *mami*. I promise if I say something, it's true." His lips drop kisses along my jawline, trace down my neck and land on my breast, and he begins suckling on my nipple.

"Yeah, I'm starting to pick up on that." I moan as he swirls his tongue, and with his other hand he squeezes my other nipple, rolling the pebbled skin between his fingers.

"You like that, *mami*?"

My hand finds his, and I guide it between my legs. I'm panting as his fingers rub circles and then penetrate me, hooking up.

"*Siempre tan mojaíta.*" My hips rise, searching for more pressure, and he inserts another finger while his thumb circles my clit. "I could make love to you all day."

We're walking along the shoreline back to our villa after dinner and I've been itching to ask him about his parents since last night but was waiting for some privacy. Now that it's just us along the short stretch of beach, I say, "Tell me about your family."

His grip tightens on my hand briefly before loosening. "My parents died when I was twelve, and me and my sister moved to Puerto Rico *con mi abuela.*"

"How did they die?" My head turns to meet his eyes. His Adam's apple is prominent as he swallows.

"My father was drunk and was driving, killed them both."

Instinctively, my hand tightens around his. The words are heavy and my heart aches for that young boy whose world was turned upside down. For the man who still carries the weight of that loss. "Oh, wow. I'm so sorry."

"Hey." He halts and cups my face in his hands. "You don't have to be sorry."

I nod and take in the crashing of the waves.

"Then *mi abuela* died a few years ago. Now, it's just me and my sister."

He's lost nearly his whole family. "I'm sorry, I can't even imagine what that feels like for you."

"It was rough at times, but most days I'm good." His eyes are soft, and they remain steady on mine.

"I didn't know. Sorry if I brought up stuff you'd rather not discuss." The slap and pull of the water soothe as the waves crest.

His head is shaking. "You didn't. We're getting to know each other, *por supuesto* you'd ask about my family." He brushes his lips with mine. "I like you asking questions."

"You sure about that? I ask questions for a living." I smirk.

He nods. "The more you ask, the more I get to ask." Our gazes linger, possibility swirling in the breeze.

The rest of the short walk back to the villa is quiet, filled only with the constant sound of water shifting. I wanted to ask more about his family and his parents but chose not to pry anymore. Although he said he's okay with me asking questions, I'll have to be ready to answer his questions too.

I finish brushing my teeth, and I enter the oversized bedroom where Xavier is undressing, his back to me. I lean against the wall, admiring as he exposes his inked skin. A memory of the online search I did pops up, reminding me I didn't see any pictures of him bare chested, which is odd considering he is sculpted and beautiful. Not to mention that incredible eagle tattoo adorning his chest.

He and Victor are different in every way imaginable, not just their looks. Where Victor was clean-cut and almost always wore a business suit or business casual attire, Xavier has an edgy look to him, looks almost dangerous with that five o'clock shadow he's always sporting. The night at *La Gata*'s release party, he was wearing a slim, all black suit over a fitted t-shirt and sneakers. I always thought Victor looked good in a suit, but now that I've seen Xavier in one, I'm questioning all my past decisions. The further I get from my life with Victor, the more I question why I put him on a pedestal for as long as I did. In hindsight, we seem so incompatible, and I wonder if I only feel that way because of Victor's betrayal.

"What are you thinking about?" Xavier asks as he crosses the room, snapping me back to the present moment.

Fuck. Should I be honest? Telling him about Victor could very well ruin the entire weekend, but I'm not good at faking it and Xavier reads me like a book. I lift my eyes to meet his and say, "My ex-husband."

His eyes widen and his back straightens. "Strange thing to be thinking about right at this moment, no?" he asks, his tone even and gentle.

"Yeah, for sure," I respond, nodding. "But as I watched you, I couldn't help but think how different you are." My fingers snake their way under the elastic of his underwear.

"I don't know him, but he let you get away, so I already know we're different. *¡Por qué yo protejo lo mío con toda mi alma y tú eres mía!*" My heart flutters as he stakes his claim, saying he protects what's his. "*Dime*, why do you think I'm different?" His eyes bore into mine, probing and inquisitive.

"You're kind, thoughtful, attentive, generous, and perceptive. Not to mention gorgeous. And if I had never caught him cheating on me, I wouldn't have gotten divorced and I never would've met you. I'd be missing out."

Xavier's hands rest on my waist, and he swallows, his Adam's apple prominent. His gaze hardens and nostrils flare as he asks, "He cheated on you?"

Xavier repeating the words back to me causes a pang in my heart; even after all this time, Victor's betrayal aches. I nod. "Yes. And apparently, he did it for years."

His jaw tightens as his hands ball up in fists. He closes the space between us, my back flush to the wall, enveloping me in his safety net, causing a flutter in the pit of my belly.

"I have no idea how many women there were over the years," I say, looking up at him. "The only reason I found out was because I settled one of my cases the day trial was starting and returned to our office early. To my surprise, he was fucking another woman inside his office. She was gorgeous with her dark silky hair. Younger than me, too. I wish I could've yelled or insulted them, but I had nothing. I felt empty and so stupid." My eyes drop. "Humiliated as I stared at them with tears streaming down my face. Watched as she hurriedly dressed, and on her way out, her hand grazed my shoulder as she whispered, 'I didn't know, I'm sorry.'" The entire thing played out like a bad film as shame crept into my every fiber. Even sharing that he was unfaithful for years makes me sound like a fool.

Xavier's hand reaches up and cups my face, forcing my eyes to meet his. His thumbs swipe away the tears gliding down my cheeks. "He's not worth your tears, *mami*. He's like every other weak, selfish person that chooses themselves first. He's done it his entire life and will continue to do it until the day he dies. That day you felt like your world shattered, *pero él te hizo un favor*," he tells me, trying to convince me that Victor did me a favor. "He gave you your life back *y aquí te tengo a mi lado*. Cowards like him *no merecen na*." His thumbs dry the wetness.

It's true that he's a coward, but because he's Cata's father, I don't wish anything bad upon him. Cata would be devastated, even if her relationship with him is strained.

"It's funny because there was a time that I wouldn't have agreed that him cheating was a blessing in disguise, but the further away from my life with him I get, the clearer it becomes. Weird how that works."

"Time and clarity *son hermanos* who bring out the best in each other."

"I like that," I say, because it's true that siblings often bring out the best in each other.

"Yeah"—he leans in, his nose brushing mine—"well, I like

you. *Déjame enseñarte cuánto.*" Leave it to Xavier to flip the script from me thinking about Victor to telling me how much he wants to show me he likes me.

His mouth covers mine, and with slow, deliberate motions, he sucks first my top lip, then my bottom. His left-hand shimmies under my top and finds my nipple, which he rolls between his fingers, causing me to gasp. Desire pulses through me, and I wrap my arms around his neck, closing the space between us. His mouth lands at my ear, and he licks and sucks his way down until he reaches the collar of my shirt. He tugs the hem up and I shimmy out of the tee. His large hands force my heavy breasts together, licking and sucking on one nipple then the next. My hand finds his hardened length, and I begin stroking.

"I need you to fuck me," I plead.

Grasping my waist, he turns me, drops to his knees, and shoves his face between my legs. His tongue searches for my puckered hole. His fingers press into my fleshy glutes, and he spreads the skin, the tip of his tongue teasing the tightness. He drags his tongue slowly along the divide, up the sacral region, my spine, and finally, he's flush behind me, his cock hot and hard as it rubs against my lower back. As he kisses my neck, he pushes his fingers in my mouth, swirling them around my tongue. Before I can suck them further, he pulls them out and drops them to my ass, spreading my cheeks apart. One of his digits draws circles on the tight opening.

"*Mami*, one of these days I want to fuck you here, *por qué to lo tuyo es mío.*" His finger penetrates and I gasp. I've never let anyone touch me there, but I'd let Xavier do anything to me.

I nod. "*Yes.*" I'm whimpering as I push my ass out, my body screaming for him to make me feel.

"*Acho, mami, que rica tú estás. Te quiero cojer ese culito.*" My limbs feel like they're gonna give out, and I have to steady myself with the wall. When I think he's going to continue stretching me, his fingers are gone.

"Why'd you stop?" I'm panting, the haze of lust and desire making me dizzy.

"We don't have any lube, *pero* don't worry, *ese culito te lo voy a romper bien rico*." His words a pledge of promised desire. "For now, *dame ese toto que te voy a dejar temblando*."

My ass pushes back, begging for him to penetrate me. The crinkling sound tells me he's about to give me what I want. His hands grasp the globes of my ass, and he positions the head of his cock at my entrance.

"*Inclínate*, and open up for me," he commands as his cock plunges into me, causing a yelp to escape.

His grunts are loud and possessive as his fingers press into my hips. He's ramming from behind, my ass meeting his punishing strokes with wanton desire. Suddenly his strokes slow, becoming even and measured, and he leans over me, his fingers playing with my sensitive nub.

"*Eres hermosa cuando estás bellaca*." His fingers pick up their pace. "*Quiero que te vengas* all over my cock. *Todita pa mi*."

His plea for me to come for him dizzies me and electricity courses through me. I have to steady myself as the pulses at my center intensify with each stroke of his dick, each swipe of his finger. I'm panting and pushing as pleasure crashes into me, weakening my limbs.

Xavier grasps my hips and increases his pace, our bodies slick with sex and sweat and desire. His body stiffens, and he collapses over me. "*Tuyo, mami. Todo tuyo*."

Being back in Miami after spending three days doing nothing but soaking up the sun and enjoying the high of Xavier ravaging my body has been rough. Monday, I had a full-day mediation scheduled. It dragged on for what felt like hours, with clients on both sides being unreasonable at different stages of the process. There were times I wanted to scream at my client, but it had nothing to do with her and everything to do with the state of mind I was in. I had no desire to be working that Monday, and I was just spreading my misery. Thankfully, by late Monday evening the clients were able to reach a settlement, and we finalized the agreement and got everything signed. Xavier wanted to see me, but I was so drained from the day I had, I told him no. Yesterday wasn't much better with depositions scheduled all day. Last night, I was in bed and snoozing by nine o'clock. This morning I still felt tired when I turned my alarm clock off and slept in until nearly nine. Luckily, today was an office day.

It's Wednesday but already feels like Friday. If I didn't have plans with Cata, I would've cancelled. The drive from downtown to South Miami was bumper to bumper, and I'm finally pulling up to her house, ready for our sushi date. After seeing her in my building a few weeks ago, she was eager to see me again, and I wanted to make sure I set aside time for her.

"Hi, Rocky," Lorena says, her dark hair pulled back in a high ponytail. "Cata said she'll be down in a minute." She closes the door behind us as we walk into the kitchen.

"Thanks. How are you, Lorena?" When Victor and I were still together, I made a lot of effort to be on good terms with her. Working with so many families involved in family court, I see firsthand how children are negatively affected by parents and stepparents who are incapable of putting aside their differences for the best interest of the kids involved. I did not want to be responsible for anything that could negatively affect Cata. After all, her world had already fallen apart when her parents separated.

"I'm good." A smile stretches across her face but doesn't meet her eyes. "I'm sure Cata will share the news with you, but she wanted to attend a summer program at Boston University for high school-aged kids, and she was accepted. She's ecstatic about it."

Every year I visited Boston to see family or friends, Victor and Cata would come with me. Cata learned to love Boston, so it's no surprise she wants to go to school there. "That's incredible! She always did say she wanted to attend Boston University for undergrad."

Not too long after my separation with Victor, Lorena called me to thank me for being a constant positive figure in Cata's life. It was something I never expected yet everything I needed to hear. With Cata being so hurt by the impending divorce, I was glad to know that Cata—and Lorena—still wanted me around.

"She loves Boston because of you, but I'm not ready for her to be so independent."

"It's a great city—"

"What's a great city?" Cata interrupts, barreling into the kitchen.

"Hey, kiddo," I say, kissing her hello. "Boston, of course."

"Did Mom tell you about BU?"

Nodding my head, I say, "Yep, and I'm wicked proud of you. You can tell me about the program over dinner."

"Okay, bye, Ma." She leans in to give her mother a kiss.

"Enjoy sushi," Lorena says.

"Bye, Lorena. We'll be back in a couple hours."

Cata chose the sushi restaurant that we always ate at when I was still with Victor. It's been her favorite spot for as long as I can remember. The drive to the restaurant in Sunset Place is quick since we're not too far from Lorena's house. Cata spends the short drive telling me about her basketball team making it to divisional playoffs.

After we order a variety of sushi rolls, I say, "Tell me about the summer program in Boston. I want to know everything!" The restaurant is quiet tonight. The soft blue walls look brighter with a near-empty dining room and only three other tables seated.

"It's an academic immersion program, and I chose Introduction to Medicine. You know I've always wanted to be a surgeon."

"That's awesome, Cata. I'm really excited for you, not to mention proud. Will you get to do any non-academic stuff while there?"

"Yeah! The one weekend while there we're taking a field trip. There were two options, one was to go to New York City for the weekend, and the other was a weekend in York Beach, Maine. I chose Maine."

"York Beach is beautiful! When I was growing up, my friend's family had a house there so I used to go up with her in the summers."

I always remember spending a week there during the summers growing up. My friend's family has a cabin just two blocks from the ocean. We'd walk to the beach every day, swim and look for seashells and sea glass. There was an ice cream shop on the corner that had the best strawberry ice cream.

"Then we'll get free time in the evenings but can only participate in organized activities. Some are on campus and others off campus. They have a bunch of stuff we can sign up for. I signed up for a duck tour and a food tour in the North End." Cata's eyes illuminate in joy as she rattles off her plans for her time in Boston.

"Well, you know the North End well since we ate at all my favorite places every time we'd visit."

"Yup. The food tour will take us to Modern Pastry and I'm super excited to have a cannoli."

"Where will you be having a cannoli?" Both of our heads turn to see Victor standing next to the table, pulling a chair out to sit with us. Heat climbs up my neck as I watch Cata's nostrils flare while grinding her teeth.

"Dad, what are you doing here?" Her pursed lips form a tight angry knot.

"I called your mom to ask if I could take you out to dinner, and she said you were out to dinner with Rocky. So here I am, saying hello to my two favorite girls."

"Kiki divorced you. You don't get to call her that anymore," she retorts, looking at me with sadness in her eyes.

"It's fine, Cata," I respond, resting my hand over hers.

"It's not fine! He never hung out with us when you were married, and now he's just here to ruin our night."

"I'm not here to ruin anything. Like I said, I called Mom and she told me—"

"Mom would never tell you where we're having dinner."

"No, she wouldn't. But she doesn't have to, your phone shows me where you are all the time."

Cata rolls her eyes and crosses her arms.

"Victor, I would really like to enjoy a dinner with just Cata tonight. So, if you don't mind, I'll walk you out."

"I was hoping I could join you."

"No, you can't. We already ordered and it's a girls' night," I say, resting my napkin on the table and pushing the chair back. "Cata, let me walk your father out. I'll be right back." I rise, stride past Victor, and turn my head to ensure he's following me. He leans over to kiss Cata goodbye and then turns on his heel. Once outside the restaurant, I face Victor. "What the fuck was that?" The small group of people crossing the street glance over.

"What was what?" he responds, as if him showing up wasn't intrusive.

"Really, that's the way you're gonna play it?" I shake my head, irritation bubbling.

"Lorena told me she was having dinner with you, and I

figured I'd stop by." The smirk that once stirred the butterflies in my belly just grates on me.

"As usual, you figured wrong! I'm really not sure why you thought that was a good idea." My hands wave in the air. "First, Lorena didn't tell you where we were, you tracked us here. Second, Cata was right; when I was your wife and wanted to have dinner with you, most nights I was home alone or with Cata. You weren't so interested in having dinner with us then while you were out fucking women left and right. Now what? The thrill of the chase is back?"

"Please lower your voice." His hand wraps around my forearm.

I yank my arm away from him. "Get your hands off me!"

"I fucked up, I know." His gray blue eyes look sunken in and have dark circles shadowing them. He steps closer to me, closing me in with the glass behind me. I'm trembling from the anger bubbling inside. "It's taken me losing everything to realize it."

"Well, you're a day late and a dollar fucking short so I'm not sure what you expect." His hand reaches for mine but before he can grasp it, I pull it away and wrangle out from between him and the glass.

"C'mon, Rocky, we were so good together."

"Were! Very much past tense." Tears burn behind my eyes, but I refuse to let him see me shed any more for him. "Go home and let me enjoy dinner with Cata. She's the only good thing that came from all the years I wasted with you. Too bad you're too wrapped up in yourself to see how incredible she is…No thanks to you!" My hand grabs the door handle but before opening it, I say, "Stop being such an asshole and start being a father."

Back inside, Cata is typing on her phone when I take my seat across from her. When she's done typing, she places her phone on the table and looks up. "I was texting *mamá* to tell her what happened. I'm sorry he ruined our dinner."

My head shakes. "He didn't ruin anything," I tell her, stretching my hands in search of hers. When she extends hers across to meet mine, I grasp them and squeeze. "It was just a brief interruption. We're still here and we're still gonna eat all that sushi we ordered."

She forces a smile and nods. "Yeah, we are. I just wish he weren't such a jerk."

"We can't change others, Cata. Each of us is responsible for our actions and our words. If your father isn't willing to acknowledge that, then we adjust."

"But how do I adjust? You divorced him and don't have to see him ever again. He's my father, I can't divorce him." The emotional weight behind her stare is heavy, years of disappointment built up around the weary gaze looking back at me.

"Someday you'll be an adult and able to make your own decisions about the people you want involved in your life. In the meantime, I think your mother is the perfect person to lean on when your father's behavior is negatively affecting you. She is a psychologist, after all, so who better than her to give you the sage advice you need."

Her head nods in agreement. "I love you, Kiki," she says with a smile, squeezing my hand. In that moment, the waitress appears, holding two large white dishes with the sushi rolls we ordered.

"Love you too, kiddo. Now let's eat."

CHAPTER SEVENTEEN

Xavier

IT'S BEEN several days since we got back from the Bahamas and I haven't spent any time *con mi mujer*. Between both of our schedules, we haven't been able to spend the time I want together. Her job also requires her to be up early, which makes it more difficult since I'm a night owl and have no set schedule. I don't like the feeling of not seeing her every day—not to mention, I can't get used to hearing the word no. She's my girl and I need to share the same space as her, even if it's only a few minutes. This is the exact reason I took her to the Bahamas—no work, no phones, no distractions, just me and my woman.

I told Adrián I'd drive today because it's been a minute since I took Brisa, my arctic gray Cayenne, out for a drive. The traffic on Collins Avenue southbound is unusually light for a late Thursday morning, which is a good thing, considering my studio is in the Design District. I'd usually make the eighteen-mile drive down 95, but for some reason I find myself cruising down Collins Avenue right by Rocky's apartment building, even though she's working. She got me pussy whipped without even trying. As I slow for the red light, I push one of the rock station channels. She's even got me listening to her music.

My phone rings, silencing the guitar riffs, and when I look at the center console, Maritza's name pops up, and I push the button on my steering wheel. "*Dímelo*."

"You close to the studio yet?"

I'll be meeting with Rio Castillo and Belú, two other reggaeton artists at the studio. We attended a *Ficha Mundial* Label Party several weeks ago when Rio pitched a collab he had in mind for the three of us. I watched as the flicker of creation crossed his eyes, focusing in on the beats floating around us, Belú's raspy voice pulling him in, but it wasn't the right place to get into too many details. Since Rio's tour is in Miami, we decided to have a meeting for Rio to share his vision for the song. Rio and I go way back to my early days. I met him through his best friend Niko *El Rebelde*, reggaeton's biggest name right now. Niko's the artist who's taking our genre to the next level, taking our music mainstream across English language charts just as much as the Latino charts—creating the crossover that many believed would never happen.

"Nah, *¿por qué?*" The tree-lined strip of Collins Avenue, sandwiched between the Atlantic Ocean and Haulover Park, whizzes by as my foot leans on the gas pedal.

"I'm a few blocks away, but I just saw your billboard at North Miami Avenue and NE 41st Street. I have a picture, but it's not great."

"Damn, that quick?" We were just in Brazil ten days ago.

"Yeah, guess that's why they work with that photographer, Efigênia Santos. They know she gets shit done. Plus, when we were planning the marketing strategy, they told me they already had everything in place here in Miami. 305 Marketing was just waiting on the prints."

"I'll swing by on my way there, see if I catch a glimpse."

"For this ad, they chose a picture in front of the palm trees with your denim jacket and the tan beanie. It looks awesome!"

"I hope so—shot over four days. Thought it would never end."

"What time are Rio and Belú getting here?" she inquires.

"Rio had a show last night, which means he'll probably show up in the early afternoon."

"The show was incredible, better than the first night," Maritza says, her tone bubbly. Meeting other artists hasn't phased her much, but when I told her Rio was stopping by, she was ecstatic because she's a huge fan.

"He always kills it *en la tarima*." For as long as I've known Rio, he's sold out stadiums with his lyrics that make *las nenas* shake their *nalgas*, especially when he's on the stage. After being gone for about two years, this comeback tour is taking him to the next level—it's like he's never missed a beat.

"This is what your tour will be like. Tickets have been selling like crazy at the confirmed venues and there's buzz *en todo Latinoamérica*."

"Yeah, but I don't sell out stadiums like Rio."

"You will. After that double platinum con *La Gata*, I have no doubt."

"From your mouth to God's ears."

"I can't believe Belú will be here too! She's been killing it lately!"

"Yeah, her sound is tight."

"I downloaded her album *La Teniente* and it's fire. If I had to identify her, I'd call her the romantic Ivy Queen." Maritza's way of describing Belú is perfection.

Although Belú is her artist name, she also goes by *La Teniente*, because she's recognized as the daughter of *El General*, one of the most iconic Latino musicians of our time. Her self-titled debut album went double platinum within weeks of its release.

"My sister was supposed to send some stuff over. We get it yet?"

"Someone dropped them off earlier. It's a hefty stack. Xiomary said to read them and then call her."

"Yeah, she's working on the contracts for the collab with Rio and Belú. Rio's lawyer sent them to her the other day."

"Okay, I'm crossing the bay at 195, where's the billboard at again?"

"When you're driving north on North Miami Avenue, look up and to your right at 40th Street, you'll see it perched at the top of the building on 41st Street."

I exit at Biscayne Boulevard and cut through the Design District, the streets lined with designer boutiques and restaurants. When I make a right onto North Miami Avenue, I slow down, lowering my head to peek up. There I am, plastered across the side of the building—my face replacing the last ad for some big personal injury law firm. I'm looking at the camera with a serious expression, my lips slightly pursed. My right arm lies across my abs and my left elbow rests on my hand, with my left thumb barely grazing my chin. The diamond-studded watch adorning my left wrist sparkles in the natural light. "Damn, I do look good."

"Told ya. We'll have to drive by with Adrián so we can snap a pic. I want to drop it on socials." Maritza is always taking pictures, saying we need them because she can always use them to create content. If it weren't for her, not sure how much I'd use my social media accounts. When I do use it, I find myself scrolling or posting stories. Although Maritza reminds me that if anyone is going to engage with the followers, it should be me to make it authentic. Whatever she does, it's working because we're now at nearly ten million followers.

"*Bueno*, I'll see you. Let's order lunch from *El Típico*—for when Rio and Belú get there. Get my usual, please." *El Típico* is a Dominican restaurant a few miles from the studio that we order from all the time. Maritza's cousin worked there for several years, so when she started working with me, she introduced me to the best Dominican food in the neighborhood. No matter how many times we order, I always order *chicharrones de pollo y tostones*. "Call their assistants and ask what time we should expect them and what to order for them."

A few hours later, Rio strolls through the front door, his hat turned backward, with Tito, his six foot five bodyguard, trailing behind him. He extends his hand, giving me a grip and slide shake and pulls me in for a side hug. "*Hermano*," he says.

"Good to see you again, *mi hermano*," I say, hugging him back. Maritza is standing to my right, her eyes gleaming as her lips curl upward. Although she went to both of Rio's concerts here in Miami, this is her first time meeting him in person. "Rio, this is Maritza, my assistant."

"Hi, Rio," she says, pushing her hair behind her ears. "I'm a huge fan."

"*Placer*." He leans in, kissing her cheek hello.

"Lunch is almost here," Maritza says, glancing at her phone.

"*Y Belú*, where she at?" Rio asks.

Maritza's eyes dart to mine then back to Rio's. "When I called her manager to ask about lunch, she said Belú couldn't join the meeting today but that she'd reach out to reschedule." She scurries out of the room toward the front door to meet the delivery driver.

"*Coño*, I thought we took care of that!" Rio exclaims.

"We shouldn't be surprised. Luna warned us that night at the *Ficha* party. Everyone knows *La Patrona* runs a tight ship. If we haven't cleared it with her, it won't happen," I say.

Ángela Guerra, known in the Latin music world as *La Patrona*, is one of the most sought-after managers in the industry. She's a shark with a sharp, analytical gaze that's always on. Word is, she discovered Belú. She helped her debut album hit double platinum within weeks, skyrocketing Belú to worldwide fame in a flash. But *La Patrona* keeps her artists tucked tightly under her wing, and everything goes through her or it's not happening.

"This collab needs to be released," Rio says. "Her sound *está bien cabrón*. We need to collab with her first before anyone else does."

"No doubt. I'll have Roly talk to Ángela. They go way back to the early days."

"Let's hope she comes around after talking to him." His gaze shifts to his phone and he inhales sharply. "*¡Coñazo! Lo que me faltaba.* Are you fucking kidding me?" He holds up a hand to excuse himself.

What the fuck was that all about?

Maritza dashes into the front room, a worried look on her face and phone in hand. "Xavi, Alba just texted me."

Alba Muñoz of *Poderosa Media* is my sister's friend and a publicist. When I got clean, Roly and Xiomary made me hire her to help clean up the mess I'd created.

My eyes dart to Maritza's. "What about?"

"A blind item was just released talking about some big *reggaetonero* getting a girl pregnant. Is there something we need to know?" she asks with raised eyebrows.

"What? Nah, that ain't me! I wrap my shit up!"

"I figured as much. Any idea who it is?"

My head shakes. "Half these motherfuckers sleep with a new girl every night. Could be anyone."

"I'll tell Alba we're good," she says, typing furiously on her phone as she leaves the room.

I grab my phone to search for the blind item site when I see a text from Alba with a screenshot that reads:

The Confluent Heartthrob apparently used those sexy hip moves a little too well. Sources tell us the saintly one is just starting to show her orb. And you know, they always say the strongest turbulence occurs between water and air.

Rio shuffles in looking like he saw a ghost when my phone vibrates in my hand. I glance down but the blind item is still open. My eyes lift to Rio's and it clicks.

"*Déjame preguntarte*, Alba sent me a blind item." I extend my phone out for him to see my screen. "It ain't me. You know anything about that?"

His eyebrows shoot up and his shoulders slump. "*Esa vaina está chicle, mi hermano.*"

That's dope if it's his girl who's pregnant, but fucked up that these bullshit gossip rags release such private information. Always crossing lines to make their next buck.

"*¿Por qué está complica'o? ¿Katya no está contenta?*" Their relationship is new, but I didn't know it was complicated.

"*No es con Katya,*" he says with finality, then goes back to what he was doing on his phone.

Him telling me it's complicated with Katya is no surprise. I'm still questioning why he let Luna go, because he was definitely happier with her. I'm gonna let it go for now because I already know if Rio ain't sharing, he's not ready. "Let's eat while we figure shit out."

We meander to the kitchen area of the studio, where Maritza placed the food that was delivered. I reach for the first container and open it, the smell of *chivo encendío con moros de gandules* tickles my nose. "*Este es tuyo,*" I say, extending the clamshell container to Rio. "Smells delicious."

"I'm missing DR right about now and this dish takes me back," he says, as if he's in a world of his own.

Maritza appears with some Cokes and water bottles, placing them on the table, and then takes a seat along the opposite side of the rectangular table.

"It's been a minute since I've been in DR. Need to change that," I say.

"*Coño, igual que mi país*," Rio says, complimenting how authentic the food tastes as he finishes chewing his first bite.

"Yeah, *El Típico* is legit," I add, nodding while chewing on the crispy yet tender *chicharrón de pollo*.

Rio reaches for a Coke, pulling up the tab, its crisp snap breaking the seal. After pulling from the can, he says, "Here's what we'll do. I have some lyrics in mind that I've been working on. Once the legal shit gets handled, I can send them over for you and we can get into it. Then, after Roly convinces *La Patrona*, we'll rope Belú in and then plan on meeting back here at your studio."

"*Dale*," I say, as I sink my teeth into a crispy *tostón*.

CHAPTER EIGHTEEN

Rocío

"Turn right," my GPS instructs. As I turn onto NE 2nd Avenue, the landscape changes telling me I've arrived at the Design District—the luxury stores and upscale restaurants are housed in buildings showcasing modern architecture, many with contemporary art murals painted on them. One of my clients requested a meeting to discuss some things he recently learned and asked if we could do it over lunch at The Sazón Syndicate near his office, instead of him driving downtown to my office. I had planned to stop by the office after court ended to drop off case files, but my hearing started nearly an hour later than it was supposed to, which set back my entire morning. Thankfully, the drive from the courthouse to the Design District is only a few miles away.

As I make a left onto NE 41st Street, a car is pulling out of its parking spot. Nice, and it's opposite the restaurant, too. Now I don't have to look for parking or valet, which I hate doing because it always takes forever to get my car. I don't come to the Design District often, but usually try to avoid it on Fridays because it's always so busy in anticipation for the weekend. There are throngs of people crowding the sidewalks and the area around where I'm parking, reminding me why I hate being around here on a Friday.

When I walk into The Sazón Syndicate, the entrance is flanked with potted paradise palm trees, the lounge bar on the left, a long stretch of marble and brass edges. As I approach the hostess stand, my client appears. "Hello, Mr. Alonso," I say, extending my hand out. "Thank you for your patience in waiting for me."

"Your office called to let me know you were running late. It's okay. My office is in the building across the street, so I haven't been waiting long."

Mr. Alonso is in his late fifties and hired me a few weeks ago after his wife served him with divorce papers. He said he didn't see it coming after twenty-five years of marriage and has been extremely anxious about the whole process, so it's no surprise he requested an in-person meeting. We're following the hostess through the dining room filled with reclaimed wood tables and aged leather banquettes. I'm about to take a seat when Xavier appears in my purview, striding toward me in charcoal gray slim joggers with a white design up one leg, a black shirt, and his denim jacket. When he's close, he leans in and says, "Hi." His warm lips land on my cheek and linger as his hand rests on my hip. "I miss you, *mami*," he whispers, before putting space between us.

"Hi," I respond, meeting his questioning eyes. "Xavier, this is Mr. Alonso. Mr. Alonso, this is Xavier."

Xavier's hand extends to shake Mr. Alonso's. "Xavier, good to meet you."

"Pleasure to meet you, Xavier," Mr. Alonso responds.

"Mr. Alonso, if you would give me just a moment," I tell him.

"Sure, take your time," he responds as he settles into the booth.

Xavier walks away from the table, and I follow, stopping at the end behind a low wall of the last booth.

"What are you doing here?" I ask, surprised to see him. His woodsy scent tickles my nose, and I inch closer to him.

"Having lunch with Landy." He turns and points to the back wall, where there's a guy sitting with a red jacket and baseball cap turned backward. "We were getting ready to leave when Landy got a call. You?"

"My client asked to meet here instead of him driving to my office, because this is close to his office."

"I miss you." He stuffs his hands in his pockets.

My heart flutters at his words, but I need to focus. "You already said that."

"I haven't seen you all week. And you didn't respond, *pensé que no me habías escuchado*."

"I heard you the first time, but I'm with a client."

"That means you can't respond?"

My eyes scan his face, and his lips are in a straight line. I'd be lying to myself if I said I didn't miss him too, but I've had to focus on work and have been exhausted, which makes me irritable. "What's really happening here, Xavier?"

His stance shifts, bringing him slightly closer to me. "I miss my girl, and I'm feeling a little jealous of that dude sitting over there waiting for her." His fingers intertwine with mine.

My tone may have been a bit short, but I'm feeling off since I'm running behind schedule. "I miss you, too, but work's been crazy. Besides, it's taken me all week to recover from last weekend in the Bahamas."

Memories of his neatly trimmed beard scratching my thighs flash through my mind, spreading a tingling sensation between my legs.

"Come over after work," he says, then leans into me. "*Yo sé que tienes esa chocha mojaíta*," he whispers, "and I wanna taste. I can help cure that Bahamas hangover you're feeling." His words send shivers down my spine.

I take a deep breath, trying to keep myself in check when all I want to do is give in and allow myself to indulge in everything he's offering. "I'll call you when I'm done working and let you know." It would be nice to spend some time with him again. I've had a dull ache between my legs all week, and he's the only one that can soothe it.

"Excuse me, *Flaco*." A short man with rounded cheeks interrupts us.

"Yeah?"

"I'm the restaurant manager. I wanted to let you know the paparazzi is out front waiting for you to exit. If you'd like, we have a rear entrance you can leave from. It's in the alley, so if you have someone who can meet you with a car, they can pick you up there."

Panic sets in at the mention of paparazzi. César did say the media is always looking to sell their next story so it makes sense. A flash of the people surrounding *La Gata* the night we met her scurries through my mind, and I remember the crowding sensation it gave off. What the heck did I get myself into?

"Thanks, man."

After the manager returns to the front, Xavier's eyes land on mine. "Hey, don't do that." He's shaking his head. "*Sin que me digas na*, I can see you're freaking out."

I have no poker face and the panic swirling must be evident. "A little bit, yeah. Why would they be here?"

He shrugs. "Maybe someone spotted me and Landy. They're looking for the next money shot. Nothing new."

I nod. "Okay. Do you think they know about us?"

His eyes widen and he purses his lips. "They might." His eyes scan the room and he shifts his stance. "Here's what we'll do.

When you're ready to leave, call me and Adrián will pick you up at the back entrance."

"Why would they know about us? We haven't seen anyone taking pictures." My days of being an anonymous person in a restaurant are numbered. Ever since I found out he's not just any guy, but one who millions of people know and love, my brain has worked overtime with worry for the day they figure it out. But my heart and body remind me that none of that matters, because he's sharing himself with me and none of them get to see the side that I do.

"They might not, but it's the media and they're like vultures. It's better to be safe, otherwise they'll follow you right to your car, and then home." His words cause a chill to shoot up my spine, for an entirely different reason than they did just a few seconds ago.

I nod. Logically, I understand what he's saying, but I'm not really sure I fully grasp what this means.

"Go have your business lunch. I'm gonna head out. I'll ask the manager to have the valet bring my car out back. I'll call Adrián and tell him he should head this way."

"Okay."

He drops another kiss on my cheek and then turns toward the back of the restaurant. As I walk toward Mr. Alonso, I'm now acutely aware whether the seat where I'll be sitting across from Mr. Alonso is visible from the front, and I don't think it is. I don't think his is either. This whole thing is crazy. I should've known it was just a matter of time before the media wanted some juicy scoop on the famous guy and the girl he's into.

When my lunch with Mr. Alonso finished, I had the restaurant manager check whether the paparazzi were still outside the restaurant because I wanted to leave. When he confirmed they were, I called Xavier to have Adrián pick me up outside the back door, because I'm not ready for whatever may be on the other side of that heavy mahogany door. Xavier must've given Adrián my phone number because a few minutes after hanging up, I receive a text from a number I don't recognize.

I'm outside the back door in a black SUV.

I locate the restaurant manager and ask for the back entrance. He escorts me through the kitchen where there are several people bustling around. As the door swings open, Adrián appears, an air of danger hovering. His imposing height towers over me as he opens the rear SUV door. It all feels so shady, like something I'd see in a movie.

"Do you need my address?" I ask as I clip the seatbelt into place. Since I drove here, I'll have to pick up my car later, considering the photographers are standing around the area where my car is parked.

"No, ma'am. Boss asked me to take you to his apartment."

"Please call me Rocky." I grab my phone to text Xavier because he just assumed I could go to his place, didn't even ask. But as I'm typing out my message, I realize I haven't seen him all week and it would be nice to spend some time together—not to mention I could go for a few Xavier-induced orgasms. I just wish he would've asked me first. It's Friday, and my staff knows not to make appointments on Friday afternoons so my calendar should be free. When I confirm it is, I text my paralegal to let her know I won't be returning to the office and they can leave early. That's why I'm my own boss, right? When I'm done, I drop my phone into my pockabook.

"So Adrián, have you worked for Xavier long?" I ask. We're

sitting on I-95 in bumper-to-bumper traffic, may as well chat with him.

His eyes lift, meeting mine through the rear-view mirror. "A little over a year."

"Where are you from?"

"Miami."

"305 till you die?" I grin, see if I can get him to relax.

His eyes flit up and meet mine again through the mirror. "Yes, ma'am."

All righty then. He's obviously not into chatting, or maybe he's not allowed to talk while working? I've never had a driver, so I have no idea if there is driver etiquette or something that I'm supposed to follow. Either way, I'll just keep to myself the rest of the ride.

Thirty minutes later, we pull into Xavier's familiar building, the sign outside reading Regalia Residences. Adrián walks through the lobby with me, and inside the elevator, he swipes his card and pushes the 34 button. "Good afternoon, ma'am," he says, then turns on his heel, sending me up on my own. When the door opens, the rhythmic beats of music fill the air. As I step into the foyer, Xavier is waiting for me, jeans hanging low with a fitted black t-shirt, and bare feet.

"Come here, *mami*," he says, grasping my hips and pulling me to him, our lips colliding. His kisses are urgent, his grip tight, and I can feel his erection pushing against me.

"Hi," I say, tucking my unruly curls behind my ears.

"I'm surprised you didn't protest." His fingers guide my gaze up to his. "*Esperaba* a call or text telling me you couldn't come and that you told Adrián to take you home or to your office." Good to know that Adrián would've taken me somewhere else had I asked.

"Almost did. I was gonna bitch you out"—my finger pokes

him in the abdomen—"but it's your lucky day because I'll cut you some slack…today. Don't do it again."

He smirks. "It's good to be *la jefa*. Do what you want, when you want, with who you want." He drops a kiss on my cheek, turns and with my hand firmly grasped between his, guides us through the open door behind him.

"Yeah, it is. But next time you need to ask, because I can't just drop everything. Sometimes I have things that can't be rescheduled or a deadline to meet."

He halts and spins, his mouth mere centimeters from mine. "When that happens, just tell me no." His breath is hot and anticipation coils in my belly. Do I even want to say no to this man? I'm not sure I do. His lips peck mine, and then he turns to continue into his apartment, our hands still intertwined.

The first night inside his apartment, I was engulfed in a haze of desire and didn't bother looking around. Right now, it's wicked bright in here with the floor-to ceiling windows streaming light throughout. I'm trying to not let my jaw drop at how stunning it is, but it's proving difficult. "Holy shit, look at that view!" It's like a completely different world from the view at my apartment. Sparkling turquoise for miles, and to the right, the entire Miami coastline. "My apartment has an ocean view. But this, this feels like I'm suspended over Miami."

"I'd prefer if you were suspended over me," he says, wrapping me in his embrace from behind. He slides my curls to one side and then drags his tongue from the top of my shoulder up my neckline, landing below my ear, causing me to writhe in his arms. He reaches down, his fingers finding the hem of my skirt, and he tugs, first the right then the left.

When he doesn't continue, I push my ass into him, his hardness pressing into me. "Why'd you stop?" I'm panting at the thought of him inside of me.

"*Dime lo que quieres*," he commands in a tone that teeters

between asking me what I want and ordering me to tell him what I want.

My hands settle on the glass in front of me, and again I push my ass out against his hardened length, moving it side to side in tune with the electric drum rhythm. "*Quiero que me garches.*"

"Look at my rocker girl, ready *pal perreo.*"

"Does that mean you're gonna fuck me?"

His hands shimmy my panties down and he slides two fingers in. "Always so wet for me, *mami.*" His words tickle my ear as his fingers explore inside me.

My ass pushes back into him as I steady myself. "Your cock, fuck me with your cock." I whimper as his fingers curl up.

"*¿Quieres que me pegue a ti?*" He continues jutting and swirling inside of me.

I nod, dizzy from the wanton desire he's stoking by depriving me of his cock.

"*Pídemelo,*" he instructs, his tone low and feral.

I'm not one to beg, but right now I'd do anything. My pussy throbs and a moan escapes me. "Fuck me, Xavier, please. I want to feel you buried inside of me."

He withdraws his fingers and the cool air brushes my heated core. The familiar crinkling sound signals he's about to give me what I want. I lean forward, opening up for him as he grasps my hips, hissing as he stretches me.

"More," I gasp, pushing into him to feel his entire length.

"There's my greedy girl. *Como me gusta* when she comes out to play."

After having his way with me in his living room, we made our way to his bed where I straddled and rode him until I couldn't see straight. As I lie in a lust-induced haze, Xavier returns from the bathroom and sidles up next to me. I sit up to face him. "Can I ask you something?"

"*Lo que tú quieras, mami.*" He crosses his arms behind his head.

"After I found out you're a super famous singer, I searched your name online."

His breath is steady and his eyes soft. "Don't believe the bullshit they write. They take one true thing and manipulate it to sell."

I shimmy closer to him and trace the black ink across his chest. "That's why I wanted to ask you about it, because I'd rather hear the truth from you."

He nods, his eyes dropping to meet mine.

"What they wrote about your drug addiction, is any of it true?"

His breath quickens as his hand rests on the inside of my thigh. "I don't know what they wrote because I don't read any of it, but it is true that I'm an addict."

He's still an addict? Is he still using? "What does that mean?" I ask, placing my hand over his.

His Adam's apple bobs, and his gaze drops. A hollow quiet drifts between us, and his deep breaths fill the space as he massages the sensitive skin on my thigh. "It means—" He pauses, then he lifts his eyes to mine again. "I'm clean, have been for two years, three months, one week, and four days, but I'll always consider myself an addict. *Para nunca olvidarme* of those dark days." His soft voice contradicts his piercing stare as he shares that exact amount of time he's been clean and that he continues to identify as an addict as a reminder. He adjusts his position, pulling his legs up and leaning into his knees. "Percocets became the center of my world, and I chose them over everything and everyone, allowed them to consume me *y perdí todo*."

"I'm—" His thumb lands on my lips, asking me to let him finish.

I nod and wrap his hand between mine, allowing my fingers to lazily drag along the backside of his large hand.

"I hurt a lot of people. Pushed everyone that mattered away, even *mi abuela*." His eyes glisten as he mentions his grandmother.

A jolt rushes through me as my eyes widen at his declaration.

He nods. "I know. I'm ashamed I allowed myself to be consumed."

Questions swirl, and my curiosity wants all the details about his grandmother, and about the woman he was dating. But I want him to share those intimate details on his terms, not mine. If I were in his shoes, I'm not sure how I'd deal with all the probing. Instead, I squeeze his hands and urge him to continue.

"*Mi abuela* died when I was strung out on drugs. If it weren't for my sister, I wouldn't have even made it to her funeral. She showed up at my apartment and forced me on a plane to Puerto Rico. I was super high at the wake. *Qué vergüenza* to show up to honor my grandmother like that. More than anything, this is what I regret the most." His voice cracks and a tear slides down his cheek as he recalls the shame he felt.

I search for words to comfort him but come up empty. Instead, I swipe away the moisture.

"Her death is what finally made me admit how fucked up I was. After her funeral, I told my sister I was ready to get clean. Between *mi abuela*'s death and detoxing, there were days I wanted to end it all."

I can't hold back the tears dripping from my eyes. My heart aches for the loss of his *abuela* amidst his self-induced drug chaos.

"I'll never be able to take any of it back and hope that when I see her again, she's forgiven me. In the meantime, this ink is for her." He pushes his right bicep forward, caressing the black ink of a woman in a frog pose.

"What is it?" My fingers trace the lines coloring his golden skin.

"It's *La Mujer Caguana*. *Mi abuela* was Taíno and the Woman of Caguana is a Taíno ancestral spirit with numerous names depending on the energy of what she's doing. I always remember *abuela* making offerings to her." His hand rubs the ink on his arm. "When I betrayed *abuela* the way I did, I couldn't take it back. I regret the choices I made but it's too late. I got this tattoo as a way to help me feel connected to her."

As he shares about the tattoo he got for his grandmother, I rest my head on his chest and intertwine my legs with his. If I can't find the words to soothe his ache, I'll try with touch instead.

CHAPTER NINETEEN

Two weeks later

Xavier

I'M ABOUT to get in the shower when my phone rings. When I see Xiomary's name, I press the green button. "*Dímelo*," I say.

"Hi, *chiqui*," she says.

"What's up?" My arms extend, turning the water off.

"I got a few calls today about some pictures that have popped up on the gossip sites." Her tone is serious.

"Why'd they call you and not Alba?"

"They called her first but since she didn't have any information, they call everyone they know."

"So, what kind of pictures?"

"Pictures of you with a woman at The Sazón Syndicate." Fuck, they must've snapped pictures a few weeks ago when I ran into Rocky at the restaurant. Rocky is going to crash out when I tell her. That day in the restaurant, worry spread across her face at the possibility. I can't say I blame her for it. These people are relentless and oftentimes make it nearly impossible to feel normal. I'm trying to get her to understand that she can't let them control her, but I'll have to be patient with her. It took me time to get used to it too.

"And?"

"Who is she?" she huffs.

"Someone I'm seeing." I love my sister, but sometimes she wants to know too much.

"That's it? You're not gonna tell me anything about her?"

"Soon. I plan on introducing you to her."

"When's that happening?"

"I don't know yet." We're still kinda new, and I don't want to freak Rocky out.

"Well, I didn't think I needed to tell you this, but you need to have her sign an NDA."

"She's not like that." Do I need to have her sign one? My gut feeling is no because Rocky isn't out for fame—I mean, when I saw her at the restaurant, she was concerned about being with a client and seeing me while working.

"Most women are out to make an easy buck. I'd hate for this woman to be into you simply because she hopes she can get something and swindle you. I don't know, show up suddenly pregnant, you know, like that chick you were messing around with last year. If she's not like that, she should have no issue signing an NDA."

"I said, she's not like that!" Annoyance bubbles but I also know Xiomary is protecting me, like she's done her entire life. Last year, I met this woman when I was out with Landy. Turns out the woman had her sights set on me and planned the entire thing. She tried to say I had gotten her pregnant, but the DNA test proved otherwise.

"Also, don't forget to wrap it up."

"Enough, Xiomary!" She's always acted like my mother, and

all these years later, it still irks me sometimes, even if my past behaviors warrant her speaking to me this way.

"What? If you're still kinda new, how do you know what kind of woman she is?"

"Because she had no idea who I was when we met."

Xiomary is cackling on the other end. "Yeah, okay. And you believed her?"

"I did because it's true. Not everyone listens to reggaeton."

A loud sigh escapes Xiomary. "*Ay, hermanito*, sometimes I wonder about you."

My eyes roll up as I lean into the wall. "Nothing to worry about, sis. Really. She's not like that. She's making me work for it."

"I'm not just your sister, I'm also your lawyer and my job is to protect you."

"*Lo entiendo*, but I'm telling you with her it's not necessary. She's a lawyer, like you."

"Oh, do I know her?" she asks, curiosity laced in her question.

"Nah, she's a divorce lawyer."

"Lawyer or not, I want her to sign an NDA."

"*Déjame pensarlo*," I say, hoping if I tell her I'll think about it she'll ease up. "Anyway, send me the picture. Do I at least look good in it?" I chuckle.

"You make my job a lot harder than it has to be." She huffs. "Sent it." A message pops up, and I press it to open the picture. They captured me dropping a kiss on Rocky's cheek, my hand pressing into her thick waist in a way that shows the intimacy between the two of us. Her face is not visible because she was leaning in, her curls hanging across her face. But now that the vultures sniffed something, they won't let up. I wonder how much they sold this photo for. Bastards!

"Angle could've been better," I say.

"You're so frustrating!"

"Love you, too!" I hit the red end button and turn the water back on.

"Hi, *mami*," I say, as Rocky climbs into the backseat behind Adrián. We swung by her apartment to pick her up. I had invited her to the listening party tonight, but she declined, said she has to finish up some documents she's working on and has court in the morning. I convinced her to at least have dinner with me. Once she's seated, I reach for her, needing her warm lips on mine. As soon as we connect, my body relaxes—her proximity calming me.

"Hi," she says, separating from me and reaching for her seatbelt.

"*Te extrañé*," I tell her.

"We just saw each other the other day."

"It's been a week."

"I was in trial."

"Right, which is why I missed you."

She exhales and searches my eyes. She puckers her lips, words teetering on the edge of her lips, but she swallows them.

"It's okay for you to miss me, too," I say, then suck her bottom lip between mine.

"Maybe I missed you a little, too." Her breath is labored between her words.

My erection pushes at the seams, and I shift, trying to adjust myself to ease the discomfort. Rocky takes that moment to put space between us, her eyes darting between Adrián and me. I know me being intimate with her while he's in the car makes her uncomfortable, making me wish we were back at my place.

"Where we going for dinner?" she asks.

Rocky loves Italian food and pasta. Last week, she shared that her mother made it a lot growing up so I knew I had to bring her to this restaurant. "Macchialina. When you told me your mother made pasta a lot growing up, I thought about this restaurant and bringing you here. You're gonna love it."

"I've never been but have heard good things. So, what's this listening party you're going to later?"

"One of Roly's artists new album drops in a few weeks. They just finished production on it, so we're gonna go listen."

"Is that a thing artists regularly do?"

Nodding, I say, "Yeah." I lean into her, my lips grazing her ear as my hand slides beneath the hem of her skirt, causing her to squirm. "You should come."

Her breath quickens, and she removes my hand from its warm spot between her legs. Despite knowing her discomfort of intimacy around others, it's hard to keep my hands to myself when she's this close to me. "Maybe next time," she says, breathy.

Inside the restaurant, we're greeted by a man in a light gray suit and pink tie with thick rimmed glasses. "Hello, Mr. Delgado."

Rocky's shoulders soften as her eyes scan the empty dining room.

The man escorts us to a table in the back corner, and Rocky sits on the banquette. She peeks at her watch and then raises her eyes to mine. "There's no one here. That's weird."

I drop my phone on the table then stretch my hand across in search of hers. "I reserved the entire restaurant for us."

Her eyes widen. "Oh."

I nod. "Yeah, now we can focus on each other and not worry about anyone else." I know she's been worried about the paparazzi since that day at The Sazón Syndicate. After I share what my sister told me, it'll only heighten her anxiety.

She gives me a lopsided grin. "Thank you."

After ordering our dinner, I say, "My sister called me today to share some news."

"Yeah, what kind of news?" she asks before sipping her wine.

"Remember when I saw you at lunch a couple weeks ago and the paparazzi were outside? Someone was able to get a picture of me kissing you."

The blood drains from her face, and her back straightens. "Kissing me? We didn't kiss! I was with a client!"

Her words sting like a fresh paper cut. "Why do you got to say it like that?"

Rocky's shoulders soften. "I didn't say it to hurt you. But I was working, and I've worked really hard to earn a good reputation for being an outstanding lawyer. As a woman, it's hard out in these lawyer streets, so I have to protect my name and my reputation. That's all I have."

The last thing I want is for my life to negatively impact her or what she's worked for. "I want to protect those things, too, and don't want your relationship with me to affect everything you've built for yourself. If anyone knows the importance of that, it's me. *Aparte, yo protejo lo mío*, and that includes you." I scoot closer and lower my head. "But I would never be ashamed of anyone seeing me kiss you."

Her eyes search mine and she leans in, stretching her hand across the table, searching for mine. "I'm not ashamed, Xavier. It's not like that."

I grab my phone and open the picture my sister sent, handing it to Rocky so she can see. Her fingers touch the screen and she's scrutinizing the image. She lifts her eyes to mine and hands the phone back. "At least my face isn't visible."

She sounds relieved, except now they'll be thirsty for more. "But now that they know I have a girlfriend, they'll circle like the sharks they are." I lift her hand to my lips and drop a kiss on its backside, allowing them to linger.

"Fuck. What does this mean for us?" she inquires.

"You referred to us as *us*." My other hand stretches under the table and squeezes her knee.

Her eyes are searching mine. "That's what you got from what I said?"

"Yeah. *Us* means we're in this together."

She tilts her head and assesses me. "But we can't ignore the media, their soon-to-be hunt for pictures, and the battle to print the juiciest story."

"We're not ignoring them, just what they write. I used to be in your shoes. It's hard, but I promise it gets easier."

A long sigh escapes her. After pulling from her wine glass, she says, "That sounds easier said than done."

"There's nothing they haven't written about me."

"Except I'm new and shiny. They'll dig up whatever they can to write about me. I feel like my whole life is about to change."

"We'll figure it out, *mami. Si estamos juntos*, everything else will work itself out." Sticking together is key for us getting through this. She's freaking out about something that hasn't happened yet, although knowing how the Latin media salivated over writing whatever they could about me, she's not far off in her thoughts. But I don't want her night ruined thinking about what-ifs. "Anyway, enough about them. I wish you were coming with me tonight."

"Yeah, it would've been nice. Although, with this news, maybe it's for the best that I'm staying home." Her shoulders rise in unison.

"You can't hide forever."

"Yeah, that's what I'm afraid of."

"Afraid of what?"

"No longer being anonymous."

Anonymous is the last thing I want her to be. "*Eres mía y quiero que el mundo entero lo sepa, pero cuando tú quieras que el mundo te conozca.*" Yes, I need the entire world to know who she is, and that she's mine, but we'll do it on her terms.

We're at the listening party, wrapping up the last song. The turnout was good and the album was dope. It hyped me up for when mine will be ready since Macho sent it back to the mixing engineer, because he didn't like the way it turned out. I'm in the backyard talking with some acquaintances when I spot my friend Axel.

I meander over to him, where he's standing by the pool lounge chairs. Axel and I became friends years ago when I was recording my first album, "*Igual a Ninguno.*" He's a sound engineer and works with a good number of well-known artists. "Yo, Axel, what's up?" His hand extends to meet mine for a grip-and-slide shake.

He brushes the back of his hand across his nose. "Good to see you, *Flaco*. Didn't know you'd be here."

"You talked to me yesterday, what do you mean you didn't know?"

"Sorry, brother. Must've forgotten," he says, sniffling.

"You don't look good." His foot starts tapping in place as he's glancing around us. He's acting the same way I did when I used to be strung out. Fuck.

"This party seems fucking dead."

Axel has bloodshot eyes and dilated pupils. Fear circles as thoughts of being high flood me. I try to avoid being around people high on drugs since I've gotten clean. I need to leave, being around Axel while he's strung out is messing with my head.

"It's fizzling out, we've been here for hours. I'm actually getting ready to leave, and you should, too."

"I just got here. I'm not ready to go home yet," he quips. "I need a drink, first." He runs the back of his hand across his nose again.

"You don't need anything else," I say, leaning into him. "You're so fucking high right now, I'm surprised you're still standing. What happened, man? You've been clean. I haven't seen you like this in a while!"

When I was hooked on Percocets, Axel had been clean and he helped me find a Narcotics Anonymous meeting to attend. Although he's not my sponsor, he's always been supportive in my sobriety journey. Seeing him blitzed right now is shocking and unexpected because he's always been proud of his sobriety.

"Renata. That's what's wrong! She was supposed to be out of town for work, but I found out it was a lie, and she was with some dude. I was in her neighborhood for a meeting when I thought I caught a glimpse of her. When I followed the woman, it was her and she was sucking face with some guy I've never seen before. Turns out they've been fucking for months!" His hands are trembling. "Our wedding is set for later this year, and I can't fucking believe she pulled this bullshit."

"Wow, man. I'm sorry to hear that." She stuck it through with him when he was getting clean, so it makes sense that finding out about her infidelity would cause him to relapse. What would Rocky do if I ever relapsed, not that I have any intentions of it.

"Not as sorry as me!"

"How'd you get here?" I ask.

"Drove."

"You're too fucking high to drive!" I say in an attempted whisper, but instead my words are harsh and sharp. I glance around, and it seems no one heard my failed attempt to keep our conversation quiet.

"You could've killed yourself, or worse, someone else!" Memories of the night of my accident flash through my mind. The driver that hit us was as high as a kite when he rear-ended us, sending us into a tailspin, literally and figuratively. The driver's toxicology report came back with extremely high levels of cocaine, ecstasy, and alcohol. Each time I think about it, I'm reminded of how lucky I am to be alive.

"What-the-fuck-ever, bro. What was I supposed to do?"

Arguing with him right now will get us nowhere. "Alright, here's what we're gonna do. I'm gonna drive your car and take you back home and Adrián will follow us. You need to get home, man." I scan the area for Adrián and when I don't see him, I grab my phone and shoot him a text message.

"Fuck that, *Flaco*. I want to party right now."

"This is wrapping up here, the party's over." Adrián finds me, and I explain the plan.

"Where are your keys, Axel?" I ask.

"You're killing my buzz, bro!"

I lean in and rest my hand on his arm. "If you drive like this, you're gonna fuck up your whole life, man. What are you gonna do then?"

His stare is blank as he sways in place.

"What do you say?" I extend my hand. "Keys?"

"They're in my pocket," he says, shoving his hand in to draw them out. He drops them in mine then stuffs his hands into his pockets.

"Let's go," I say, walking through the yard so we can exit without going through the house. Although there are a few people I should say goodbye to, I decide to skip it because I need to get Axel out of here while I have him convinced it's a good idea. When we reach the front of the house, I ask, "What car did you bring?" When he doesn't respond, I halt and ask again.

"The Rover." We walk the length of the driveway, and as I approach his car, I notice the shit job he did parking—strewn across the patch of grass, over the small stones, and crushing the bed of flowers. He probably has no idea he parked like an asshole. I ensure he climbs into the passenger side and then scurry to get into the driver's seat.

"Adrián," I say.

He stops and turns back to me. "Yeah?"

"I'll text you the address, just in case we get separated."

"You got it, boss."

Once inside the car, I strap my seatbelt on, place the keys on the center console, and push the start button.

The drive from Key Biscayne to Miami Beach is quick at this time of night because there's no traffic. As we're driving northbound on Alton Road, blue lights appear and when I slow down to let it pass, the cop pulls up next to me, signaling to pull over. *Motherfucker, just what I needed tonight!* We had almost made it to his house too—57th Street was the next turn. When I look in the rearview mirror, Adrián stopped not too far behind us.

"*Flaco*, what the fuck did you do? I'm fucking high, bro. I got—"

A tapping on the window interrupts Axel mid-sentence. "Be quiet and don't say shit," I command.

I press the window button and place my hands on the steering wheel. The blinding beam of the officer's flashlight cuts through the dark and hits my face. "Good evening, sir. Do you know why I pulled you over?"

"No, sir, I don't," I respond.

"Your vehicle has an expired tag."

"Oh, man, I'm sorry officer. I had no idea. I'm driving my friend here home. He lives on 57th and North Bay Road," I say, hoping maybe he'll let us go because we're mere blocks from Axel's place. "My car is actually behind us." I point to Adrián stopped behind us.

"Who's in that car?"

"My driver."

"Just one person in that car?"

"Yes, sir."

"License and registration, please. And open the passenger window for Officer Rodríguez."

I press the passenger window button and then reach for my wallet in the inside of my jacket. After pulling out my license, I ask, "Axel, where's your registration?"

The officer at Axel's window is sweeping the backseat with the flashlight. "In the center console," Axel responds, picking up his keys. He pulls the registration out, closes the lid and then drops his keys onto the console again, when the small silver vial that's hanging from his keychain snaps open, spilling white powder across the console.

"Step out of the vehicle!" the officer at my door commands with his weapon drawn. Fucking A! All the shit I put myself through and I'm about to get arrested while helping someone else?

My pulse quickens and I raise my hands. "Officer, like I said, I'm driving my friend here home and—"

"I said, get out of the vehicle!" he yells.

"You too, sir. Step out of the vehicle!" the officer at Axel's door commands with his weapon drawn.

My heart is racing as I exit the car. I glance down and read Ofc. Ruiz on the name plate on his shirt. "Up against the car and place your hands on the side," Officer Ruiz says to me. "I'm going to pat you down." As I lean into the car, I can't help but think about what the media will do when they find out I was arrested. They're gonna have a fucking field day with this. I can already see the headline: "*El Flaco Casanova*'s Quick Fall from the Top," or some bullshit like that! Across the other side, Axel is leaning against the car, his head hanging as the officer pats him down as well.

"I'm going to detain you while we search your vehicle." He slaps the cuff onto my left wrist, then my right, the mechanical clicking sound of the metal ringing in my ears.

"It's not my vehicle," I say, hearing my sister's voice in my ear. *Keep your mouth shut. If you ever get arrested, don't say anything and call me.*

Officer Ruiz is searching the vehicle with the light from the driver's side, while Officer Rodríguez is leaning in from the other side. "The white residue looks like cocaine," Ruiz says.

"Are there any other drugs in your vehicle, sir?" Ruiz asks.

"I'm not answering any questions. I want to call my lawyer." I say.

"What about you, you know if there any other drugs in the vehicle?" Officer Rodríguez asks Axel.

"I want to talk to my lawyer," he responds.

"You're under arrest," Ruiz says, and tugs to indicate he wants me to move in the direction of his police cruiser. The strobing red and blue lights blind me, and I drop my head. "You have the right to remain silent. Anything you say can and will be used against you in a court of law. You have the right to an attorney. If you cannot afford an attorney, one will be provided for you."

We arrive at the vehicle but before we get in, I look over to Adrián, who's exited the SUV but is standing on the door jamb looking over the door at us. "Call my sister right now," I yell. He gives me a curt nod and gets back into the tight space of the vehicle. Shame crawls up my neck that I've landed here, even if I know it wasn't my own doing.

Once inside the back of the cruiser, Axel slides in next to me from the other door. Both doors are closed and the officers are standing in front of the vehicle. "*Perdóname, Flaco.* I'm so fucking sorry."

CHAPTER TWENTY

Rocío

My day has started off on the right foot. This morning, I had a contempt hearing for a client who hasn't received the money he was owed from his former spouse. At the conclusion, the judge held my client's ex in contempt because she hasn't paid. She has five days to pay the amount owed to my client, plus she has to pay my attorney's fees. Great way to start the day! Once my client leaves, I'm in the elevator checking my phone and see I have seven missed calls, four from Nikki and three from Alondra. Something must be wrong. As I'm walking out of the courthouse, I dial Nikki's number.

"*Mujer*, why haven't you been answering your phone?"

"I've been in court all morning. What's going on?"

"I saw you've been in court, but damn, you could've at least texted me back," Nikki protests.

"Have you seen the news?" Alondra asks.

"Alondra, you're on the call, too?"

"Yeah, I merged her because I was on the phone with her when you called."

"What's happening? Is everything okay?"

"So you haven't seen the news?" Nikki asks.

"No, I've been in court all morning. What's in the news that has you both calling me incessantly?"

"Xavier was arrested last night!" Alondra says.

"What?" I shout, causing the two people walking in front of me to turn their heads. "Where? What happened?" I'm scurrying to my car in the garage so I can drop my things and search online for information about Xavier.

"César told me about it because he works with Xavier's sister. When I searched his name, I saw a picture of his mugshot," Nikki says.

"And the craziest part—" Alondra adds.

"It gets crazier than him being arrested?" I interrupt. I push the elevator button, and the door to my right immediately opens.

"Victor is his criminal lawyer!" Alondra says.

"What? How the fuck did that happen?"

"César said his sister knows Victor."

"What the fuck! This can't be happening right now."

I toss my tote onto the passenger seat, sit, and kick my heels off. Putting the phone on speaker, I open a web browser and type in Xavier's name, and recent news articles appear with headlines that read:

Sobriety shattered! Reggaeton star's demons return in shocking drug related arrest.

Exclusive: See the mugshot of famed reggaeton star *El Flaco Casanova*, who was arrested for possession of drugs.

The comeback is over! Reggaeton icon Xavier Delgado, known professionally as *El Flaco Casanova*, arrested because of his complicated relationship with drugs.

I click on the second link and the first thing that pops up is his mugshot. Xavier's neatly trimmed beard looks darker than usual, and his eyes are red and angry as he's staring at the camera with pursed lips, his chin lifted. But even in this awful picture, he's still my Xavier.

"I can't believe this. Drugs?" There's no way he would've relapsed. He cried as he told me about the ruin it caused, and the regret he's felt. I won't believe anything that's published until I look him in the eye.

"The articles all say he's a drug addict," Nikki says.

"In all the times we've spent together, he's never been high. He doesn't even drink alcohol."

"Maybe he only does drugs when he's not with you?" Alondra asks.

Is that possible? Wouldn't I have noticed? But then again, sometimes we don't see each other for days at a time, so he could be high as a kite and I'd be none the wiser. Has he pulled the wool over my eyes like Victor did? Ugh, thinking about them in the same sentence makes me nauseous. "No, that's impossible. An addict is an addict all the time, no?" Maybe if I say it out loud, I'll convince myself.

"Addicts can be good at hiding their addictions, so it's possible," says Nikki. "I see it a lot at work."

"There's gotta be some misunderstanding! Besides, he told me not to believe any of the stuff they write about him," I add. "We shouldn't be jumping to any conclusions. We already know how the media salivates over shit like this then spins it for profit."

"You're right. We shouldn't. Especially since César told us most of the crap they write about celebrities is planted or sensationalized," Nikki says.

"Have you guys ever talked about his past drug use?" Alondra asks.

Words teeter on the tip of my tongue. Do I share that Xavier told me he's an addict? Even though they're my closest friends, it still seems kinda personal. He trusted me. Although they're my besties, this is something I'm keeping to myself. "Not really.

Haven't gotten around to it. Been waiting for the right time." The lie slips from my lips as I remember how he called himself an addict to remind him of the darkest days of his life.

"Seems like the time is right," Alondra chimes in.

"To be fair, he was only arrested for possession and none of the articles say anything about whether he was high," Nikki adds. "I'm sure if he was, that is something they would not leave out."

After hearing the way Xavier spoke about himself, it's hard for me to believe he's using. His words seemed sincere, but do I really know him? Am I being fooled—again? I hate that I'm doubting him after what he shared.

"Are you gonna call Victor?" Alondra asks.

"I don't know. I'd rather not if I can avoid it. Besides, he's not gonna give me any information." Even considering dialing his number makes me uncomfortable. He'll almost certainly want something from me in return.

"Why not?" Alondra inquires.

"Attorney client privilege," I respond, glancing through my mirror at the people getting into the car parked behind me.

"Right, because Victor is such a stand-up guy. You think he wouldn't share any information with you?" asks Alondra.

"It's his ethical obligation not to, so probably not."

"HA! Victor and ethics in the same sentence. That's laughable!" Nikki adds.

"He just might, if you sweet talk him enough," Alondra says.

"Eww, no! Girls, I'm not gonna call him. He'll probably ask for a blowjob in exchange for information, and that's never happening again." Disgust churns as the words fall from my mouth. "Xavier has a driver, and I have his number. I'll call him and see what he knows."

"A driver?" Alondra asks.

"Oh, is he sexy? Maybe you can hook him up with Alondra."

"Focus, Nikki," I retort.

"What? It's always the right time to talk about a sexy man."

"This is all so crazy, and I think the craziness is just getting started. We had dinner last night, and Xavier told me there was a photo recently published in the tabloids of him kissing a woman on the cheek. That woman is me! Now with his arrest, it's just a matter of time before they find out who I am." My head drops back as I squeeze my eyes shut. The chaos that's on the brink of unleashing is unimaginable.

I was itching to talk to Adrián, but needed to get back to the office for a settlement conference. As soon as it ends, I grab my phone and shoot him a text.

ME

Hi, can I call you? What's going on with Xavier?

Instead of responding via text message, my phone lights up with his name.

"Hi," I say.

"Ma'am." His voice is deep and raspy.

I hate that he calls me that. Xavier said he addresses everyone with the same formalities—remnants of his time in the military, I suppose.

"I saw the headlines about Xavier. What happened?"

"It's a misunderstanding. He was driving a friend home and got pulled over, but the cops believed the drugs were his." Adrián continues explaining how the night unfolded and how he ended up arrested. *I knew he wasn't doing drugs.*

"Well, if the drugs weren't his, it should be easy enough to resolve," I say, hopeful that it's true. I may be a lawyer, but I know very little about criminal law.

"Yeah, his sister thinks so, too. I called her last night and she hired a criminal lawyer she knows."

Victor. My ex-husband, who I can't seem to get away from. But I don't think that's information I need to share right about now. "That's good to hear! Is he out yet?"

"Not yet. Bond was already paid, and we're just waiting for him to be released. I'm outside the jail, but his lawyer said it could be a few hours." He's wicked meticulous and must be going nuts in there. "Media is already set up waiting for his release."

Shit, this means the vultures will be circling waiting to snap pictures of anything and everything. "Will you let me know when he's out so I can call him?"

"Sure thing."

"Thanks, Adrián." I push the red end button and slide back in my chair, allowing my head to rest on the cushioned part. There's no way I can be at work the rest of the day. How am I supposed to concentrate knowing that Xavier is just waiting to be released? I grab my phone, search for Victor's name, but when I see those letters my fingers twitch and hover. Do I really want to go there? If I call him, he'll want to interrogate me before he shares any information, if he even shares anything. Knowing his asshole personality, he'd ask me twenty questions, get what he wants from me and then end up saying he's not at liberty to share. Manipulative asshole that he is, and I'm the dumbass who may just fall for his bullshit—again! I press the lock button and drop my phone on the desk. I don't need the added stress of Victor right now.

My eyes scan the calendar on my computer to see what's scheduled for today. *Shit, I have a deposition this afternoon!* My eyes dart to the clock. Still have a couple hours before it starts. Thankfully it's via Zoom instead of in person, which makes it easier. They're taking my client's deposition. So, while I have to be ready to defend it, it's not as much work as when I'm the lawyer asking all the questions.

I change my shoes to my office flats and meander out toward my paralegal's office. Before entering, I call for the receptionist. "Vero, come here please. Let's decide what we're having for lunch."

Inside the office, Milena is at her desk. "What should we order?" I ask them.

Milena has been my paralegal for eight years. I hired her while she was still in college earning a bachelor's degree. Although she had work experience, she didn't have any legal experience, which is exactly how I like to hire my staff. This way I can teach them the way I like things done and not worry about them coming with any bad habits from previous law firm jobs.

"That place with the kabobs, what's it called again? I always forget the name," Veronica says.

"Shahs of Kabob," Milena responds. "Their grilled chicken kabobs are to die for, and the basmati rice is super good."

"We haven't ordered from there in a while, I'm in." My eyes peruse the menu. "Get me the chicken, the one that has rice and a side salad, and also a Coke Zero. I need some caffeine."

"I'll get the beef kabobs with the rice," Veronica adds.

After ordering lunch, we set everything up in the conference room since my client chose to come to my office, rather than appear by computer from her house. She's anxious about the deposition, so having her in the office with me will help keep her grounded throughout the process. Now we're in the kitchen unpacking our food, the aroma of the sumac making my belly growl. I'm about to take my first bite when "Armageddon" by Def Leppard starts playing, alerting me that Xavier is calling. I rise, quickly grab the phone and push the green answer button as I scurry to my office.

"Hi," I say, trying to hide the anxiousness in my voice.

"It's good to hear your voice, *mami*."

Closing the door behind me, I slide into the chair at my desk. "Are you okay?"

"*Bastante*. For all the shit I put myself through, *nunca estuve preso*," he says in a coarse tone as he tells me he's never been in jail.

"Where are you?"

"*En camino a mi casa*. First thing I'm doing is getting in the shower. Then, I'll try and catch some shut-eye *porque no dormí na*." The exhaustion is clear in his gravelly voice.

"I can't even imagine."

"*Y ni te quieres imaginar*," he says. "You coming over?"

As much as I want to, I'm reluctant because of all the media buzz surrounding him. But he sounds so down if I tell him no, it may break him. To make matters worse, I have a trial coming up and I pretty much isolate myself until it's over, which means if I don't see him soon, I'll see very little of him until it's done. "I hadn't really thought about it because I was waiting for you to get out and call me."

"*¿Qué tienes que pensar?*"

What do I have to think about? Well, that's a loaded question. Being plastered across the front page of every news outlet's website and social media? Having paparazzi swarm outside my office, the courthouse, and my apartment building? I'm sure I'm only prolonging the inevitable, but I want to avoid them as long as I can. Oh, how I've complicated my life by having feelings for a wicked famous reggaeton artist when I told myself I wasn't getting involved with anyone. This may be the first time I've allowed myself to acknowledge that whatever is happening between us is more than friends with benefits.

"Won't the media be outside your building?"

"Probably, but they can't come onto the property so they'll likely be on the sidewalk. Building security is tight."

My response hangs, and the silence is palpable. I realize the longer I take to respond, the more doubt builds. I really want to see him, feel the pressure of his arms wrapped around me, the tenderness of the kisses he drops along my hairline. But the possibility of seeing swarming paparazzi sours everything. If I don't go to avoid them, they win. They dictate how I live my life. That's exactly what Xavier keeps telling me I shouldn't allow. Ugh, I hate this.

"Is that what you're worried about? The media?" His words are sharp.

"If I'm being honest, yes."

"*Si los dejas*, they'll dictate how you live. Don't let them."

If I had a choice in the matter, I wouldn't allow them to dictate anything. I realize he's used to all the media stuff but also, now isn't the time for me to get into it. "Will you send Adrián to pick me up?"

CHAPTER TWENTY-ONE

Xavier

"We can swing by and pick you up on our way." The softness of her voice when she answered my call flowed through me, instantly relaxing me. I hate that she considered not coming to my penthouse because of the paparazzi, even knowing she wants to be here. I'm eager to see her and wrap her in my arms. Inhale her unique floral scent at the nape of her neck.

"*No podés venir ahora,*" she blurts out. "I have a deposition and a few things to finish at the office. *Yo te aviso cuando termino.*" Her Argentine accent turns me on, even as she's telling me no.

If there's one thing I'm learning with her, it's patience. "*Dale.*" I force the word, trying to pretend I'm not bothered because I have to wait for her to finish the workday before coming over.

Forty minutes later, Adrián is pulling up to my building and the fucking paparazzi are crowding the sidewalk. Not really sure what for, because they won't be able to access the property. Security here really is tight and the way the front entrance is set up, if they're lucky, they'll get a picture of the back of my head. Besides, these motherfuckers were outside the detention center waiting on my release, shoving their microphones and cameras in my face. They have enough material to print bullshit stories for days.

Once inside, I head straight for the shower to wash the night in jail off my skin. After the cops arrested us, they took us to the TGK Jail. By the time we got processed, it was well past midnight when I was taken to the holding cell with seven other guys, including Axel. I was frustrated and angry with him, so I mostly kept to myself, because I didn't want to get into it around prying eyes. I wasn't sure if anyone in the holding cell recognized us, and the last thing I needed is for one of the guys in there to sell whatever they witness to the press. I knew Adrián called Xiomary so it would just be a matter of time before I was bailed out. But the officer that escorted me to the holding cell told me I wouldn't have a bond hearing until the afternoon, since we had arrived after midnight.

My sister hired a lawyer who was able to get me released before the afternoon bond hearings started by paying the requested bond amount. When I talked to Xiomary on the way here, she told me, between her and Alba, they've been getting bombarded with calls and email requests for statements. I'll have to check in with Alba later and see what she has in mind to tame the media beast.

A few hours later, I'm in the kitchen cutting plantains. I haven't eaten since dinner last night with Rocky, and I'm starving. She texted me that she was ready for Adrián to pick her up, and he's already on his way here. The rice cooker is going, and the white rice will be finished soon. *Las habichuelas guisadas* are simmering and nearly ready. I've already seasoned the *chuletas* and placed them in the fridge. I'll fry up the *plátanos* and smash them in the *tostonera* so they'll be ready to drop and fry. Let's hope Rocky likes Puerto Rican food.

Growing up, I loved spending time *con mi abuela* while she cooked for us, even while I was creating the image of being a kid of the streets. She would explain what she did as she prepped and cooked. In between, she sprinkled tidbits of family stories—of when she met my mother for the first time and how much my father loved her, before their love ended in tragedy. Whenever he came up as a topic, I'd either change the conversation or leave because I didn't like speaking of him. Still don't and try avoiding it when I can. My grandmother's and my image of my father were at odds because, despite his misgivings, she held him on a pedestal. He was her only son, after all.

Meanwhile, I remember him as the man who drank too much alcohol and made my mother cry night after night because of his infidelities. They would argue nearly every day when she would beg him to stop seeing other women, to dedicate himself to his family. Hearing her weep for him made me angry, but I was powerless to do anything about it. On the night they were killed, they were at a friend's house partying when they started arguing. My father hated when others saw him for who he truly was, and so he forced my mother to leave. Except they never made it home, because he lost control of the vehicle and struck a tree, killing both of them instantly. All these years later, and I'm not sure I've ever been able to move past the fact that my mother suffered in life because of his infidelities. As if that wasn't enough, she's dead because of him. Dead because of his drunken state that caused their fatal accident. I've gotten good at keeping memories stuffed deep down and hidden away. Whenever thoughts of him sneak up or someone mentions his name, my heart pounds and heat spreads across me—reminding me of everything I lost because of him.

My phone pings with a text from Rocky. They're almost here.

Shit! The plantains are gonna burn. I quickly remove them from the pan, dropping them on the dish lined with a paper towel. Once cooled, I squish each one in the wooden tool designed to flatten them and cover them up with a dish towel.

Adrián texts that they're downstairs. I wash my hands and scurry to the great room, my foot tapping as I wait for the elevator. When it dings, the doors open and my girl's face appears. All the exhaustion and hunger disappear, and warmth fills me as I admire her dark curls cascading around the angles of her jaw.

"*Mami.*" My hands instinctively fall to her rounded hips, covered in the black fabric of her dress, and my lips fall on hers, sucking and pulling.

"Hi," she responds, separating from me. Her palms rest on my cheeks. "You okay?" Her eyebrows are drawn together, tension rippling across her forehead.

"I will be." Closing the space between us, I wrap my hands over hers and let them fall to our sides. "The drugs weren't mine," I declare, keeping my eyes firm with hers.

Her breaths are steady. "Okay." Her vibrant green eyes shimmer with the late day sun.

"They were my friend Axel's, not mine."

"I didn't think they were." She blinks but her eyes never stray.

My thumb draws circles in her palm as my heart pounds. "I'm still sober."

"I believe you."

My shoulders drop. "You do?" Relief floods through me.

"Is there a reason I shouldn't believe you?" she inquires, her eyes probing.

My head shakes. "No, I mean, besides the bullshit the news is reporting."

"Well, you already told me I shouldn't believe everything I read, right?"

I nod. "*Seguro que no.*"

She gives me a lopsided grin. "Then we're good." Sincerity surrounds her emerald irises.

Since the moment I was arrested, thoughts of Rocky have been spinning. Although the circumstances are different now than when Lisandra left me because I was strung out, I've been anxious about losing Rocky before we've had the chance to continue growing what we've started. The sensationalized headlines could be overwhelming and push her away. My lips brush across hers. "You hungry?"

"A little."

"I made us dinner." But if she isn't hungry, then I'll build up her appetite.

"Dinner?" She glances at her watch.

My thumbs drag across the apples of her cheeks. "If you're not that hungry yet, maybe I'll make love to you first."

Her eyes widen, and she purses her lips. "Make love to me, huh?"

I nod and push her curls to the side, kissing the skin along the side of her neck where her soft floral scent always lures me in. "Unless my greedy girl is here. Because I'd be happy to fuck her first, before making love to you."

A whimper escapes her as she extends her neck and pushes her hands beneath my t-shirt.

"¿*Cuál tú quieres*?" I push her jacket off and let it fall to the floor.

She shoves her hands in my shorts and wraps her fingers around my cock. "*Elegí vos*." Her words are short and breathy, and her accent ignites me from within.

"If that's the case, I'll fuck you then feed you. *Y después más tarde, te hago el amor*." I grasp her hips while promising to make love to her later. "*Virate*," I command, turning her toward the large couch.

She yanks up the hem of her dress and bends over the back of the couch, spreading her legs for me.

I make quick work of wrapping it up, then slide her panties and penetrate her while grasping her generous hips. She's hot and tight and wet. I pause, then pry her open so I can fill her to the hilt. A moan escapes her then she pushes back, the pressure of being fully seated inside of her send shivers across my body.

Rocky is leaning on the kitchen counter, her cheeks flushed and her hair tied up in a messy bun. She's barefoot, her red panties visible through the thin white fabric of my t-shirt. I flip the pork chops in the frying pan and drop the *tostón* in the heated oil.

"You made this all yourself?" She lifts the lid off the pot where the *habichuelas guisadas* are simmering. Growing up, I loved my *abuela*'s *arroz con gandules*, but my favorite was when she made stewed beans. Mine are good, but nothing will ever compare to how *abuela* cooked.

I give her a sideways glance and nod. My phone dings, and when I peek at it, I see Lisandra's name in the message bubble. I ignore it, and my eyes meet Rocky's. "Why do you sound so surprised?"

Her shoulders rise and fall. "Not sure. Seems too good to be true that you'd be sexy, a super rockstar, and a good cook." She bites her lower lip, rolling it between her teeth.

I lift a pork chop to check the temperature and then raise my eyes to find her staring at me. "You think I'm sexy?" I smirk.

"Sometimes." She gives me a half grin.

"What about the rest of the time?"

"Wicked sexy!"

I raise an eyebrow. "What's the difference?"

"Sexy means you look good. Wicked sexy means you look fucking delicious and I want to devour you."

My heart hammers in my chest at her declaration. "Then I got work to do."

A few minutes later, I've served each of us a dish and we're seated at the counter. Rocky scoops some rice and beans up with her fork and raises it to her mouth. "Oh my god," she mumbles, covering her mouth with her hand as she finishes chewing. "That's delicious."

Pride swells. "*Abuela*'s recipe, if you can even call it that. She just eyeballed everything. Knew exactly how much *sazón* everything needed."

She cuts into the pork chop, and the fork hovers at her mouth. "When did you learn?"

"When I was a kid, I loved spending time with her in the kitchen. I'd be in there with her almost every day when she cooked for us." A pang shoots through me as memories of my grandmother resurface. Her small white house in Carolina stood at the end of the block, across the street from a natural habitat. We'd cook together nearly every night in her tiny kitchen.

Rocky's hand reaches for me, resting on my forearm.

"Every night after dinner, we'd sit on her wrap-around porch listening to *los coquís* serenade us." The open fields across from her house spanned for miles and their sound carried us into the night.

Her eyes light up and she tilts her head. "What's that?"

"A frog that's native to Puerto Rico. It's called *coquí* because that's the sound the male frogs make when mating."

When we moved to Puerto Rico after my parents died, it took me months before I became accustomed to the noise. With my *abuela*'s house being across the street from the natural habitat, the call of the *coquí* was loud, something I wasn't used to when living in the suburbs of Boston. I would lie in bed awake for hours, until the frogs lulled me to sleep. Eventually, I became used to their singing, and it only took me minutes to find slumber.

"When's the last time you were in Puerto Rico?"

My *abuela*'s funeral where I disgraced her by showing up strung out on Percocet. The guys from my *abuela*'s neighborhood had to drag me out to my sister's car, where they left me to sleep off my high. "*Abuela*'s funeral." My voice cracks, and I push the rice on my plate around, mixing it in with the bean mixture covering it.

"I'm sorry." She squeezes my arm.

"It's okay. You don't have to apologize. I fucked up by showing up to her funeral Perc'd out, and part of my addiction recovery is acknowledging the people I hurt. *Abuela*'s gone, and I'll never be able to take back what I did, so the least I can do is talk about that day. Maybe she can hear me, wherever she is."

Her eyes are steady, and I'm searching for signs that she's freaking out as I'm unloading my drug-laden baggage onto her. But all that stares back is understanding.

"Anyway, enough about me." I snake my arm out from under her hand and grab my knife. "Tell me about your family *ya que* when I asked in the Bahamas, you avoided the topic."

Her back straightens and she grabs the napkin, swiping it across her mouth. "My parents live in Pembroke Pines. They moved here when I graduated from law school, and I have two sisters. One lives in Maine and the other is still in Boston."

"Are you close to them?" I scoop some rice and beans up and into my mouth.

She contemplates my question, her head giving the slightest of nods. "I'm close with my father, and my younger sister. My other sister is seven years older. We have a good relationship, but we were never super close because of the age difference."

I rest my knife on my plate as my fork hovers at my lips. "What about your mother?"

"It's complicated," she quips, nudging her plate away.

"Why's it complicated?" Her quickness to dismiss the relationship with her mother bothers me, although I'm not one to judge. I've chalked it up to feeling envious of people who have an opportunity to have a relationship with their mother but don't. The reason doesn't matter, envy churns in the pit of my stomach at their lost opportunities, an opportunity my father stripped me of.

"She's judged and criticized me my entire life and it's built a massive wedge between us. She doesn't know how to just accept me for me, and I don't know how to get past that."

"At least she's still here."

Rocky sips some Coke Zero then places the can on the counter, her eyes piercing mine. "What does that mean?"

"Exactly what it sounds like. Whether she's judging you or not, she's alive. You should cherish that."

Her nostrils flare and her back straightens. "Who says I don't?"

I stretch my hand across in search of hers, but she slides it back, tucking it under the counter. "I'm not saying you don't. Maybe it came out wrong." My hand snakes beneath the quartz stone in search of hers, and when I graze her skin, I thread our fingers, resting our hands on her thighs. "I didn't mean to upset you. But talking about mothers makes me feel some type of way."

"What type of way is that?"

The thumping in my chest intensifies. "My mother died when I was twelve and I'd give anything to see her one more time."

Rocky's shoulders soften, her hand gently squeezes mine, and she takes a deep breath. "Sorry. I get defensive when my mother comes up, but I'm working on it, I promise."

"All I'm saying is, *la mamá es única.*" I tug her hand up and gently kiss her palm. Hopefully me telling her that mothers are one of a kind won't upset her. "Just try to remember that *cuando tu mamá* is making you mad."

Rocky pulls her hand away and reaches for a fried green plantain, sinking her teeth into its crispy exterior as she considers my words.

"You sound like my father."

CHAPTER TWENTY-TWO

Three Weeks Later

Rocío

AFTER A FULL-DAY TRIAL YESTERDAY, I came to the office this morning with plans to work and get ahead on a few things. But as I clicked through the calendar, excitement spread as I learned I have no deadlines to meet this week or next and no hearings or trials scheduled either. That's a rarity! My next deadline is thirteen days from today. It's practically cause for celebration. I peek at my watch and then back at the calendar. Xavier's words, *you're la jefa*, ring in my ears. Fuck it, I'm going to pull a page from his book. The chair slides back, and I stride toward Milena's office, calling for Veronica.

Milena swivels in her chair, her eyebrows furrowed. "Is everything okay?"

The concerned look on her face tells me I'm making the right decision. "Of course."

After Veronica scurries in, my eyes bounce between the both

of them. "We have no hearings, and no trials scheduled for the next two weeks. Not even a deadline."

"What?" Milena grabs the mouse and opens the calendar, clicking one day at a time. "Wow, I don't think that's ever happened before!"

"Exactly, which is why we're taking the rest of the day off."

"Really?" Veronica adds, her eyes widening as a smile spreads across her face.

"Yes, really! Tomorrow is Wednesday and we'll start the day fresh. We don't know when, or if, this will ever happen again so let's seize the moment." The long days and nights of preparation and trial hit me harder each time I have one, and I'm not loving my job as much as I used to. Maybe it's my age speaking, but litigation isn't as exhilarating as I once thought it was. I've only seen Xavier twice since having dinner at his penthouse a couple weeks ago, and I'm craving him and his presence.

"True, we could get a call that would change that instantly." Milena's head bobs up and down.

"It's almost lunch time, anyway. Let's finish up what we're doing, then call it a day. Vero, please transfer the calls to the answering service."

"Will do." She spins and walks back to her desk.

"Is everything okay?" Milena inquires as she rises from her chair. After so many years by my side, Milena knows me well. I'm generous and flexible, but I've never decided to close the office on a whim for a half day, but also never remember having the opportunity to do it. Maybe I wasn't paying attention, or maybe Xavier is rubbing off on me.

I nod. "It is." A smile stretches across my face. "I'm trying to remember that work is important, but we also need to enjoy life and take time for ourselves. When I saw the calendar without deadlines, it felt like the right decision." Her concerned tone makes me think Xavier's right—life is short and we need to take the opportunities to enjoy it as much as possible.

Forty-five minutes later, I'm in the car exiting the garage. "Call Xavier." The ringing reverberates as I make a right onto NE 1st Avenue.

"Hi, *mami*." His deep, raspy voice fills the space and goosebumps spread as I recall him whispering that in my ear when we're naked.

"Hey you, whatcha doing?" When the light turns green, I make a right and start driving north.

"I'm at the studio, approving the final mockups for tour merch. It kicks off in less than two weeks." He's been talking about his tour here and there, but other than the cities he'll be performing in, I don't know much. "*¿Y tú, qué haces?*"

"I'm leaving my office, told the girls to take the day off." I smile, knowing he's rubbing off on me.

"That's my girl." Warmth spreads when he calls me that. "What are your plans?"

"Thought I'd come by and say hi, if you're not too busy." The words slip before I have a chance to change my mind.

"*Siempre tengo tiempo para ti, mami.*"

My heart swells at his declaration. As much as I tried to talk myself out of getting into a relationship with him, I know I made the right choice. Not sure where we're headed, but I'm enjoying the ride. "Have you eaten lunch?"

"*Todavía no*. But don't worry about it. Get your ass over here, and I'll order us lunch when you get here." I love that he loves to feed me. Seems we're always doing something related to food.

"Okay. Send me the address."

There's tons of construction in downtown Miami and the GPS didn't account for road closures. A drive that should've taken me twenty minutes took nearly an hour. I park the car a block away from his studio in the Design District of Miami. The houses in this neighborhood are what many consider "old Miami"—homes designed with stucco walls, arches, and wrought iron detailing, with most donning barrel tile roofs. My eyes scan the area, and it seems it's still mostly a quiet residential neighborhood. Interesting choice for him to have his studio here.

I'm about to ring the doorbell when the door opens. Xavier's wearing dark slim cut jeans that hang low and a white tee that's a bit too short, showing a smattering of the black ink on his belly. "Hi, *mami*." His large hand grasps my hip and pulls me to him, pushing the door closed with his foot. He's sucking on my bottom lip and squeezing the generous skin beneath his hands.

"Hi." My eyes scan the large open room. To my left, a vibrant blue sectional adorned with colored pillows—pink, yellow, turquoise, and a few flowered ones too. Behind it hangs a large brightly colored canvas that reads *el ritmo es mi alma* in block lettering on one wall, the other wall covered in black and white pictures in black frames. In the far-left corner there's a grand piano, the keys open and a notebook splayed across the flat area to the right of the music rack.

"*Te extrañé*," he mumbles between kisses. His warm breath caresses me.

"I missed you, too," I confess, meeting his energy. Now that I'm in his arms, I realize how much I've craved spending time with him.

"Welcome to my studio." His smile reaches his eyes as he grasps my hand and tugs. "Let me show you around." I toss my pockabook on the couch and scurry behind him down the hall, passing a small open kitchen. "This is the recording studio itself." We're peering inside a room that's covered in black padding from floor to ceiling and across the ceiling. A thick, dark rug covers the floor. There's one wall at the far back with a painting of an empty stretch of beach. A lone microphone stand and headphones in the middle, next to a stool and a music stand.

"What beach is that in the picture?" My eyes find his.

He shifts his eyes toward the picture and stares at it as silence hovers. Leave it to me to always ask a question that takes him off to a distant place. "*Piñones*. It's where *mi abuela* took us all the time."

Of course my question relates back to his grandmother. I hate that asking questions could stir up stuff he'd rather be avoiding. "It's beautiful."

The corner of his mouth lifts. "Yeah." He turns on his heel toward the adjacent space and pushes the door open. "This is the control room." In the middle is a large wooden table with a mixing console in the center, flanked by computers, amplifiers, and monitor screens. The far wall is exposed brick with various framed pictures, and there's a slender dark gray couch behind the table, a door leading to the recording room wedged kitty corner from where we're standing.

"Did you always want to be a musician?" I shift toward him, looking up, waiting for his eyes to find mine.

His shoulders rise. "Not until I was living in Puerto Rico. I was sixteen when the guys in our neighborhood were performing *en las marquesinas*, and I was hooked. It was then that I knew, I had to be a part of it too." His eyes shimmer as he shares memories of his younger days. "I had a lot of anger *con mi papá*. The first lyrics I sang were years of pent-up rage I felt toward him and releasing it was so freeing. I never looked back."

"Did you think you would get to where you are today?"

He shakes his head. "Nah, at least not initially. I was just rapping and singing with the guys. But then I met Roly. He made me believe I had talent."

My arm reaches for his waist and I close the space between us. "Guess he was right. Look at you now." I smirk, then rise up on my toes to swipe my lips across his.

"Let me finish showing you around." He wraps my hand in his and then tugs me toward the hall.

I follow him and glance at the painting on the wall outside the control room. The silhouette of a female dancer against a backdrop of neon-colored, graffiti-tagged brick walls, a perfect blend of blues, purples, reds, and pinks.

"This is my office." His words bring me back to him as we step into another vibrant room. The wall to the right has a floor-to-ceiling custom mural that resembles colorful street art. It's a stylized Puerto Rican flag that blends with Boston's skyline, the Prudential Tower proudly on display with art deco accents throughout. On the wall opposite, there is wood paneling with bright neon lights in the middle reading "*Modo Perreo*," flanked with a gold record on one side and a platinum on the other. There are floating shelves on the wall, a colorful high-top sneaker sitting on each of the shelves. In front of the window is a modern desk with a glass table to the right. There is a small stack of paper on the right and the rest of the desk is neat. Stark difference from the scattered papers of my disorganized office.

"What's '*Modo Perreo*'?" My eyes raise to meet his.

"My second studio album that went gold, then platinum."

My hand reaches for the platinum record hanging in a black frame. "That's impressive." The frame has a plaque at the bottom that reads, "Presented to *El Flaco Casanova* to Commemorate a Platinum Certification, 1,000,000 RIAA Certified US Sales Units for the Album '*Modo Perreo*.'" Above the plaque is a picture of the album cover, the white block letters outlined in pink reads "*Modo Perreo*," a turquoise blue frog with a pink eye below it, sitting atop a low concrete wall covered in graffiti. The background is a tropical street, pastel-covered buildings and two tall, skinny palm trees, with string lights hanging between the buildings. There are random blurred out people standing in the cobble stone street. Across the top, the album cover reads *El Flaco Casanova* in simple white lettering. The most prominent feature is the large platinum-colored disc with the same album cover in the center circle.

He's silent, and when I glance at him, he's staring at the wall. "Too bad I threw it all away for drugs."

Instinctively, I thread our fingers together and squeeze. "That may be true, but that doesn't diminish the work you did to earn these records hanging on the wall. They're still your achievements. And you should be proud of them, regardless of what came after. Besides, you've been clean and none of us should be defined by our past."

Silence hangs as he stares at the platinum-colored disc. "Yeah, tell the Latin media that. They make sure that no one ever forgets every single fuck up I've ever had."

"You're the one who told me not to pay attention to anything the media writes. Maybe take your own advice on this one." My shoulder nudges him.

"Using my own words against me." He smirks and his eyes light up. "I see how it is." His fingers grasp my chin as he brushes his lips across mine.

"Sometimes we just need a reminder." My fingers trace one of the colorful shoes adorning the wall. "What's with the sneakers?" The shoes displayed on the wall of his office point out the stark difference between him and me—he's vibrant and colorful in his work, and I live inside a legal box with constraints.

"Customs I had made when I started making money. I was young and that's where I decided to blow the cash rolling in."

"That's the beauty of you making your own money though, isn't it? Nobody can judge you for where you spend it."

His eyes search mine and he shrugs. "That's what I tried telling my sister."

Mentioning his sister makes me think of Victor, and he's the last person I want crossing my mind right now. I turn toward the opposite art covered wall, my hand resting on the vibrant colored flag. "Tell me about this mural. It's wicked awesome. I love the blend of all the elements."

"The artist is Puerto Rican. I first saw his work a few years ago at Art Basel. When I bought this place, I commissioned him to create this piece and it's what I love most about my studio."

"I don't blame you. I'd spend a lot of time in here if it were my office, too."

"You can come here anytime you want to work in this office." He grasps my hips and his nose finds the crease of my neck, and I extend it up, exposing my skin for him.

His touch ignites me from the inside. "Doubt I'd get much work done if that happened."

Instead of continuing, he separates, and I instantly feel the cool air brush my skin as he drags me out to the front room again. "That's the studio. Now we can chill up here."

I meander to the piano and peek at the open notebook, seeing writing scribbled across the page. "Do you play the piano, too?" I inquire.

"Yeah, not a lot but enough. Sometimes I sit there and write." This man is talented in so many ways.

"Is that what you were doing when I called you?" My hand

slides the notebook toward me, and I catch a glimpse of the words "age difference" before his hand gently closes it.

He nods but his eyes don't meet mine. "It's something I just started working on."

"What inspires your music?"

"Everything. Anything. But usually it's something that's going on in my life." His fingers thread with mine and our arms stretch out.

"What's got you inspired lately?"

His eyes light up. "You." My heart feels like it's going to explode at his declaration. He moves our hands down to the piano keys, the sudden clang of overlapping musical notes escape from the piano.

I rest my left hand along the dark wood and turn my body to lean over the piano. "What have I done to inspire you?"

He pushes himself into me. "Damn, *mami. Tú sabes cómo calentarme* right quick."

My body turns and I reach for his belt to free his straining cock from his jeans. "*¿Yo qué hice?*" I shove my hand in his briefs and grip him as heat spreads from my core pulsating with need.

"*Ese acento me vuelve loco.*" The night we met, he told me he loved the Argentine accent, but I haven't heard him say it again until now. It stokes my desire for him even more.

"*Quiero sentirte*," I tell him. My body burns for him.

"*Eso es tuyo* and you can have it *cuando tú quieras*."

My heart hammers in my chest as he tells me his cock belongs to me. In all my years, I've never had a man give himself to me like Xavier has. Feeling like I have this much power over a man is a first for me. It's both frightening and addicting.

He pushes his jeans down, then hikes my skirt up and slides my panties to the side. His large hands cover the globes of my ass and lift me onto the ivory keys, the thwack of my ass cheeks causing a messy mixture of jumbled tones. "I've been thinking about you fucking me all day." My words are a blend of urgent desire and moaned pleasure.

"The condoms are in my office." He releases me, but my hand firmly grasps his wrist.

"We don't need a condom." My foot rests on the bench, opening up for him.

His head tilts back, his eyes assessing me. "There's no going back, *mami*. Once I fuck you raw, that's it. *Eres mía*."

"I thought I was already yours." The tip of his cock is hot and wet as he nudges into me, opening me up inch by inch.

"Ahh, you're so fucking tight." His eyes roll up and the clanking of the multiple piano keys pressing down create an unpleasant sound amidst the most pleasurable sensation of him inside of me with nothing between us. I pull my blouse up over my head and remove my bra, and Xavier's lips instinctively fall to my nipple. He sucks and swirls as he strokes in and out.

My hands slide under his shirt and grip the muscles in his back as his length fills me. "Xavier, yes, just like that!" Warmth spreads as he continues his punishing strokes, a tingling spreading from my core and up my back.

"*Esa chocha es mía, mami. Ya no te me escapas más.*" He's staking his claim and it lights a fire within me. My hips rise to feel him deeper inside of me, creating out-of-tune notes with each clank of the piano keys. His hands squeeze my ass and I come undone, which only makes Xavier increase his pace until he grunts and fills me with his seed.

As he's catching his breath he sits on the bench and brings me with him. I straddle him and his cock remains deep inside of me as I wrap my arms around his neck, while staring into his hazy, lust-filled eyes.

"*¿Y esa cajita de sorpresa?*"

I surprised myself as well so I'm not sure how to answer that. I shrug. "It just felt right, so I went with it."

"I'm here for all your surprises, *mami*." His lips curl up.

"I'm a victim to my overthinking and indecisiveness. I'm working on it."

"*Conmigo*, you can work on it as much as you want."

His lips cover mine, but my stomach growls interrupting his exploration.

"Hungry?"

I nod. "Starving. Let's order lunch before you meet Hangry Rocky."

"I want to meet all the versions of you." He drops one more peck on my lips then lifts me off of him. He jogs out of the room and quickly returns with a small towel in hand. His left hand nudges my thigh while he cleans up the remnants of us and then adjusts my underwear.

We're sitting on the couch waiting for our food to arrive from *El Típico*. He said it's his favorite Dominican food that he orders a couple times a week, and since I've never had Dominican food, I want to try it. I order *carne frita* with rice and beans and he orders *rabo guisado* with rice and a side of *tostones*. Says it's the best oxtail stew he's had in Miami.

I'm strewn across the couch, shoes kicked off and legs extended. My head lies in the crease of his leg and his fingers tussle with my curls.

"I'm leaving for my tour in less than two weeks, and you still haven't told me what cities you're coming to."

"Cities? As in, you want me to go to multiple concerts?"

"*Mami, si fuera por mí*, you'd be with me every day." His head lowers, and he hovers centimeters from my face. "And after today, *ya te dije que eres mía*." His lips peck mine as he reminds me that I'm his.

I lean my head back and search his eyes. "It's not about that, Xavier. I want to go to a show, but I also have to work."

He holds my stare, his gaze heavy with unspoken thoughts. "*Qué necesitas de mí* in order to get you to as many shows as possible?" It's not lost on me that he's asking what I need from him but he hasn't addressed my statement of only attending one show.

"How long is the tour?"

"This first leg is seven weeks. We kick off in Mexico City, then play our way through Central and South America. We'll take a couple weeks off then start the North American stops and end in the Caribbean. So, another four weeks."

My back straightens. "That's almost three months! There's no way I can take three months off from work."

"You could work when we take a break." He chuckles.

"Sure. Let me file for continuances in my scheduled cases citing my newly planned reggaeton tour."

A deep-throated laugh escapes him. "It's not the worst idea."

I don't know what's worse, him thinking I can take three months off at the drop of a hat, or that somewhere in the back of my mind I wish I could figure out a way to be able to actually pull something like that off. "Send me the dates and the cities and then I'll check them with my calendar. I will buy a flight for the show I can attend."

"I get it, you can't come to all my shows, but you can at least make it to a few. *¿No?*" His eyes widen, pleading with me.

"Once I see the dates, I'll see what I can do." He swallows and then grins, but his smile doesn't reach his eyes.

"*Y no tienes que comprar boletos.* I have a plane that'll fly you to the shows you're coming to."

I've never been on a private jet but won't protest if he's sending it for me. "Sounds fancy. I—"

The doorbell interrupts us. That seems quick for the food to be here already, but I'm not complaining. "Hold that thought." He jumps up and jogs across the room, opening the front door. "Hey, man." Xavier extends his hand to someone behind the door. "Come in, I'm just here with my girl." My heart flutters when he refers to me as his girl.

The door opens and Victor appears. My mouth goes slack because I was not expecting to see this motherfucker. He's wearing his usual slim-cut dark suit, white shirt and colored tie—today it's blue. His eyes narrow when they meet mine.

"What the fuck is my wife doing here?" Victor shouts while sprinting across the room.

My heart races as anger seethes. I shoot up, planting my bare feet on the wooden floor. "You must be confused!" I shimmy closer to Victor, stopping him in his tracks, glaring down at him. He appears shorter than I remember, even with his shoulders squared back and chest out. "I'm your ex-wife, remember?"

Xavier blinks, his eyes jumping between Victor and me as confusion spreads. Moments later, he shakes it off and strides across the room, fixing himself to my left. "Victor, you need to leave!" Xavier commands.

Victor ignores him and wraps his hand on my forearm. "Rocky, what the fuck are you doing with this guy? He's a drug addict, for Christ's sake!"

Anger churns in the pit of my stomach, and I yank my arm from his grasp. "Allegedly, right? Besides, what I do is none of your fucking business!"

"I'm not leaving until you answer me!"

"Answers? You're not entitled to answers!" My voice quivers. "You lost that right a long time ago."

He's apprising me with a cold, sharp glare. A short, clipped "HA" escapes him as he takes a step closer to me and raises his chin. "You have that freshly fucked look on your face! I know it all too well." He smirks but it doesn't reach his eyes.

Rage simmers and instinctively my knee flies up, landing between Victor's legs.

"Ahhhh! You fucking bitch!" Victor keels over as he cups himself.

"In all the years you fucked me," I say, my tone even and flat, "I never once felt as satisfied as I do with Xavier. Maybe that'll give you an adjustment to up your game."

"Hey," Xavier interjects, inserting his body between Victor and me. "It's time to go, there's the door." His arm extends toward the exit, creating a barrier between Victor and me.

"Don't fucking touch me, man." Victor forces himself up and shoves Xavier, which causes me to stumble back. Victor's face is red and swollen from the pain I inflicted.

Xavier begins lunging toward him when my hands grasp Xavier's arms. "Please don't." My head shakes. "It's exactly what he wants." His gaze meets mine and lingers as I watch his chest rise and fall.

He turns back toward Victor. "*Vete*," Xavier yells. "Get out of my fucking studio. You're fired."

"Good luck with those criminal charges." He cracks a dismissive laugh, his hand still between his legs as he limps toward the door. "There's no other lawyer that will get you the deal I will."

"I don't need a fucking deal. So I guess I don't need you! Now get the fuck out of here before *te rompo la cabeza* for disrespecting my girl!" Xavier's hands are balled in fists at his side.

Victor limps out the door, and Xavier slams it behind him then strides across the room back to me. "*¿Todo bien, mami?*" He pushes my curls behind my ears.

I nod. "Yeah. I'm fine." My heart is beating a million miles a minute. Tears threaten but I refuse to let Victor be the source of one more tear. I never imagined I'd run into Victor here of all places. "Thought I was done with his ridiculous behavior, but I guess I'm not so lucky. He's the reason I've been seeing a therapist. Now you know why."

"I'm sorry. I had no idea." His shoulders slump.

"You don't need to apologize. You had no way of knowing." I snake my hands underneath his arms and tighten them. "I just wish your criminal case would've been over. He's a good lawyer."

Xavier's head is shaking. "*Me consigo uno mejor*. Someone better. But he's right, you know."

My eyes widen. "What do you mean?"

"He called me a drug addict. That's something I'll always be." Xavier rests his forehead on my head, his eyes sullen and wet.

"I won't pretend to understand everything that goes with drug addiction and recovery, but what I know is you're clean today." I put space between us and meet his eyes. "What was it you said a few weeks ago? Two years, three months, a week, and four days?"

His eyebrows shoot up. "You remember that?"

I nod. "Of course, you were sharing important parts of yourself." I bite my lip as our gazes linger and unspoken sentiments hang.

The doorbell interrupts us again, breaking the heavy silence. Xavier crosses the room and grabs his phone from where it's resting on a shelf. His fingers swipe a few times and then he says, "Our food is here."

CHAPTER TWENTY-THREE

Rocío

"*Nena, no tengo pan*," my mother says from the kitchen. Bread is a staple in my parents' house, and since I'll be in Vegas this weekend, I wanted a true home-cooked meal before I left. We've never had a meal without bread on the table so I already know my mother is slightly panicking, especially after I showed up a few days before our usual Saturday lunch. "I didn't notice earlier when you called."

"It's fine. I'll run to the store real quick. I can pick up some Coke Zero while I'm there." I need some bubbles and caffeine to power through the rest of the night so I can start packing for Vegas.

A few weeks ago, Xavier told me his friend is headlining a heavyweight boxing match in Vegas, where he'll be performing a song for his walkout, and invited my friends and I to go. Nikki is in trial this week and next, but Alondra was able to make it happen. We're leaving on Friday morning, but because I took Tuesday off and will be out on Friday, I have a full work day planned for tomorrow and won't have much time to pack.

"Gracias. *Chispa y Espectáculo* starts in a few minutes and I don't want to miss it," my mother says. *Chispa y Espectáculo* is the late day gossip show that airs on Spanish language TV that my mother religiously watches every day.

My head shakes as I grab my pockabook off the back of the chair. "Not sure why you love that show so much. All they do is gossip. And they don't even know if what they're saying about the celebrities is true." I was never a fan of the show, but once I got involved with Xavier and realized how much of the celebrity reporting is fake, I dislike it even more. "Anyway, *vuelvo enseguida.*"

I'm in the checkout line at the grocery store when the two older women in line at the next register start looking at me while whispering to one another. What the heck is their problem? I glare back at them with a fake smile plastered across my face and give them a curt shake of the head.

As I'm paying for my groceries, "Armageddon" starts playing, a picture of Xavier filling my phone's screen. "Hey, you," I respond while tapping my credit card. "I'm paying for groceries, let me call you right back."

"Okay, *te espero*," Xavier responds. "It's important."

His voice has a serious tone to it, I hope everything is okay. I scurry to the car and toss the groceries in the back seat.

"Call Xavier," I instruct the voice command while sitting in the parking spot.

"Hi, *mami.*" He answers before the first ring is complete.

"What's up, is everything okay?"

"Yeah, I'm fine." Silence hangs.

"But? What are you not telling me?" My hands grip the steering wheel.

"Yesterday when you left the studio, there was paparazzi hiding somewhere out there. They know about you. About us."

"What?" Instinctively, I glance at each of the mirrors

searching for someone. "I didn't see anybody. How is that possible?" This must be why those ladies were staring at me inside the store.

I type his name into the search bar on my phone and photos of us on his front porch appear—him kissing me and hugging me, but with his right hand palming my ass cheek in all the stills. Even amidst this chaos, a surge of desire pulses through me remembering how good he felt with nothing between us. As I was walking out the door, Xavier came outside and pulled me in for one last kiss while his hand cupped my ass. Damnit, he should've known better, considering his recent arrest.

"They're shady like that. Hiding in bushes or vans just to get their next shot."

"You can't really see my face in these," I say, scrolling through the pictures.

My phone beeps, signaling my mother is calling me. I can't answer right now but decide to start making the short drive back to my parents' house.

"Keep looking."

My heartbeat increases. "They got my whole face?"

"*Si, tu rostro hermoso.*"

"Focus," I quip when he tells me I have a beautiful face. When the car rolls to a stop at the light, I peek at my phone again and keep scrolling. My stomach twists when my flushed face fills the screen.

"It's gonna be fine." I know he's trying to keep me calm but now isn't the moment. "Right now, you're new and shiny so they're interested. Once there's a new story for them, they'll let up."

"Do they know my name?" I make a left on my parents' street.

"Not yet. We can get with Alba, my publicist, and she can help tame the situation."

I sigh and park in the driveway, dropping my head on the

steering wheel. Once they figure out who I am, what happens then? Will they find my parents? My sisters? Will they show up at my law firm? Try to speak to my employees? My clients? Pretend to be a future client to gain access to me? Oh God! "A publicist? Everything will be different now, life as I've known it is over."

"*No digas eso, mami*. We're still us, and the media knowing about us won't change that."

My heart thunders in my chest. "Easier said than done, you're used to them." We knew this day was coming, and I've been dreading it. Now that it's here, I wish I were better prepared.

"I'll send Adrián to be with you. He can drive you tomorrow and when we're back from Vegas."

"What do I need him for?" Having him around all day will be so awkward. He barely talks and never smiles.

"To make sure you're okay. I know you're worried *y quiero asegurarme que estés bien*, at least for the time being." Him wanting Adrián with me means he's concerned for my safety.

"We can talk about that later. I'm at my parents' house and need to go inside."

"Hey, everything will be okay. *Llámame* when you leave your parents." His voice is so calm right now while my insides are flipping all over the place.

"Okay." I scan the mirrors to see if anyone is outside, but as I'm walking to the door the neighborhood is quiet, like every other time I've been here. The soft hum of the electric poles tickles my ears.

Before I'm even through the front door my mother yells, "*Nena, no me contestaste el teléfono cuando te llamé.*"

She always scolds me for not answering her call as if I don't call her back, or in this case, show up at the house. "Yeah, I was paying for groceries when you called."

"*¿Por qué no nos dijiste que tenés novio?*"

My heart is beating so loudly I feel the pulsating in my ears as she's asking me about my boyfriend. "*¿Qué?*" I'm not really sure what I want to say about the whole thing so I decide to play it off and see where she's headed.

"*¡No te hagas la tonta!* You know what I'm talking about." Her lips are tight as she waves her finger up at me.

My mother is about to give me a tongue lashing, but I want to know what she saw first. I drop the groceries on the table and turn to her. "No, really. I have no idea what you're talking about."

"*Tenés que saberlo porque* you're all they're talking about *en Chispa y Espectáculo.*" The Latin media made quick work of selling those pictures. Great! This is exactly the way I didn't need my mother to find out about us.

My fingers start rubbing circles on my right thigh. "What did you see?" I'm trying to be nonchalant but it's not my strong suit, especially when talking with my mother.

"*El personaje* they call *El Flaco Casanova. Te estaba toqueteando toda mientras te besaba.*"

I'm not sure if I'm more annoyed at her tone as she describes what she watched or that the paparazzi was hiding outside of his studio yesterday and landed us in this predicament. This is the same way she'd yell at me when I was in high school, after she didn't like an answer I had given her. She's already worked herself up and no matter what I say, it'll end the same way—me leaving angry.

"*¿Y no tenés nada que decir?*"

I have a lot to say, but I'd like to avoid a huge argument, if I can. If I tell her he's just a friend, she'll call me a floozy. And if I tell her we're serious, she'll call me that or worse because we were caught on camera making out. Doesn't matter what I say because she's already made up her mind and is judging me despite knowing only whatever they're reporting.

"We met a few a months ago and—"

"Months? And you never told us?" She huffs then looks at my

father while she repeats my words, as if he wasn't standing three feet away from us. The lines around her eyes crinkle as they dart between my father and me.

Because she can't see me, I roll my eyes. "No, I didn't, because I wasn't sure if we are serious but—"

"Not serious!" She quickly turns back to me and closes the space between us as she's waving her finger up at me. The soft skin on her cheeks hangs a bit looser than it used to but her words are as sharp as ever. "You're not serious *y andás zorreando como una cualquiera?*"

It's crazy how I'm forty-one and stand nearly a foot taller than my mother, but her words can still make me feel like the seven-year-old little girl that wanted to please her at every turn. I swallow the words on the tip of my tongue and take a deep breath. "Ma, I'm not doing this with you right now. Especially if you're going to keep insulting me."

"*Ay, nena, no digas pavadas*. I didn't insult you." She feigns being offended and her tone gets under my skin. I'm measuring my breaths to keep myself calm, but as her words slice me, it's proving ineffective. Her inability to recognize how she talks down to me is infuriating and one of the biggest issues I have with her. She's incapable of understanding how her words cut me.

My nostrils flare. "You basically told me I'm whoring myself around, but sure, you didn't insult me." My breaths are short as my heartbeat increases. "We can talk about this another time after you calm down. I'm gonna leave and—"

"*Nena, ni se te ocurra irte*," she commands, grabbing my wrist. Part of me knows that she's right, I shouldn't leave because it will only infuriate her more and then she'll be mad at me for an undetermined amount of time, making herself the victim for something she created while giving me the silent treatment. But rational me knows better, because if I stay, I'll start yelling, end up having an anxiety attack, and then I'll leave. Regardless of my choice, it always ends in us getting nowhere. With her, I always lose so much for the sake of protecting my mental health, I've started choosing the silent treatment.

"You're right, I shouldn't leave. But guess what, I'm old enough to do what I want. So this is me leaving." I grab my pockabook from the chair and stride toward the door.

"*¡Siempre faltando el respeto!* It's no wonder you allow a man like that to disrespect you!"

My jaw clenches. I'm torn between continuing out the door and turning around. But she knows how to push my buttons, and I fall for it every time. I whip around and face her. "What does that mean?"

Her cheeks are flaming red and her hands are on her hips. "You let him touch you like that for everyone to see, *solo las putas hacen eso*."

"Yes, Ma. I'm a whore. What can I say?" My heart hammers in my chest.

"*Aparte, se ve que no es un hombre decente. Si lo fuera,* he would sing real music, not that garbage he does!"

"Let me guess, a decent and good man, like Victor." I grind my teeth as anger seethes.

"Yes, just like him. You let him go and for what? *¿Para estar con un cualquiera? ¿Vos pensás que él te será fiel? ¡Ay, qué ingenua que sos*!" Her head shakes as her hands fall to her hips.

She's unlocking my biggest fear with Xavier—that, like Victor, he'll be unfaithful. After all, he's a megastar with women pining after him at every turn. I storm to the front and slam the door behind me. As I'm getting in my car, my father appears in the driveway.

"Roo, wait."

Tears stream down my face. "Papi, I'm sorry, I can't do this right now."

His arms widen as he approaches me. "Don't leave when you're upset."

"I have to." I put space between us. "I can't be here anymore."

"Your mom, she—"

"Stop making excuses for her!" I scream. It's not his fault, but when it comes to my mom, he's never stood up for any of us. Not me, not my sisters, and not himself. "I wish you'd defend me just once when she talks to me the way she does. You stand there and say nothing, let her belittle me and cut me with her words. I'm leaving. I'll see you when I get back from Vegas."

My hands are trembling as they grip the steering wheel, but I force myself to back out of the driveway. As soon as I turn the corner, I pull over and allow the tears to flow as I try to recompose myself.

My sister Micaela called me a few minutes ago, after my mother called her to complain about her tramp daughter being on TV with the reggaeton singer guy. I lie back on my bed and kick my shoes off, extending my legs.

"So who is this guy, and why haven't you shared anything about him with me?" Her tone is questioning, but she doesn't sound upset.

I wasn't ready to do all this with my family yet. "You've been traveling, and since he and I are still kinda new, I wasn't ready to. I'm sorry."

"You don't have to apologize. I get it, especially since you're recently divorced. How long have you been seeing each other?"

"A little over three months." Thinking back on our time together, it seems much longer than that, and I'm not sure when I shifted from barely wanting a friend with benefits to feeling a heavy warmth in my chest when I'm with him.

"He's your boyfriend then?"

I roll over on my side, pull the pillow he slept on a few nights ago to my nose, his woodsy scent still lingering in the pillowcase fibers. Yesterday was the first time we had sex without a condom, and he made it clear that if we took that step, there was no turning back. "We haven't used those identifiers, but I think so."

"Woman, you need to ask him!"

Does it matter what we call each other if we've chosen to be exclusive? "As long as he respects me, I don't care about labels."

"You might not, but his fans do." She's right. The media is already speculating about me, calling me everything from his latest hookup to his next fiancée. "Now that you've been outed, what's the plan?"

"I have no idea. Before all this went down, we planned a weekend in Vegas. We're going to a boxing match."

"Since when do you like boxing?"

"I don't, but his childhood friend is headlining the fight and Xavier's performing as his friend makes his entrance, so I said yes." What I'm not sharing is that the more time I spend with him, the more I want. I'm not sure what he did to break down the barriers I was building, but somehow, he managed it.

"When do you leave?" she asks.

"Friday morning."

"Wow, taking the day off from work and everything."

"You make me sound like a workaholic!" She's not wrong. She's been trying to convince me for years that I work too much, but I always brush her off.

"If the shoe fits."

"Yeah, yeah. I think you and Xavier would hit it off because, according to him, I work too much and we don't spend enough time together."

"I've been telling you to lighten your workload for years so I'm glad someone else is finally doing it too. Besides, if I were a dude, I'd want to spend more time with you too!" She cackles.

"Yeah, maybe, but we also see each other nearly every day of the week. I think we see each other plenty."

"But if you're working, it's not the same. You don't get the same quality time in. Not to mention, you never go anywhere."

"I don't have time. Work is busy."

"Exactly, you don't have time because you're letting it pass you by while you're working day in and day out."

Micaela has created a life where she can work from anywhere, and works around her travel schedule, not the other way around. She's a digital marketing guru and graphic designer, allowing her the flexibility to travel and explore the world whenever she wants. Although she calls Boston home, she's rarely there. I'm a little envious, if I'm being honest.

"I love my job, though," I say, more to convince myself.

"Just because you love what you do doesn't mean you should work as much as you do. We've talked about this so many times, you can do what you love while still doing more for yourself!"

She's right. After my separation from Victor, Micaela came to Miami to stay with me for several weeks. During that time period, we talked about what I wanted to do now that I had a new journey to set out on. Traveling was something I've always wanted to do more of but never made the time for. Once I snapped out of the funk I was in from my separation, I took to rebuilding the same law firm, just in a different location. What I should've done is pivot to a different area of law—one that will allow me to work remotely and not be tied to a court's calendar. Not to mention, one that is less stressful. I have a love-hate relationship with litigation. Although I love being a trial lawyer, it's also an extremely stressful job, in particular because the clients have a lot at stake, and they're relying on me to get through one of the most difficult stages of their lives. "You're right."

"My favorite words," she says, giggling.

"Yeah, yeah. Now that I've finally been divorced for four months, and that chapter has closed, maybe I can start thinking about transitioning away from litigation."

"I'm here for it, and ready to travel and explore whenever you are! Now, back to your Vegas trip. Any plans other than the fight?"

"Xavier hasn't mentioned much."

"Do you know anything about the trip?"

"Nope. Not even where we're staying. But knowing him, we'll be at some bougie hotel."

CHAPTER TWENTY-FOUR

Xavier

The feeds from my studio surveillance cameras cram my home computer screen. Paparazzi crowd the perimeter of the studio, scoping the area like hungry eagles. How long have they been camping out and how much longer will they be there? I have no desire to deal with any of them, so I'm working from home today.

Despite Rocky's protests, I sent Adrián to pick her up and spend the day with her. After our pictures were plastered everywhere, I asked him to be her detail until their thirst for information about her settles. They like to get into people's faces, and I want to make sure she'll be okay. If he's there as a buffer, maybe she'll freak out a little less about how intense they can be. Adrián will have to bring someone else from his team in to work with us so that she can have her own detail. Right now, he's the only one I trust with Rocky, and I would never forgive myself if something were to happen to her.

As I'm waiting for the coffee to finish brewing, my phone rings and Xiomary's picture pops up on the screen. *"Dímelo."*

"Hey, *chiqui*. I'm waiting to board my flight to LA, but real quick—Katia called and told me the contract for your performance in Vegas was never signed. Gaby's lawyer never sent it over."

Gaby lived next door to my grandmother. I had met him during my short visits to Puerto Rico as a kid, but we never had enough time to hang out longer than a few hours here and there. When my parents' death forced my move to the island, he was my first friend. We'd walk to school together and he introduced me to everyone in the neighborhood. Although I moved to Miami in my early twenties, we kept in touch as we each pursued our careers—him as a boxer and me as a *reggaetonero*.

"It's fine. I'm sure they'll get it over soon."

"It's Thursday, and you're performing on Saturday. I hate when these lawyers don't do their jobs. Will you call Gaby?"

"Why don't you just call the lawyer?"

"You think I didn't try that already?" She exhales loudly. "He hasn't responded to my calls, texts, or emails."

"Then call Lisandra. She'll get it done for you. Gaby is busy training for Saturday's fight." When Gaby was just starting out, Lisandra was already working as a boxing manager. She saw his potential early on and signed him as a client while he rose through the ranks. Lisandra and I met at one of Gaby's first fights after she started managing him.

"I didn't want to have to drag her into this, considering your history."

Xiomary loved Lisandra, and when Lisandra dropped me like a bad habit, Xiomary was furious with me, because Lisandra chose to cut her off too. Lisandra told her she needed a clean break from me and my world.

"I'm performing at her client's fight. She's already involved in this."

"I'll try. But if that doesn't work, then you have to call Gaby."

"Fine. Listen"—I grab the coffee pot and pour into my cup—"Roly said the marketing team for *Pulso Urbano* called him. Now that the tour merch is in production, they're interested in a partnership—maybe a capsule collection or something."

"Okay, I'll talk to Roly and get details. If it's something you're interested in, I'll reach out to their lawyer. They're about to call the flight, I'm gonna go."

"That's it? You're not gonna ask about the pictures that have surfaced? Ask about my girl?" There's no way Xiomary doesn't know about the pictures that have been posted everywhere.

"Of course I saw the pictures. Alba sent me an email with them. You already know I want to talk to you about them. About her."

That's the sister I know. "Always looking out, sis."

"They're calling my flight, we'll talk later?"

"Before you go, you wanna hear something crazy? I fired Victor yesterday because it turns out he's Rocky's ex-husband."

Xiomary is silent, her breaths all I can hear when she finally says, "What are the odds?"

"We can talk when you return. Will you be back before the gala?"

A few weeks ago

"What's the occasion?" I ask Rocky, while sliding a dish of sorullos de maíz *across the counter.*

Nikki and Alondra are swinging by my place to pick Rocky up because they're going dress shopping at the Aventura Mall. As

Rocky was getting into the shower, she mentioned being hungry so while she got ready, I made some sorullos.

"Nikki is receiving an award at the Federal Bar Association's annual gala." *She reaches for a cheese-filled corn fritter on the plate, still steaming hot. After grabbing a napkin to hold it, she bites into it, the crispy exterior flaking as the hot cheese oozes.*

"You flying solo to this gala?" *I reach for my water bottle and pull from it, but my eyes never stray from hers.*

She nods. "Yeah, that's what I had planned."

My jaw clenches and I swallow, pushing down the angry words sitting on the tip of my tongue. "Guess you don't need a date?"

Silence hangs as her eyes flit away from mine while she purses her lips. She takes a deep breath then lifts her gaze back to mine. "I'm sorry, I didn't even think about it, because I just assumed you wouldn't want to attend a legal thing."

Her indifference twists me up inside. "A legal thing, huh? Not a special event to honor your best friend?" *My attempt to keep my tone soft fails as my words are sharp, causing Rocky's eyes to widen as she crinkles her forehead.*

Her stance shifts from side to side as her fingers circle on her upper thigh. "Xavier." *She scurries around the counter and nudges me so that we're standing flush to one another.* "Truly, I hadn't thought about it." *She drops her head back, green eyes searching brown.* "I'm sorry. We learned about her award around the same time we met. I hadn't really thought about it since then."

I'm not sure I want to know the answer to the question I'm about to ask. "Would you rather go without me?"

"That's not what this is." *Her fingers grasp my hips and squeeze.*

I swallow the lump in my throat. "So, what is it?"

She shrugs. "Honestly, the event hadn't crossed my mind until *last week when we were planning our shopping day. Then I just assumed you wouldn't want to go, especially because I'm not really sure where we're headed."*

It's like she stuck a knife in me and she's twisting it to make the wound bigger. I swallow, wanting to mask the hurt and anger that's churning inside. "You're my girl, that's where we're headed."

She nods and whispers, "I know, and that scares the shit out of me."

At least she admits understanding what I'm feeling. "What are you scared of?"

"When I met you, I thought it was a one-time thing." Her voice trembles. "Feelings weren't part of the plan. In fact, I was dead set on completely avoiding them. But then when I saw you again, the pull I felt toward you was unavoidable. The more time we spend together, the more I want. Except I'm just waiting for the other shoe to drop."

My fingers seek out hers, threading them with one another. "It's like you're half in, half out, even though you admit having feelings. I don't get it. Are you ashamed of me or to be seen with me?" Nearly every time I suggest inviting her friends out with us, she says no, offering no explanation. The time I asked about her parents, she shut me down real quick and changed the subject. Seems I'm moving at a quicker pace than she is.

"Why would you think that?" she retorts, confusion spreading across her face. "I could never be ashamed of you!"

"Because you'd rather stay in than go out. And you still haven't taken me to meet your parents."

She swallows and takes a few deep breaths. "Remember when we talked about my ex-husband, how profoundly he hurt me, and how that scar impacts my decisions? I told you then that the unfortunate reality of having anything with me would be my reluctance to be more. It has everything to do with how deeply my trust was shattered, and my slow journey back toward building it up to a place where I can truly allow myself to fully let someone in. I don't mean to hurt you but I have to protect my heart. My emotions can't handle that level of heartbreak again. I just can't." A tear slides down her cheek.

As much as I want from her, I also need to understand how her asshole ex-husband broke her. It makes me want to find him and strangle him for the hurt he's caused.

My thumb swipes away the tear. "Lo sé." I lower my head, meeting her eye-to-eye. "I'll never hurt you the way he did. Eso es una promesa. *I know those are just words right now, and I have to earn your trust. You're the only one that knows when we get there. If you want to go to the gala with your friends, I will accept your decision, no questions asked.* Pero quiero que sepas, *I want nothing more than to be with you every day, whether we're watching TV or celebrating your best friend."*

Without hesitation, her hands shoot up to rest on my cheeks and her eyes glisten. "I want to be with you too. Please forgive me and come to the gala with me." My heart pounds, a heavy rhythm bursting from inside.

"Yeah, I get back the night before the gala," Xiomary says. "My firm gets a table every year, so I'll be there. Listen, they just called my flight again. We'll talk soon."

"*Dale.*"

With my coffee in hand, I meander to my office, grab my notebook off my desk, and sink into the couch along the sidewall. Like every room in my penthouse, my office has floor-to-ceiling windows, with this room only having a partial ocean view since its window faces north. Last week I was driving when inspiration hit, and I started working on a new song. Although I wrote an entire album that's dropping soon, I finished writing that album months ago and haven't written anything since. Feels good to have my creativity flowing again. I only wrote a few lines down and want to add a few new ones that've been brewing. I don't have a piano here so I grab the bongo drums from the shelf behind the desk and start rapping my fingers across the drumhead as I reread the words I've written so far.

La fama, the age difference *te llenan de doubt*
Inventas razones to keep us apart
You hold yourself back, *eres reacia*
Evitas y te mientes to protect your heart
Escondes tu deseo y creas angustia
Pero tu cuerpo te traiciona, begs for my touch
My fingers explore, *calmando tu ansia*

I tap the skin of the drum with the rhythm I hear for the words I've written, humming the tune as I imagine it coming to life. I grab the pencil and notate the words floating in my head before I lose them.

You let yourself feel
Te entregas con gracia
Your curves *me llaman,* creating a frenzy
Tu figura, tu piel, toda tu esencia
Overpower my senses, blinding me
No se controlarme, creando una frenesí
There was a time *que pensé* I'd never love again
Pero tu tacto y mirada me queman
Me caíste como un rayo
And I'm done flying solo

My phone rings, interrupting me. Alba's name appears. "*Dímelo.*" She tells me she's pulling up to the valet, and I call down to the security desk so they know to let her up. I scribble a few notes down so I don't forget what's in my head then close the notebook, grab my coffee cup, and walk to the kitchen. While waiting for her to reach the foyer, I shoot Adrián a text to check in on Rocky.

> **ADRIÁN**
> We're at her office. Paparazzi were outside her building this morning. We need to work on some enhanced security features for the office. She's good and working with her staff.

I want to see Rocky, gauge how she's handling the situation.

> **ME**
> Tell her to call me if she can. Bring her here when she's done.

The elevator dings, signaling Alba's arrival. She struts out of the elevator wearing her signature charcoal gray skirt suit, her dark hair cascading down her back. Every time I've seen Alba, she's always in a dark colored skirt suit with a vibrant blouse—today, it's fire engine red.

"Hi, Alba." I lean in, our cheeks meeting for a quick hello.

Alba and my sister met in law school and became fast friends. After law school, Alba worked for a cutthroat entertainment PR firm in LA for several years before opening up *Poderosa* Media. She's earned the respect of numerous big name Latin artists and is now one of the most sought-after publicists.

"Always keeping me busy. First you get arrested and now you got a girl. What else?" She drops her bag on the table in the center of the great room then continues to the window.

A low chuckle escapes me. "I'm sure I can come up with something."

"Tell me everything about her. Why isn't she here to meet me so I can assess her for myself?"

"She's working. She's a lawyer, works for herself, and—"

"What kind of law?"

"She's a divorce lawyer."

"Is she married?"

My eyes widen. "Uh, no. Why the fuck would I date a married woman?"

She's still as she stares at me with dead pan eyes. "Don't sound so shocked, it happens every day. Does she have kids?"

I shake my head. "No, but she is divorced."

"What's her ex-husband's name?"

I'm still in shock that Victor is the lawyer Xiomary hired. With all the lawyers in Miami, why'd it have to be him? "It's that asshole Xiomary hired as my criminal lawyer. I fired him, so you can add that to your list, too."

She shakes her head. "How old is she?"

"Forty-one."

"Anything I need to know about her?"

"Yeah, she's fucking amazing and I don't want this media hype about my girl to ruin it for me."

Her face is stoic but then her lip curls up. "Hope she has thick skin."

Several hours later, I'm getting out of the shower when I hear Rocky's voice. I throw on a gray tank top and black pants and follow her voice until she appears. My eyes trace her curvy lines as she paces barefoot the length of the glass in the great room. Her curls are unruly today as they poke out in different directions all around her head. She's gorgeous and she's all mine. When she pivots and our eyes connect, her smile stretches across her face while she lifts her hand, one finger outstretched. I nod, acknowledging her request.

A few minutes later, she puts her phone on the ledge of the couch and strides across the room to meet me. Her hands grasp my face and her lips crash with mine. She pulls me flush to her and drapes her arms on my shoulders, my cock hardening inside my pants. Her kisses are desperate as her fingers press into my back. "I missed you," she says, her breaths short.

"*Así me siento yo* every time I'm not with you. Welcome to the club." My lips peck her cheek, grab her hand, and tug her toward the kitchen. "I've been waiting for you *para comer*."

"What's on the menu?"

"*Pollo guisao*." I turn the knob on the stove to warm up the stewed chicken I finished making a little while ago.

"Another one of your *abuela*'s dishes?"

I nod. "*Siempre*. Everything I know how to make is because I learned it with her."

As we're sitting at the counter with our dishes, she says, "Today was crazy. When we pulled up to my office, there were dozens of people outside, some of them set up with their cameras like when they're reporting on important things."

Nodding, I respond, "*Son exagerados*. The paparazzi are always extra in their pursuit of the perfect picture."

She pushes the rice around on her plate. "I haven't said a word to them, and they know my entire life history—where I grew up, the schools I attended, my majors in college, and about my divorce. Victor made an appearance, too, when they flashed a picture of him as they reported on my divorce. Somehow, that asshole always pops up. They even found pictures from my old social media posts. Thank god I never posted much."

"*Mami*—"

"Listen to the headlines they're writing." She grabs her phone. "Have you read them?"

"No, I don't read any of the stuff they publish, and you shouldn't either."

"Since you haven't read them, let me share. 'Is *El Flaco Casanova* Ready for a 'Real' Woman?' and 'Rocío Fontana, the Cougar that Captured *El Flaco Casanova*!'" She shifts in her seat. "You'll like this one. '*De Niño a Hombre*: *El Flaco Casanova* Finds Love with a Woman 10 Years His Senior!' And my favorite of the bunch, 'Cradle Robber? Social Media Reacts to *El Flaco Casanova*'s New 41-Year-Old Girlfriend.'" Sarcasm drips from every word.

"*Mami*, you shouldn't read anything they write." I stretch my hand across the counter and thread my fingers with hers. "They don't know you, or us. Let them say whatever they want."

"How am I supposed to ignore all this?" She places her phone onto the counter as her shoulders drop.

"*Es difícil*, I know, but you gotta try because none of it matters. *Lo único que importa* is what's happening here"—my hand gestures between the two of us—"*tú y yo*, nobody else."

She sighs. "Well, when you say it like that." She pulls her lip between her teeth. "You and me. I think I can handle that."

"You'll get used to it. Just remember that the people who are writing these things have never met you and they have no idea what they're talking about. They don't care about us. They only care about making money. That's why you need to ignore all of it." I know what I'm telling her is easier said than done. My first couple years in the limelight had their fair share of headlines, and I would read everything that was posted about me. But Roly finally convinced me to stop for my own benefit.

She's shaking her head. "Okay, I'll do my best."

"*Recuérdate, tú y yo*. Nobody else."

"You and me." She tilts her head and gently kisses me.

"Ready for Vegas?" I want to tell her that Lisandra will be there so there are no surprises. Although she's texted me a few times since I've gotten clean, we've not seen each other. I'm a little nervous for her and Rocky to be in the same room because Lisandra's text messages have hinted at getting back with me. I haven't confronted Lisandra, giving her the benefit of the doubt. Maybe I was reading into her texts too much. Regardless, that ship sailed. Rocky's my girl now.

"Yeah, I'm actually excited to see the boxing match."

"It's a good time, even if the fighting gets intense."

"Have you been to a lot fights?"

I nod as I finish chewing. "Yeah, with my ex-fiancée, Lisandra. She's a boxing manager for a lot of the well-known boxers."

"That's a pretty cool job for a woman."

I shrug. "Gaby is one of her clients, so she's gonna be in Vegas."

She stiffens. "Oh." The word barely a whisper.

"I'm telling you because we're gonna run into her, and I don't want any surprises."

Rocky swipes the napkin across her lips. "What does 'run into her' mean?"

"She'll be at both events, so we'll see her."

She pushes her hair behind her ears. "Okay. Thank you for telling me."

My eyes remain locked with hers, searching for any signs of hesitancy, but they're warm and soft.

"What's the plan for Vegas and the paparazzi?"

"No plan. We just roll with it." I scoop some rice into my mouth.

"What's that mean? Do we just go about our lives as if they don't exist?"

Nodding, I respond, "Yeah. At the Vegas events they'll have plenty of opportunity to photograph us."

"Are there red carpets or anything like that?"

My head shakes. "Yeah, more so for the Friday night preshow celebration since it's to promote the fight. On Saturday, we'll get to the venue early and probably enter through a private entrance."

She shifts her seat. "So, we're making our debut." Her lips curl upward.

"Yeah." I scoot closer to her. "We let the world know we're together. *Que eres mía.*"

CHAPTER TWENTY-FIVE

Rocío

ADRIÁN PARKS the car at the foot of the boarding stairs leading up to Xavier's private jet. There are a handful of smaller jets scattered across the small Opa Locka airport. It's quiet and secluded, a stark difference from Miami International Airport. This seems so far out of my league, yet here I am. Never in a million years would I have imagined I'd fly privately, but Alondra's reminders that I deserve this as much as anyone else are tucked away in the recesses of my thoughts.

I stare up at the six steps before me while my hand grips the handrail. "This is so surreal," I whisper to Alondra on my right.

Her head shakes a quick no. "Nah, chica. This is your life." She heads up toward the entrance.

"*¿Todo bien, mami?*" Xavier sidles up behind me, his fingers spread across my lower back.

I peek back at him and nod. "Yeah, more than okay."

Inside the plane is luxurious—cream-colored plush leather seats, a long sofa along one side, and across the aisle is a high gloss mahogany table and chairs.

"You ladies can sit anywhere," Xavier says as he goes around me and drops his things on the second chair to my right.

"Hello, Mr. Delgado. It's nice to see you again," the flight attendant says, then turns to me and Alondra. "Ms. Fontana, Ms. de Cardenas, welcome aboard. My name is Sonja and I'll be taking care of you during the flight." She slips past us and toward the back of the jet.

"Where do you want to sit?" I ask Alondra. My eyes dart around the jet. There's a single captain's chair across the aisle from the one Xavier chose. A long couch stretches behind the chair right in front of me, directly across from a large TV screen behind Xavier's seat. Behind the couch is a table with four captain's chairs, followed by one more row of single chairs and a door that the flight attendant just walked through.

"You sit up here with him, I'll go back to the table. This way I can get some work done during the flight and be done with it."

"Okay, that works. Let me know when you're done and then I'll join you." When we planned the trip, Alondra said she could join but would likely need to work while in flight because she had a few deadlines this week.

"We should be airborne soon," Adrián says to Xavier, then slips past us.

"Does that man ever smile?" Alondra whispers as she watches him pass by.

My head shakes. "Not that I've seen, but then again, he's always working when I see him." I shrug.

I dig through my bag, searching for the small pouch with my lavender oil. Dr. Pérez recommended I take prescribed medication, but I was hesitant to try strong meds. We've been trying lavender oil as a way to help calm my nerves, but this is the first time trying it for a flight.

"You good?" Xavier asks, grasping my hips as he stands before me.

My head bobs up and down. "I will be once this kicks in." I flash the contents of the open pouch.

"Flying private isn't like flying commercial. Hopefully you'll be more relaxed *ya que estarás más cómoda.*"

As if the comfort of flying is what makes me anxious and not soaring through the air at high speeds with zero control. "I'm pretty sure it's flying in general that I hate."

His lips graze my cheek and his hands tighten at my hips. "*Bueno, cualquier cosa,* I'm here."

I apply the lavender oil to my pulse points and then deeply inhale its aroma.

As the plane taxis, I tighten the seatbelt across my waist. When my stomach alerts me the plane is ascending, my hands grip the armrest to the point my fingers turn white. Xavier's hand stretches across the aisle and covers my hand with his large fingers. "It's okay, *mami. Respira.*"

I've been measuring my breath to keep myself relaxed and my eyes skirt to his, giving him a half smile that doesn't reach my eyes. Once we reach cruising altitude, my body should relax so long as there isn't any turbulence. I rest my head and close my eyes, wishing for sleep to take over, even for a short while.

When I open my eyes, I glance over to Xavier's seat, but it's empty. Turning in my seat, I see him sitting with Alondra at the tables. I stretch and then make my way toward them.

"Hey, gonna use the bathroom then I'll join you."

"Sleep well?" Alondra asks.

"Almost forgot where I was," I respond, my head bobbing up and down. I turn toward the back. As I'm opening the door, Xavier's arm wraps around me. "*¿Todo bien?*" His lips fall on my temple.

"All good." I nod.

"If you're hungry, Sonja can get you something to eat when you're done."

"Thanks." I slip into the bathroom.

Back at the table, Alondra is looking at her phone, and Xavier and Adrián are standing near the front by his seat. "Hey," I say, as I slide into the seat across from Alondra. "Did you get all your work done?"

She places her phone face down onto the table. "Yep. Officially off for the weekend."

"Sweet. How long did I sleep for?" My fingers reach for my wrist, but I didn't wear my watch today.

"About two hours."

"Still about three hours left till we get there. Wish I would've slept longer."

Her eyes flit away then meet mine again, and she whispers, "Girl, you're in trouble with that man."

Did something happen while I was sleeping? "Why, what happened?"

"Nothing. But the way his eyes light up when he talks about you. He was asking about when we met, our friendship, what we like to do. Basically, getting to know you through me."

My belly stirs and I smirk. "I agree, I'm in so much trouble. I find myself missing him when we're not together. I really don't know how it happened. I went from telling him we could be friends with benefits to this"—my right hand makes circles in the air—"whatever this is."

"Doesn't matter." Her hands reach across the table, grasping my left hand between hers. "You're the happiest I've seen you in a long time. That alone makes me love him for you."

"Let's see how it goes in Vegas at this event with the paparazzi salivating." I'm still nervous about the situation, but talking with Xavier yesterday helped to take the edge off.

"It's Vegas. Let's just have fun." Her eyes skirt away from me and up to somewhere behind me.

"That should be easy."

"Yeah." Although she responds, she's still not looking at me.

"Did you eat something?" I ask.

"Yeah."

I shift in my seat, intrigued by what has her so entranced and then turn back to her. "What are you looking at?"

"What?"

"What are you looking at? It's like you're far away."

Her eyes meet mine again, and she slides forward in her seat. "He finally smiled," she whispers.

"Who?"

"Adrián."

"Why are you so concerned whether he smiles or not?"

"He's cute. Even more when he smiles. It makes me want to see more. Is he single?"

"Don't know." My shoulders lift. "But happy to ask Xavier, if you want me to."

She smirks. "Nah, I'll ask him myself this weekend."

Tonight is the pre-fight celebration at *El Cabo Rojo* Restaurant and Lounge on the Vegas Strip that's being hosted by the fight's promoter. Outside the venue, a jumbotron reads, "Welcome Heavyweight Champion Gabriel '*El Huracàn*' Nieves to Las Vegas," a picture of the dark-skinned boxer with braids to the left, his glove-covered hands lifted.

"Wow, there's a lot of people here," Alondra says, glancing out the window as our SUV rolls to a stop. There are barriers to each side of the door creating a walkway. Behind the metal dividers are throngs of people with phones in their hands.

"Holy shit." Xavier said there would be a lot of people, but this is not what I envisioned. Adrián and the other security guy with him are already outside surveying the area. We're waiting for them to give us the okay to get out and make our way inside.

"This is it, *mami*." Xavier's lips graze my cheek.

The knots in my stomach twist and tighten. "You saying that makes me more nervous."

"Don't be nervous." He nudges my chin to draw my eyes to his. "*Tú y yo*, nobody else." He gently swipes his lips across mine.

You got this, I remind myself as Adrián opens the door to piercing screams. Xavier hops out then extends his arm. With my hand in his, I step out, my Doc Martens hitting the red carpet. Xavier's hand envelops mine, tightening as we walk toward the entrance. Alondra is to my left, while Adrián and the other security guard flank us.

High-pitched cries calling out Xavier's name hurl in from every angle, asking him to stop for a picture and telling him they love him. My heart thunders in my chest as the butterflies swirl in my belly. When we reach the middle point, there are professional photographers waiting for us, with some of them calling for us. "*Flaco*! Rocío! Over here!"

This morning, Alondra and I went to a boutique to get our outfits for the event tonight. I chose a metallic bronze jersey wrap dress that emphasizes my waist and creates a beautiful v-neckline. I paired it with a sharp-shouldered black blazer that's draped over my shoulders. My curls are loose and have a bit of extra volume. Alondra went with a black leather pencil skirt that hits just below her knee, paired with a sheer, high-neck mesh bodysuit over a black lace bra. She paired it with an oversized floor-length duster coat that's ruby red, black ankle boots, and chunky gold hoop earrings.

Xavier stops and drapes his arm behind me as we pose for the pictures. In typical Xavier fashion, he's sporting an all-black suit that's fitted with a black t-shirt underneath, his eagle tattoo peeking out at the top. The shutters of the cameras click in rapid fire. I gesture for Alondra because I want a picture with her as well and she joins us, with me in between her and Xavier.

Inside the venue, we trade the loud screams of fans for the pulsing reggaeton beats. Xavier halts and turns to me. "You look beautiful, *mami*. You okay?"

I nod. "Yeah. That wasn't as bad as I imagined." Last night, I barely slept as my thoughts churned in overtime, creating scenarios of what I thought this moment would look like. People yelling at me and insulting me, or worse, throwing things at me while accusing me of stealing their superstar.

He grins. "That's what I was waiting to hear." His eyes shift to Alondra. "You good?"

She nods. "Yeah. This place is incredible." Her eyes shoot up and scan the high ceilings of the multi-level venue.

"It is. Now wait until the party starts. It's gonna get crazy."

"Is this where you're performing?" Alondra asks.

"No. That's tomorrow night at the arena." His smiles reaches his eyes. "Before the emcee introduces Gaby, I'll come out and start singing. Then about halfway through the song they'll introduce him and I'll finish the song as he enters the venue."

"I had no idea they did stuff like this for boxing," I add.

"Yeah, it's all about the hype," he responds.

We enter a roped-off area and drop our things at a table reserved for us before heading to the bar to get drinks. Xavier stays behind, talking to a group of people.

"Two Hendricks and soda, please," I tell the bartender.

As we're waiting for the drinks, Alondra asks, "Who's that?"

My head turns to see a tall woman with dark tight curls. He leans to give her cheek a kiss then shoves his hands in his pockets. When she shifts, I recognize her from the many pictures online. "It's his ex-fiancée, Lisandra." Jealousy churns as I watch them talk to one another. Does Lisandra still have feelings for him? Does she want to get back together? She left him at his darkest moment but now he's back on his game.

"Her outfit is fire!" Alondra comments. She's wearing silver metallic pants, a black corset top, and black blazer with quarter sleeves and leather booties.

"It really is. She's gorgeous." She has tattoos on each of her arms, and her neck, although from here, I can't tell what they are.

Alondra's hand reaches for mine and she nudges me. "Hey, don't do that."

"What?" I say, meeting her eyes.

"That thing where you get in your head and create a whole scenario of what's happening over there."

"It's hard not to. We're surrounded by women that would give anything to be with him. And that gorgeous, bad ass woman was supposed to be his wife." I was never this insecure about myself and relationships, and I hate that this is what I've become after Victor betrayed me the way he did.

"Stop. She's not his wife and he's here with you, my gorgeous, badass friend." I love Alondra for always keeping it real with me.

"Your drinks," the bartender says, placing them on the bar top.

"Come on," Alondra says, and strides toward Xavier and Lisandra.

"Here goes nothing," I mumble under my breath.

As I approach the small group, Xavier spots me, then threads his right hand with my left. "Lisandra, this is Rocío. Rocky, this is Lisandra."

"Pleased to meet you, Lisandra." My hand juts out to meet hers. Her grip is firm, and she pulls me in, giving me a cheek-to-cheek kiss. From here, I notice the tattoo in the middle of her neck is a sun, and below it to the left is the word *invicta*. On her right arm, there is a flower and barbed wire wrapping around her wrist and up her forearm.

"*El placer es mío.*" Her hand holds mine a bit longer than necessary and her dark eyes remain steady.

I break the awkward silence and tug my hand back. "This is my friend, Alondra."

"Hi, nice meeting you," Alondra says, after giving her a cheek kiss.

"I was telling Xavier that when we announced he would be performing during Gaby's entrance, the fans went wild. The fight is sold out but resale ticket values doubled."

My eyes shift to his, and his cheeks are flush. "That's incredible."

"Anyway, I have to keep making my rounds before Gaby gets here. It was nice meeting you. Enjoy the party." She slips into the crowd behind her, the small group she was with following suit.

Alondra separates from me and meanders over to Adrián, who's standing to the side of the seating area.

"She's beautiful," I say to Xavier.

He shakes his head and leans into me. "Don't do that."

"What? Tell you she's a beautiful woman?"

"She is, but that's not why you're saying it." His fingers graze my chin and guide my eyes to his. "*Tú y yo. No importa quién sea*, that doesn't change." He drops a light kiss on my lips. His reminder that it's just him and me no matter what stirs something inside of me. I hate myself for feeling insecure, especially because he hasn't given me a reason to feel this way.

The venue for the boxing match is loud as people begin filling their seats. The ring is set up right across from where Alondra and I are sitting. Xavier will join us after he performs tonight. He told us he'll come out from the same walkway that Gaby is exiting from, except Xavier will walk out alone singing and then Gaby will join him while Xavier finishes, both of them ending at the ring.

"I'm gonna run to the bathroom real quick," Alondra tells me.

I grab my phone and as I'm unlocking it, I feel a hand on my arm.

"Hi, Rocío. It's Lisandra, we met yesterday."

My head snaps up, and my eyes meet hers as she gives me a soft smile then leans in, our cheeks meeting.

My stomach twists. "Hi, Lisandra. Of course I remember you." Ugh, why did I say it like that? Did I sound snarky?

"Have you been to fight night before?"

My head shakes. "No, it's my first."

"They're high energy and a lot of fun. Hopefully it won't be your last."

"I'm actually excited for it. Apparently it's a big deal." When Xavier told me we'd be attending this boxing match, I did a deep dive online to try and learn about boxers and the sport. Gaby is defending his title tonight and they're streaming this live.

"Quite a big deal. Gaby's been training months for this particular fight. His opponent has been on a winning streak. The stakes are high."

"You being a manager for fighters like this is pretty badass." Will she think I'm weird that I'm basically fangirling over her?

She chuckles. "It has its days. My father was a well-known fighter, so it felt like the right career for me."

I catch a glimpse of Alondra approaching us and relief floods me. Small talk isn't my strong suit.

"Anyway, I saw you and wanted to come say hello." Her hand grips my upper arm and she leans in. "Xavier's a great guy, it's good to see him happy again." She gives me a crooked smile that doesn't meet her eyes, then slips into the crowd.

"Were you just talking to Lisandra?"

I nod. "Yeah. She popped up outta nowhere."

"What did she say?"

"Small talk about the fight tonight and her being a manager. But then, as she was leaving, she grabbed my arm and quietly told me that Xavier's a great guy and that it's good to see him happy again. It was weird, and wicked random."

"She's probably just being friendly. I wouldn't worry about it."

My eyes widen as I smirk. "Sure, being friendly. The divorce lawyer in me thinks otherwise. Or maybe it's the new jaded version of me after my ex-husband fucked half of Miami."

"Girl, Xavier is not Victor."

"I know."

"Doesn't sound like you know," Alondra quips.

My body shifts toward Alondra, and my hands wrap around her wrists. "I don't know what's wrong with me. I suppose her being drop dead gorgeous has nothing to do with it."

"You better go see Dr. Pérez when we get home and work on that. Jealousy looks ugly on you woman!"

"I hate Victor for making me so insecure about myself. I thought I had worked through it all, but apparently I still have homework to do."

She wraps an arm around me and pulls me to her, our heads leaning into one another. "You'll get there. Just make sure you don't punish Xavier for Victor's indiscretions."

The lights dim and the crowd roars. Guitar riffs and drum beats stream throughout the arena and the spotlight beams down to the end of the walkway where Xavier will exit from. The crowd chants "*Flaco*," knowing he'll make an appearance soon.

Xavier emerges from the black curtain, his sultry voice filling the arena. He's wearing black pants, a white t-shirt, and a black jacket, his signature bandana wrapped around his left wrist peeking out. He wore a thick, white gold, blinged out chain with a cross on it, white sneakers, and a baseball cap turned back and to the side.

"Tengo vibras de fuego
But what do they know
De esta vida that's flipped
Like a motherfucking tornado. "

He continues singing, and I glance at the crowd entranced by him as they sing along with each of his lyrics. Loyal fans of a man who brings their culture to them by way of urban Latino hip-hop. This entire arena loves *El Flaco Casanova*, the reggaeton artist they adore for the edgy street lyrics he raps in Spanglish that flows *como el Río de la Plata*. But to me, he's Xavier, the sexy man who is vulnerable behind closed doors and talks dirty between the sheets but is a perfect gentleman when we're in public. He's practically a walking contradiction.

Xavier turns, and the beat of the music increases. The entire venue goes dark except the spotlight shining down where Gaby will exit.

The emcee's voice fills the space. "Ladies and gentlemen, the reigning, defending, undisputed heavyweight champion of the world, Gaby '*El Huracán*' Nieves."

The black curtain pulls back, and Gaby appears in the spotlight to a roaring crowd. The beats of Xavier's music fill the arena as Gaby greets the fans he passes as he descends the walkway. When he nears Xavier, they hug each other, then turn toward the center of the arena. Xavier brings the microphone back up.

"Cero miedo en la mirada
Focus in my eyes
Desde el barrio vengo luchando
I've felt all the highs and lows
Pero hoy I'm at the top of my game
No hay quien me baje

I'm the king of the ring
En esto soy salvaje."

Cheers erupt at the last lyric as they approach the ring. Gaby removes his hood, exposing his braided hair and neatly trimmed beard. His robe is red with blue and white accents. The back reads "*El Huracán*" with a Puerto Rican flag below it.

Gaby gets into the ring, and Xavier finds the seat next to me. "That was incredible," I tell him.

"Thanks, *mami*." He kisses me, then wraps my hand in his tightening grip.

CHAPTER TWENTY-SIX

Xavier

OUR FLIGHT from Vegas landed early afternoon, and I asked Rocky to come back to my place. Although we spent time together in Vegas, Alondra was there, too, so I didn't get her all to myself. Right now, she's in the shower and I'm stretched out on the couch texting with Alba.

> **ALBA**
> What do I need to know about the pictures of you and Lisandra?

Of course the cameras were snapping away when we were saying hello. One of the pictures Alba sent me is of me leaning in to give her a cheek kiss.

> **ME**
> Nothing. I was just saying hi to her since she'd come over to us.

> **ALBA**
> Did you see the picture of her smiling? She looks mighty happy to be with you.

Vegas was the first time I've seen Lisandra since she walked away when I chose my Percocet highs over her. When I finally got clean, I wanted to reach out to her and apologize for my selfish behavior, but she was in a relationship at the time and I decided against it. Vegas wasn't the time for it either. At this point, I'm not sure it'll ever happen.

> **ME**
> That may be true, but it has nothing to do with anything I said or did.

> **ALBA**
> Have you read what they're saying about you two?

Once Lisandra came to say hello, her intentions were written all over her face, at least to me. The way her eyes searched mine and her body was in close proximity, it was clear she was looking for an angle to work her way back in with me.

> **ME**
> You know I don't read any of that shit.

> **ALBA**
> I know. You've told me you're a one-woman kind of guy, but it's my job to ask.

> **ME**
> We good.

> **ALBA**
> Check out these pictures of you and Rocky.

She sends me a dozen photos or so from when we paused on

the red carpet to pose. That dress she wore made her look more beautiful than she is. It accentuated her curves and made her tits look amazing.

ME
Thanks for sending these. Rocky's gonna love them.

ALBA
When am I meeting her?

ME
Soon.

ALBA
Not soon enough.

"You look so comfy on the couch," Rocky says as she strolls into the family room wearing one of my t-shirts, her thick thighs on full display making my dick twitch.

My hand pats the gray fabric. "I'll be more comfortable when you're lying next to me."

"Alondra texted me asking if I saw the headlines today." She settles into the couch on my left and rests her head on my chest.

I gather her curls and pull them to the side. "I hope you told her no, and that you won't be looking."

"I know I shouldn't read them, but man, these fuckers don't stop. Although I did see they reported your criminal charges were finally dropped."

A few days ago, my new criminal defense attorney gave me the news that the State Attorney would be dropping the charges against me. The attorney thought that they'd be pursuing charges against Axel, but my lawyer wasn't sure. I wanted to reach out to Axel, but the lawyers instructed me not to speak with him while this criminal stuff was still pending. "Yeah, the State got their shit together and did the right thing."

"At least the reporting on that was accurate. Wish the same could be true for the rest of it."

During my early years of fame, the media splattered me all over the headlines with whatever they could find. I would spend time scouring the web searching for everything they published about me. Maybe it was the newfound fame that made me do it, but it got old quick when I read the way they'd twist a truth to profit from it. "That's why I told you not to read any of it."

"Ugh, I know. I'm my own worst enemy. But there's pictures of you and Lisandra talking when you said hello to each other. So, of course, you already know the types of headlines they wrote."

Their headlines are always misleading, the sole purpose being to get more clicks. When I was living the Percocet life, they loved trashing me and talking about how far I'd fallen since the days of having platinum records.

"I can imagine, but we know that whatever they wrote is bullshit, so don't waste your time." My fingers squeeze her leg.

"How do I reach your level of 'I don't give a fuck'?"

My shoulders rise. "One day it'll just hit you." I had stopped caring long before I succumbed to drugs, after Roly shared stories of his other artists allowing the media to control them. I wanted to be different. But once I got clean and got my shit together, I felt stronger. The world had a front row seat to my epic failure and they'd written and said everything they could. There's nothing they can write worse than what I've already been through.

"Great, I also have to be patient. Another thing I'm terrible at." She laughs under her breath.

"*Mami*, look." I grab my phone and unlock it, search for the pictures of us on the red carpet that Alba sent me. "Look at how stunning you look." I hand her my phone.

"We look good." She bites her lip.

"Damn straight we do. Alba just sent these to me. Scroll, there are a few more."

"This one with Alondra came out cute!" She lifts my phone to show me which one she's referencing. "I'm gonna send it to myself so I can text it to her."

"See, these are the types of pictures you should be looking at online. Not the other shit they post about."

In that moment, a text message from Lisandra appears. Fuck, what bad timing.

> **LISANDRA**
> This is why you're one of the good ones 😊

Rocky stiffens when the message window appears. I take the phone from her, drop it on the couch and then shift toward her.

Her nostrils flare. "Have you been talking with Lisandra?" She jumps to her feet.

My head shakes. "Well, yeah. But no." My hand reaches for her, but she swats it away.

"Which is it? Because it can't be both!" The rise and fall of her chest tells me she's trying to keep herself calm.

I grab my phone, punch in the code and hand it to her. "Here, read it for yourself."

Her lip curls, and she snatches the phone from me.

> **LISANDRA**
> It was SO good seeing you in Vegas this weekend. Wish we could've had more time to talk. We have a lot of unfinished business 😉

> **ME**
> It was good to see you too.

> **LISANDRA**
> I'll be in Miami in a couple weeks, maybe we can meet up?

> **ME**
> That's not possible. I'll always respect you, but Rocky's my girl now and you know I'm a one-girl type of guy.

> **LISANDRA**
> I knew you'd say that, even if I wish you hadn't.
> 💔 Can't blame a girl for trying.
> This is why you're one of the good ones 😊

Her eyes lift to meet mine. "That's it?"

"*No tengo nada que esconder.*" She already knows I have nothing to hide, but it's worth repeating given the circumstances. I close the space between us, grasp the generous skin at her hips, and drop my forehead to connect with hers. "*Tú y yo*, nobody else."

"I hate that I feel this way," she mumbles. "I'm sorry."

"It's okay." I cup my hands around her face and suck on her bottom lip. "I promise I'll never be unfaithful to you."

She blinks rapidly in tune with her quick breaths.

My eyes remain steady on hers as my heart rate rapidly increases. "For as long as I can remember, my father cheated on my mother." My hands search for hers, threading our fingers. "I hated listening to her cry herself to sleep almost every night while my father was out *mujereando por ahí*. As a young kid, I didn't really understand why he was barely home, and she never told me. She'd cover for him and would tell me she's crying because she didn't feel well. But after my mother's death, her friends would share stories about my parents, and how my father was a well-known womanizer *en el barrio*. I already hated him for causing my mother's death, and that made me hate him more."

Her shoulders soften. "That must've been hard."

"Yeah. When I found out, I made a promise to my mother and myself that I'd never be anything like him, and I'd never be the reason a woman felt what my mother did." I rest my forehead against hers.

"I believe you." She drapes her arms over my shoulders. "It's gonna sound cliché, but me feeling this way has nothing to do with you. I was never like this until I caught my ex-husband fucking around. He screwed with my head so bad." She shrugs. "I guess I just need to keep working on it."

"You'll get there. In the meantime, I'm here." My thumbs drag across her cheeks and she lifts her chin, brushing her lips with mine.

She pulls my bottom lip between hers and sucks as she slides her hands under my shirt. My skin burns beneath her touch and heat spreads when she lifts the fabric up and off. Her lips drag along the outlines of my eagle tattoo. "You're so fucking beautiful," she whispers. My heart hammers in my chest as she explores. She pushes my pants down, my stiff cock springing free, and she grasps it with both hands. "*Tengo gana de vos.*"

My fingers tug the hem of her shirt. "*Mami, quiero verte desnuda.*"

"If you want me naked, you're gonna have to do something about it." Her sultry voice pulses through me. I remove her shirt, letting her heavy breasts fall, and push her underwear down. Her skin is soft and supple and warm beneath my touch.

I allow myself to fall back on the couch and start stroking myself. I'm hard as a rock and need to feel her. All of her. "*Tráeme ese toto, mami, que te voy a dejar temblando.*"

She strides across the room until she's standing before me, pushing her tits together as she licks her lips. "Now what?"

"*Móntate encima y haz que esa chocha me lo exprima completo.*"

She straddles me and then grabs my dick in her hands, positioning me at her entrance, then impales me. Her eyes roll back as I fill her, and she adjusts herself. "Ah, you're so fucking hard."

"That's it, *mami*. Ride me *pa que te vengas todita pa mi.*" I grab her breasts, one in each hand. While I suck and swirl on her left nipple, my free hand squeezes the right one and she squirms as she rolls her hips. "*Eso mami, dame cintura.*" Her pace increases as I encourage her.

She throws her head back and screams, "I'll give you whatever you want."

My hands cup the globes of her ass, guiding her up and down as I glide in and out of her. With each stroke of my cock, I give myself to her a little bit more.

"God, Xavier, I love feeling you like this." She moans, pushing me over the edge, and I empty myself inside of her.

CHAPTER TWENTY-SEVEN

Rocío

THE GALA TO honor Nikki is tonight. Rather than getting ready at my place and having Xavier pick me up, I brought my things over to Xavier's penthouse for us to get ready together. After snapping the front of the bra and adjusting my ladies into place, I step into my dress. "Can you help me zip up?" I ask Xavier, pulling up the straps of the dark gray trumpet-style dress. When Nikki, Alondra, and I went shopping a few weeks ago for dresses, the glimmer of this dress caught my eye. As soon as I tried it on, I knew it was the one because it's not often that a full-length dress falls past my ankles, dusting my foot's dorsum.

Nikki is being honored with the Scales of Liberty award tonight. As a federal public defender, she is a member of the Federal Bar Association for the Southern District of Florida. Each year, the organization hosts a gala at the Intercontinental Hotel next to Bayfront Park to honor outstanding lawyers, with the criminal defense section honoring an attorney dedicated to upholding the Constitution. Nikki has always been an advocate, fighting for the rights of those facing criminal charges and severe criminal sentences. Even before we graduated from law school, she knew she wanted to be a public defender. She became certified as a legal intern during law school to be able to work on cases during our last year of law school. There was no other path for her, and she's never thought about working anywhere else. Receiving this award is fitting, because Nikki works tirelessly against injustice and has a profound belief that true justice cannot exist unless everyone has their rights protected, regardless of their circumstances.

"Yeah, I can zip you up," Xavier says, squeezing my hips as he drags his nose along my neckline. "But seeing you in this dress makes me want to fuck you first."

My arms lift, landing behind me to rest on his neck. "Mmm, don't tempt me. If we weren't already running late, we could've gotten a quickie in."

"*Estoy siempre listo pa ti, mami.*" His erection presses into me. "But Adrián is already on his way. *Por más que quiera*, we'll have to wait." I'm always ready for him to explore and ravage me. He zips me up then slips out of the closet.

With my shoes in hand, I walk into the bedroom, but stop in my tracks when I see him across the room, his dress pants unbuttoned and hanging, revealing the trail of hair that peeks out of the top of his briefs. Black ink covers most of his sculpted abdomen and chest, the eagle taking up most of the real estate across his pectorals and spilling over to his arm. The tip of the eagle's wing brushes the head of the Woman of Caguana tattoo on his bicep. My eyes follow as he adjusts his slacks and closes the button, then slips his arms into the black fabric. I'm in awe, and still surprised, at how this beautiful, young, virile man is with me—a woman ten years his senior. He's given me every reason to feel secure, and I'm finally trusting him with my heart. He's shown me he's a man of his word. Xavier is everything Victor wasn't.

As the elevator descends, my eyes assess him in his black,

fitted suit, accentuating his lean, fit length. He chose to forgo a tie, opting for the top button open, exposing a smattering of his golden-brown skin at his collarbone. My belly stirs in anticipated desire, knowing he's all mine. "I can't wait to get back home," I say, pulling my bottom lip between my teeth.

"*Y yo*," he responds, kissing my temple.

"You look incredible!" I tell Nikki, who's adjusting her deep sapphire blue dress in the full-length bathroom mirror. It embraces her contours and accentuates her hips, the slit on the right leg gives the illusion that she's taller than she is.

"That dress is pretty amazing!" Alondra adds, then swipes the red lipstick tube across her bottom lip.

I dry my hands and toss the paper towel into the trash. "I'm really hoping Victor isn't here. I'm not up for his antics after our run-in at Xavier's studio. Who knows what bullshit he'd come up with if he sees us here." A hollow feeling settles at the pit of my stomach.

"I haven't seen him at this event the past few years. Unlikely he'll be here tonight," Nikki says.

"Let's hope you're right."

As we're walking back toward the ballroom, where Xavier and César are waiting for us, I halt, and my hands shoot out, grabbing each of their arms. Across the way, a woman with long black silky hair approaches the ballroom entrance alongside a balding, slender man, and they greet a group standing outside the door. "Holy shit!"

"What is it?" Alondra asks.

A memory of the office I shared with Victor flashes through

my mind—Victor and this woman naked on my couch. It's like everything I felt that day rushes back. "That's the woman who was fucking Victor the day I walked in on them. The woman who ruined my marriage."

"Which one?" Nikki inquires.

My body shifts away from the woman, and I lean into the girls. "Don't make it obvious that you're looking," I whisper. "The one wearing the dark green sparkly dress." My eyes rake down her accentuated silhouette.

"The one with the black hair?" Nikki asks.

"Yeah. That's her."

"Damn, she's pretty."

My eyes dart to Nikki at her declaration and misplaced jealousy creeps in. "Ugh, why'd you have to say it like that?"

She shrugs. "Because she is, but girl, you're gorgeous so it shouldn't bother you."

"Besides"—Alondra interlocks her arm with mine—"she isn't the woman that ruined your marriage. Victor did that all on his own."

Alondra's right, of course. My marriage was over long before I caught them that day, but in this moment, it all rushes back. Even all this time later, Victor and the shitstorm that he created makes its way into my life, trickling into a perfectly good night. "It's been months since we've officially divorced, so I'm not sure why I'm reacting this way."

"It's like new evidence found in a case," Nikki chimes in. "It isn't always exculpatory, but it's definitely got shock value."

Alondra unlinks our arms and scoots closer to Nikki. "I know we're keeping it on the DL, but what did you say? I couldn't hear you over the music."

"Just that it doesn't matter that she's been divorced for three months or three years, seeing this woman will make her feel some type of way."

"Let's go," I say, turning on my heel. Victor is old news and I'm not gonna let this woman ruin our night. "We're here to celebrate you, Nikki."

Inside the ballroom, people are gathered, laughter and chatter floating around us. As we finagle our way through the crowd, we spot César and Xavier off to the right, near the table reserved for us.

"Looks like it's a full house for you tonight, *mi amor*." César wraps his arm around Nikki's waist.

"You'll just have to share me with everyone tonight." She winks, then softly bumps him with her shoulder.

"Hi, Rocky! How are you?" When I turn, Soledad Caruso, the interpreter I use for all my clients' court hearings, appears, arms interlocked with a tall, dark-haired man.

"Soledad. Hi, it's good to see you." Our cheeks meet, kissing each other hello. "This is Xavier, my boyfriend." My heart bursts that I get to call him that. It's the first time I'm introducing him as my boyfriend to someone other than my friends. I'm trying it on for size, and although it's a bit uncomfortable, it fits like a glove. "This is my friend, Alondra. Nikki here is tonight's honoree, and César, her husband."

"It's nice to meet everyone. This is Amaury, my husband." She glances up at the man with a prominent scar over his left eye.

"Hi. Nice to meet everyone." He extends his arm, shaking everyone's hand, one by one.

As we're chatting, Xavier is eyeing his phone then slips it into his pocket. "*Mami*, come here." He drapes his arm around my waist. "My sister's here, let's go find her by the bar."

"Excuse us. Xavier's sister is here. We'll be right back," I say as we turn toward the crowd.

When we reach the bar, the area is crowded with people waiting to order drinks. He types a quick text and then slides his phone back into his pocket. "She's getting a drink, so we'll wait for her here."

"I'm not gonna lie. I'm a little nervous." My hands smooth my dress down then my right hand rests at my thigh, my thumb and index fingers drawing small circles. "Too bad we have to meet at this gala the first time, instead of a dinner. It would've been nice to have time to sit and get to know her better." We had talked about meeting his sister, but between everyone's schedules, we haven't been able to pull it off.

"*Tenemos tiempo para eso.*" My belly stirs at his claim that we'll have time. "But tonight, don't be nervous. You're the two most important women in my life, and I can't wait for you to meet each other." His eyes crinkle in line with his smile.

Xavier often speaks of Xiomary and how much he admires her. Since losing their parents at a young age, and then losing their grandmother, it's just them. When he told me she'd be attending this gala as well, my stomach fluttered. Knowing the important role she plays in his life, plus my being older than her by a few years, makes me anxious. Will she like me? He told me she knows how old I am but what if she hates me? Is their bond strong enough that her thoughts and feelings about me will influence him? All these unknown factors race through my mind, fueling my anxiety over it.

"That's not helping." A shaky chuckle escapes me. The music buzzes around us, the low hum of conversations mince in the air, like the build-up moment of your favorite movie.

He leans into me and whispers, "Don't be nervous, *mami*. She's gonna love you as much as I do." My eyes dart to his while my heart thunders in my chest at his words.

My lips slightly part. "Um—" He searches my gaze.

"It's okay, *mami*." His thumb draws circles in the palm of my hand. "You don't have to say anything. *Sé lo que sientes sin que me digas las palabras.*"

I swallow as my heartbeat rattles in my ribcage, his declaration one I'm not ready for, which he knows because he's telling me he knows what I feel without me saying it.

His eyes are darting around in search of Xiomary. I catch a glimpse of the woman in the green dress walking toward us. I shift my stance, looking to turn the other way, hoping to avoid her.

In that moment, Xavier releases my hand and waives his arm. "Xiomary." The woman in the green dress walks up to him and Xavier wraps his arm around her back, dropping a kiss on her cheek. My heart plummets and heat rushes over me.

This.

Cannot.

Be.

Happening.

"Xiomary, meet Rocky. The woman I've been telling you about."

He turns, putting me face to face with her, and it's like he's punching me in the gut. What are the fucking odds? "We've met before." I lift my chin.

She tilts her head, her widened eyes flitting between mine and Xavier's.

"When? Where?" Xavier asks, his forehead creased.

"She's the woman who was fucking my husband!" The pounding in my chest is incessant. Heat burns at the nape of my neck. The balding man to her left stares at me, unfazed by what I just shared.

Xavier's head swivels back toward Xiomary as her mouth opens then closes. "What?" he demands, his eyes widening in anger.

"Not here, please," Xiomary whispers as her head shakes.

A deep crease forms between his brows. "So it's true?" Xavier inquires.

"Of course it's true," I scoff, even though his question was directed at his sister. "I'll never forget her face."

Xiomary's hand lands on Xavier's forearm. "*Chiqui, por favor. Hablemos de esto después.*" Her plea to talk about it later is barely audible.

"That's rich!" My tone is wrapped in sarcasm. "Now you're pretending to be modest." I huff and turn, snake my way through the crowd in search of a door. I need some fresh air.

"Rocky, wait." Xavier calls for me from behind, but I continue toward the door I spotted.

When I reach the glass door, I push it open and step outside, the humid air filling my lungs. As I descend the concrete steps, I can hear Xavier behind me.

"*Mami*, please."

I halt and look toward the amphitheater lighting up the night sky across the park, music floating through the air. Tears sting and glide down my cheeks as a lump fills my throat.

His fingers wrap around my wrist. "I didn't know." The look of shock that overtook him when he heard what I said confirms his words. I'd never seen him look so pale.

In an effort to calm the erratic feelings churning inside, I exhale through pursed lips. I nod. "I know, but it doesn't matter."

"What does that mean?" He steps closer his body taking up the space between us.

Thunder crashes, and when I look up, the night sky is dense with clouds. Great, just what I need right fucking now. "I'm not sure. But knowing one of the two most important women in your life is the same woman who was fucking my ex-husband is something I never imagined. I don't know what do with that information." I glance around us to ensure we're alone. "I just hope the paparazzi doesn't find out about this because that's all I need. They already follow me practically everywhere; this new bit of information will only make them hungrier."

He's nodding while also threading his fingers with mine. His free hand reaches for my other hand doing the same.

"*Mami*, I'm just as shocked as you."

"If it shocked you, it annihilated me." My head drops as tears drip.

His grasp loosens and he quickly cups my face and begins furiously kissing me. His kisses are urgent in their search and exploration. Rain begins falling and the fat drops sting as they lick my skin. Xavier's grip tightens and my arms wrap around his neck, pulling him closer to me as the sky opens up, drenching us. Xavier's hands drop to my ass as he grasps the globes and lifts me, hoisting me up above him and tightening his arms beneath my ass. I wrap my legs around him, gripping tightly to steady myself as I reciprocate his onslaught of kisses. My carefully styled curls have turned into a wet, matted mess stuck to my face and neck and back.

Thunder crashes as the rain intensifies. I separate just enough to say, "We should probably go inside."

"I'll go anywhere, as long as I'm with you." His breath is quick and short.

"Let's go underneath the overhang," I say, pointing toward the hotel.

He sets me down and interlocks our fingers as we ascend the stairs toward the covered area of the hotel.

Once protected from the rain, Xavier whips his phone out of his pocket and types a quick text. "Adrián will be here soon to pick us up and take us home."

My heart hammers and I swallow the lump in my throat. "I need to go to my place. I need time."

His eyes widen and his nostrils flare. "What? *¿Por qué?*"

Water slides down my face, and I push the soaked strands away from my eyes. "Are you really asking me that right now?"

"What happened between Xiomary and Victor has nothing to

do with us." He reaches for me, his hands squeezing my rounded hips.

My head tilts back and I exhale. "You're right, it doesn't. But she's your sister and the most important woman in your life. I'm not sure how to reconcile that with what I'm feeling."

He closes the space between us, our soaked bodies flush. "What are you feeling?"

A muddle of confusion, anger, sadness, and love churn and bubble, and I don't know which way is up. "That I don't want another day to go by without you by my side, but also that I cannot imagine seeing her face because of everything she represents and because of that, I can't be with you. My heart is literally ripping right now, and it's overwhelming."

His thumbs drag across my cheek. "You already know *lo que siento*."

While waiting to meet his sister, he basically told me he loved me, and when he saw the frightened glint in my eyes, he coddled me so I wouldn't feel obligated to respond. I'm definitely not ready to respond now, even if deep within the fibers of my heart, I know I've fallen in love with this man. "I'm not doing that right now." Tears stream down my face.

His jaw tightens. "You're shutting me out!"

"I'm not." The lie slips from my lips.

"That's bullshit!" His brows furrow as his nostrils flare.

"It's not. I just need time."

He swallows, his Adam's apple bobbing as his chest rises and falls. "*No estoy de acuerdo con tu decisión*, but I'm gonna roll with it—for now." He grabs my hands and threads our fingers, lifting them between us. "*¿Qué necesitas de mí?*"

I have no idea what I need so I'm not sure how to answer his question. My thoughts are a jumbled mess. Confusion feeds the ache in my heart, and I'm at a loss with how to handle this chaos of emotions. The only thing I know is that I need to process everything to figure it out and the only way I can do that is alone. Even now, Victor's indiscretions trickle in and are destroying what I've been building with Xavier. Will the effects of his destruction ever end?

I straighten my back and take a deep breath, searching for the strength I need for the words I'm about to say. When I see the moisture around his eyes, my heart flutters. "You leave for your tour next week. Go be amazing while I work through all this shit in my head and when you're back, I'll let you know where I land."

His eyes widen. "I'll be gone for six weeks!"

The ache in my chest twists as pain spreads across his face. "I know," I respond, forcing the words out.

"What the fuck am I supposed to do for that amount of time *sin saber* where we stand?" He raises his voice, but the only thing I recognize is fear and panic as his hands shoot up and circle his skull.

"Whatever you think is best."

"What I think is best is for you not to do this!"

"That's not an option."

"Please, *mami*, don't do this." His voice trembles while he wraps his arms around me, and my face nuzzles his chest as the tears drip. After recognizing Xiomary as the same woman who was with Victor, everything has blurred. My mind is protecting me and forcing my heart to separate from this man that makes it swell and burn with love and desire, and I don't know how to tame the storm that's brewing.

Adrián picked us up, and we're inching our way up Biscayne Boulevard toward the McArthur Causeway. Silence hangs, heavy and loaded with unspoken words. I type out a text to Nikki and Alondra that I left and briefly explained why, with a promise to catch up tomorrow.

The drive to my apartment is quiet, the hum of the car on the road coupled with the heavy rain, the only sound filling the space between us. Now that we're in the car, I've started shivering and Xavier scoots across the seat and drapes his arms over me.

"*Ven acá, mami.* You're shivering." I wish I didn't want to feel his touch, but I do, more than anything, so I don't push him away. I savor it for the rest of the ride to my apartment, especially knowing it could be the last time his arms soothe me.

Adrián pulls into the rounded drive of my building and I reach for my bag.

"I'll be right back, just gonna walk her up."

"No," I say, grasping his arm. "This is good."

Xavier's gaze locks with mine, his brown hues shimmering from the tears he's fighting back. "*Mami*, this isn't right."

"It is. I promise that once I work through all this shit in my head, you'll hear from me." I force myself from the car and to not look back for fear that the look on his face will make me regret the decision I've made for us.

CHAPTER TWENTY-EIGHT

Xavier

"Did you fucking know?" I yell at Xiomary while pacing the great room in my penthouse. She's been avoiding my calls since Saturday night when Rocky left me. This morning, I called her office, and when I was transferred to her voicemail, I was gonna crash out. She showed up at my apartment a few minutes ago, after I texted and threatened to show up at her office if she didn't make an appearance.

Her head is shaking as she keeps a distance between us. "No, I had no idea. Not until I saw the pictures of her outside your studio."

I'm trying to not totally lose my shit but her response isn't helping. "Why the fuck didn't you tell me?"

She's trembling as she stands at the foot of the couch, her shoulders slumped. "I wanted to talk to you but was in LA and that's the type of conversation you have in person. I was gonna do it before the gala, but then my flight was delayed. I'm sorry."

"You were fucking a married guy! How can I believe a word you're saying?" I let out a dry huff. "You turned out just like him and he isn't even your real father. I guess all that nature versus nurture bullshit they taught us in school is real."

Growing up, Xiomary was a daddy's girl, even if she wasn't my father's biological child. Since her sperm donor, as she likes to call him, disappeared when she was two, she craved my father's attention once our mother started dating him. Anybody who saw them would've never known they weren't blood related. Once our parents died and people started sharing stories, Xiomary became angry with him.

She rushes toward me and gets in my face. "I'm nothing like him!" Anger laces her words.

"Could've fooled me." I shake my head and cross the room to put some space between us.

She storms behind me and screams. "What the fuck, Xavier?"

I spin and glare down at her tear-soaked eyes. "Do you get off on being the other woman?"

"What? No, it's not like that!"

A humorless huff escapes me. "No? What's it like then, because Victor isn't the first married guy you've slept with."

"That's not fair. It only happened one other time."

"That's two times too many."

Her voice cracks as her pitch increases. "You're being unfair. Both times the men lied to me. I had no idea until it was too late." It's true. I am being unfair, but right now, she's the only one I have to blame. The last time this happened to her, she and I were out to dinner when a woman confronted her, identified herself as the wife. After that, Xiomary didn't date for over a year.

I scoff. Angry that she's put herself in this position. Put me in this position. "You need to fix your daddy issues!"

"You're being such an asshole right now." Black streaks cover her cheeks.

I drop my forehead on the window that looks west. "You're lucky that's all I'm being."

Xiomary comes up behind me and rests her hand on my back. "*Chiqui*, I promise you I had no idea he was married. When I moved to Miami, I didn't know many people." Her voice softens and her shoulders drop. "I went to a lawyer event one night and met Victor there. After that, we met a few times and he acted very single in the way he flirted. He didn't wear a wedding ring and the people we were with didn't mention anything about him being married. How was I supposed to know?"

Seeing Xiomary defeated hurts because she's the only family I have left, but her behavior is like a thorn in my side.

"I don't know, Xiomary. But she left me." My hand smacks the glass. "She fucking left me, and I'm crashing the fuck out." My voice cracks.

"Why would she do that? You had nothing to do with it."

I tilt my head and glance at her sideways. "Maybe because I told her I wanted the two most important women in my life to meet, and it turns out you're the reason she's divorced."

"I'm not the reason she's divorced," she quips. "He did that all on his own. I'm collateral damage."

"Whatever. You were fucking him and she saw you, and now she left me."

"She probably just needs some time."

"I leave for my tour tomorrow, and she won't see me." My voice cracks.

"Give her space to sort it all out."

My chest tightens. I've barely slept since dropping Rocky off on Saturday, because I can't bear to think about her ending it. "What if she doesn't?" I choke up at the sound of those words because it's the outcome I refuse to believe is possible. The last time I lost the woman I loved, it was on me. This time, if I lose Rocky, it's out of my control, and I don't know how to fucking deal with it.

It's been two weeks since the gala.

Two weeks without seeing my girl.

Two weeks of uncertainty.

Two weeks of persistent heartache.

We just wrapped up our show in Panama City, Panamá, the fifth city of our Latin American tour. The past few shows we'd fly out the same night as the show, but because our next show in Medellín, Colombia isn't for three days, we're staying the night. So far, all the shows have been high energy with the crowd carrying me through. The fan-filled arenas are the only thing that's made it possible. But despite the love and adoration of my fans, there's still a gaping hole in my heart that only Rocky can fill. I've called and texted her every day over the past two weeks. She needs to know I'm here and waiting for her to come back to me. Although she hasn't responded to my calls or video calls, she has texted back, albeit at the bare minimum. It's fucking killing me, but I know that I can't pressure her and need to give her the time and space she asked for, otherwise I'll push her further away.

We're backstage in a large room in the underbelly of the venue while roadies take down the stage. There are about forty people in the room milling around, chatting, and drinking, while I sit alone on a couch in the back of the room, spinning in my own anxiousness. My leg bounces incessantly in rhythm with my heartbeat as my eyes track the people moving around me. Adrián is outside the room handling a matter, and Maritza already left for the hotel.

"*Ey, tienes cara de nervioso. ¿Quieres algo para calmarte?*" a guy offers as he slides into the seat on my right.

Nervous doesn't begin to explain what I'm feeling. Restlessness courses through my veins and I could really use something to take the edge off. Maybe I'll take him up on whatever he's offering. I glance at him but don't recognize the face. Who is this guy? Can I trust whatever he'd give me? But also, I'm so anxious about everything that's happening with Rocky, checking out for a few hours sounds pretty good right about now.

"What do you got?"

His eyes scan the room then meet mine again, and he leans over and whispers, "*¿Quieres una línea de perico?*"

I haven't done a line of cocaine since the early days of chasing my Percocet high. I'd probably wig out if I did one now. Or maybe it would give me that euphoric feeling I chased for years and take away all of the uneasy pain stirring inside of me. When I lift my head up, I catch a glimpse of Adrián in the corner of my eye. Do I want to do a line and then suffer the consequences of a hangover? Or worse, into a habit of drug use again? Not to mention ending the length of time I've been sober. My sponsor's voice rings in my ears as I repeatedly whisper *play the tape through* under my breath to myself as my fingers drum along the armrest. Fuck, I haven't craved getting high like this in a long time. I give him a curt nod then jump to my feet.

I need to get out of here before I make a mistake. When I spot Adrián again, I slip through the group of people over to him. "Hey, man, I'm ready to call it a night."

"Sure thing, boss. There's a car waiting for us outside."

A few people stop me as we work our way toward the door, and when we reach the car waiting for us, it's parked under an overhang protecting us from the heavy rainfall. The air is damp and heavy, similar to Miami nights. I pull my hood up as we stride toward the waiting vehicle. We both jump into the backseat, the silence ringing loudly in my ears. As we're driving toward the hotel, vivid pictures of Rocky flip through my mind, the torrential rain reminding me of that fateful night she closed the door in my face. The night of the gala has replayed in my mind like a broken record. I don't think there is anything I could've done to change the outcome. *Fuck!* I drop my head back on the headrest, gently tapping it repeatedly.

"You okay, boss?" Adrián asks.

I glance across the seat at him. "No, I'm not okay. None of this is okay."

"Marcos checks in with me every few hours. She's going through it, too. If I've learned anything over the years, it's to give women the space they ask for."

Marcos is part of Adrián's security team. After the paparazzi started hounding Rocky, I insisted she have her own detail, despite her protests. After the gala, she tried telling him to leave but I wasn't having it. She wouldn't talk to me, but I texted her and convinced her he needed to continue with her for her own safety, at least until I'm back and we figure our shit out.

"That doesn't make me feel much better, because it just tells me this shouldn't be happening."

Back at the hotel, I lie restless in bed after a scalding hot shower. My thoughts race back to when Lisandra left me, and I don't remember feeling anything close to the unbearable pain causing the heaviness in my chest. Was I that fucking high the entire time that it didn't phase me? The drugs must've skewed everything I did and thought and felt. I don't have anything to numb that feeling right now. Don't want to numb myself. The only way I'll feel better is by getting my girl back. I reach for my phone and push the camera icon, hoping Rocky answers.

CHAPTER TWENTY-NINE

Rocío

My body hums as I sip on my Hendricks and soda while sitting cross-legged in the middle of my couch, staring up at the painting of the woman wearing a tear-soaked dress. To think I acquired it because of all the tears shed for my ex-husband, and here I am again, shedding tears for another man, yet somehow it connects back to Victor. Xavier's album, "*Modo Perreo*," is playing, and the rhythm of the kick and snare of the drumbeats reverberate across my body. He flows seamlessly between English and Spanish lyrics, and his voice is deep and sultry, just like when he's buried deep inside of me while talking dirty. Tears stream down my face as I remember how he claims me in public by firmly holding my hand or the way he kisses my temple. Not to mention, the sexual chemistry between us is off the charts. He always puts me and my needs before his, which makes me want to give him everything. Of the millions of people in the world, why the fuck did his sister have to be the same woman I walked in on with Victor. "Why?!" I scream out into the void.

My chest is heavy and I grab my phone, opening up the text

message exchanges we've had since we last saw each other two weeks ago. It's the only way I've allowed myself to communicate with him for fear that seeing and hearing his pleas will cloud my ability to think clearly. I've seen Dr. Pérez twice since that night. Both times she asked me if I believe avoiding Xavier is the best way to deal with what I've learned. When I made the decision, I was absolute in my conviction to not speak with him. Today, I'm questioning myself and that choice. I'm seeing her again first thing Wednesday morning, and I'm sure she'll ask me again since my answer has changed each time.

His first text message was minutes after they dropped me at my building.

> **XAVIER**
> Mami, this isn't right. The way we work through this is together, not apart.

> **ME**
> I can't think clearly when I'm with you, which is why I need space.

> **XAVIER**
> You can't think clearly because you love me, you're just not ready to admit it to yourself, or me.

When I read his last message the day he sent it, I knew he was right. But I'm terrified of what that entails and of giving my heart to another man. I probably should've thought about that before willingly participating in a friends-with-benefits arrangement. With my emotions maxed out, I chose not to respond and left him on read. In hindsight, that may have been a bad idea, because if the roles were reversed, I would've had a meltdown.

Over the past two weeks, he's called me every day and when I'd reject the call, he'd immediately text. Because I care about him, I would respond but also tried to keep it light. He'd send me short messages, like "*Buenos días, mami*" or "I miss the way your nose wrinkles when you're laughing." Sprinkled throughout texts like those were ones that read, "*Quiero saborear* that pussy" and "I miss my greedy girl." But the one he sent every day, without fail, is, "*Tú y yo*, nobody else." This one got me every time. Still does.

When we got back from Vegas and Lisandra's text popped up, I thought it was over, there and then. In the two seconds I saw the message and jumped from the couch, I had already played out the scene in my head. Except I now realize the scene I imagined was as if it had been with Victor, not Xavier. When Xavier shared the story about his mother and how he made a promise to her, and to himself, that he would never be the reason a woman goes through and feels what his mother did, my heart cracked a little—for the little boy he was and the man that he is.

"Armageddon" starts playing and his name appears on my screen, indicating an incoming video call, and I stare at my phone. I put my glass on the table and hit the green button before I can think twice about it.

"Hi," I say.

He sits up, seeming as if he wasn't expecting me to answer. His beard is longer than it usually is, and the dark circles under his eyes tell me he's not slept much.

"God, it's so good to see you, *mami*." His gorgeous smile stretches across his face, illuminating his dark brown hues. I've missed the way his eyes crinkle at the corner when he smiles.

"How are you?"

"You already know the answer to that question, so I'll just say I'm better now that you finally answered my call."

Relief floods through me as I would rather pretend the past two weeks never happened, even if just for a few minutes. "What city are you in right now?"

"*Ciudad de Panamá*. We stayed here after the show tonight

since there are three days between this show and Medellín. We're flying out tomorrow."

"Are you being amazing?" I know he loves being on stage. I've been scrolling social media every night for videos from his concerts, and it looks like he's giving his fans the show they're expecting. I just hope what's happening between us hasn't taken the joy of performing from him.

His shoulders rise and fall. "As much as I can be. *Te extraño*. My entire body literally hurts for you. *Necesito verte. Sentirte. Tocarte. Hacerte el amor*." His voice cracks as his fingers touch the screen.

Even if I wanted to avoid him, he's not making it easy. Being able to touch him and stare into his eyes as he makes love to me would wash away all the chaotic feelings that have taken up residence within me. "I want those things, too." He gives me a half smile, his eyes lighting up as they widen. I bite my lip and pull my legs up against my chest.

"I'll send the plane for you. Meet me in Medellín."

I take a deep breath because, yet again, I have to say no. "I can't. I have a full work calendar this week. Plus, I'm seeing Dr. Pérez on Wednesday. I can't make any decisions until after my session with her." Although I'm capable of making the decision, I've learned that talking it out with Dr. Pérez assures me I'm making good decisions that support my mental health.

He swallows, his Adam's apple prominent. "Okay. *Entonces el miércoles* we'll talk and make a plan?"

I nod. "Yeah, I can do that." I've already decided how I want to move forward, I just need to confirm it with myself, and I'll do that with Dr. Pérez on Wednesday.

"*Mami*."

"Yeah?"

He gives me a soft smile. "Thank you."

"For what?"

"Answering my call tonight."

I'm in my office working on a memorandum of law that's due next week when Veronica knocks on the door as she enters my office. "Rocky, there's an attorney named Xiomary Silvestri calling. She said it's urgent she speak with you, but her name isn't in our system and she wouldn't give me any information." Why is Xiomary calling me? I'm not ready to talk to her yet. But what if something happened to Xavier? If something happened to him, Adrián would've called me, not her. Maybe I shouldn't answer. But also, I'm not the one in the wrong.

I shake the erratic thoughts from my mind. "Okay, I'll take the call. Thanks, Vero. Please close the door on your way out." *Please dear god, let him be okay*, I say softly before pressing line one. "Hello, this is Rocío."

"Hi, Rocío. It's Xiomary, Xavier's sister. Thank you for taking my call."

"Is he okay?"

"Oh, yeah, he's good. I mean, physically he's okay. Emotionally, not so much."

My shoulders drop and I lean back in my chair. Her words are a relief, even though he's going through it because of me.

"I thought about just showing up to your office but figured you probably wouldn't appreciate it."

"Thank you."

"My office is just two blocks from you. I happen to be across the street from your office at Julia & Henry's Food Hall. Would you be able to come down and meet me? We can grab a coffee from the place on the first floor."

Asking for a meeting isn't something I was expecting or ready for. Since the night of the gala, I've been thinking about my eventual conversation with her, but I thought I'd have time to come up with a game plan, except life doesn't work that way. Dr. Pérez asked if I wanted to talk to Xiomary about this entire situation. During my first session, I flat out told her I wasn't ready. As usual, after my session ended, I contemplated Dr. Pérez's questions. Why don't I want to talk to her? Do I think talking to her or not talking to her will help me move past the situation? Do I think speaking to her will help me understand the situation better? Will speaking to her help bring closure to the life I had with Victor? Will it help me get back on track with Xavier?

One of the biggest things I tell my clients is that communication is key. I'd be a hypocrite if I just told them that but didn't actually practice what I preach. I knew at some point I would have to speak to Xiomary, especially because I know I want to make it work with Xavier and I'll need to figure out how that will work. I had planned on making that happen sometime after my next session with Dr. Pérez, but I suppose we can do it today and get it out of the way.

I peek at my calendar, then my watch. "Sure, give me a few minutes."

"Thank you, Rocío. You'll see me at one of the tables across from the coffee shop."

I grab my pockabook from the bottom right drawer and tell the girls I'll be back.

"Marcos, I'm going across the street to Julia & Henry's." I hate that I have a permanent shadow with him, but also appreciate that Xavier was concerned enough that he has him with me.

"Yes, ma'am." I've asked him to call me Rocío or Rocky because he makes me feel old when he calls me ma'am. But he doesn't listen. Same as Adrián. Per usual, he follows in silence as I exit the office.

As we descend the elevator I stare at my reflection in the scratched mirror. "You got this, Rocky. You're a badass trial lawyer, you can handle a conversation with his sister," I say under my breath, then release a deep exhale before exiting into the lobby. At the entrance of Julia & Henry's, I glance up at the sign before stepping inside, pushing my shoulders back as I stride across the busy food hall. Xiomary is sitting at a small round table with attached stools. She's wearing a green blouse, and her hands twirl a paper coffee cup. Seems nerves are visiting her just as much as me.

"Hi," I say, sliding into the chair across from her.

"Hello." She gives me a warm smile that reaches her eyes. "Who's that?" Her chin juts out gesturing toward Marcos where he's standing against the wall behind me.

"Your brother has Marcos with me while he's away. Says he doesn't trust the paparazzi right now."

"Sounds just like him." She smirks. "You gonna grab a coffee?"

I shake my head. "I'm good."

"Okay. Well, thank you for coming on such short notice."

My gaze searches her dark brown eyes and regret stares back at me before her eyes slide down. "Of course. It was inevitable for us to have this conversation, so today is as good a day as any." I hang my pockabook on my knee then rest my hands on the table.

She takes a deep breath then looks up again, where my eyes are waiting for hers. "I'm sorry, Rocío. When I met Victor, I had no idea he was married. I had just moved to Miami and met him at an event I attended." Her voice trembles and she shifts in her seat, but her eyes remain steady on mine. "Not once did he wear his ring and his behavior was not that of a married man. I never would've entertained him, had I known. Never! It doesn't make what I did right, but I owe you an apology for it." Her hand stretches across the table, landing on mine, and my foot begins tapping under the table. "Truly. I would never intentionally do that to you, or anyone."

A memory flashes through my mind of a day I found Victor's wedding ring in our bathroom and asked him why he'd taken it off, since I believed he wore it all the time, even in the shower. He made up some lame excuse about removing it while showering because the gold was wearing down after so many years of consistent use. Hindsight is twenty-twenty. "Thank you for that. I imagine it wasn't easy for you to come here today, especially to say those words." Her apologizing doesn't change what happened, but I realize that we're all pawns in the game of Victor.

She shakes her head. "It wasn't. I'm ashamed that I allowed myself to be put in that position, that I hurt you. I had no idea until you walked into the office that day. I'm sorry."

My heart hammers in my chest as Xiomary takes responsibility for her role in the day my marriage crumbled. But Alondra, Nikki, and even Dr. Pérez have repeatedly reminded me that Victor is the one primarily responsible for the demise of our marriage, not the multitude of women he slept with along the way. Sitting across from Xiomary, I can say I believe the words she's telling me. Sure, I may never forget the role she played in my past life, but that doesn't mean I should allow Victor, through his affair with her, to continue tainting my current life. "Victor was hurting me long before I walked in on the two of you. I now know my marriage had ended way before that night."

"I'm sorry." Despite her perfect lipstick and silky hair, she looks tired. She has dark circles under her eyes, and she's hunched forward. Her words are laced with regret and sincerity.

"Really the only person who owes me an apology is Victor, but his ego will never let that happen." All the times we tried having conversations after that fateful day, his apologies were empty and meant nothing. It's not that I wanted an apology because I was going to forgive him and continue our relationship.

I was hoping he would have the decency to apologize for how badly he'd hurt and betrayed me over the years. "I appreciate you reaching out and I accept your apology."

"Thank you." Her hands remain on mine, and we stare at each other in silence; two women hurt in starkly different ways by one man's selfish behaviors. Listening to the cracks in her voice as she told me how she met Victor tells me she has demons of her own to deal with. I suppose we all do on some level. She pulls her hands back and then adjusts herself in the seat again. "Maybe you can find it in your heart to not hold the mistake I made against my brother." She pauses and tilts her head. "Since the night of the gala, he—"

"Did he ask you to come see me? Talk to me?" If he did, that might change the entire way I perceive the conversation we've had until now.

Her eyes widen, and she shakes her head. "What? No, he doesn't know I came to see you."

"Why didn't you tell him?"

"Because this is a mess I created, and I'm the one who needs to handle it." A woman who handles her shit. I can respect that and, in turn, respect her for being woman enough to sit across from me and look me in the eye to have this conversation.

My head slightly nods, and my shoulders soften. "I miss him. He's a really great guy."

She's nodding. "He is, although I'm biased." A smile stretches across her face.

"How's he doing?" We briefly spoke last night but we didn't get into any of the heavy stuff.

She shrugs. "I mean, he's pushing through, but not knowing where he stands with you is killing him."

Sitting across from Dr. Pérez today is different. There is no uncertainty and no indecision swirling in my thoughts. Instead, calm spreads over me.

"Tell me, Rocky. What's new since last week?"

"I talked to my mother about the blowout we had."

Last week

"Hi Ma." I drop a kiss on her cheek then place the box of facturas, Argentine pastries my parents like to eat when drinking mate, on the table. I left the office early today and drove to their house. I haven't been over since the day we had our huge blowout because we went to Vegas, then had the gala, and then I was avoiding them. But I couldn't evade my parents any longer.

"Hola, nena," she replies.

I say hello to my father who's filling the gourd with yerba to prepare el mate. "Hola, Roo."

"Hace tiempo que no venís," says my mother as she turns the stove off.

"I know." I slide the chair out and sit. "I don't want to yell or argue, but I need to talk about the last time I was here. I need you to listen to me."

"Okay," she responds, but doesn't look at me.

"Ma, can you please sit down?"

Her eyes fall on mine, and they're steady. She stares at me for what feels like an eternity then turns toward the table and slides out the chair to my right.

"Thank you."

She nods and adjusts herself in the chair.

"My whole life you've judged me and my decisions. I don't understand why."

"Nena—"

"Por favor, Ma, dejame terminar." I hope she agrees to listen to everything I have to say before talking. Otherwise, I don't think it'll happen.

She nods as she takes the mate *from my father, who's sitting across from me.*

My pulse quickens and I take a deep breath. "I'm not here to ask permission for my life choices. Tengo cuarenta y un años *and I own a law firm." I rest my hands on the table. "I survived a marriage that was a lie. You care more about the shame of a divorce than your daughter's happiness." My eyes burn, and I can't hold back the tears as they slide down my cheeks.*

I get up to grab a stack of napkins from the counter and slide back in my seat.

My mother is gazing at me, her lips pursed. She looks older today than she did three weeks ago, the wrinkles around her eyes more prominent. "Now, for the first time in years, I'm happy. Xavier is thoughtful and respects me. And because the paparazzi posted pictures of him kissing and touching me, you called me a whore who allows herself to be disrespected." I dab the napkin under each eye to swipe away the tears that drip then exhale through pursed lips. "If I had stayed married like you wanted, I would've disrespected myself. Me divorcing my cheating ex-husband is how I respect myself."

My mother hands the gourd back to my father, then stretches her hand on the table toward me.

"I'm not a little girl anymore. You don't have to like my life,

or my choices, but I also don't need your permission or approval. I want to keep coming here and spending time with you, but I deserve to be respected, not controlled." I release a deep breath as my heart hammers in my chest.

"Nena, no llorés." *My mother telling me not to cry only makes the tears fall harder.*

I reach for another napkin, swipe the tears, then blow my nose.

"Hija, *I didn't want to hurt you."* *I stretch my hand across the table and she rests hers over mine.* "Soy vieja y me crié en otros tiempos. *Life is different than when I was your age."* *While I agree she's from a different era, it can't be her excuse for everything. That'll have to be a conversation for another day.* "I'm proud de todos tus logros." *Her being proud of all my accomplishments is nothing new.*

She tilts her head as her eyes search mine. She blinks several times, then says, "You are the woman I always wanted you to be. Smart. Independent. Beautiful." She straightens herself, pushes her shoulders back. "Sos la mujer que yo no pude ser." *My mother isn't one to apologize. Right now is no different. But her telling me that I'm the woman that she never could be is as close as it'll get.*

I slide my chair back and kneel next to my mother, drop my head in her lap.

Dr. Pérez is wearing a light purple sleeveless blouse today, and her dark brown wavy hair hangs over her shoulders. "That's a huge boundary to draw with your mom. How did she take it?"

Exhaling deeply, I lean back in my chair. "She didn't scream or argue. She didn't even defend herself." I expected her to at least do this. "She just stared at me before telling me I'm the woman she could never be." My head rolls back, and I take deep breaths to calm my erratic heartbeat.

Dr. Pérez crosses her legs and adjusts the position she's sitting in. "We've often talked about her judgment being a reflection of her own limitations. How'd it feel to hear her say that?"

My heart thumps in my chest as I recall her words. "It broke me. I ended up with my head in her lap, crying like a little girl." I kick my shoes off then rest my feet on the edge of the sofa. "It's complicated. On the one hand, her saying that felt like an apology I've waited my entire life for. The flip side is that her being proud doesn't erase that she called me a whore. It was so typical of her. She is a Latina mom, after all. She didn't actually apologize, she just admitted she's jealous of my freedom."

Dr. Pérez writes something on her notepad then lifts her eyes to me. "Is that enough for you?"

I've been thinking about the answer to this question because I knew she'd ask it. "I'm not sure. It's a first for my mother. For now, I'm taking it as a win."

She nods. "And your father, where was he?"

"There, at the table, like the good wallflower that he is."

Her lips purse and she scribbles something. "Have any thoughts about him from that day?"

I take a sip of water from my cup then place it back on the side table. "He didn't say a word. No surprise there. But for the first time, I didn't expect him to. After our argument three weeks ago, I realized that if I keep waiting for him to defend me, I'll be waiting forever. I had to speak up for myself. I think seeing me finally stand up for myself actually made him look...relieved? Or maybe shocked? Like he was watching a younger version of my mother."

"You do say he always tells you that you and your mother are identical." When my mother said those words to me the other day, it clicked that my father has been seeing it all this time.

"Where are you with Xavier?"

The million-dollar question. "Xiomary asked for a meeting, which we had yesterday."

Dr. Pérez's face is always steady and free from emotions, but I'd like to believe that I see a glint of happiness on her face when I share that news. "How did seeing her affect you?" Her hands are crossed and lie on her notepad that rests on her legs.

"When she called me, I wasn't sure how to feel." It felt forced, and maybe it was. But as she sat across from me, and her facial expressions showed regret and anguish for what she'd done, I almost felt bad for her. My marriage was over long before Xiomary. She may not have known that the day I walked in on her and Victor, but she may have believed it for a long time. That's a heavy burden to carry. "I hadn't prepared anything and was worried our meeting could take a wrong turn. But she wasted no time and apologized for her role in how it all went down with my ex-husband. I was a little surprised, although maybe I shouldn't have been, because she was so direct in her words."

Dr. Pérez scribbles a few notes down then lifts her eyes to mine. "Did you ladies discuss Xavier?"

"Briefly. She asked if I would be able to not hold her mistake against Xavier. When she told me that, I immediately thought he'd ask her to speak to me. But that isn't the case."

"Are you satisfied that she went to you on her own?"

I nod. "Yeah, I am."

"What's next?"

"Before everything went down, we had discussed me going to a few of his shows in South America. I'm moving some stuff on my calendar to meet him on his tour and I'm trying to pull it off for next week when he's in Buenos Aires. I haven't been back home in a few years so it would be nice to go, even if it's just a few days."

"And what about Xiomary? Have you decided what your relationship will look like with her moving forward?"

I cross my legs. "I'll be cordial with her. I'm not likely to text her to hang out anytime soon, but I think I can be in the same room with her if it's necessary." Over the years, I've had to work with some opposing counsel who were downright nasty to me, and still my job required me to be professional at all stages to represent my clients' interests. I can treat this situation the same. "I'm sure it'll need to be gradual, but it's better than the alternative."

"What's the alternative?"

"Me never seeing her, which would only be possible if I also end it with Xavier, and I'm not willing to do that. At least not right now."

"Why's that?"

Spending three weeks away from him hurt. I spent many nights crying, thinking about the relationship we'd built in our few months together and how much I craved sharing time with him. I know I needed time away from him to be able to think clearly, but I also wish I hadn't missed so much time away from him. Time is the one thing we can never get back. "I think I love him. I set out to have some fun with a guy I met at a bar and had zero expectations, and here I am."

"Can you share why you think you love him?"

I nod. "He respects me. He's thoughtful in his words and in his actions. He's confident. I feel safe with him, emotionally and physically. I love that he allows himself to be vulnerable, a side he shares with only me. He's intuitive and perceptive. He makes me feel whole again. Like I was never broken to begin with."

Dr. Pérez writes a few things down and then looks back up at me. "Have you told him how you feel?"

"Not yet."

As I pull my pajama pants on, my phone pings with an incoming message from Xavier. My heart flutters when I see his picture pop up. God, I've missed him. Now that I've finally admitted to myself that I love him, I feel lighter. It's like the sun shining after weeks of rain.

XAVIER
It's Wednesday.

ME
It is.

XAVIER
Today's the day we make plans.

ME
I know.

XAVIER
Entonces, what's the plan?

ME
I was able to clear my calendar next week. I'll meet you in Buenos Aires on Saturday.

CHAPTER THIRTY

Xavier

Rocky's flight from MIA landed at six a.m., an hour behind schedule. I wanted to fly to Miami, pick her up, and then fly back to Buenos Aires, but she told me she didn't want me flying that much when I have to perform. I told her I'd only agree for her and Marcos to fly commercial if I paid for the flight. We timed our flight to leave Medellín so that we'd land in Buenos Aires around the same time as her. We're here now and Adrián is inside waiting for them, while I sit with the driver. I'm anxious to see her and have her next to me, even if it's only going to be for the week.

Last week, I called her after the *Panamá* show like I had done every night before since the gala incident with the expectation that she wasn't going to answer. Except she surprised me by picking up and also telling me she wanted the same things as me. There are no words to describe the way my heart exploded. I wasn't able to sleep that night because my mind raced all night with possibility.

As I see the three of them approaching the vehicle, I hop out to wait for my girl. She's wearing black leggings and her Doc

Martens. She adjusts the scarf around her neck, then tucks her hands into her pockets. As she strides toward me, my dick hardens at the sight of her curves, which are visible even under the black coat she's wearing. "*Mami*." Despite the weary look of travel, she's more beautiful today than any other time I've seen her. My hands reach for her, and I wrap her in my embrace, burying my nose in her hair to inhale her unique floral scent. I was starting to forget what she smelled like, and it was making me angry. "It feels like forever since I've seen you."

She tucks her hands into the top of my jeans and she raises her eyes up to mine. "Hi." She bites her lip then gently kisses me. "I hate that it's been so long." Her eyes dart to Adrián. "Hey, can you give us a minute, please?"

Adrián glances at me, and I give him a nod. He scans the area then gets into the front seat of the SUV. I rest my forehead against hers, our noses brushing. "*Dime*."

Her eyes settle on mine. "Our time apart made me realize I'm not carrying my past anymore. You make me feel respected and safe in a way I've never felt before, regardless of what's happening around us. I never want to be without that again. Without you." She drags her lips between her teeth. "*Tú y yo*, nobody else."

Her words settle in the fibers of my heart, spreading warmth over me as I trace the line of her jaw. A smile tugs at the corners of my mouth, then I brush my lips with hers. As hard as the past few weeks without her have been, her realizing the depth of my commitment makes the torture all worth it. "*Siempre*." I bury my nose in the crook of her neck, her floral scent invading me. "Let's finish this conversation at the hotel."

We climb into the backseat of the SUV and I tug her toward me, draping my arm around her as we cruise down the road. "How long to the hotel?" I ask.

"Thirty minutes," Adrián responds.

"Where are we staying?" she asks.

I grab my phone and search for the text from Maritza. "*Puerto Madero*. A hotel that's waterfront but also has a view of the city *y del Obelisco*."

She peeks up at me and asks, "Have you been to Buenos Aires before?"

"I did a few shows back in the day, but it was always in and out so I never really saw much. Now that I'm here with my girl, who happens to be from Argentina, I was hoping she'd be my tour guide." My lips drop to her temple. Her presence filled the gaping hole in my heart, and I can finally breathe again. Whether we spend the next three days inside our hotel room or exploring the city, I really don't care as long as it's with her.

"I mean, I'm not from Buenos Aires so not sure I could be a tour guide, but I do have some favorite places."

"What part are you from?"

"I was born in Mar del Plata but moved to the States when I was five. We came back almost every year, but definitely not the same as when you live your entire childhood somewhere."

"Where's that in relation to where we are?"

"About a four-hour drive south. It's a waterfront city known for its beaches."

"We'll have to come back in the summer then, so you can take me there."

She bites her lip. "I'd like that."

Maritza already checked us into the hotel and we stop at the front desk.

As we're being handed our keys, the young guy behind the

desk calls Adrián over. When Adrián turns back to me, he says, "He's asking if you'd be willing to take pictures with him and the front desk staff. They said they have tickets to the show on Tuesday night because they're all very big fans."

Nodding, I say, "*Mami*, give me a minute."

I release her hand and turn toward the small group working at the desk. We take selfies and group pictures and then one of them has me sign a "*Modo Perreo*" t-shirt he has from my tour back in the day.

"Adrián, here"—my thumb gestures toward him—"will come back before Tuesday so we can get you seats by the stage."

"*¡Guau! Qué bueno. Mil gracias*," he responds with a grin stretching from ear to ear.

"That was really nice of you," Rocky says as she threads her fingers with mine.

"If it weren't for my fans, none of this would be possible." When I was at rock bottom and the only thing I cared about was my next high, they supported me. They're the ones who allowed me to have this career a second time.

We ride the elevator up to the tenth floor in silence as I tighten my grip on Rocky's hand. When we arrive at the room, I tell Adrián, "I'll check in later." Considering it's barely eight in the morning, we have all day. But first, I need some privacy with my girl so I can devour her and end the fast she forced on me.

As soon as the door closes behind us, I grasp her face in my hands and cover her mouth with mine. "I fucking missed you."

"Makes two of us," she mumbles, her hands falling at my hips. Her kisses deepen and her hands cup my cheeks.

"Hold that thought." I separate from her and run to the restroom quickly, leaving my jacket and shoes behind.

When I get back, Rocky is lying back on the bed on her elbows in her bra and underwear. The black lace digs at her rounded hips and her tits spill out over her red bra. My dick strains in my jeans, and I loosen my belt to let it free.

Rocky's gaze moves between my cock and my eyes as she licks her lips. I'm about to crawl onto the bed when she says, "I brought something for us." Her chin gestures to the nightstand where a clear bottle of lube sits.

"What's that for?" If it's what I think, she's ready for me to take her from behind.

She removes her underwear then rises up on her knees to unclasp her bra, freeing her heavy breasts. "I'm ready for you to own every part of me." She turns around then spreads her ass cheeks while gazing at me from over her shoulder.

I swallow and my heart thunders as I continue stroking myself. With my free hand, I grab the small bottle and squeeze some onto my cock as my hand glides up and down. "*Ponte en cuatro,*" I instruct.

She bends over and moves her ass side to side as she does. With my left hand, I palm her ass cheek and spread it, while my lube-covered finger traces her puckered hole. A moan escapes her as she pushes her ass out toward me. "More," she pleads.

My index finger penetrates her, her tightness gripping me. Heat spreads as I draw slow circles with it to stretch her, making room for a second finger. "*Dime lo que quieres, mami.*"

Her breath is quick as she moves her ass in tune with my hand and I insert a third finger, continuing to widen her. "I want to feel all of you." My heart swells, knowing she's trusting me enough and allowing me to penetrate her this way.

I lean into her and whisper, "Tell me when you're ready."

"I'm ready," she responds without hesitation.

"*Relájate.* The more relaxed you are, the better it'll feel." As the head of my cock nudges her, she gasps and I pause, allowing her to take in the pleasure, and pain, she's probably feeling.

"*Más,*" she whimpers as her head drops forward. I grab the

lube and add a few more drops to my cock, stroking it before pushing into her. Her breath hitches as her tight hole grips me, sending shivers across my body.

The pleasure is blinding as her bound muscles tighten around my shaft and her leg twitches. The globes of her ass are soft and plump and inviting. "*Esas nalgas están hechas pa mí.*" Her body tightens as I continue penetrating her. When I'm fully seated inside of her, I ask, "Does it hurt?"

She groans. "Yes."

"Do you want me to stop?"

"No, please don't stop." Fuck me. My girl is submitting herself to me completely, allowing herself to feel the pleasure and the pain of anal sex to allow me to have my way with her. Her submission. My ownership.

I slowly glide out, then back in and she whimpers. "Oh god," she cries out as she pushes back against me. "I had no idea it would feel this good." As my strokes move in and out, her body moves in tune with mine and it feels like my dick is being crushed, yet it's pure heaven. I lean forward to rub her clit, and she moans.

The pleasure of her moans, her tight hole, and her submission is too much and I come undone, a lot quicker than I would've wanted. "*Me estoy viniendo, mami. Todito pa ti.*" My fingers tighten at her hips as I empty myself into her and I fall forward, kissing her back.

I pull out of her and my hands loosen, leaving red marks on her curved hips. She drops to the bed and stretches her legs, her skin glistening. "That felt wicked good." Her words are breathy and her eyes are burning with lust.

"*Ahora quiero perderme entre tus piernas.*" My hands spread her legs and I bury my nose in her, letting my tongue do the work.

Her curls are splayed across the white sheets. A soft snore escapes with the rise and fall of her chest, and her dark nipples are puckered underneath the fabric. I'm starving but don't want to disturb how peaceful she looks. Instead, I bury my nose in the crook of her neck and inhale her floral scent. The contour of her neckline is my favorite spot on her entire body. Whether she's wearing perfume or freshly showered, it's always the same scent that lures me in like a drug.

She grumbles and stretches her legs, rolling her ankles. "What time is it?"

I peek at the clock on the nightstand. "One fifteen."

"Mmmm, I'm sore, but I'm also starving. We should go eat something." She rolls over and opens her eyes, the slumber at odds with her movement.

"Got any places in mind?" I ask, dragging my finger up and down the length of her torso.

"I've been craving *una fugazetta* since I knew I was coming to Buenos Aires." My girl is hungry and wants to share a meal. All is right in the world again.

"What is that?"

"Pizza that's a local favorite. It has double crust that's stuffed with cheese and then is topped with more cheese and lots of onions."

"I could go for some pizza and an ice-cold Coke."

"We can go to *El Cuartito*. It's wicked good there."

We're about twenty minutes out from starting the first of the two shows at the Luna Park Arena in Buenos Aires. The last time I performed here was when "*Modo Perreo*" hit platinum. When Roly chose this venue, I was worried about sale numbers, but the two shows sold out in minutes.

We're backstage, the crew scurrying around to finalize everything. With Rocky's hand in mine, we stroll toward the side of the stage where I'll make my entrance tonight. A black curtain separates us from the crowd filling seats and the nerves in my stomach hum, the way they always do before a show. "*Mami*, you can watch from here if you want or Marcos can take you out to the front row along that side." My finger points across the stage.

"I think I want to watch from here tonight, if that's okay. Then, tomorrow night, I'll watch from out there." She swivels toward me and gazes into my eyes.

"You're here *y eso es lo único que importa*." The past few weeks of the tour have been robotic for me, with thoughts of Rocky consuming me. It wasn't necessarily about her not being at the shows, but her decision to take time apart left me in limbo and really fucked with my head. I was withdrawn and barely socialized before and after the shows, and that's not like me. "You can watch it from wherever you want. Just make sure you're always wearing this." I give her all-access lanyard a tug. "Everyone here knows you're my girl, but just in case."

The dancers meander into the backstage area as they begin gathering for their initial performance. They wear black body suits with black thigh-high stockings and silver boot covers that make their dance shoes look like boots.

"Hey Rocky," Maritza says, approaching us. "You ready for an incredible show?"

She nods and squeezes my hand. "Yeah. Excited to see *El Flaco Casanova* on full display."

"He's incredible on stage, you're gonna love it." Maritza then turns to me. "We gotta go."

"Okay, *mami*." I drop a kiss on her temple and head back to the dressing room with Maritza.

As we walk back, Maritza says, "Your outfit's ready. They just finished pressing it. Also, Misu is here tonight. He'll be in second row to your left when you're on the stage." Misu is a huge Argentine producer who's been recording with all the artists. He told me he'd be coming to one of the shows, I just didn't know which of the two. Before leaving for Montevideo, we'll be laying down a new track with him for the series he's working on.

Inside the dressing room, Roly is with my stylist and barber waiting on me. Although I got a trim this morning, he's here to touch up my fade to make sure it looks sharp on the big screens. Once he finishes, I pull on the black tracksuit and t-shirt that was hanging and grab my cap and turn it to the back and side. I unfold the chrome-colored bandana and wrap it on my left wrist, tightening the knot. On my way out, I grab the crystal cologne bottle and pull the silver cap off, pumping once on each wrist, and twice on my neck and chest area. It cuts through all the smells of pyrotechnics and stage fog and sweat. Its earthy scent has always been my concert cologne that I only wear when performing—a touch of armor before being met with my fans.

Back at the side of the stage, I watch as the dancers get in their spots. Rocky is several feet away, and when I glance over at her, my eyes meet hers. I pucker my lips out, sending her a kiss, then turn back to the stage. The lights in the arena go dark, and the crowd screams as the rhythmic beats of "*Dosis Peligrosa*," the second biggest hit off the "*Modo Perreo*" album, fill the air. The curtain rises and the dancers *perrean* as the snare hits the off-beats, signaling my entrance. Smoke begins surrounding us, and I bring the microphone to my lips.

"Este juego is just starting
Soy el mejor en el ranking
Las nenas me buscan
Porque saben who's king."

The dancers part, and I emerge to the fans singing along with every lyric. The sound pressure of my fans knowing every word is a physical force that hits my chest like a wave, carrying me with their energy.

Almost two hours later, I exit the stage, soaked in sweat and delirious exhilaration. The fire felt under the rafters and lights almost mirrors the one I chased by popping pills, only it's more.

More intense.

More satisfying.

More visceral.

Rocky's eyes light up when she spots me, and her gorgeous smile stretches from ear to ear. "That was incredible!"

The pure joy of performing is irreplaceable. Knowing my girl is there experiencing it with me heightens my concert high, in a way only her presence is capable of.

CHAPTER THIRTY-ONE

Rocío

ADRIÁN IS DRIVING us to Alondra's house in Miami Lakes for her daughter's fifth birthday party. Last week, when Xavier returned from the first leg of his tour, he may have slept for three days straight. He told me he caught the flu while in Rio de Janeiro and performed the final show with a fever of 101. Since he was sick, I wanted him to recuperate, and we didn't see each other until last night.

"I've never been to a kid's birthday party," he tells me as the car heads west on the Palmetto Expressway.

"It's basically a bunch of high-energy tiny humans running around, screaming, laughing, and swimming since it's a pool party."

"Should we have brought our bathing suits?"

I shake my head. "Nah, I'd rather not be in the pool with a bunch of five-year-olds."

"Good point."

"So, what's the protocol when introducing you to people?" With him being such a well-known reggaeton artist, I'm not sure if he likes to be introduced a certain way or how people will react when they meet him. I suppose that's why Adrián is coming with, which Alondra will be ecstatic about. She told me that when we were at the pre-fight celebration in Vegas, while Xavier and I were talking with some of his friends, she was chatting it up with Adrián. "I got him to smile a few times," she'd said with dreamy eyes. I was surprised to hear she was able to talk with him, because he's always so quiet and serious. Or maybe he's only that way with me.

Xavier's eyebrow shoots up. "Uh, I'm your man?"

My hand reaches out and rests on his thigh. "That's not what I mean. Do I just introduce you as Xavier?"

Genuine confusion crosses his face. "What else would you say?"

I shrug. "I don't know, I've never dated a wicked famous reggaeton rockstar before."

"*Mami*, I'm just a guy who happens to also be a music artist."

Sometimes I wonder if he even realizes how famous he is. At the three concerts I went to a few weeks ago in Buenos Aires and Montevideo, he performed to sold-out crowds who sang along to every song he performed. It was crazy impressive to watch, so I cannot imagine what it must be like for him to be on stage and have the masses sing along with music he's created. "You're so humble."

"I guess. Think of it this way"—he turns his body toward me—"if we were to go to one of my friend's homes, would I introduce you as Rocky or as a lawyer?"

I understand why he's giving me the example, but it's not quite the same, at least I don't think it is. "You're comparing apples to oranges. I'm not famous."

"It doesn't matter. Being a lawyer is your job, it's not who you are. Same goes for me. Being a *reggaetonero* is my job."

I nod. "I get it. Your job doesn't define you. Makes perfect sense because when I meet people, I don't usually share that I'm a lawyer until I get to know them. For whatever reason, it changes the way they interact with me. I just thought maybe it was different because of your fame, but now that we're talking about it, I suppose not."

"Nobody needs to know who I am. If they recognize me and say something, it's fine. If not, I'm just Xavier. Or your boyfriend. Preferably boyfriend." He gives me a toothy grin.

"I think I can handle that."

Adrián parks the SUV in front of Alondra's house, which is in the same neighborhood as Nikki and César's house. There are very few cars here, which is exactly what I wanted. In my head, I rationalized that if we are one of the first to arrive, there would be less eyes on us. As I'm grabbing the gift from the back, I hear Adrián tell Xavier, "I'll be out front if you guys need anything."

I close the trunk. "What? You're not joining us?"

"No, ma'am."

"Xavier, why isn't he coming inside?"

He lifts his shoulders. "Don't know."

"I told Alondra you'd be with us. She'll be disappointed to know you are outside and not inside enjoying the party." She'll probably be pissed that I said that, but oh well.

Xavier gestures with his head to join us. "Come on," he adds, wrapping his hand with mine as I guide us toward the house, Adrián following.

The door is unlocked, and I follow the voices toward the kitchen. When I turn the corner, Alondra is standing at the refrigerator with the door open, her mother is at the sink washing dishes, and her sister is taking groceries out of the bags. "Hi everyone!"

"Hey, Rocky," Alondra says, closing the fridge. "Hi, Xavier." When her eyes meet Adrián's, her voice softens. "Hi, Adrián."

"*Hola, señora,*" I say to Alondra's mother, leaning in to kiss her hello. Her glasses are too large for her soft rounded face, and her dark brown hair is clipped back. "This is Xavier, my boyfriend, and Adrián, his friend." I didn't ask Xavier how I should introduce Adrián so friend it is. People may freak out if he gets introduced as security.

"*Hola, mija*, it's good to see you." She turns to Xavier who also leans in to kiss her cheek, and she takes his hands in hers. "*Hola, Xavier*. Alondra told me about you." I'll have to ask her about that later.

"*Bendición*," Xavier responds.

"*Tú eres el que cantó esa canción con La Gata, ¿verdad?*" She recognizes him because of the song he collaborated on with *La Gata*. That's wild! I didn't expect that from Alondra's mother, although I suppose if she watches the gossip shows like my mother then she would.

He nods in agreement. "*Sí*."

"*Me encanta ella como artista. Canta bien lindo.*"

"*Si, ella es tremenda artista.*" It's true that she's an incredible artist. Before I went to her show the night I saw Xavier on stage, I had listened to a few of her songs. But after I knew she collaborated with him, I went down the rabbit hole and listened to all her music and watched her music videos. She now has a permanent spot on my playlists.

Alondra's mother turns to Adrián and leans in to also give him a kiss on the cheek. His body is stiff, and his eyes dart to Xavier and back to her mother as discomfort settles in.

"Where's the birthday girl?" I ask Alondra.

"She's outside in the pool because a few of her friends are already here."

"We're gonna go say hi and drop the gift off, then I'll come back and help."

"I'm good. Everything is all set up. Coolers are full of drinks. The big white one has water, soda, and juice. The red one is for adult beverages. And before you ask, yes, I got you Coke Zero."

"Aw, I love you, too." I sweep in to give her a quick kiss on the cheek before heading outside.

There are only a few people on the patio, none of whom I know. They must be parents of the other kids in the pool. When Alaia sees me, she jumps out of the pool and scurries across the deck. "Tía Rocky, you're here!" Her dark hair is wet and matted to her head and back. She's missing one front tooth and has freckles splattered across her nose and cheeks.

"Happy birthday, kiddo!" I hand the gift to Xavier then kneel to hug her.

"Thank you. I'm five now."

"I know, such a big girl. These are my friends, Xavier and Adrián." My hand gestures toward the two of them standing just behind me.

When I peek at Xavier, his grin stretches across his face. He joins us down at Alaia's level. "Hi there."

"Mommy says you're Tía Rocky's boyfriend. Is that true?"

Xavier and I both chuckle. "Yes, that's true," he responds.

She turns to me and asks, "So why did you say he's your friend?"

Only five years old and already questioning everything. I always tell Alondra, we're training her to be a lawyer and I love it. "Because he's also my friend."

"Is that present for me?" Alaia asks Xavier.

He nods. "Yes, we brought it for you."

"You'll have to put it with the other presents on the table. Mommy said I can't open any of them until later."

"I'll put it with the others now." Xavier rises and walks toward the gift table.

"My mommy says she has a friend named Adrián, is that you?" Alaia asks Adrián as she's staring up at his six-foot-five stature. Has Alondra been talking to Adrián and keeping that secret all to herself?

He nods and then kneels down. "Yes, that's me." For the first time since I've met Adrián, he smiles, albeit a small one that barely shows his teeth.

"If you're Mommy's friend, that means you're my friend too."

"I'd like that, Alaia. And happy birthday."

"Thank you. Okay, my friends are waiting for me. I'm going back to the pool." She turns and runs back toward the water.

Adrián is standing and back to his serious face. I'm staring at him, but his expression doesn't budge. "You and Alondra, huh?" My smile stretches across my face as he tries to avoid eye contact. "I approve."

Xavier is walking back with two bottles of water and a Coke Zero. "Here you go." He extends his hand to me, then hands Adrián a bottle. He thanks Xavier then turns on his heel and goes back inside. "You missed it. Alaia told Adrián that her mother has a friend with that name and then asked if it was him. He told her yes. Did you know anything about that?"

He shakes his head. "No, I had no idea."

A little girl runs outside followed by a young couple, who I presume are her parents. They meander to where we're standing. "Hi, I'm Lourdes and this my husband, Miguel. We're Amelia's parents." She gestures toward the pool.

My hand extends to shake hers and then her husband's. "It's nice to meet you, I'm Rocío, a friend of Alondra's, and this is Xavier, my boyfriend." A smile spreads across his face as he introduces himself.

"You look familiar," the husband says. "Do I know you?"

Xavier shakes his head. "No, don't think we've met before." He stuffs his hands in his pockets. Does it get weird for him when people think they know him but then don't make the connection that they've probably seen him on TV?

"You look familiar, it'll come to me," the husband says.

My eyes cross with Xavier's, but I remember our earlier conversation.

In that moment, Nikki and her two kids walk out of the house. The kids head straight for the pool and when she sees me, she strides toward us. "Hi, Rocky." She drops a kiss on my cheek, then Xavier's. "Hi, Xavier."

I introduce her to the parents I just met, but they excuse themselves when their daughter calls for them.

"Where's César?" I ask when I notice he's not outside. The other day she told me she'd be coming to the party with César and the kids so I'm surprised he isn't here.

Her eyes flit from Xavier to me, meeting my gaze. Her chest rises and falls as she contemplates her answer, which is not like her. "Don't ask, I don't want to talk about it. Let me get my kids situated and I'll be back. I need a drink." Her voice is terse. She sounds angry or annoyed.

Something's off, but this isn't the time or the place to get into it. When I see Adrián come back outside sans Alondra, I tell Xavier, "Gonna go inside and see if Alondra needs help."

Inside, Alondra is putting the finishing touches on a charcuterie board she's making. "I thought you didn't need any help," I say to her.

"Yeah, I know. But now this is really the last thing, then I'm coming outside with you." She lays out some crackers.

"Girl, when were you gonna tell me you've been talking to Adrián?"

Her eyes dart up. "How'd you find out?"

"Uh, your daughter asked him if he was Mommy's friend."

She smirks. "My Alaia girl is something else. She saw me texting the other day and asked who it was."

"Who you texting with?" Nikki asks while strolling into the kitchen.

"Perfect timing. Now spill," I tell Alondra.

"Adrián," Alondra responds. "We messaged a few times while he was away on tour. Since I knew when the tour ended, I texted him once he was back and asked if he wanted to hang out."

"I had no idea," Nikki says. "What did he say?"

"We had breakfast a few days ago. We were there for four hours until he had to leave for work."

"A breakfast date. Damn, that's how we know we getting old." Nikki throws her head back in laughter.

"Did you have fun today?" I ask Xavier as I'm undressing in my bedroom, while Xavier sits in the armchair across the room. After the party ended, I told him I had to come home because tomorrow, I have an early court hearing. He chose to come with me instead of going back to his place.

"Yeah, I actually did. Alaia's cute. I can't believe she's only five. She asks a lot of questions for being so little."

She's a smart kid who's well ahead of all the kids in her VPK class, but because her birthday is in the middle of September, she can't start kindergarten for another year. "I tell Alondra all the time, she's gonna be a lawyer like her two *tías*."

He chuckles. "I can see that. She took charge with all her friends."

"You were great with all the kids today. Playing games with them, making them laugh. They loved you!" Watching him play the party games with them and being goofy caused my heart to pang. I'm sure he wants to be a father, except I've never asked him, although I've been wanting to bring it up. But once the whole thing with Xiomary happened, it took a back seat.

"Speaking of, we've never really talked about kids. Do you want any?" In my mind, of course he does, he's only thirty-one. After today, I know he'd be an incredible father.

"*En verdad, nunca lo pensé.*" He's never thought about having kids? I guess with his career and then the battle with drugs, that makes sense. He rises from the chair and strides across the room to me. "Now that you mention it, I'd like to have kids." His hand falls to my belly. "But with you."

My heart hammers in my chest. "You do remember I'm forty-one, right?"

"And?"

"I don't even know if I can get pregnant at this age."

"Well, if you don't, then we don't have kids." He says it like he's talking about not having pizza for dinner, as if it's not a big deal.

My eyes drop. "But if you want kids, me not getting pregnant is a problem."

His hands cup my cheeks. "Why are we talking about things that aren't happening today?" He tilts his head down, searching my eyes.

"Because this is huge." I swallow and straighten my back. "My age may be the thing that keeps you from being a father, and I'd never be able to live with myself." Victor and I never had kids, and initially it wasn't for lack of trying. But when he started coming home later and arguments increased, I took precautions not to get pregnant. Turned out to be a good decision because I would've had to co-parent with him for the rest of my life. *Thank you, Madame Universe, for looking out.*

"I don't know where this is coming from, but if you can't get pregnant because of your age or something else, there's other ways we can have kids. You know how many kids are out there who need adopting?"

His words surprise me. "You'd be okay with that?"

"Of course I would." His eyes are soft, and sincerity spreads across his golden-brown skin. He wraps me in his embrace and drops kisses along my hairline. "When the time comes that we want kids, we'll talk about our options."

This is a subject we'll have to talk about with more time, because I'm not sure he understands the magnitude of what he's saying. I separate from him and stare into his dark brown hues. "Okay." I drop a kiss on his lips then say, "I'm hungry, let's go have a snack." I grab his hand and tug as I walk to the kitchen.

As I'm searching for the yuca chips I bought earlier this week, Xavier's phone buzzes. He shoves his hand in his pocket and peeks at the screen. "*Dímelo*." He beams and jumps up and down. "What? That's crazy!" His eyes are wide and he's smiling as if he just won the lottery "*¡No lo puedo creer!* When is the official announcement?" He's pacing with one hand rubbing the top of his head. "*Dale*. I'll talk to you tomorrow."

"What was that?"

He places his phone on the countertop and interlocks his fingers behind his head. His eyes are bright and smiling. "'*Sombra Fiel*' is being nominated for Latin Billboard song of the year!"

CHAPTER THIRTY-TWO

Xavier

Since learning that "*Sombra Fiel*" was nominated for the Latin Billboard song of the year last month, we've been in full awards show planning mode, and it all came together today.

The makeup artist just finished with Rocky, and she's now with the stylist in the bedroom getting dressed. The barber left a few minutes ago after he touched up my fade and beard. I'm wearing a John Varvatos suit with a new custom pair of sneakers, designed specifically for the song title. They're white with black rhinestones, made to look like the emblem is casting a shadow.

"I'm really nervous about tonight," Rocky says, as she walks into the great room.

"Wow, you look fucking incredible!" She's glowing, and the late-day sun streaming through the glass illuminates her stunning green eyes.

"I don't think I've ever worn a dress this beautiful. Or expensive," she says, looking down at the dress as her hands drag along the fabric. It's a cabernet-colored Silvia Tcherassi gown. It emphasizes her voluptuous curves. The plunging neckline is lined with detailed lace designs and small crystals, accentuating her breasts, while the dramatic slit up the right side reveals her thick thigh. *Now's not the time for a hard-on*, I remind myself.

She's been working with the stylist for a couple of weeks to get the perfect dress. The label wanted to ensure that the color Rocky wears also compliments the color Roxana will wear, since we'll likely be photographed all together throughout the night.

Her curls are swept up with ringlets loose and hanging all around. I drop a kiss on her temple, and her floral scent tickles my nose. I'm not used to seeing her wear anything other than lipstick. They've lined her eyes and put on lashes, covering her lips in a color that matches her dress. "Don't be nervous. It's gonna be an incredible night."

"That's easy for you to say. You're used to these glamorous events."

Marcos is driving the SUV as it approaches the Jackie Gleason Theater in Miami Beach to drop us at the blue carpet. The sidewalk is lined with fans waiting to catch a glimpse of their favorite artists and screams of adoration float through the air. The SUV rolls to a stop. Adrián jumps out, and I slide across the seat, tugging Rocky's hand. "Ready?"

Her chest rises and falls, and she gives me a quick nod but doesn't meet my eyes.

With my finger, I guide her chin up, forcing her to look at me. "*Tú y yo*, nobody else."

She gives me another nod accompanied by a smile this time.

Outside the vehicle, I reach for Rocky's hand to help her out.

When she steps out of the SUV, flashes from the multitude of cameras blind us, accompanied by calls to look every which way. I tighten my grip on her hand as we stride down the blue carpet. Fans call out, "*Flaco, te amo,*" and "*Flaco,* can I get your autograph?" But the cries that stand out the most aren't for me; they're for my girl. "Rocky, you look beautiful," "Rocky, can I get a picture with you?" and "Rocky, we love you and *Flaco* together!" My heart thunders at the words that I too want to scream out.

We take a slew of pictures along the step and repeat as we make our way into the theater. Although there are also photographers milling around, it's calmer in here than outside because the throngs of fans are only outside the venue. I search the area for Roly, but he's nowhere to be seen, neither is Maritza. When I glance at my phone, I see Maritza's text telling me their ETA is fifteen minutes. I spot Roxana across the way in a dark pink glittery dress, standing with a small group of people. We cross the lobby toward her, stopping to say hello to several people along the way.

"*Hola*, Roxana." I lean in and drop a kiss on her cheek. "Congratulations again. This is Rocío, my girlfriend."

Rocky leans in and gives her a kiss. "Please, call me Rocky. It's nice to see you."

"We've met before, right?"

Rocky nods. "Yeah, the night of your concert at the stadium where Xavier was your surprise guest."

"Were you already dating that night?" Roxana glances between the both of us.

Rocky's head shakes. "No. We had met a few weeks before that concert. My best friend's husband works with his sister, which is how we ended up at the concert."

Roxana's eyebrow raises. "Wait, César?"

"Yeah," Rocky responds.

"That whole six degrees of separation theory really is a thing," Roxana says.

"Such a small world. Congratulations, by the way. The song is incredible and the nomination is well deserved," Rocky adds.

"It's both of our first nominations so it's exciting regardless of the outcome!" Roxana responds with excitement.

"Roly called me earlier," I chime in, "told me they may want us to perform at the Grammy's next month."

"Yeah, my manager told me the same thing," Roxana adds. "You know what they say, when you get invited to perform, it's because you're likely going to be nominated."

"*¡Eso estaría bien cabrón!*" I respond. I always dreamt of a Latin Grammy, but "*Modo Perreo*" didn't make the cut. The album I made while strung out on drugs flopped so I thought that dream was dead. If "*Sombra Fiel*" gets the nomination, it's not exactly what I dreamt, but incredible just the same.

A soft bell rings and the lights dim on and off, indicating it's time to take our seats.

"I'm just gonna wait for my boyfriend who is using the restroom," Roxana tells us. "I'll see you inside since our seats are together."

Inside the theater, an usher escorts us to the third row along the left side. We say hello to the attendees sitting around us then settle into our seats. I've attended concerts at the Jackie Gleason Theater and always loved the vintage vibe it evokes with its deep red curtains and plush velvet seating. The crystal chandeliers hanging from the rafters finish off the Golden Era glam look.

"I've always wanted to see a show here," Rocky says. "I never could've imagined it would be the Latin Billboards."

"It's a beautiful historic venue. And you'll get to see lots of performances tonight. Best of both worlds." My heart swells knowing she's sharing this night with me. Regardless of how it ends, I get to go home with her.

Two hours later, the emcee announces, "Let's welcome Solmara *La Imparable* to the stage to present the award for Latin Billboard Song of the Year. Solmara is a Dominican-American *reggaetonera* whose song was nominated for a Latin Billboard last year.

This is our category. I shift in my seat, nerves flipping in the pit of my stomach. Rocky squeezes my hand as Solmara crosses the stage in a black, low-cut lace gown, leaving very little to the imagination.

As Solmara begins speaking, I lean into Roxana, rubbing our shoulders. "Good luck," I tell her.

"Whatever the outcome, we kicked ass this year," she responds.

"And the nominees are," Solmara announces, opening the black envelope with metallic letter embossing, her long black nails struggling to get it open.

"Niko *El Rebelde*, 'Biologia.' Zao el Dominante, 'En lo Mío.' Valeria Leyes y el Orden, 'Sin Documentos.' La Gata y El Flaco Casanova, 'Sombra Fiel.' Noryel DD, 'Por Donde No Brilla.'"

A clip of each of the nominated songs plays after Solmara announces the artist name and song, prolonging each of the announcements.

"And the Latin Billboard Song of the Year award goes to..." A deep rhythmic hum fills the auditorium as she opens the card, and it seems like an eternity waiting for her to announce the winner's name. "¡*La Gata y El Flaco Casanova*! ¡'*Sombra Fiel*'!"

The crowd erupts in cheers, whistles, and clapping filling the space. I shoot up to my feet and meet Rocky's eyes. They're glistening as they crinkle in line with her megawatt smile. I pull her to me and tighten my arms. "Congratulations, I'm wicked proud of you," she whispers, her lips at my ear.

"*Gracias, mami.*"

I brush my lips against hers and then turn to hug Roxana. "Congratulations, Roxana. This is huge for us!"

"We fucking did it, *Flaco*!"

I follow her as we descend toward the stage, taking the three steps up toward the podium. Solmara congratulates both Roxana and me by giving us each cheek to cheek kisses. She steps to the side, allowing the trophy presenters space to present our awards. My hands wrap around the sleek, glass trophy with the billboard etched above our names and song title. It's heavier than I anticipated when watching the trophy presenter carry it across the stage.

As Roxana is giving her thank you speech, my eyes scan the auditorium and pride swells. I've dreamt about standing on this stage for years. Although it's not the path I envisioned, it's still incredible. My gaze crosses with Rocky and she's beaming, her hands intertwined and resting below her chin. A few weeks ago, I was spiraling, but in this moment, I'm sitting at the top of my game with the woman I love by my side, celebrating the biggest achievement of my career.

"*Gracias*," Roxana says as she wraps up her speech, then slides over making room for me at the podium.

I adjust the microphone for my height. "This year has been incredible for a lot of reasons, this award being one of them. Thank you to Juan Pablo Colón, without your vision we wouldn't be here. My label, *Ficha Mundial*, your support of Latin artists is taking us to the next level. Thank you." I turn my body toward Roxana. "Roxana, working with you *ha sido una de las mejores experiencias de mi vida. Gracias.* We should definitely make more music together."

I turn back to the audience, searching for Roly who's standing to Rocky's left, a smile stretching from ear to ear. "To my manager, Roly. You're more than a manager, you're family. You've believed in me my entire life, even on the days when I didn't believe in myself. Thank you." I shift my eyes to his left. "Maritza, you keep my life in order and run a tight ship. Thank you. To my sister Xiomary, thank you for always being there, supporting me, protecting me, and loving me, even in my darkest hour. I love you, *hermana*." I raise my eyes up to the heavens and lift the glass award. "A *mi mamá y mi abuela* who are hopefully looking down on me from heaven, *esto es para ustedes. Nos volveremos a ver algún día*." I lower the trophy and lock gazes with my girl, who's still beaming with joy. "*Y a mi mujer Rocío, te amo.*"

Rocky purses her lips as if blowing me a kiss.

Music begins playing as we're escorted off to the left side of the stage, and the emcee says, now for the first time in the Latin Billboard history, the *Alma y Verso* award, a special achievement presented to a visionary musician whose pen is as powerful as their voice. This award honors…

The emcee fades as the noises backstage take over. People scurrying around, issuing instructions into earpieces, and a blue carpet crowded with photographers. Roxana and I pose for several photos with our awards. I walk toward the exit when Solmara stops me. "*Flaco*, congratulations again on the win." Her smile doesn't reach her eyes and her shoulders are stiff. "I'm sorry to stop you here, but I don't know what else to do."

"What's up?" Her eyes scan the area and then she steps in closer. "I need you to connect me with your sister. I need a new lawyer, like yesterday." Her voice is trembling as she continues looking around us.

She looks terrified. "Yeah, I can do that. Let me—"

"*Flaco*, we need you for a few more pictures," a woman in a suit says.

"Solmara, I got you." She nods as I'm escorted away from her.

We're waiting to give a brief interview with TV-eMMe when one of the presenters approaches me. "*Flaco*, I was told to give this to you for Rio Castillo. He's the recipient of the *Alma y Verso* award, but he's not here."

I glance at the award, a black marble base with a rose gold metal ribbon that looks like a quill. *Damn, my boy Rio is killing it. Proud of him.* "I'll be sure he gets it."

After the award show ended, we came to The South Beach Rooftop Bar for the afterparty. It was packed and the music was loud. I'm wrapping up a conversation and notice Rocky has wandered off and is gazing off into the Miami night, the dark sky barely illuminated by a sliver of a silver moon. A steady light breeze rolls off the Atlantic, and her loose curls tussle in the light wind. The air is crisp, and Rocky tugs her shawl over her shoulders. "*Mami*, you good?" I stand flush behind her, resting my hands on her rounded hips.

She nods and peeks back at me. "Yeah, it's been an incredible night."

I slide her curls to the side and bury my nose in the crook of her neck. "The best."

She turns, and my arms fall at her lower back. "You told me you loved me while giving your speech. You haven't said that before." She bites her lip as she rests her arms on my shoulders.

My heartbeat races and heat spreads. "I've been showing you how I feel since before I left for my tour. Today I just said the words out loud, to you and the whole world. *Te amo, mami*." My lips brush hers and I want to devour her, but with so many eyes around us, I have to keep it simple.

Her hands intertwine at the nape of my neck as her eyes search mine. "I love you, too. I've been feeling it for some time now but was terrified of trusting myself and wasn't ready to say it out loud." Her lips brush against mine. "But with you, my heart is safe."

My heart explodes when she finally vocalizes the words her body has been expressing every time we're together, and I can't hold back the smile. It's like her words lit a fire inside of me, and I want to jump up and down and scream victory. Instead, I lean into her and hover at her lips. "*Tú y yo*, nobody else."

EPILOGUE

Rocío

A Few Months Later

WE'RE STANDING OUTSIDE MY PARENTS' house, grabbing our things from the trunk of Xavier's SUV to bring inside, where we're celebrating *Nochebuena* with my family, since Christmas Eve is the bigger day of celebration for us. "I'll grab the gifts and you take in the rice and dessert."

When we decided to spend Christmas Eve with my family, he immediately offered to make *arroz con gandules* and *tembleque*, his favorite dessert. I had never heard of Puerto Rican coconut pudding until he mentioned it. I was immediately intrigued and loved it when he made it for me the next day.

"You nervous?" I ask. I didn't sleep much last night thinking about how it'll go with my mother, since she's really the only one I'm worried about.

His head shakes. "Nah, you're more nervous than me."

I chuckle. "That's because you've never met my mother."

He sets the food containers back down and cups my face with

his warm hands. "I know you've already created the whole scene in your head. But don't, you're worrying yourself *por gusto*. Everything will be fine. She's gonna love me." His lips brush against mine. "And if she doesn't, it's okay *también* because I love you. *Nunca te olvides, no importa quién sea,* it'll always be *tú y yo*, nobody else.*"*

I nod, his measured tone easing the bundle of nerves tightening in my belly. He started saying that phrase when the paparazzi splattered pictures of me everywhere and I was freaking out. Now he reminds me of them whenever my mind works overtime. The calmness of his words has a way of settling the swirl of anxiety that builds up when I start overthinking. Micaela told me she's talked to our mother and that I shouldn't be worried, that she's already started preparing the house for my new man. But I suppose old habits die hard. "Okay." I take a deep breath. "Let's do this."

We stroll toward the front door, but before I can open it, it swings open and Micaela's face appears. She's practically my twin with her dark curly hair and large green eyes. We both look like our father, but the only difference is at five foot eight, she's shorter than the both of us. "Hi, Rocky." My shoulders instantly relax at the sight of her. She takes a few of the gifts from my hand and then gives me a cheek kiss.

"Hey." Xavier slides in next to me. "This is Micaela." I've introduced them by video so they've briefly met, but today is their first time meeting in person.

"I finally get to meet the man my sister's been raving about." My eyes widen as Micaela raises up on her toes to give him a cheek kiss.

"Raves?" His eyes cross mine briefly before turning back to my sister. "We'll have to hang out later and talk more *para que me des todo el bochinche*," he says, then flashes her a toothy grin.

"I like him already. We're gonna get along just fine." She

turns into the house but halts once inside. "Xavier, our mom isn't as bad as Rocky's made her out to be, but if you find yourself being interrogated, find me and I'll save you." His shoulders are relaxed, and his laugh reaches his eyes. It's like none of this is phasing him, just another day meeting more people. Maybe all his years under the microscope of the media has made him good at this kind of stuff.

Inside the kitchen, my mother is nowhere to be found and Julieta is cutting a red onion. She takes after our mother. Short, thin nose, brown eyes, and pin straight brown hair, which is currently tucked beneath *un pañuelo*. Xavier places the food containers onto the table. "Rocío!" she says, wipes her hands on the apron and pulls me into her.

"Hi!" I kiss her cheek. "Where are the kids?"

"Their dad took them to the store for a few last-minute things. They should be back soon," Julieta responds.

My hand lands on Xavier's arm and he steps forward. "Xavier, this is my older sister, Julieta."

"Ugh, you love calling me older, don't you?"

"Well, you are older than me. And don't forget, when you're fifty, I'll still be forty-three." I nudge her with my shoulder.

"*Hola, Julieta*. It's nice to meet you." Xavier kisses her cheek.

She rises on her toes then kisses him hello. "Nice to meet you too, Xavier."

"*Hola, nena*," my mother interrupts. My heart hammers in my chest at the sound of her voice. She's coming in from the patio, where my father is probably lighting the grill for our *asado*, our traditional *Nochebuena* meal that consists of various cuts of meat and sweetbreads.

A couple of weeks ago, when I was at my parent's house for our Saturday lunch, I told them I'd be bringing Xavier home to meet them on *Nochebuena*. All my mother had to say was, "It's about time."

"Hi, Ma." I kiss her hello. "*Mi novio*, Xavier. Xavier, this is my mother, Mirta."

"*Bendición*," he says, then kisses her hello.

"*Sos más lindo en persona que en televisión*," she tells him while stretching her arm up to palm his cheek. Heat rises to my cheeks because of course, the first thing she would comment on are his good looks.

"*Gracias*." He smirks then turns toward the table, resting his hand on the food containers he brought in. "*Hice arroz con gandules y de postre, tembleque*."

My mother's eyebrows shoot up. "You made them?"

He nods and gives us a half grin. "Yeah. *Mi abuela me enseñó a cocinar y es unas de las cosas que más me gusta hacer*." A lot of times while he's cooking, he shares stories about his *abuela*. But what I love the most about it is, he not only enjoys cooking, but he does it to feel closer to her.

My mother shifts toward me and says, "He cooks and is good looking. *Ya me cae bien*." She rests her hand on Xavier's arm and tugs. "*Vamos, para que conozcas al papá de Rocío*." He flashes me a smile and follows my mother through the French doors.

"He's in her good graces in the first few minutes, I'd say he's safe. She loved Andrew the first time she met him too. Look at how she dotes on him now," Julieta chimes in, then grabs the knife to continue what she was doing. In my heart, I want to believe Julieta is right. But there's always a small part of me ready for the next battle with my mother.

I set my stuff down and then use the bathroom quickly before going into the backyard. As I'm exiting, I halt. My mother is resting both hands on Xavier's forearm and they're both laughing and looking at one another. He's so much better at this than me. I push the door open. "*Hola, Papi*," I say, dropping a kiss on his cheek.

"*Hola, Roo*."

Xavier's gaze shifts to find mine. "Your father is telling me about his grill." The grill in my parents' backyard is the one my father built years ago since he couldn't find the exact Argentinian style one he wanted here in the U.S. It's his pride and joy. "He asked if I know how to cook an *asado*. I told him I've never tried, but that I make some mean Puerto Rican food."

I'm nodding. "He does cook really well. Has me spoiled with all the stuff he makes."

"I love feeding you." The crinkles at the edge of his eyes turn up in line with his smile. "They're coming over later this week while your sisters are still here. I invited them to our place for dinner."

My lips curl up. After the Latin Billboards, Xavier asked me to move in with him. There was no hesitation in my decision to say yes. It's only been a few weeks, but I've settled in nicely.

My father wanders over to me and leans in. "*¡Es un buen pibe, me cae bien!*" My heart swells. Yes, Papi, I agree, he's incredible. So much so that my heart trusted him enough to fall in love in a way I thought I'd never love again.

THE WORLD OF FICHA MUNDIAL LATIN ENTERTAINMENT™

Ficha Mundial Latin Entertainment is a fictional world where *Reggaeton Rompe Barreras con Romance*. Immerse yourself in a world of interconnected stand-alones infused with culture, Latin heat, nostalgia, *y el sabor de nuestra gente*, created by Latinx authors J.L. Lora, K.L. Hernandez, K. Rodriguez, and Shelly Cruz.

In our shared world, *Ficha Mundial* Latin Entertainment is the higher arching music label representing the shared world's most prominent Reggaeton artists.

Current Works under *Ficha Mundial*:

Wishing for La Luna - J.L. Lora - Available now
Staying for La Lluvia - Shelly Cruz
Lost Between El Rio y El Mar - J.L. Lora - (coming soon)
Shooting for Las Estrellas - K.L. Hernandez (coming soon)
Falling for El Cielo - K. Rodriguez (coming soon)

Learn more about *Ficha Mundial* on our website: https://www.FichaMundial.com

RESOURCES

If you've seen yourself or someone you love in the pages of this story, please know that you're not alone. Recovery is a journey that doesn't have to be walked in silence. If you are struggling with substance use or need someone to talk to, the following organizations offer professional, confidential support and a path toward healing.

Substance Abuse and Mental Health Services Administration (SAMHSA): 1-800-662-HELP (4357)

Resources for Parents & Families: Partnership to End Addiction: www.drugfree.org

ACKNOWLEDGMENTS

To my *Ficha* Girls: **J.L. Lora, K.L. Hernandez, K. Rodriguez, and Windy Johnson:** We've created something special here. I'm beyond lucky to call the four of you friends *y ahora somos hermanas del alma*. **J.L.**, I'm grateful for our "failed one-night stand" trope where dinner blossomed into a beautiful friendship. You're a creative queen that dreamt of a shared world, *y de ahí nació Ficha*…and here we are. **K.L.**, your triple fire keeps me young, and your editing prowess helped make this story the amazing novel it is today. **K.Rod**, what started with a bond over terrible coffee ended with you saying, "I can assist." You're a design savant and make everything you touch beautiful. **Windy**, thank you for always pushing me to "look again." This book may never have been written had it not been for you. I'm fortunate to be the beneficiary of so many "Windy Wins." Keep them coming.

To those who helped make this book shine:

Silvia Maria Gonzalez, thank you for being so generous with your time, your wisdom, and your experience. Your knowledge helped keep this story realistic. **Jonathan Vega**, my paralegal, who read early chapters and gave incredible feedback. You're amazing in all that you do and I'm lucky to work with you. **Estefania Cecchetto**, *mi prima* and legal assistant, who read an early copy and gave feedback. *Gracias por toda la ayuda* with keeping an authentic voice for Rocío and her family. **Antoinette Nichols**, thanks for making sure I'm understood. **Doctora Darlene Flores, Taíno Cultural Advocate and Medicine Keeper**, thank you for sharing Taíno stories and culture with me. I have so much more to learn. **Laura Brown, LCSW**. Thank you for lending your wisdom and your heart to this story. You helped me find the words for Rocío's healing and ensured her journey was walked with truth. **Marietere (@thisboricuareader)**, wicked grateful for your beta-reading magic. Thank you for holding space for the heavy parts of this journey and for making sure the Boricua heart of this book beat loud and true. You are a true protector of stories.

Mi *mamá*, my siblings, and family, thanks for always supporting my crazy dreams.

Alex, my husband. *Tu apoyo, y paciencia*, means everything.

ABOUT THE AUTHOR

Shelly Cruz spends her days navigating the courtroom and her nights igniting the page. She writes stories that capture the vibrant pulse of her Latina roots and the complexities of modern love. A lawyer by trade and a storyteller by heart, Shelly weaves Spanglish flair and deep emotional connection into every page. When she isn't at her desk, she's likely traveling, sipping a cafecito, spoiling her rescue pup, Dalia, or catching the breeze on the back of her husband's Harley.

ALSO BY SHELLY CRUZ

Nine Years Gone

Amor in the 305

En Español

Nueve Años de Ausencia

Amor en el 305

www.ingramcontent.com/pod-product-compliance
Lightning Source LLC
LaVergne TN
LVHW041618060526
838200LV00040B/1332